THE PROFESSOR

ALSO BY LAUREN NOSSETT

The Resemblance

THE PROFESSOR

Lauren Nossett

FLATIRON
BOOKS
NEW YORK

This is a work of fiction. All of the characters, organizations, and events portrayed in this novel are either products of the author's imagination or are used fictitiously.

www.flatironbooks.com

Designed by Susan Walsh

Library of Congress Cataloging-in-Publication Data
Names: Nossett, Lauren, 1986– author.
Title: The professor / Lauren Nossett.
Description: First edition. | New York : Flatiron Books, 2023. | Series: Marlitt Kaplan ; 2
Identifiers: LCCN 2023017642 | ISBN 9781250845351 (hardcover) | ISBN 9781250845375 (ebook)
Subjects: LCGFT: Thrillers (Fiction) | Campus fiction. | Novels.
Classification: LCC PS3614.O7838 P76 2023 | DDC 813/.6—dc23/eng/20230417
LC record available at https://lccn.loc.gov/2023017642

Our books may be purchased in bulk for promotional, educational, or business use. Please contact your local bookseller or the Macmillan Corporate and Premium Sales Department at 1-800-221-7945, extension 5442, or by email at MacmillanSpecialMarkets@macmillan.com.

First Edition: 2023

10 9 8 7 6 5 4 3 2 1

For Gray, forever and always

Feathers are for the birds, my boy.
Flaking, peeling, scale-ridden wings,
now that's what real beings wear.

—**George Pendle**

THE PROFESSOR

Prologue

Her

This isn't how I imagined it. In American movies, professors have offices lit by warm lamps and cozy leather armchairs nestled under towering wooden bookshelves. Crisscrossed windows overlook brick buildings choked by ivy or a park where students curl up to study on benches. These professors have analytical conversations over coffee, broaden students' minds through lectures. From their podiums, they see nothing but rapt faces nodding and hands scribbling notes. They are well-respected members of their communities, content and secure, knowing they're making the world a better place and will do so until retirement and, if they're lucky, a few years beyond.

My office is in the basement. There's a window, but it's obscured by a bush and an air-conditioning unit. The space is heavy with the mildew that grows in the carpet from the two-inch flood that races through the building every time it rains. And it's springtime in Athens, Georgia, so it rains daily in heavy bursts like the sky has been slit open. Lecture halls morph into cramped classrooms with students staring at cell phones, half listening, barely acknowledging one another, furious to be called upon. The only students who know how to find me are the angry ones, the sad ones, the desperate ones.

I always leave my door open. Always. This is important. *I have never been alone with a student.* Yes, it allows these students to drop in at all hours, to interrupt my research, grading, lunch at my desk, lesson planning, and whatever else the world throws in my direction that day. But like others before me, I learned from personal experience and endless anecdotes. Students who stalk their professors, students who accuse professors of unwanted advances or blackmail them for better grades. It happens. Almost as much as professors make unwanted advances, curve numbers, and place their hands on the knees of their graduate advisees. That is the burden of being a professor: so many years spent on both sides of the desk. You over-empathize with students and take on their pain as your own. Some of them tell you everything—the anxious thoughts, the friend who committed suicide, the grooming experience and childhood rape, the family excommunication, the loneliness; and you don't stop them from sharing these horrors, because how can you interrupt? They leave your office unburdened and free, and you gather up papers to grade, articles to review, and all the heartbreak they left at your feet. You send alerts to counseling services and wonder if you said the right thing. You try not to think about the students alone in their dorm rooms, the easy access they have to firearms, the girl discovered last year by the lake with a cocktail of anxiety medications in her system. You worry about the students who keep these thoughts to themselves. The ones who linger outside your classroom with haunted eyes and silent lips. And you worry about the damage their secrets are doing to your own already-overloaded psyche. After all, you're a German professor, not a therapist. You're not trained to recognize warning signs, to give advice, or to bury what they've told you someplace it doesn't hurt. This is why you feel heavy on your way home, why you can't meet your boyfriend's gaze or answer his questions about your day. Instead, you bend down to squeeze the dog tight because he doesn't ask anything of you. Because, really, you have nothing left to give. Then you sleep. And the next day, week, month, you wake up and do it all over again.

PART I

One

Monday, March 2, 10:00 A.M.

The steering wheel's cold under my fingertips, but my palms are sweating.

I can do this, I think as I slow to a stop in front of the crosswalk.

"I just need to explain what happened," I say to the windshield. "That I overreacted."

My eyes flicker to the rearview mirror. They jump back to the road but not before my mind registers the red-raw skin and stubbly patches of newly grown hair, as soft and fine as an infant's. I've never considered myself a vain person, and yet I continue to gaze at my reflection as if one day I might find something different.

I draw my attention instead to the university arches, watch the students with their flushed faces and pale flesh shooting out of freshly ripped jeans. Like featherless baby birds, they perch precariously on brick ledges and yell to one another across the soft grass. A year ago, I believed their youth made them carefree and weightless, no more tethered to the earth than falling leaves. Now I know this lightness can make them cruel, frightening in their inability to understand the consequences of their actions. I wear the proof of this on my skin.

The light changes from red to green, and I blow out a breath, accelerating again.

The station's only five minutes from the students and shops of downtown Athens but might as well be a world away. I could drive here with my eyes closed, and yet, for the past few months, I've been tracing large circles around it, taking back roads, and looking straight ahead when I can't avoid passing. It's embarrassing, actually—the ways I've allowed its central location to dictate my days.

But now I'm here, turning into the parking lot, drawn like a magnet, succumbing to the inevitable pull of my shame. I swallow, but no alarms sound and no one rushes out to chase me away. The building's as nondescript and unimposing as it was the day I walked in as a newly minted detective, and as squat and gray as the morning I walked out in disgrace.

Out of habit, I drive toward the back. A deep flush rises up my chest when I see a familiar bike locked to the steps. The lieutenant's silver Charger is parked aggressively across a white line. And even Oliver's VW Golf is in its usual space, as straight and rule-abiding as the owner himself pretends to be.

Nothing's changed, I think.

But then, for me, it has. Because instead of parking dangerously close to the lieutenant's beloved vehicle, I circle around the lot and pull in the front. Today I won't be entering through the key card rear entrance. Instead, I'll go through the lobby and check in at the reception desk, where I'll sit on the hard wooden benches and twiddle my thumbs like an idiot waiting for someone to escort me to the bullpen.

If they let me that far, I think as I turn off the engine.

The silenced scream of a siren echoes as I open my door. A white sedan with a blue racer stripe takes the corner too fast. They must be new—no one leaves their siren on that long unless they want an ironic round of applause at their entrance. I crane my neck but don't recognize the driver or the woman in the back—she's merely a flash of dark hair whirring past, the edge of a gray shoulder, her face turned inward and blurred by the smudged handprint on the glass. The blue lights disappear in a swirl of sunshine; and then she's gone, and I'm walking through the front doors of the station, bludgeoned by the familiar scent of damp ceiling tiles, astringent cleaner, and heavy memories of the life I left.

A predictable crowd gathers in the lobby—it's a mixture of hungover students, recent retirees, and strung-out junkies. And as I move toward the front desk, I avoid the glances that flick to my skin. Focus instead on the laminate tiles, the light flitting across the scuffed walls and layers of faded paint. It's been four months since a misguided young man slipped into my house and set my bedroom on fire, and I've hardened myself to the curiosity and looks of disgust, but I still can't stand their pity.

I didn't use to be this way. When I was on the force, I strolled across town, eyes on everyone, looking for suspicious activity—telltale signs of a disturbance, teenagers disappearing into dark alleys, the convertible weaving across the lane, the bloodshot eyes and the slurred speech. Now I keep my eyes down and try not to notice the plastic bags slipping between the fingers of junkies, the thumbprint bruises on the woman's neck, scrape marks on the entrance door, and signs the lock has been tampered with, because I no longer have the power to stop a person or to investigate, and the last thing anyone at Athens PD wants is a disgraced former detective showing up every time she thinks she sees something.

I mutter as I sign my name on the visitors' sheet and grudgingly check my watch to add the hour. I've never been good at waiting. But now I have time. Time that gnashes its teeth like a leviathan, a never-ending battle to keep myself busy, to avoid thinking about how badly I screwed up my job, my life, and any chance of friendship with my old partner, Teddy.

I choose a chair near the window and a good distance from the others. A woman blinks at my face and then away before sneaking another glance. There's a prickly sensation of eyes on the side of my neck, and I scan the room for the glint of a knife, the flick of a match. But all I find is the woman, her mouth now hidden by a magazine, a steel-blue gaze watching me.

My mobile rings, and the woman clears her throat, a quick gesture of her hand to the paper sign taped to the desk—a boxy phone with a giant X drawn across it. Her eyes dart between me and the sign in noiseless reprimand.

I silence the call without apologizing. It's my mother. Unusual. She teaches in the morning and dislikes talking on the phone almost as much as answering student emails, unnecessary modifiers, and department meetings.

It's nothing, I tell myself as I slip the phone back in my bag. But before I can resume my practiced disinterest, it rings again.

I hear a clucking from the front of the room and look up to find Amy, the station's long-suffering admin, smirking crookedly at me.

I decline the call a second time and stand.

"The prodigal child returns." Amy's laughter turns into a wheeze. She picks up the lobby phone. "Lieutenant Truman," she says.

"Not Truman," I tell her. "Teddy."

She wags a bony finger at me. "Yes, sir," she says with barely disguised glee. "There's someone here to see you."

"I don't want Truman," I grumble, but Amy's already returning the phone to its handset.

"Have a seat," she tells me brusquely. "Someone'll bring you back."

I swallow the bile in my throat. I don't like taking orders from Amy, and Truman is the last person I want to see. But maybe this is better. Teddy might have refused to meet me.

The guy they send as my escort is tall and gangly, and the pants of his uniform twitch above his ankles as he hurries to my seat. I don't recognize him, and no one must have warned him about my burns because he does a predictable double take at my face.

"Follow me," he says, gaze shifting to the floor.

When we round the corner, my eyes go straight for Teddy's desk. My stomach clenches. His profile is toward me: the same dark, warm skin, strong jaw, and high cheekbones. There's a sharpened pencil tucked behind his ear as he stares at his computer screen. And I know he's registered my presence by the way his shoulders go rigid.

I open my mouth, but the gangly new hire steers me toward the back.

"Kaplan." Truman's voice booms from the dark hole that is his personal office. "Well, isn't this a surprise."

And there he is: my old lieutenant standing behind his mahogany desk, the light from the outer room illuminating his bald head. He rocks back on his toes to study me.

I clench my jaw as his eyes rove over my face, my T-shirt, and my ripped jeans.

I don't have to impress you, I want to say, which is ridiculous, because of course I don't, but a part of me wants to all the same.

He looks pleased to see me, and suddenly I realize that he's been waiting for this moment, perhaps since the day I left. He thinks I'm here to grovel, to beg for my job back.

"To what do we owe the pleasure?" He beams.

"I'm here to see Teddy."

"Even Teddy can't help you with this," Truman says, still smiling. "But let's hear it."

"What?"

"I want to hear how you've rationalized your actions and now have the audacity to ask to be reinstated."

"I'm not—"

"Because from where I stand, you put both your job and your partner's at risk, you jeopardized an investigation by breaking and entering into a fraternity house, and then continued to harass its members while given strict instructions to stay away from the case. Am I missing anything?"

I breathe through my nose. Breaking and entering is a bit of an exaggeration. Last November, I investigated a hit-and-run fatality of a fraternity brother and crashed one of their parties. The doors were open, and I was more or less invited in. But three days later, I resigned instead of risking termination. I made mistakes Truman never discovered and I have no plans of illuminating him now. But I also know that I was right. About the fraternity, the lack of justice, and that this department was too busy kissing the university president's ass to do anything about it.

When I remain silent, Truman rubs his finger along a framed photograph on his desk.

"You know, if it weren't for me, you never would have made detective. The first woman in the homicide unit. Everyone thought you'd lose your nerve and throw your gun at a suspect, but I gave you a chance—"

"I had top marks in my class—"

"I advocated for you." His voice lifts to drown mine out. "And you made a fool of me." He hammers a thick forefinger on his desk. "Or did you think enough time had passed that I forgot you arrested a suspect while suspended?"

Fury ripples over my skin. If I hadn't followed leads while suspended, the perpetrator would still be walking free. But what's worse is that those who enabled the crime will never be punished. And Truman knows this.

"I'm not here to get my old job back," I say through clenched teeth.

"You're not?" His lips flatten, and he frowns, too startled to mask his surprise.

"No." I fold my arms across my chest. "I'm here to see Teddy."

Teddy, who hasn't answered my calls. Teddy, my partner for three years, whom I haven't seen in months.

Truman stares at me. Then he collapses in his chair as if exhausted by our conversation. "You can fraternize later," he says gruffly, and begins thumbing through the papers on his desk.

"He won't talk to me." It costs something to tell Truman this, but he's no longer listening.

His phone rings. His palm hovers over it.

"Figure out your relationship drama on your own time," he says, and reaches for the handset.

Dismissed, I turn on my feet. An officer I don't recognize glances in my direction and then away again. He's striding toward the interview room with a pinched look around his mouth. And I think of the woman in the back of the cop car when I arrived. On another day, in another life, I might wonder about her, what she did, what evidence I could gather to put her away. But today, my eyes scan the bullpen only to find Teddy's chair now empty. In the corner, the new guy wavers, loath to escort me out.

Every workplace has its pariahs—the people whose presence sends those at watercoolers scattering, whose name is toxic by association. I never minded being an outsider. In an over-politicized system lacking accountability, I believed more got done on the margins—not so much coloring outside the lines but on top of them, over them, so the border moved a little every time. What's unfair is that the sole person who understands the egregiousness of my error is Teddy. The rest don't know what happened—not really—but the station gossips like teenagers at a slumber party, and by now, rumors about my resignation will have spread like a bad game of telephone, spanning everything from assaulting a fraternity member to a gender-coded psychotic break.

I hear the back door slam and move toward it. See the edge of Teddy's shoulder as he jogs down the steps to his bike.

"Wait." My voice is muffled, not as strong or as sure as I want it to be, but it rings between us.

Teddy stops.

I move around the metal handrail to face him.

His expression is heavy and shuttered. And something in my stomach tightens when he turns to me.

"I'm sorry," I say. "The fire . . . ," I begin, trying to remember the words I practiced. "I overreacted. I know that. I shouldn't have forced you to take me to that cabin. I put your job at risk, messed up the investigation—"

Teddy shakes his head, and I quit speaking.

Our eyes meet and I have a flash of driving around Athens, him laughing at something I said, breaking a granola bar and passing him the other half, sharing a cup of coffee, fingers touching as we shiver in the cold. I see him at my hospital bedside, his head in his palms. Him teasing me about being a secret agent. There was something there, something real and pure and so tangible I could have held it in my hands. But I took our friendship for granted, and now I'm searching his closed face for it, refusing to believe that it's gone.

"Is this about Cindy?"

I had brought his girlfriend with me to the fraternity party Truman accused me of breaking and entering. I wasn't totally up-front about my motives and left her to follow the organization's treasurer. I found out later that one of the brothers was responsible for the fire in my bedroom, but I already knew they were dangerous. And as I blink at Teddy, I realize that not only does he think I'm a bad partner, he also must think I'm a bad person.

"I know it was wrong—selfish," I say, repeating the word Teddy used to describe my behavior last year.

Teddy's jaw clenches. "And yet here you are." He gestures between our chests. "You can't keep apologizing and expect everything to be better. I made it clear I needed space to think." He looks past me to the traffic on Broad Street. "But you want everything on your timeline, at your initiative, and"—he lifts his voice when I start to interrupt—"you don't respect boundaries."

"Boundaries?" I open my mouth and close it again, caught off guard by the therapy speak.

He scans my face as if looking for something redeemable in me. For the partner he knew, the friend he trusted. But then he's pedaling away, and there's nothing I can say to stop him, because he's right. I had my own agenda in solving last year's case and people got hurt in the process. I thought if I could just get out the most perfectly worded apology, everything would be okay. But maybe my error was too egregious, maybe I don't deserve his friendship or his forgiveness.

I watch his edges fade into the sunlight.

My phone vibrates again, the third time in the last fifteen minutes.

"What?" I say, a bit harsher than I intended.

"Marlitt? *Gott sei dank*." My mother's breathless, thanking god, and so out of character that my heart starts to hammer.

"I've been trying to reach you all morning." Her voice is tight and accusing, a slash of her German accent coming through.

Something clenches in my stomach. "What happened?" I ask.

She lowers her voice. "I can't say over the phone."

I grit my teeth. "You called me three times," I say impatiently.

"I know." A quick inhalation as she decides something. "Can you come to the house?"

"Now?" I feel the weight of Teddy's accusation and the childish obstinance only my mother has the capacity to unleash in me.

"It's Verena," she says. There's a shuffling as the phone moves against her chin. "The police came to her office this morning. Took her to the station for an interview." I see a flash of dark hair, a dirty back window, a cop car taking a corner too fast. Think of Verena, my mother's junior colleague, and try to reconcile her face with the one smudged in the reflection of the glass. "It's horrible—" Her voice is muffled as she navigates some outdoor space. "Verena would never—and—with a student—it's just not possible."

"What do you mean 'with a student'?" I ask, but my words are lost in the noise on the other end.

"Just come home," she says. "Please." And then she's gone.

Two

Monday, March 2, noon

Home is a few tree-lined blocks from the university.

There was a time when I'd be met by a wave of nostalgia driving these streets, but I've been living with my parents in the months since the fire. My house, a shotgun-style cottage in Normaltown, is still recovering from its wounds. The fire marshal told me the inspections and repairs could take half a year. I'm not allowed on the property; the perimeter is circled in yellow tape, an eyesore for my neighbors that turns our peaceful street into a perennial crime scene.

I sigh and try not to think about the look on Teddy's face, the implication that my sins go beyond a propensity for skirting boundaries and shitty apologies, and that he's seen something dark and irreparable deep within me. Instead, I concentrate on my mother's call—her insistence we meet at home instead of her office.

I can imagine a million things that could go wrong at the university—professor turned predator after an article rejection, student turned gunman after a bad grade, admin gone rogue after a misplaced travel reimbursement—but nothing that wouldn't have already turned the campus into a nightmare of screaming sirens and students hunkered down in classrooms. Certainly nothing that would involve one of my mother's junior colleagues or explain her cautious tone and audible expressions of gratitude to a god she doesn't believe in.

I drive through a tunnel of oak and elm branches. Power lines dip beneath their heavy limbs. Quaint cottages with wicker furniture and prayer-flag-lined front porches sit comfortably next to restored painted ladies with plastic toys strewn across their lawns. An older couple waves at me from their stoop. A dog races along an invisible fence. And between maple leaves, I recognize my mother—five foot eight, still long and lean at sixty-seven, silver hair cropped at her chin, wearing her usual no-nonsense tan slacks and cream blouse—pacing the length of the brick porch. She hasn't seen me yet, and when I pull alongside the curb, she flinches.

I step out of the car.

"Marlitt—" Her voice catches, and I register it—the sudden doubt in her eyes, the thought that maybe she shouldn't have called, that maybe I'm not ready for anything beyond library trips and note-taking. But then, whatever's worrying her surpasses the angry scars on my skin.

She motions me inside. "Please talk to her," she says, her voice clipped. "These accusations are completely unfounded. And I know—" Another hesitant look at my face. "I know you can help. You can find out what happened."

I note the appeal to my ego, but after my abysmal meeting with Teddy something trembles and warms in my chest—*At least someone needs me*, I think.

I follow her into the sun-bleached entry hall. French doors open to the living room on the left and dining room on the right. The smell hits me like it always does—coffee, books, old leather furniture—threatening wistful childhood memories, but I push them away. Focus instead on the subtle change in the house, the chill that sweeps through the foyer like a draft.

Like my mother, Verena is a professor in the German Department at the University of Georgia. I saw her a few months ago. It was Thanksgiving, and she was exclaiming in delight over everything, while I was a complete wreck with weak lungs and fresh burns. But today, it's she who's white-faced, sitting at the long farmhouse table next to my father, who also seems paler and thinner than usual.

I offer what I hope is an encouraging smile, then take my mother by the elbow and lead her through the open French doors into the bookshelf-lined living room.

"I think you should tell me what happened," I say.

She nods, gray eyes flitting under her glasses from me to the sound of my father coughing in the kitchen. His offer of tea. Music. Silent company. We sit on the sofa facing the large windows.

"Start at the beginning," I tell her.

My mother hunches her shoulders. "I arrived on campus around eight this morning," she murmurs, closing her eyes briefly. "It was quiet, and I left my door open in case any students needed to drop by and ask questions before class. They had a test today," she says distantly, and her eyes fly open. "With everything that happened, I forgot to cancel." She blinks furiously around the room. "They'll be wondering what to do."

"They'll be fine," I say.

But I've lost her. There's a tiny movement in her jaw as she whips out her phone, eyes scanning, fingers pecking at the screen.

"Tell me about Verena," I prompt again.

She clicks Send and throws the phone back on the couch.

"Right."

She stands, and I watch the trajectory of her shadow as she paces the room.

"Around a quarter to eight, a police car passed under my window." My mother scrunches her brow, remembering. "Not long after, I heard a commotion in the hall. There were three men, Ray from campus security and—" A quick glance at me.

I tense, bracing myself. "Teddy and Oliver," I breathe.

I picture Teddy, tall in his bright running shoes; Oliver, a few inches shorter, his hair swooped back with so much gel it looks like he's prepared for a windstorm.

She meets my gaze. "Not Teddy, no. But Oliver, yes. And another man I didn't recognize."

I swallow the lump in my throat. Oliver was in the interview room with me on my last case, even though it should have been Teddy. The other man must be my replacement. And I wonder if it was the same man I saw walking into the interview room this morning. I resist the urge to ask more about this guy—his credentials, qualifications, height—and let her finish.

"They were looking for Verena's office."

I frown. Oliver works Homicide, and the university has its own law enforcement. He wouldn't come onto campus without a good reason.

"So I told them it was in the basement. And—I don't know why—I was still preparing for class and answering emails—but I just thought it was strange, so . . . I followed them." Splotchy color returns to her cheeks.

"And?" I ask.

"And then they went to the basement—Verena was there—and they said she was wanted for questioning in the death of a student."

I sit up straighter. "A student died? How?"

"I don't know." She hesitates. "I assumed . . . overdose."

"Why overdose?"

My mother purses her lips. "Are you interrogating me now?"

I breathe through my nose. *Patience*, I remind myself. "I can't help without all the information," I tell her.

My mother rubs her hands down her arms. "Verena said the detectives asked if she did drugs, if she'd ever given any to her students. And . . ." She takes a breath, and I see the switch, the shift from person to professor, as if she's beginning a lecture. "Over a hundred thousand Americans died from drug overdoses last year. Suicide is the second-leading cause of death of college students. It's only natural to assume—"

"Does Verena do drugs?"

"Of course not," my mother hisses. "And she certainly wouldn't distribute drugs to students. Some professors might fraternize, but Verena—" She shakes her head. "No."

"Then why did Oliver want to talk to her?"

She rubs the side of her jaw. "They wouldn't give details, but they seemed to believe that Verena and the student were having an affair." Her glasses slip down her nose and her shoulders sag. But then she lifts her chin and stares hard at me.

"Verena?" I repeat incredulously. "Was having an affair with a student?"

My mother casts a pointed look at the French doors and motions for me to lower my voice.

"It's ridiculous," she whispers. "Verena would never—" She gives another shake of her head, the thought impossible to consider. "You have to help her."

She's still staring at me, a faint slash of hope lifting the corners of her eyebrows.

And it's there in spite of myself—the sliver of disappointment. It's wrong, I know, but I was hoping for a murder, a coldhearted killer and ulterior motives—not an overdose and a misguided affair. And maybe it's because I'm used to searching for justice for the victim, but there's something distasteful about my mother's request, her asking me to help Verena, when it's her student who's dead.

I unfurl myself from the arm of the sofa. "What do you want me to do?" I ask.

"You can prove she didn't do it." She folds her arms over her chest. "She's been suspended pending a Title Nine investigation. An affair with a student . . ."

"I mean . . ." I touch the scars on my face absently. "I know that's frowned upon—the potential for exploitation, unfair bias, academic integrity issues." I shrug. She knows the reasons better than I do. "But it's not like she teaches high school. The students are above the age of consent—unless he was a fourteen-year-old genius or something?" I lift an eyebrow.

"He was twenty."

"Right. So?"

She takes a breath. "This could ruin Verena's life—be the end of her career."

I sigh. Of course, for my mother the two are indistinguishable—life and career, career and life, one does not exist without the other. I know, because I used to be the same. The job is like a briefcase with metal cuffs—to be free you must saw off your own hand.

But I'm not a detective anymore. I don't have access to lab reports or crime scenes, and it sounds like my mother wants me to play some kind of reverse-style private investigator, except instead of snapping photos of writhing bodies from the bushes, I'd be put in the impossible position of demonstrating such unrespectable behavior never happened.

"Please," my mother says, her voice softening, "she's had a horrible year already. Her boyfriend left, dog ran away, and now this . . ."

Her eyes flicker to my face. "You know I wouldn't ask, if—" She stops when she sees my expression.

Say it, I will her. *Say you don't think I can handle it.*

Instead, she puts her head in her hands, talks into her palms. "When I picked her up at the station," she murmurs, "I parked across the street, I don't know why . . . I guess, I didn't want anyone to see—" She clears her throat, straightens her shoulders. "But walking back to the car, Verena, she looked"—she gestures toward the kitchen—"strange. Not like herself at all." She sighs. "I know she's been under a lot of pressure lately. I should have paid better attention."

I frown. "Whatever this is," I say, "it isn't your fault."

She shakes her head impatiently like I've missed the point. "When we reached the sidewalk," she says, "there was a car coming. Verena hesitated, but then," her eyes flash, "it was just a fraction of a second, but I thought she was going to step out into traffic, and it would be just like the fall—only I was there and did nothing to stop it."

I suck my bottom lip between my teeth. She means my last case—a boy who walked into the street and didn't make it to the other side. I close my eyes and see a body on the asphalt, yellow tape, students circling.

"You have to help her," my mother says. "Otherwise . . ." She casts an anxious look back at the kitchen. "She's all alone."

I take a deep breath. "What's the student's name?" I ask.

"Ethan." Her mouth twists sadly. "His name was Ethan Haddock."

In the kitchen, Verena's still sitting at the table, arms wrapped around herself. She doesn't move at the sound of my footsteps.

"Verena," I say cautiously.

"He was my favorite student," she murmurs, mouth crumpling. A tear rolls down her cheek.

My father pats her hand.

I chew my lip. Part of me wants to tell her that this is information best kept to herself. That her favoritism may be the reason she's suspected of having an affair to begin with.

"I know this is hard," I say, glancing at my mother, who nods, "but can you tell me what the police said? It would help to know what we're dealing with."

"They said . . ." She takes a breath. ". . . that Ethan died." She looks at me then, as if hoping I'll correct her, that I'll tell her this is all a big misunderstanding—and everything will go back to normal. When I don't, she blinks hard at her hands. "They wanted to know if I'd ever been to his apartment. If he was on any medication. If he did drugs. If I did drugs. They wanted my computer and cell phone," she says, a confused furrow between her brows. "Searched my office, took my journal as evidence."

I stare at her. "They searched your office?"

She nods.

I glance at my mother again. If Oliver searched her office and took her laptop, then Verena isn't just suspected of faculty misconduct, she's a suspect.

In a split second, I picture it clearly: the alienated young woman, the obsessive young man. That desire for connection, for understanding. Is it so hard to believe she'd have an affair? If her boyfriend left, maybe she sought comfort in a student's arms? And then there was a fight. Blackmail. Maybe they did do drugs together, and Ethan took too much. Or maybe it was just a smile, a light touch of the hand when passing back a graded assignment, an encouraging word—innocuous things that compiled together were taken as romantic gestures by a young person just learning to analyze symbols and interpret dreams, who read something between the lines where there was nothing and overdosed just like my mom said.

A year ago, I wouldn't have considered it. I solved murders, not relationship problems. My goal was to find the perpetrator and get him—and sometimes, but rarely, her—off the streets, file the paperwork, and show up in court. I was never good at talking to the vulnerable, the desperate, the ones in a shock so deep they receded to some inner place; but the thought of the student, the mystery, makes something loosen inside my chest. And there's something else, too, something still reverberating from my conversation with Teddy. *Maybe helping Verena will prove I'm a good person.*

I know what my mother is expecting—that in talking with Verena's other students, her colleagues, Ethan's friends, I will discover a troubling pattern of Ethan's behavior that dismantles Oliver's proof and exonerates Verena. But the lid to Pandora's box is heavy for a reason. Prying into others' affairs rarely reveals sunshine and cheerful stacks of yellowed photographs. Instead, you're sorting through all the dark bits they slammed into drawers and shoved into the backs of closets. Even if you find the key, pick the lock, uncork the jar, you will discover only false oaths, lost faith, and duplicity. And because you, seeker of truth, lifter of urns, have dared to look, you will be the receiver of scorn, exiled to the ends of the world, and stripped of honor. Because truth, like anything buried in the bottom of a box, is rarely the balm people think it will be.

I hope my mother knows what she's asking and will forgive me for any truths I set free.

Her

When I wake this morning, I have that familiar flutter of nerves I always get on the first day of class. The fear the students will reject me, that when I walk in the room, they will laugh and point, identifying me as the imposter in their midst.

I take a breath and bring myself back to the bedroom.

I'm in Athens. On our sleepy kudzu-lined street. Christopher's side of the bed is empty. And now that I focus, I hear him trying to be quiet in the kitchen, the effort of being discreet causing him to drop and bump into things more frequently than if he would just move freely.

I slip into the bathroom for a quick shower, take more deep breaths, run through my lesson plan, forget whether I've washed my hair, and shampoo it twice. By the time I step into the kitchen, there's a bowl of muesli on the table and Christopher's holding out a cup of coffee.

"For the brilliant professor," he offers, flourishing the mug with a smile.

I step back as brown liquid sloshes over the edge.

"Sorry!" He laughs and wipes away the droplets with his thumb. "You're going to be great today," he murmurs, and my stomach clenches.

"Don't talk about it," I hiss.

His smile falters.

"I just . . ." Another deep breath. "I don't want to jinx anything."

He takes my hand.

"Okay." He smiles, and I try to ignore the hurt that lingers in his eyes. "We'll pretend this is just a normal morning. A Saturday, even."

I nod, but the pressure is already there, building in my chest, a tightness, making it difficult to breathe. *I can't do this*, I think, staring at the back of Christopher's head. *They'll see right through me*. He's chattering about weekend plans. *They'll want to know my credentials. Laugh until I run out of the room*.

Somehow, I manage to eat a few bites of granola, get dressed, and tie my shoes.

By the time I unlock my office door, the panic has receded, replaced with the urgency of all the things that need to get done before instruction begins.

When I walk into the classroom—shoulders straight, head high (they can smell fear, you know)—the students don't look up immediately. Feet bounce under desks, fingers tap on phones, two young men jostle over something behind their chairs. It's not until I reach the technology podium that there's a shift in the air. *The professor—that's her—she's here.*

No one points. But a few shush each other, scramble for notebooks, and whisper requests to borrow paper and pens.

I scan their faces. I always try to learn their names before the term begins—the rosters have thumbprint photos next to their year and gender pronouns. But more often than not, these pictures—taken during freshman orientation right after a gold-kissed summer—look nothing like the students in my classroom. Long hair now short, skinny kid now fat, rows of braces now straight teeth—all of these changes matched by the fact that the lens has missed the essence of the person—it doesn't tell you if this is the shy student who ducks her head when called upon but will write the most brilliant essays you've ever read, or the student who talks constantly but then is struck dumb by an exam question and will email your department chair to complain of unfair treatment. It doesn't tell you if this student will be the type to remind you why you chose this job, sacrificed your twenties, your financial future, and your mental health to the altar of higher education, or if this student will make you want to bang your head against the wall and wonder why you bothered—so I take a moment to breathe in their faces, their presence, to remind myself it's not about me. It's about them, teaching them, seeing them, and recognizing their potential.

We start with introductions. The basics. "What's your name?" "Where are you from?" I give them interview questions and move around the room, listening, correcting, and encouraging them to talk to one another.

"*Woher kommst du?*" Travis, one of the talkative boys in the back asks me as I make my way down his row.

"*Woher kommen Sie?*" I correct. "Since you're talking to a professor, you should use the formal 'you': '*Sie*,'" I explain.

"*Woher kommen Sie,* then?"

"*Ich komme aus Deutschland,*" I say, careful to speak slowly, to enunciate each syllable. The other students have stopped talking to listen, so I model how they should answer.

"*Woher kommst du?*" I ask him.

"From Germany," he echoes skeptically in English.

"*Aus Deutschland,*" I repeat.

He exchanges a glance with the boy next to him.

"How do you say: Where do you come from, *originally*?" he asks.

I've had a lifetime of practice, but it still takes all my willpower to keep my expression neutral.

"*Du meinst, wo ich geboren bin,*" I say slowly. "*In Deutschland.*"

He blinks at me.

"*Ich wurde in einem kleinen Dorf geboren,*" I tell him. "*In der Nähe von Bamberg.*"

A visitor might think the town I grew up in was picturesque—clumps of red-roofed houses dotting rolling green hills, not a billboard or building over two stories in sight—but I hated it since the day my father, a university-educated botanist, returned to Turkey. He begged my mother to join him. *I tried*, she always said. But she missed the tree-lined rivers, the village set between seven hills, the people who knew her name—never mind that those same people called her a race-shamer under their breaths. Never mind the open-mouthed stares at her dark-haired daughter. This is why I have my mother's last name. Sobek, the surname of my maternal grandfather, is Polish and different enough to raise eyebrows in our village, but not so different as Şahin, Özdemir, or Yilmaz. "She was my great love," my father told me once, years after he had remarried, "but I couldn't live her life." Ultimately, I said the same thing when I got on a plane for my master's degree, on the phone when I decided to stay for my PhD, over email when I accepted the job at UGA: *I love you, but I can't live your life.*

I don't tell the student any of this. Instead, I walk away before he can repeat his question. Because this is what I have, gifted to me by my mother, by my education—the ability to speak flawless high German, better than most Germans, in fact, and certainly better than the rest of our village—so that I could have been a politician, a newscaster, an ambassador, even. But I will never be accepted as German by other Germans. Just look at the violence against refugees, increasing anti-immigrant sentiment, the presence of right-wing nationalists in the German parliament. I know more about the origins of the language, its changes in syntax, phonetics, and morphology, the history and accurate pronunciation of diphthongs and the weakening of short vowels. I've read the *Nibelungenlied* in Middle High German, can list all Goethe's lost loves, and know the names of the female storytellers who inspired the Grimms' collected tales. All my learning would have delighted the old masters, had I not been born a woman and had my Turkish blood not been found guilty of diluting the German race. And even if many Germans accept their country's growing diversity, there are others who bomb mosques and salute Hitler look-alikes in the street. Americans might not be able to tell the difference between Poles, Germans, and Turks, but many of my students think Germans can only look one way: tall, blue-eyed, and blond. So I clutch at this language, this hard-earned knowledge, as I walk back to the front of the room.

"Who's been to Germany?" I ask.

A boy at the front—swoop of dark hair and bright, clear eyes—raises his hand.

There's something in the movement, a delicacy and determination, that reminds me of someone else. I shiver before I smile at him.

"*Wunderbar,*" I say.

He smiles back.

"Und wie heißt du?"

"Ethan," he says. "*Ich heiße* Ethan Haddock."

Three

Tuesday, March 3, 8:00 A.M.

That night my dreams are strange and unruly, silver wings on a black night, a man whose face blurs when I get too close, and slips of a woman—dark hair, light eyes, a glimpse of her coat sleeve—and a dog barking in the distance, but nothing solid or stable, a hall of mirrors, where only one image is real and everything else a reflection of the object at its core, and yet this is precisely the substance I cannot see.

Something wakes me, and I jolt out of bed, panting, scanning my room with all its strange furniture, smelling smoke, and tearing at my skin. But then I remind myself to breathe, that I'm safe, at the Boulevard house, where it's still dark but a faint orange light claws at the edges of the windows.

I roll my head from side to side. It's been four months, but I'm still not used to the mattress in my childhood bedroom—now the guest room—in my parents' house. I toss and turn, fighting the suffocating softness, before giving up and flipping on the lamp. Yellow light fills the room and glints off framed photographs. In the corner, an armchair contains copies of my passport and birth certificate. A tangled mess of clothes, all brand-new with price tags. Small tokens of the ever-growing list of items from the fire that need to be replaced. But as everyone keeps telling me—I was lucky. The burns on my face are permanent, but not debilitating. They should look better a year from now. My life, in fact, might have gone on as usual—scars and all—had I not decided to forgo protocol in pursuit of that hit-and-run driver.

My hands find the assortment of bottles and creams on my nightstand and begin the slow routine of applying artificial lubricant to the parched, scaly skin on my cheek. I can thank the fire for the damage to my oil-producing glands, something the doctor reminds me at every visit not to underestimate. The scabs that adorned my nose and chin in the early days have fallen away, but there are blisters on the back of my skull, and it takes all my willpower not to scratch. Instead, I open my jaw, jut out my chin, and raise my eyebrows in a facial exercise routine I would be embarrassed for anyone to witness but that ameliorates the stiffness that has settled after a night of little movement. As I remove the compression sleeve on my arm, I hear children's voices lift from the half-open windows. I massage lotion into my biceps, thinking that if the buses are running, it's a weekday and after 7:00 A.M.

That's the strange thing about no longer working Homicide. There's no rushing around the house, early-morning coffee run, trying to be the first one in. No taking phone calls, sorting through mounds of paperwork, filing affidavits of probable cause, or trips to the DA's office. Now there's no structure, no purpose, no crime to solve or families of victims looking to me for help. Nothing but a crushing sensation of nothingness.

I should be grateful. Most officers who resign don't have fathers willing to hire them as research assistants until they get back on their feet. But the monotony of it all—coffee, library, books, coffee, notes, home—is mind-numbing. And, of course, there's also the anger, seething where it always is just under the surface—an unruly, volatile beast that lashes out at the slightest provocation.

It's a long story, but the essence is: my parents lied to me. My whole life I'd grown up believing I was an only child, the sole girl alone at the bus stop, the one demanding all the attention, and the only possible suspect for the broken vase, cookie crumbs, or bad report card grade. But I had a brother. One who died at two years old, whom my parents buried and erased, hiding family photographs and footprint molds, never finding the right time to tell me. The fire forced me to form questions I didn't know how to ask, but it didn't stop me from obsessing about brothers and brotherhood, searching for lost boys, and trying to right the wrongs of the past. All-encompassing fixations that cost me my job, my partner, and any semblance of meaning in life. And yes, I'm being dramatic, but the truth is, I don't know what to do with myself anymore.

I roll over and will my body to move, to lift my chin up and not let my limbs drift away in a sea of self-pity.

My toes are just hitting the floor when I remember: Verena, the student, and the truth shimmering out there on the horizon, beckoning me.

I check my email while I brew a fresh pot of coffee. Down the hall, there's a faint click followed by the strains of a violin. I breathe a sigh of relief. My father rarely leaves the house, but he's in his office—a small laundry-sized room nestled behind the kitchen. The record player means he's working, typing away at his book, or thinking, staring out his small square window. Either is fine by me. The thought of Verena has quelled the fury in my chest, but it's still there—tail snapping.

The new emails are predictably few and I'm about to put my phone away when a message from my mother pops up. It's an Excel sheet attachment with the names of Verena's students, the ones in Ethan's class highlighted.

They'll tell you she never acted inappropriately, she's written at the bottom.

I roll my eyes.

For someone who considers herself so worldly, my mother can be incredibly naïve. Not that I'm convinced Verena had an affair with the student—there's a stopgap in my imagination whenever I try to picture her seducing anyone—but I'm not so quick to rule it out either.

And, a voice insists, *Oliver wouldn't have confiscated her laptop without a good reason.*

I take my coffee to the living room and turn on the local news. Like checking the crime blotter, it's become a habit since my not-entirely-voluntary resignation. A month ago, I was so crazed with boredom, I thought about buying a police scanner. After visions of myself driving around like a delusional cape-wearing vigilante, I decided against it, but there are times when I would give anything to be recanvassing a crime scene, skimming surveillance footage, for my phone to ring in the middle of the night and send me, heart pounding, out the door.

I put my coffee down and turn up the volume.

The television's splattered with blues and grays, and a man dressed to match stands in front of numbers symbolizing pollen count and wind speed. "We'll see plenty of sunshine today," he promises. "Temperatures will climb into the midsixties, but there will be strong winds with gusts at twenty to thirty miles per hour." My gaze flickers to the window. A leaf caught in a spider's web knocks against the pane.

The screen blinks and we're outside. It's sunny, just like the weatherman promised. A reporter pins a strand of hair behind her ear, unaware the camera's rolling. But then her smile snaps into place.

"It was here," she gestures to the storm-colored building behind her, "on Friday afternoon that the body of Ethan Haddock was discovered by his roommate." The camera zooms in on an upper-story window.

I sit forward in my chair.

Ethan's photo fills the left side of the screen. He's pretty in that soft way of youths halfway through their transformation into manhood—brown curls, wide eyes, and long lashes give him an air of innocence, and I can see why he might awaken a kind of protective maternal urge in Verena, but also why Oliver would be quick to believe the possibility of an affair. High cheekbones, a slightly pointed jaw, a smile that looks simultaneously natural and self-conscious—a few tweaks to his clothes and he could be the lead in a BBC period drama.

"Although the police are treating the death as a suicide, Channel Six

News can report that a professor at the university has been taken in for questioning."

I lean forward. There's no way Athens PD confirmed the cause of death. Not while the investigation is still ongoing. Any unattended death should be investigated as a homicide until the facts prove otherwise. Someone must have leaked the overdose theory.

I focus on the reporter's lips. "The suicide reflects a troubling trend, as more university students are reporting high rates of depression and anxiety, in addition to increased drug and alcohol use."

There's a movement in the upper window of the apartment building. A hand, I think, or a face, but the camera switches to a close-up of the reporter, and it's lost between the strands of her hair.

"More on this from Leland Thomas."

A change of scenery. A U-shaped building I recognize instantly.

"Thanks, Jana. I'm standing in front of Joe Brown Hall." Students pass behind him in pairs. Some point and make faces. *Hi, Mom!* Some stop to watch. "Yesterday morning, Professor Verena Sobek was taken in for questioning by Athens PD. We've spoken with a representative from the university who confirmed that Ethan Haddock was a student in one of Dr. Sobek's courses but refused to comment further. Here she is Monday"—a quick transition to gray-toned footage of the building from the Baldwin Street entrance. The door opens and Oliver steps out, a little pale but sharply dressed in his dark suit. He's followed by two figures: Verena, who's not in handcuffs but is visibly shaken, drawn into herself, with her head down, and my mother, who holds a folder over Verena's face and frowns out into the street.

Maybe it's the protective way she holds that folder or the firm grip she has on Verena's elbow, but something roils in the pit of my stomach. It's an image posted online, slipped into her file, immortalized for the future. And I know that whatever happens, she'll be tied to Verena—not just as her colleague but as her defender. The group turns, and the camera's able to catch Verena from a different angle. It zooms in on her face. She looks shocked, scared, and, I think, a little guilty.

So this explains why the death of Ethan Haddock gets media attention—someone caught the whiff of a scandal. The news isn't the suicide, it's the disgraced professor. And the implication that the suicide and the professor are related.

The screen flashes again. Return to the studio. A different reporter talking about stakeholders and a school renovation.

I sit back.

Oliver was there just like my mother said. She omitted the part about Verena almost needing to be carried out of Joe Brown and the fact that she shielded her from sight like a lawyer protecting a client leaving a courtroom. I draw up Verena's face again, the way her jaw quivered, her haunted expression. She had bags under her eyes, and her dark hair hung unwashed and limp at her slumped shoulders.

My phone vibrates. A text from my mother: *Did you get the list?*

And then, before I can respond, another message: *Kirsten says she'll talk to you. Meet in the Joe Brown lobby in half an hour.*

I stand and walk toward the window. On one hand, the crumpled wet face, dazed look, and sudden weakness of limbs reflect the shocked grief you would expect from someone who's just learned of a death. But the hair, the shadowy slashes of purple encompassing her cheekbones, and heavy weight around her neck point to a prolonged distress. I think of the beautiful boy with the sad eyes. Who was Ethan to Verena?

Him

He knew as soon as he saw her. Dark hair swept back, tan cheeks flushed from the cold, nerves, or both. She looked too young to be a teacher, too scared to stand at the front of the room. Her clothes were professional, but slightly frayed around the edges. Her bag was clearly secondhand. No one observed her at first. She walked to the podium quickly, like if she made it there unnoticed, everything would be okay, but if they recognized her, they might chase her away.

At first it was just that—her insecurity, obvious vulnerability—that drew him toward her. The way she flinched when a student raised their hand. The way her statements arched into questions. The others didn't understand her. Didn't listen to her. Only he—and he alone—saw her brilliance.

That first day, her golden eyes swept the room, looking for a friendly face, for someone to show her she was not alone.

Her eyes met his.

He smiled.

And she smiled back.

Four

Tuesday, March 3, 10:00 A.M.

Thirty minutes later, I slip through a side entrance and stride down the familiar carpeted floors of Joe Brown Hall. Faint scent of dry-erase markers, the rustle of paper, a professor's voice booming out a classroom door and students echoing his words. *Russian*, I think, due to the rough consonant clusters. A flash from last November, the sound of screaming, me tearing through the hall. A fleeting thought: *I shouldn't be here.*

I recognize my mother's students as the ones who smile shyly and look away. Blending in has never really been an option for me—I'm five-nine, all sharp knees and cheekbones, and in another life could have been played by a taller Natalie Portman. That's not to brag, that's just how I *used* to look. My scars appear worse today than they did four months ago. The pinkish skin has turned gray and scaly, thin tissue puckering into slivers along the side of my face. My doctor says it's temporary. A year from now I'll be golden, all new skin like a starfish, maybe a scar or two here or there and a strip of scalp where the hair no longer grows, but otherwise, you know, the picture of perfection.

The lobby is a blue glassed-in breezeway linking two departments—Germanic and Slavic Languages on one side, Comparative Literature on the other. There are couches set across from each other, noticeboards advertising tutors, a fireplace that's never lit but will be strung with tinsel in December. It's a space for students to gather between classes, one that predates laptops and cell phones. Today the students slump over textbooks and avoid eye contact. They chew their fingernails and clutch blue screens in their palms like flat beating hearts.

Toward the far end of the room, a girl sits on the edge of an armchair, nervously swiveling her head between the two main entryways but missing me in the hall.

There's something startled and defiant in her expression when I stride toward her. *Here we go*, I see her think.

"Kirsten," I say for confirmation.

She nods, a quick decisive movement, meeting my gaze for a moment before her eyes skitter away. She has small elvish features and mousy brown hair half hidden by a black beanie. Her clothes are overlarge thrift-store finds, but the laptop's new, as is the backpack, which makes me think the hand-me-down look is a choice rather than a necessity.

A nervous midmorning energy hums through the room. A student opposite Kirsten taps a pen on her knee to the beat in her headphones. Another sits propped up against a table, leg dangling, trying for nonchalance but swinging his head at everyone who glances in his direction. Outside the glass doors, a couple embraces, one girl on her tiptoes, the other breathing into her hair and blocking the entrance so that students and professors alike are forced to draw their bags into their bodies as they slide past.

Meeting here shows my mother's confidence in Verena. *They'll tell you she never acted inappropriately.* The office of the department chair is right around the corner. So is the administrative assistant's. *She has nothing to hide.* But I have a suspicion that, despite the headphones, the girl is listening. The boy is watching me from his table. And whatever my mother thinks, this building is Verena's territory, too. If the students saw something, if they're scared of retribution, they're unlikely to confide in me so close to the rooms where she teaches.

Kirsten's waiting, the unease growing in her face.

"Let's take a walk," I suggest.

"I have a class at eleven," she murmurs.

"We won't go far."

She sighs, but the response is half-hearted—more a signal of the sacrifice she's making than a refusal to cooperate.

I wait while she stuffs her earbuds into her pocket and grabs a backpack from the floor. A last glance at the others like they might save her, a drop of her shoulders when nobody looks her way.

Outside, the birds offer an unruly chorus. The couple has disappeared. And there are faint yells from a Frisbee game somewhere on the quad. A student lies on the thick concrete slab next to the stairs, eyes closed, sunning herself like a cat.

"Have you ever been to the Founders Garden?" I ask.

Kirsten shakes her head.

"It's just here," I say, and take off across the square lawn.

The garden's one of my favorite places on campus. As a child, I'd escape the narrow confines of my mother's gray office for this green space, where the rows of magnolia trees give way to ghostly blue foxgloves, voluptuous camellias, and a white arbor. I have the sudden desire to stride past the gate—not to spoil it with rumors of an affair and thoughts of suicide. I could save this place for myself and take Kirsten through the front courtyard instead. Point out the circular design in the pavers, tell her about the time capsule concealed beneath, and ask what secrets she thinks her professor is hiding.

"I like Dr. Sobek," Kirsten volunteers, breaking the silence and lengthening her stride. Gold flecks in her irises, a shimmer of something as she tilts her head up to me.

I grimace and veer toward the gap in the brick wall. *Fine*, I think to the fates or furies who want us here, and Kirsten follows me through the wrought-iron gate.

She peers around my shoulder. At the far end of the sunken garden, framed by a brick wall, stands a statue of a barefoot girl clutching a rose to her breast.

"Wow," Kirsten says, breaking the spell. "I had no idea this was here."

I gesture to the arbor and empty grounds. "It's a good place for a private conversation."

Her eyebrows lift, and she looks behind us, suddenly unsure.

"And I like Dr. Sobek, too," I tell her.

After all, this isn't an official interview. I don't have to hide the fact that I know Verena. This is simply a nice chat between a former detective and a student who's just learned that one of her classmates died and might have been having an affair with their professor.

She gives me a sidelong glance, connecting, I think, Verena to my mother, my mother to me, and me to Verena, an ellipse of sorts that seems to mollify her.

She bites her lip. "I know I shouldn't say this, given, you know, the circumstances and all, but she was a good teacher." A tight breath. "You could tell she cared." She puts emphasis on the last word, and it strikes me that she's already talking about Verena in the past tense, like she's the one who won't be coming back.

I nod and pull out a notebook. It's a long-ingrained habit, but I trust my pen better than my memory. As I scribble, I wonder how a student determines that her professor cares. Is it the numbers of hours she spends in her office? A quick response to emails? Chatting with the students before class? Over drinks? At her house?

"I appreciate you talking with me," I say, striving for sincerity. I try not to think of what I'll do if I actually learn anything. It all feels like security theater. Equality theater. Whatever you want to call it when the powers that be pretend they're impartial judges interested in the truth while going through motions that do nothing to achieve it. But I'm trying to do the right thing, and I can tell by Kirsten's sudden glance that I've struck the right tone. She wants me to acknowledge this isn't easy and to take her seriously.

"I know it must be strange. Finding out about Ethan. And then the allegations against Dr. Sobek. But they're just allegations—"

"Innocent until proven guilty," Kirsten offers.

"Right," I say. "What we're the most interested in is their relationship, so I'm going to ask you a few questions, if that's all right." I pause to meet her gaze. "Just answer as best you can."

"Okay." She nods, and her lips flatten into a grim line.

I realize a split second too late that I've said "we," as if I belong to a team and my partner's here walking beside me, that he's waiting in the car, or back at the station. The plural gives an authority I alone don't possess and the slip is as close as I'm willing to get to impersonating an officer. I'll let Kirsten make her own assumptions.

"How long have you known Dr. Sobek?" I ask.

"Since fall semester."

"You were in her intermediate German class?"

"Yeah, but I had Weber for beginners." She purses her lips. "He sucked."

I've met Karl Weber. He's another one of my mother's junior colleagues, a thin, unsmiling man, who probably thinks teaching lower-level language classes is beneath him. And she's right, he sucks.

"And was Ethan Haddock in your fall class?"

"Yeah, but I think he had Sobek the year before."

"So Ethan knew Dr. Sobek for two years, then?"

Kirsten exhales. "I guess."

"How well did you know Ethan?"

Ambivalent shrug.

One thing I learned from last fall: college students are fiercely loyal to one another. Even though they're adults, an older person still equals a symbol of authority. They close ranks. Don't bother asking—they don't know why they're doing it and will clam up even if it goes against their best interests. They need time to decide they're telling you of their individual volition, that they've applied their newly developed critical thinking skills and come to the conclusion to be helpful on their own, not because you told them to.

"Did you ever talk to him?"

She frowns, and I picture a classroom full of students sitting next to one another but not speaking, earbuds in, asleep at their desks, or awake, but ignoring one another for the tiny worlds on their phones, shoulders hunched and eyes glazed in silent screams for help, for someone to break the spell, to save them from themselves.

"Sometimes Sobek made us work in pairs."

"Okay." I note her reticence. Could be something there. "Was Ethan a nice guy? A jerk? Talkative? Shy?"

She inclines her head, her gaze moving away from me, toward the arbor. "He was smart," she says after a pause. "Always knew the right answer. Was the first person to put his hand up if Sobek asked a question. And he would nod like he understood every word she said. She'd look around the room to see if anyone else knew the answer, but she always called on him."

Strike one, I think. Preferential treatment.

"And how would you describe Dr. Sobek?"

Eyes to the treetops, annoyed glare in my direction. "You *know* her."

"I do," I concede. "But I want to hear your opinion. How you view her—from a student perspective."

She chews her cheek. "I already told you." Short puff of a breath. "She *cared*."

I nod, right, super generic, not helpful at all. I let the silence stretch between us to see if there's more.

"But . . ." She hesitates. "Maybe she cared too much, you know?"

Lift of an eyebrow, say nothing.

"Like if we failed a test, she was more upset than we were. Like she thought she had failed us somehow, when in reality we just couldn't be bothered to study. And sometimes, the way she looked at us," another pause, "it was kind of needy."

I frown. "Needy how?"

"I don't know." Furrow of her eyebrows, thinking. "Like she needed us to like her, I guess, or to think she was a good teacher. Like teaching was everything to her. And if we hadn't done our homework or weren't interested in her lecture, she'd crumble. Some of the guys—they said she was one step away from a nervous breakdown, wanted to be the ones to push her over the edge."

The frown lines deepen between her eyebrows, and her chin tilts down, not like she'll cry, but like she's suddenly older, like it's dawned on her for the first time that authority figures can't be trusted—and not because they'll get you into trouble, but because they're troubled themselves. I can almost see the new weight settle around her shoulders.

"What guys?" I ask.

"Mainly Chase and Travis, but some of the other guys were in on it, too."

"Last names?" I ask.

She shrugs. "I don't know."

"But not Ethan," I say.

Shake of her head. "It was like he tried to compensate for the rest of us. Be extra good so she wouldn't notice how bad we were."

Strike two. Ethan protecting Verena, playing knight to her damsel.

"Can you tell me more about the class itself?" I ask. "Does Dr. Sobek stand at the front and lecture or—" *walk around the room, whispering sweet nothings to her good students in private?*

"No—that's what Weber did." She throws out her hand and imitates him. "*Schlagen Sie Ihre Bücher auf Seite*—cue infinite boredom reading questions and answers out of the book."

I smile. Her accent's not bad.

"Sobek would go through grammar on a PowerPoint and then have us practice speaking in pairs. She'd come around and help if we needed it."

So, half right.

"Did you ever see her act in a way that was inappropriate?" I ask. "Toward Ethan or any other student?"

Kirsten's beanie slips over her eyebrows. "No." She pushes it up. "I mean, she smiled a lot, but not at anyone in particular. I think she just wanted to put us at ease, you know, so we would talk."

"Did she smile at Ethan?"

"Yeah, but no more than at anyone else." Her voice is both thoughtful and defensive. "There's no rule that says she can't be nice to her students."

"Of course not," I say diplomatically. "So you never witnessed anything unusual?"

"No," she says. "Except, well . . ." She pauses. We reach the arbor and turn back down the path toward the entrance. "Once, I forgot my book in the classroom, and I was halfway down Lumpkin before I remembered, so when I got back everyone was gone, but Dr. Sobek was still packing up and Ethan was there, which," she corrects quickly, "isn't that weird. I mean, some students stay after to ask questions. It's easier than waiting for office hours, you know?" A slight cock of her head at me. "But anyway, I just remember that Ethan seemed embarrassed when I ran into the room, and it kind of looked like—I don't know—like maybe he had been crying."

"Crying," I repeat.

"I'm not sure, I mean, it could've been allergies or something, but his eyes were red, and his voice had this kind of raw edge—"

"And Dr. Sobek?" I ask. "Were they standing together? Touching at all?"

"No," Kirsten says, firm, no hesitation, a slight curl of disgust at me for suggesting it. "I think she was actually relieved that I came back. She looked uncomfortable."

"When was this?"

"I don't know—a few weeks ago?"

"End of January?" I ask. "Beginning of February?"

She exhales and swings her bag off her shoulder. "Let me check. It was right before my trig test, that's why I was hurrying." She thumbs through a well-worn scheduler. "Here. February twelfth." Her hand wavers slightly as she holds out the page to me.

"You sure?" I ask, scribbling the date in my notebook.

Another impatient breath. "No, not a hundred percent sure, but yeah, like eighty-five to ninety percent."

Fast gallop of steps coming up the sidewalk, a couple pressed together, one smothering a laugh in the other's sleeve when they turn the corner and realize they're not alone. Kirsten swings her head around. I need her to focus.

"What were they talking about?"

She scrunches her nose, eyes still on the couple. I watch her face carefully.

"I can't remember," she says finally and shakes her head. "I wasn't paying attention."

I give Kirsten my phone number in case she thinks of anything else, and she races off to her next class without a backward glance. As I watch her beanie disappear, I realize two things: my mother chose Kirsten because she thought she'd confirm what she's been telling me—Verena's a good teacher, would never sleep with a student, blah blah blah; and anyone she sends my way is going to repeat this assertion. But even with my mother handpicking a student who would talk in Verena's favor, and despite Kirsten's own innocent-until-proven-guilty quip, Kirsten fell headfirst into the affair narrative. She gave me two reasons to believe it and threw in only minor caveats to muddy the waters. It didn't feel intentional. In fact, I doubt she even realized she did it, but now that the students have heard the rumor of the affair, they'll all be seeing signs, whether they were there or not.

I take one last look around the garden. The couple's disappeared into the far corner. The stone girl stands a silent witness. *Ethan and Verena both deserve better*, I think as I let the metal latch clank against the gate.

I follow the pebbled path around a redbrick building and make my way downtown. I picture Ethan walking this same path. His apartment—the one from the news report this morning—is not far from Joe Brown, a half-mile walk under oak trees and iron light posts. A half mile to Verena's office.

How might it happen? Did she work late? A light burning in her window a secret sign? Or did he watch her, crouched outside her building in the dark? A shiver sneaks up my neck at the thought of him stalking Verena in the shadows.

It must be one or the other, I think.

Real or imagined, Ethan at least believed there was something going on between them. Otherwise, why would he have been crying in her classroom? Why would Verena be relieved to see Kirsten, but then shaking and nearly paralyzed in my mother's kitchen? Why would Oliver suspect her involvement in Ethan's death?

The patio outside Walker's is occupied by a handful of regulars who nod when I approach but then return to their newspapers and black coffees. I bless them for getting their stares out of the way months ago. A man sits at the long outside bar, his back to me, but I catch a flash of orange running shoes. It's not Teddy. Of course not. He only drank obsessive loads of coffee because I did. But my mind's suddenly blank. I forget why I'm here, what I'm supposed to be doing, and stand, holding my phone in my hand until Roger—a bearded veteran of indeterminate age—clears his throat and I realize I'm hovering above his table. I grab a seat farther down, glancing again at Teddy's doppelgänger, before I pull up my mother's list on my screen.

One thing I didn't notice earlier—she's put asterisks next to some of the names. Her star witnesses. Kirsten is one of them.

I shake my head. German's a small program. My mother would know the good from the bad. And she may be thinking the good ones are more likely to be helpful, but they're also the least likely to say something negative about a professor. They're no dummies. They've learned to be impartial—at least with strangers—and to hold their tongues lest word get back to the professors themselves. I'm not interested in the ones who've learned diplomacy, to keep their mouths shut and ears open. I want the opposite. The ones who still think shit-talking is cool, who like the sound of their own voices and think others do, too. I send emails to the students without asterisks.

The first to respond says he can meet in half an hour. I type the address for Walker's in case he's never been, click Send, and then sit back to wait. I tilt my head and examine the pub's hulking garage-style windows and chipped maroon paint. A bird with speckled wings swoops across the aluminum awning, and I let my eyes close briefly.

The student—olive skin, dark glossy hair that's swept back into a lacquered frozen custard swirl, cocky upturn of his lips—arrives twenty minutes late, tells me my burns are "fire," and that there's nothing wrong with professors sleeping with their students.

"It's just sex," he says loudly and with a quick glance around for approval. "In Europe, it wouldn't even be a big deal."

Roger snorts but doesn't look up from his paper. The student swivels his head but can't determine the source of the sound. I suspect one summer his parents took him to Italy and now he considers himself an expert.

"Did you ever see Dr. Sobek act in a way that was inappropriate?"

"Nah." Shrug of his shoulders. "But sometimes she'd lean over to help you, and you could see down her shirt. She wore these lace bras—"

"Did it seem intentional?"

"What?"

"Did it seem like she was trying to get you to look down her shirt?"

Twitch of a smile. He likes the idea of Verena as an exhibitionist, but he shakes his head. "I doubt it. Probably would have been super embarrassed if she knew."

"Did you ever see Dr. Sobek act inappropriately with Ethan Haddock?"

The head shake is slower this time. "Nah, but you could tell she liked him—smart kid and all."

"Do you think they were having an affair?" I ask him.

He leans forward. Smiles at me. "Sure," he says, "why not?"

I resist the urge to roll my eyes. "Thanks," I say, not bothering with sincerity this time. "You've been a great help."

I wave him away, and he stands, looking disappointed.

"Riley said she'd come by at two if you're still around."

"I'll be here," I tell him.

Riley's tearful. A wisp of a girl with slumping shoulders, she's trailing scarves and tissues, like she's worked herself up for this conversation the entire walk here.

"I sat next to him." Her brown eyes are wide. "I just—I would have never thought. I mean," sniff, "if I had known," sniff, sniff, "I would have said something."

"Like what?" I lean back and fold my arms over my chest.

She gives me a wide-mouthed stare. "I don't know . . . anything. You know, like, 'Don't do it. You have so much to live for. There are other girls—'" Her voice breaks, and I wonder if maybe she was a little in love with Ethan. "I mean," pinched mouth, "why would he kill himself over Dr. Sobek? She's not even that hot—and she's old." Look of revulsion.

I raise an eyebrow.

"No offense," she says quickly, eyes flickering over my scars, trying to guess my age.

"None taken." I fiddle with my pen. The tears, I notice, are gone.

Behind her, a dark-haired man strides across the sidewalk and glances backward as he slips through the coffee shop door. It's my old colleague. Oliver Graves.

I frown.

Despite working Homicide two years together—he was promoted a year after me—we don't trust each other. It wasn't always this way. We got along fine—a little teasing because he was new and so determined to make a good impression, but otherwise a nice working relationship, an occasional drink if one of us got a solve, a sympathetic grimace if one of us—usually me—got on Truman's bad side. But the last case changed that. I'm partly to blame, but so is he. He recognized pretty early that I had personal reasons for believing a prominent fraternity on campus was involved in the death of one of their own, and I broke protocol in my desperation to prove it. My actions got me suspended and nearly implicated him and Teddy. But while I was stalking fraternity members and crashing their parties, Oliver was pointing in any and every other direction. Although I can't prove it, I still think he was compromised—getting pressure from the outside to wrap up the case—and undermined the investigation.

I have the feeling he's not here for the caffeine, that instead he's keeping an eye on me. But there's no way he could know that my afternoon coffee has anything to do with his case. And while I might not have access to lab reports or witness statements, I can talk to anyone I want. *And he can't stop me*, I think.

I focus my attention back on Riley and ignore the sense that Oliver's somewhere inside, watching.

"So you think they were having an affair?"

"I mean, that's what the note said. Why would Ethan lie?" She furrows her brow. "Except, wait." Her hands flutter excitedly to her chest. "What if he didn't write it? I mean someone could have written it after the fact—"

"Who said there was a note?" I ask.

"I don't know." She shrugs. "I think I saw it online."

"Where?" I ask.

"I don't know," she repeats. "But if you think about it, there must have been one, right? Otherwise, how do the police know it was a suicide? And how do they know about Dr. Sobek?" She lifts her hands. "All I'm saying is anyone could have written it as long as they had access to his apartment. Or, I mean, they could have slipped it in the mail?" Her voice arches into a question.

I resist the urge to roll my eyes. In the days of *CSI Name-Your-City*, everyone thinks they're a detective. People make assumptions. Even officers are warned when responding to a potential suicide not to let the initial report bias their findings. But it happens. Detectives take shortcuts and rush the investigation. And for Verena, the public speculating about her involvement is even more dangerous.

"So I mean—" She blows her nose and then continues breathlessly. "Someone could have snuck into his room after and written— Oh my god," she exclaims, "I mean, how do we even know he killed himself? Maybe someone killed him and just made it look like—"

She's going fully off script now, but I don't stop her.

"Why would someone do that?" I ask.

"I don't know. I mean, aren't you supposed to figure that out?" She shakes her tissue at me.

I grimace, knowing this is the notion I've allowed. Still, it doesn't sit right. "Let's return to your idea that there was a note and someone else wrote it in order to accuse Dr. Sobek," I say. "Why?"

She shrugs. "Maybe she gave them a bad grade? Or, I don't know, maybe they just didn't like her."

"But you're talking about someone breaking into Ethan's apartment, killing him, forging a note, all just to get back at a professor for a bad grade? That seems like a lot of effort."

Careful, a small voice warns. Hypothesizing with a student could lead to her quoting me to anyone who'll listen, changing the narrative without a shred of evidence. But it's been months since I ran through theories with anyone and it feels good—even if my conversation partner leaves much to be desired. I close my eyes briefly and let the sun turn the backs of my eyelids gold. *It's not a real case anyway*, another voice argues. *The same rules don't apply*.

She shrugs again. "Sometimes students really hate their professors." She leans in conspiratorially. "Once, my friend Melissa tried to get her professor fired because he embarrassed her in class. I think it was math and he called on her and she didn't know the answer—she probably wasn't paying attention, she's like addicted to her phone—anyway, I guess he gave her a look that more or less said she was an idiot and the rest of the class laughed, and so she wrote an anonymous email to his boss or whatever saying he was using racist anecdotes in class, like talking about Black people and welfare checks, and she even convinced one of her friends to make a similar complaint, accusing him of saying the N-word."

"Seriously?" I breathe.

"Yeah," she says, as if only now realizing how bad it sounds. "She can be a real bitch sometimes. Anyway, long story short, she got called in to academic affairs, and it became pretty clear she made it up, so I think she's on academic probation or something." She stares at me evenly. "I'm just saying, it could happen."

"Can you think of anyone who hated Dr. Sobek that much?" I ask her.

"Yeah, actually," she says slowly. "I can."

Riley tells me the names of two students who she claims tried to make Verena's life miserable—Chase Warren and Travis Hubbard. I assume they're the same Travis and Chase Kirsten mentioned. She references another—Madison King—whom she overheard saying she wished Dr. Sobek would die in a fiery car crash, even though she was sure she didn't mean it.

I watch Riley cross the intersection in front of the university arches and then turn my attention to the handful of crumpled tissues she's left on the table. I'm gathering them up with the pages of a discarded newspaper when I hear my name.

Oliver leans against the back of the wrought-iron chair across from me, a drink in one hand that might be coffee but is smothered with so much chocolate syrup and whipped cream, it should be considered a different drink entirely.

I smirk.

"Interesting conversation?" he asks, nodding at the tissues.

"Just a friend with boy issues," I say half truthfully, irritated to have my suspicions confirmed that he was watching.

"A friend, huh?" Oliver sips his drink. "Are you friends with a lot of Professor Sobek's students?"

I glare at him. But, of course, he would have studied Ethan's class list and recognized Riley right away.

I fold my arms over my chest. "I don't know what you're talking about."

He smiles. "Good," he says. "Because if you did, it might look like you were interfering with a police investigation. Witness tampering. Intimidation." He ticks each off with his fingers. "You could be arrested for obstruction of justice." He shrugs. "Of course, that's just hypothetical, since you and Riley Jenkins are friends."

He tilts his hand to his forehead in a mock salute. "See you around," he says as he walks away.

I purse my lips. His threats are empty. I know that, but I can't help wondering why he's so interested in a suicide case.

I think over my conversation with Riley. Her theory of a student forging a note has a lot of logistical holes. How would the student have known where Ethan lived, never mind how to break into his apartment and compose a note in his handwriting? There are easier ways to terrorize your professor than murder and note forging—like Riley's friend Melissa. And despite what Riley says she saw online, Athens PD would never release information about a note. But if it exists, chances are that Ethan wrote it. And if some of Verena's students hated her, maybe he did, too.

* * *

It's just after four in the afternoon. My mother's standing at the kitchen counter, grading papers. A rare occurrence for her to be home early on a weekday. The light from the window flickers across her face, shadows shifting with every strike of her pen, and I wonder if she's avoiding her office, what her colleagues think of the allegations, and if they know she's gotten me involved.

"I talked to three of Verena's students," I tell her.

"And?" she asks, writing a large C on the top of the page.

"And nothing. It sounds like a few students didn't like her, but they didn't see any unusual behavior, even if some wouldn't rule out an affair from the realm of possibilities."

She sighs. "They have no idea how serious this is. I heard two young men gossiping outside my office today claiming one in five professors sleeps with their students." She shakes her head. "I asked if they were quoting from a reliable, peer-reviewed source."

I smirk as I pour myself a cup of coffee. Of course she did.

But being a professor is no proof of anything. No proof of higher morals, liberal-mindedness, or progressive tendencies. No proof of good intentions. Some professors are assholes. Some aren't. Some get tenure. Some don't. Some dutifully sacrifice themselves on the altar of higher education, subjecting themselves to peer review, agonizing over lesson plans, and losing sleep over student absences and substandard participation; while others embarrass and harass their students, stalk them, sleep with them, and get nothing more than a slap on the wrist, a note in their file, or a transfer to another university.

I know a woman who married one of her students. She was in graduate school; he was a senior. They waited until he wasn't in her class to start dating. There were some suggestive comments, a few headshakes, but all in all, it wasn't a big deal. Having an affair with a current student falls more into the moral gray area. Yes, if we're talking about college, then the student is an adult, but such relationships have all kinds of ethical and legal concerns. They have the potential to create unhealthy power dynamics, opportunities for bias and retribution. So if Verena did have an affair with Ethan Haddock, it raises a few questions: Did Ethan feel pressured to do things because she was his professor? Did he get special treatment? Did it detract from his learning in any way? Did it lead to his death?

I sip my coffee, thinking if this were a murder investigation, it would be a lot more straightforward.

"So what's next?" my mother asks.

I've been wondering the same thing, but the question still rankles. *I don't work for you*, I want to say, which doesn't make sense because I'm clearly doing this for me.

"Three students claiming they didn't witness anything doesn't prove Verena's innocence," I tell her, resisting the urge to scratch an itch under my compression sleeve.

If Verena was having an affair with a student, I doubt she'd be foolish enough to give any indication of it in class. And after the thrill wore off, who could stand being so secretive and snubbed on a daily basis? If Ethan thought he loved her, maybe he wanted her to acknowledge the relationship. Maybe she refused. And then he took matters into his own hands. *Blackmail*. That would explain why Oliver was interested in her laptop.

I drum my fingers on the table. My head's wrecked, and yet I feel like I haven't learned anything. I want to know more about Ethan, what the techs found in his apartment, if there was, in fact, a note, and if there's any reason to believe someone else wrote it.

My mother rummages through her purse and holds out a rectangular object.

"What's that?" I ask.

"A voice recorder. I use it whenever I'm working on a new article."

"You have a smartphone," I tell her. "There are apps for that."

She shrugs. "I'm old-school, as the students say. Anyway, it works for me." She extends it across the table. "Here."

"And what am I supposed to do with this?"

"I thought it might be useful when you talk to the students. You could put it in your purse—"

I laugh. "You know it's illegal to record a conversation someone reasonably expects to be private, right?"

She thinks I'm being difficult, but it's true. Most privacy laws fall under the Federal Wiretap Act. And although there are loopholes—Georgia has a "one-party consent" law, meaning that I could record the conversation without the other person's permission so long as I was taking part in it—the fact that she'd ask me to record my student conversations means she's getting desperate.

She sighs, the long-suffering exhalation of a stubborn-child parent. "It's just in case you hear something relevant to the Title Nine investigation," she says. "Verena's not standing trial. She just needs," she gestures to the recorder, "someone to believe her."

"Fine," I say. I don't have the energy to argue. Instead, I slip the recorder in my jacket pocket with absolutely no intention of using it.

"Couldn't you—?" she begins.

I frown at her. I know what she wants—for me to call in a favor. To see if I can find out more about the case and about Ethan. But I can't. I burned those bridges, scuttled the boats, and took off from a muddy runway while loaded with 2,700 pounds of aviation fuel. Teddy's made it clear he wants nothing to do with me. And Oliver's just threatened to arrest me for obstruction of justice. There've been no phone calls from Dara or Aisha, Athens's best digital and crime scene forensic analysts, whom I once considered friends. Even Cindy, Teddy's girlfriend—a nurse, whose medical insights always came in handy and whose kindness I took for granted—has vanished from my life. There's no one left.

I haven't said anything to her about Teddy. She knows I resigned, and I'm sure has some idea about the reason—you don't leave after a big win, after all—but she's never asked. Still, she knows my father's book project isn't enough to keep me going. He threw it out last December like a lifeline, and I caught on and held it tight, but my grip's been slipping for a while now.

I think of the storm-gray building at the intersection of Broad and Oconee. The woman on the news gesturing to the upper window. What I need now is less of a lifeboat and more of a ship's hull.

Artisan's Corner, the apartment building where Ethan died, juts out between a sea of traffic, an ever-changing, always-morphing structure. One story to two, cotton stores to kitchen counters, apples to table saws. Alternating faces peering out the windows—couples, sisters, lovers, friends. Layers of thick paint burying fingerprints, one catching bits of hair and oven grease, the next baby's breath and burned milk. Concrete slabs covered with hardwood, linoleum, carpet, rugs, but underneath it all is Georgia clay that runs red in water like a vein split open just waiting to spill its secrets.

And I'm certain of this more than anything else: I need to get inside.

Her

It's my fault. I moved us here.

I met Christopher on a Thursday afternoon in late January, my fifth year as a graduate student at Tufts University. It was one of those impossible winter days, where the snow turns to sludge and every few steps take so much effort you're sweating despite the freezing temperature. The kind of day that made me believe my father was onto something when he moved his new wife and family to a sunny house with a terrace near the Bosporus. I was thinking of my father, of the last time I saw him, my half-siblings crawling at his feet, and how happy he looked, thinking that I couldn't imagine him smiling like that if he lived in Germany, thinking how no one smiles like that north of the Alps or anywhere so goddamn cold, when a man bumped into me. Later, Christopher would say that I looked up with such a deep scowl, he had no choice but to make me laugh.

Two years later, I finished my dissertation, got the job offer from UGA, and held my breath as I showed the letter to Christopher, a flash of my father at the edge of my vision, whispering that mine was a life he couldn't live.

"Awesome," Christopher said instead. "I love R.E.M."

And just like that we packed up his car and headed to the Classic City.

He found a job in cybersecurity at a bank. I started teaching.

It's one of those things that only becomes clear in hindsight, but he brought joy into my life—laughter and good food, hot chocolate with marshmallows. I know that meeting him saved me in some way—from myself, my work, my self-isolation and anxious tendencies. But that's a lot of pressure to put on a person—to be your savior. It means they can't ever ask for saving themselves. And even though Christopher makes coffee in the morning, tells me to rest my eyes from the computer, and organizes hikes on the weekends, the anxiety still creeps in.

I saw the way the other professors looked when my name was announced in the list of new hires at the first meeting—sandwiched between John Smith and Mike Stanton—Verena Sobek—the middle *e* mispronounced like "teen," like "Ver-een-a" instead of "Ver-ay-nah"—and looks between the other faculty that said "not another one," eyebrows raised, wondering the nationality of the name Verena, of Sobek, calculating how much the university paid for my green card and immigration lawyer. The college never certain how much diversity is too much diversity. The human resources officer wondering aloud what the point is of hiring a woman with a Muslim background if she doesn't bother wearing a hijab. My colleagues debating the merits of affirmative action and speculating whether I checked a box to gain an advantage. If I can claim this part of my heritage even if I'm nonpracticing. The feeling I have to prove myself and work longer and harder than everyone else.

"But to who?" Christopher asked a few weeks ago.

He had cooked dinner. I could smell vegetables roasted in wine and herbs. I was hungry, but still in the living room, a stack of ungraded assignments in front of me. I hadn't looked up when he said it was ready. Didn't stir when I heard him lay everything on the table. Or when I sensed him waiting. The vegetables grew cold. Finally, he asked "to who" I was trying to prove myself.

"To whom," I replied without thinking.

That was the day that laughter vanished from our house. Not for good. It's been a slow death. But the laughter died, and I killed it—one evasive grammar correction, one weekend spent working, one missed lunch, then dinner, then date night at a time.

So that today, when I come home, I see how much effort the smile takes, the forced nature of our conversation. And he's less my cuddly giant than a large circus bear, performing all his tricks to make me laugh. I'm smiling smiles that don't reach my eyes. And we're pretending, so much pretending every day, that everything's okay, pretending like our lives depend on it. Pretending my anxiety's not a disease slowly infecting our house. A disease even Jagger senses. We take him on long walks. Hold his leash like a lifeline, a fraying tether, the last strand before everything breaks apart.

Maybe I should have told Christopher all of this. The stress. The fatigue. The fears of failure.

I could tell him that I caught a student cheating today. That she denied it—lied to my face without so much as a blink. Even though it was obvious. It was their first exam, and she made the same mistakes as the girl next to her. Wrote sentences that made no sense. When I showed her, she swore she would never do such a thing and then got mad at me for suggesting it. I could tell him about the boy who kept getting up to use the bathroom during the exam, who rolled his eyes when I told him to leave his phone, my male colleague who found a list of vocabulary words next to the sink. I could tell him how Helena said I shouldn't worry about it. To just give the girl a warning. The boy a point deduction. And so, I gave her a warning. I reduced his grade. But I'll be watching her. Him. All of them.

But I don't tell Christopher.

I thought there was an implicit understanding—that it was obvious from the bruised purple slashes under my eyes, the way I toss and turn in my sleep, that I was cracking, flailing, barely holding it all together. But today when I arrived home, he was trying on button-up linen shirts, sucking in his belly in the mirror and switching out belts.

"What's the occasion?" I asked.

"Dinner," he said. "With Mike and Julia." A questioning glance at my reflection in the glass. "At Last Resort. I asked you about it last week." The smile crumples at the edges as doubt creeps in. "Remember?"

I remember a stack of exams to grade and a pinch in my neck from bending over them. I remember him rubbing my shoulders and saying something while I wrote "dative prepositions," "spelling," and "conjugation" in the margins. I vaguely remember nodding, saying "Sounds great," while thinking if I could just get ten done before dinner, I could finish the rest before bed.

"Do we have to?" I ask, my voice a barely concealed whine.

Christopher turns to face me.

"I told them we were coming. Julia made reservations. They're really looking forward to meeting you, and I'm excited for you to meet them, too."

"But why?" It's the fatigue—it must be—but I feel pinpricks of tears in the corners of my eyes.

"Why?" he repeats. I can tell he hopes I'm joking, that he thinks if he pretends this is the case, I will go along with him.

"Because of friends, that's why."

I feel the weight of papers in my bag, the stress of my conference presentation next month, the ticking of the tenure clock, and the knowledge that if I don't succeed, I'll have to leave this job that's already swallowed a decade of my life. Just the thought of changing clothes, leaving the house again, and being around new people makes me exhausted.

"Can't we just—"

"Stay here, grade papers, work, never enjoy our lives until we die?" His voice lifts to let me know he's teasing, but there's a bite of truth to his words.

"It will be fun," he says, drawing me into his arms. He smells of toothpaste and aftershave. "Remember fun?"

"But—"

"We've lived here over a year," he says. "Don't you want to see something other than my silly face? Go to restaurants, people's houses, watch football games? Hang out with someone other than your colleagues? Not think about work for a change?"

"I like my colleagues," I say, although Helena's the only one who's actually nice to me. "And I like your face."

"Great," he says. "Then you can sit across from me at dinner."

It's not that bad. Mike's balding, in his midforties. He works with Christopher in cybersecurity and spends most of the evening telling funny stories about his boyfriend who rents a booth at a fancy salon downtown. Julia's on the pudgy side, wearing an old band T-shirt and ripped jeans. She's a little shy like me but loves cinema, and we spend the evening comparing notes on our favorite Weimar directors.

But then they ask me about work, and I start complaining about the long hours and lack of sleep (all I seem to do now is complain, I can't help it!). How I thought being a professor smelled like old books and warm sweaters, grading papers while listening to music, a mug of tea in my hand, Jagger in my lap, and Christopher by my side. When really it tastes like stale coffee and hastily shoveled snacks in front of my computer and feels like light-headedness when I miss a meal. It smells like mildew and long nights in my office and sounds like students complaining in the halls and passive-aggressive department emails. It's catching students cheating and turning a blind eye. Or confronting them and watching them lie to your face. It's the prickly feeling of students lingering just a little too long outside your door. It's colleagues pretending they don't understand you because of your accent. It's never feeling good enough, smart enough, German enough, American enough, professorial enough.

But, of course, Christopher's too proud of me to let me criticize myself, so instead he brags about my "work ethic."

"She's like a shark," he tells them. "If she stops swimming, she'll die."

I think I'm more like the snake that eats its own tail. My work, my drive, whatever you want to call it, is slowly consuming me whole. I don't know where I begin and it ends.

Him

It was his favorite class.

As the leaves turned red and gold, he memorized dative prepositions and learned that the genitive case was used to show possession. He translated phrases:

The heart of the man—*das Herz des Mannes*
The soul of the woman—*die Seele einer Frau*

He attended his other classes. Economics. Finance. Psychology. But while the professors lectured, he diagrammed the German cases. In neat square boxes, he listed definite articles, added the plural forms and possessive adjectives. He collected words without English equivalents:

Sehnsucht—the longing for some unknown thing
Zweisamkeit—the feeling of closeness between two people
Weltschmerz—the pain of the world

In the mornings, he took his time choosing what to wear. The other students rolled out of bed, hair a mess, T-shirts wrinkled, smelling of stale beer from the night before. But he brushed his teeth and slicked back his hair.

He straightened his shoulders before he entered the classroom.

"*Guten Morgen*," he said.

"*Guten Morgen*," she echoed.

She stood at the front of the room in a navy skirt and scuffed black boots. She had missed a button on her sweater so that it hung asymmetrical at her waist. He wanted to tell her. To reach out and fix those buttons so close to her skin.

They were studying adjective endings. She drew their attention to the patterns in the masculine nominative and feminine accusative cases. A green stripe from her dry-erase marker bloomed on the side of her hand.

"How am I supposed to learn German when she can barely speak English?" whispered a student in the back.

"I don't get it," moaned another in the front. "Why do Germans make everything so difficult?"

"But that's what makes this fun," she countered, her cheeks flushing. "The language is like a puzzle." Her eyes moved to his, seeking someone who understood. "But unlike in love and life, here, once you understand the rules, you always win."

She scanned the room. "Can anyone translate the sentence on the board?"

He put his hand up.

"*Wunderbar*," she said.

Five

Wednesday, March 4, 9:00 A.M.

I park my car on Clayton in front of a clothing store. It rained last night—low rumbles of thunder matched by a heavy downpour thrumming against my parents' roof—and a dampness lingers in the air. Puddles gather in the uneven dips of the sidewalk, but the sky is a vibrant, crystallized blue. In another life, on this kind of day, Teddy would meet me on my doorstep for a morning run and we'd keep the same pace until the very end when I'd sprint the last hundred yards. On another day, another morning, he might even let me win.

But today I'm met by a cluster of students laughing open-mouthed, baring their teeth. The rush and hiss of their breath curls in the early-morning air. They cup their hands around a shared cigarette and lean together as if they could shield themselves against the blows of the world. Wind whips around corners once occupied by oak trees. A server dries bistro tables. And I stride toward Artisan's Corner clenching my fists, forcing myself to reckon with this new destiny, where I'm alone and following Verena non-leads, and Teddy's at the station without me.

At the edge of North Thomas, a grizzled homeless guy with a dog asks for money, and I ask whether he's seen any cop cars here recently. He meets my gaze, an uneasy steel-blue stare under thick gray brows that takes in my burns dispassionately, and then moves away, saying he doesn't want trouble. The dog sniffs at my feet, gives a slow wag of its tail, and then slinks after him.

I linger, letting my gaze move slowly up and down the street. I don't have a plan. Not really. I just want to slip into Ethan's shoes for an hour, get a feel for the space where he lived, see if Verena left her presence like tendrils of smoke, an outline of her destruction on a wall like volcanic ash. My best bet is to slip in behind a resident, a morning delivery, or a fleeing one-night stand. If anyone asks, I'll say I'm visiting Emily, Katie, Ansley—something I can mumble my way through.

There's no movement at the front entrance, so I slip around the side. No one here either. I pull out my phone, act like there's something interesting on the screen. And while I wait for the door to open, I scan the rows of tempered glass. They're outlined with thick red paint and have grime at the edges. Prayer flags flattened with tape hang next to string lights. A black-and-white drawing of a fist. A child's rainbow scrawl. And as my gaze flicks from one to another, I catch a movement, a pale shape in an upper window, and then a sign appears. It holds two neatly scrawled words: FOR RENT.

I lean back against the wall, chewing my lip.

A moment later, the side door opens.

"Excuse me." I lift my hand, but the man is already striding past, eyes straight ahead, not a glance in either direction. The door clicks shut.

Shit.

"Wait," I say, running after him. I fumble in my bag, thinking of a missing key card, a lost phone, something to justify my presence, smack of a hapless look, a helpless grin, when my eye catches the edge of the sign again.

"Is that your apartment?" I yell.

The man stops and turns his head like I might be talking to someone else.

I point to the window. "The one for rent?"

Up close, he's all broad shoulders and pronounced cheekbones, square jaw, and slick brown hair. He's dressed in dark jeans and an olive Henley, with a leather satchel strapped across his chest.

"Yes," he says slowly.

"Is it still available?"

A second hesitation as he scans my face. Flecks of amber in his brown eyes. Serious expression as he evaluates my hair, my clothes. Careful—not free-falling through life like most students, confident there are wings stretched out somewhere beneath him, but guarded, like he's found the ground at the bottom once or twice and knows better than to let just anyone near.

I smile softly. Caution is a character trait I appreciate. These days, too many people are willing to give away everything for nothing—tell their secrets for a smile, bare their soul for a like, show exactly where they live, work, where their children play for a click of a heart that costs no more than their privacy, a bit of security, and control over their lives.

He meets my gaze. "Just the one room," he says after a pause. "For two months until the end of term."

I wait.

He shifts on his feet. "There was a—" His eyes slide away from mine, the corners of his mouth crumple, and I realize that in my eagerness to get inside, I've missed the obvious: the availability aligns with Ethan's death, it must be his room for rent. And this is quite possibly the roommate who discovered his body.

On a smaller campus, by now everyone might know everything about Ethan—where he lived, where he died. But with close to forty thousand students and dozens of apartment complexes off campus, he has no reason to suspect I know what happened. I feel a quick stab of pity followed by a surge of excitement—this is my chance, not only to get into the building, but to see Ethan's apartment, his room. "—a sudden vacancy," the man finishes. "And we're looking for a subletter."

While he was speaking, his lips have paled, and his arms have moved closer to his body, folding in on himself. His eyes are suddenly younger, less certain, less watchful than wary. He's still fresh with bruises from the ground, I realize. I need to tread carefully. Can't show too much interest in the vacancy, can't give him any reason to doubt my motives.

"Well," I say, pretending not to notice his hesitation, "this is incredible. I was just on my way to the front office to see if anything was available."

His eyebrows lift a fraction, and I wonder if there is, in fact, a front office.

"I didn't think I'd be this lucky," I continue in a rushed, slightly flighty tone in case I've made a mistake. "It's normally impossible to find anything in the middle of the semester. And I bet you'll have, like, a million calls by the end of the day, but if you have time, I'd love to see the apartment." *Pretty please*, my voice says. "Then I could submit an application before the rest of the world finds out."

I've been talking so fast I've made myself sound breathless and a little desperate, but it works. The crease between his eyebrows disappears. He checks his watch.

"I have class at nine thirty but could let you in for a quick look around." A flicker of a smile as he runs his fingers through his hair. "If you're interested, it would save me the hassle of returning phone calls and fielding applications."

"Great," I say, exhaling a small laugh.

He motions for me to follow him back into the shadow of the building and thumbs through his well-organized satchel—notebook, laptop, pens arranged by height and clipped outward to a side pocket, no gross tissues falling out, nothing rolling around at the bottom—before withdrawing a key.

A click of the lock and he holds the door open. Lean but visible muscles on his forearms. Nice hands. Fingernails clipped and clean. This is a man who pays attention to detail. A breath at the back of my neck whispers caution, no misstep, not a wasted word that won't pass his scrutiny.

I slip by him into a narrow space with high ceilings and sloping hardwood floors. There's the smell of old paint and brewed coffee, of parents who still write monthly rent checks and students who go home to do laundry. But this feeling doesn't quite match the man who lets me inside—he seems older. Independent. Or perhaps, given the strong jaw and chestnut eyes, I simply want him to be.

A gust of wind sends the door slamming behind us, and he steps inside, so close that his hand grazes my back. I feel a rush of heat spread through my skin. There's a grinding sound farther down the hall, and a heavy metal door slides open. A girl with bright red hair rolls through, earbuds in, humming a melody. She nods at me—a quick, evaluating gaze—but ignores my companion completely.

"It's up here." He indicates a flight of metal steps.

I look back toward the freight elevator.

He follows my gaze. "The mechanism gets stuck constantly. Most people don't use it unless they have to."

I frown, but he's already taking the stairs two at a time.

"I'm Spencer," he calls over his shoulder.

"Mar—" I choke on the word. But then I remind myself—not a case, not undercover, not even a detective anymore. Just a normal, if slightly nosy, woman looking at an apartment for rent. I settle on a nickname. "Marley," I finish.

We've arrived at an industrial-style landing, rough brick and steel beams, updated with oversized light fixtures and new polish, but exposing the bones of the warehouse underneath.

There's a sudden stiffness in Spencer's shoulders, and I wonder if he feels it—the last vestiges of death, the way the memory lingers and brushes its fingers against your skin.

I inhale, waiting, but there are none of the telltale signs. The body's been removed. The cleaning and biohazard crews have scraped and sanitized and erased what happened. Will they have left anything to tell me who Ethan was? If Verena was here? And if he was a liar, or if she was an irresponsible teacher, a heartbreaker, or worse?

Our footsteps echo down the hall. We pass a unit with a scuffed welcome mat and another with a small wreath. Tiny markers of individuality in an otherwise impersonal space.

Spencer stops in front of the third door on the right. No adornments on this one, just a pair of mud-caked black boots, too small and narrow to belong to Spencer. Too fresh with life to belong to Ethan.

"Here we are," he says.

And the world swings open.

For a moment, I'm struck breathless. This is where Ethan lived? Not some drab dungeon, hungry churchyard, or gaping tomb. But an open floor plan with high ceilings and tall south-facing sheets of glass. Perhaps it's just the way the light fills the space. Perhaps it's simply contrary to what I was expecting. But it seems wrong that death could haunt this place.

Paper-star-shaped lanterns hang from twine and potted plants sprout from the narrow window ledge. A faded rug hides scarred floorboards. The exposed brick and metal ductwork lend the room an odd kind of charm. To the left is the kitchen—clearly a later addition—a little plain and clunky in the otherwise retro apartment. A faux marble bar separates the appliances from the rest of the living area. The bowl of fruit and slim vase of wildflowers give the impression of a house that's been staged. But there are signs the apartment belongs to students—cream slipcovers over the sofa and loveseat, notes littering the coffee table, wine bottles lining the tops of the kitchen cabinets like trophies. It's the kind of place where roommates have weekly dinners, play board games, and laugh over cheap bottles of alcohol. It doesn't taste like death or smell of bleach and rubber gloves.

"So, Marley," Spencer says, coming to stand beside me. "Are you a student?"

I blink, drawn back to the present, the odd sensation of anyone besides Cindy calling me that name. Of course, I realize, this is a pseudo-interview. I sneak a glance at his profile. He wants to know whether I'll be a good roommate. The kind who'll pay rent on time and clean up after myself. The kind who won't disappear and leave him to pick up the pieces.

"I'm a researcher," I tell him, only realizing as I say it that it's true.

"What subject?"

"History," I say, breathing life into this new identity. "With a little bit of architecture."

"Architectural history." He nods thoughtfully. Then he smiles again, and I notice dimples I didn't see earlier. "That must be why you want to live here."

"Totally," I say. The word sounds ridiculous in my ears. "The structure's quite remarkable." It's dawning on me that even though my father's book is about the university's uncomfortable history with its Confederate past and the racist men honored with building names, I have no clue how to talk about architecture. But it doesn't matter. I'm not trying to impress him. I just need to keep him engaged long enough to show me around.

"Well, then, let's take a tour."

Perfect.

"This is one of the larger units," he says. "As you can see, it's more or less an open floor plan. Our part of the building was once occupied by a hardware store, but it was converted to loft apartments in the late nineties. Living area. Kitchen." He gestures to both unnecessarily.

I watch as he moves through the space. There's no slouching with self-consciousness or the slumping of the shoulders you often see in very tall men. His posture is poised, effortless. "The sofa's seen better days, but it's comfortable, and the upside is you wouldn't have to bring anything. Oh, and that reminds me. The room comes fully furnished as well."

I must frown, because he continues, "But, of course, if you have your own furniture, we can put the bed and nightstand in the dump. They were left"—a slight wrenching breath—"by the last tenant."

I try to rearrange my face, but my heart is hammering. At best I was hoping for a fingerprint on a wall, a strand of hair caught in the door.

Some proof one way or the other of Ethan's relationship with Verena. But if nothing's been removed, there might be more—notes, love letters, a diary. I'm congratulating myself on my luck when the strangeness of it hits me. The fact that Ethan died and no one collected his things. No grieving parent. No angry sibling. No heartbroken professor. But it's the next thought—that whoever rents his room will be sleeping on his mattress, writing on the table where he potentially composed his last words—that sends a shiver down my spine.

Spencer's waiting for me to say something, head tilting with concern.

"That would be great." I smile. "It would save the hassle of moving my things, especially since it's temporary."

Spencer looks relieved. "Okay." He claps his hands together. "Well then, let me show you the space."

I follow him through the archway at the far end of the living room and down a narrow hall. The ceiling is high here, too, but the walls are the cheap drywall kind—thin cream veneer that does nothing to dull noise between rooms and magnifies fingerprint smudges and dark scratches from moved furniture.

"They updated the light fixtures recently," Spencer says, and flips the switch to my left. A pale glow illuminates the hall. "Put in new thermostats. There are laundry facilities downstairs and package lockers for big deliveries. A study lounge, too . . ."

"What's in there?" I ask, pointing to the closed door on the right.

"Just my humble abode," he says, and keeps walking.

The door to the next room is ajar. Inside, there's only enough space for a single bed under the window and a nightstand with a box of tissues. Photos and magazine cuttings stretch the length of the wall opposite the headboard. Two more paper stars dip between a pair of flowerpots and thin curtains.

"That's Sadie's."

"Sadie?"

I lean forward for a better look. A pale-haired girl laughs from a dozen photographs, throws her arms open wide, and blows kisses at the camera.

"My roommate," Spencer says. He arches his eyebrow at me. "Yours, too, if you decide to live here."

I look back at the tiny room, the comforter kicked to the bottom of the bed and nightstand overflowing with used tissues. A metal clothing rack like you'd see at a dry cleaner's holds Sadie's clothes, which are almost entirely black. There are scuffed boots in the corner—the same size as the ones I saw in the hall. The floor's covered in a chalky white dust, scratched in ways that could never be considered normal wear and tear, a kind of violence that seems more likely to have been wrought by a large animal or sharp knife. The cuts look fresh.

"She's twenty," he says with a shrug. "Her life's a mess, but she keeps it mostly to her room."

I laugh. "That's the most you can ask from a roommate." I keep my voice light. "Is she around?"

He shakes his head. "She's spending a few days at a friend's." He hesitates, and I think maybe he'll say something—anything—about Ethan, about Sadie not wanting to be here after what happened, but he moves determinedly down the hall.

"This is the available room." He steps aside. I may imagine it, but there's a rough edge to his voice. An odd stillness in his face.

I hold my breath. But nothing's unusual or out of place. Just like Sadie's, the space is small and lacks the historical charm of the rest of the apartment. There's barely enough room for the full mattress and its heavy wooden frame. The head of Ethan's bed is positioned under the window, squeezed against the right wall, so that the foot almost reaches the threshold. On the left is a standing fan and a small rolling nightstand. Exposed brick on the outer wall, but the rest of the interior is thin particleboard, hastily built and tilting inward. An illusion of privacy, but one that wouldn't muffle a whispered confession or squeaking mattress. If Sadie was in her room, she would know everything that went on in here.

"This is one of the best units," Spencer says in the silence behind me. He shifts on his feet. "Some of the others don't have windows in the bedrooms. There's one without any windows at all."

I raise my eyebrow.

"I know," he says. "They think students won't care, which I guess"—he smooths the cuff of his shirt—"some don't."

I look back at the room. There are no photographs. No hanging stars or green tendrils, no personal touches at all. A strange sadness fills my stomach. *Who are you, Ethan? Who were you?* Two boxes sit at the foot of the bed—what must be the last of his belongings. It takes all my strength not to kneel down and lift the contents from their depths. But I feel them stirring—Ethan's secrets—beckoning me.

"How many bathrooms?" I ask.

Clench of his jaw. "Just one."

Cool breath on the back of my neck. I look behind me, but nothing's there.

"It's here." Spencer returns to the hall and indicates a door on the left.

Like the bedrooms, it's half the size one would expect for a room shared by three adults, and contains a pocket-sized sink with the same faux marble countertops as the kitchen, a toilet, and a standing shower so narrow you'd bump your elbows on the plastic sides when you washed your hair.

I glance at Spencer, but he's turned resolutely away, lips pinched, looking down the hall toward the living room.

How can he bear it? I wonder. To return so soon after his roommate's death? To return at all? In a space this small, every inch must be haunted with Ethan's memory. The lingering smell of his shower gel. His favorite coffee mug, the place where he used to throw his keys, stow his shoes, tuck his feet beneath him on the couch.

Back in the living room, I see the spaces he once occupied, all the potential memories springing from their sources. I turn to the windows. I can just make out the wrought-iron edges of the university, the tips of ivy that have crept up the sides of the brick metalworks building, and the tops of students' heads bobbing beneath ginkgo trees. But I can also see the cracks and crevices in the rough stone rooflines of Broad Street. The crumbling rotten stucco on the opposite building.

Which did Ethan see, I wonder, the blue sky or the disintegrating rooftops?

I'm still staring at the flat roof of the neighboring building, the crates that have been forgotten there, when Spencer steps behind me.

"It's a great view," he says appraisingly.

In another life, he might have been talking about me. I squash down the warmth, an old memory, a different Marlitt, laughing, turning with a smart remark, knowing that he's not referring to me at all, but the way the apartment's positioned to catch the light, the sweeping oak trees, and the uneven brick sidewalks.

"It's one of the reasons I wanted to live here. And it's a short walk to the university."

I nod, realizing he's trying to sell me on the place.

"Do you smoke?" he asks.

I shake my head, feeling a dead thing curl inside me. That person I was before, she's gone. Not dying, but decayed, sinking her teeth into the earth.

Suddenly I can't look at him, can't turn my face with all its scars and anger to meet his amber-flecked eyes.

"That's for the best," he continues. "The unit is nonsmoking, and you can't smoke directly outside either. You'd have to stand on the corner." He motions in the direction of the front of the building. "Also, Sadie's allergic to pets, and I don't think it would be fair to her—"

"No pets," I say. The excitement has left my voice. I feel suddenly tired—defeated. Not sure why I'm here, how I convinced myself any of this mattered.

"What else?" He moves back toward the kitchen and I follow him, wondering whether there's a rule that says you have to inform a potential occupant if someone died in a residence—I remember seeing something about stigmatized properties online when I was researching buying my own home. But that was for buyers. Renters probably have less access to that kind of information.

"I'm completing an MBA, so I'm gone a lot. Sadie's an undergrad, but works part-time at a grocery store, so she's in and out a good bit, too. You'd have the apartment to yourself during the day. Cable and trash services are included in the rent. We split water and electricity every month. The ground floor has staff offices, maintenance, laundry facilities. There's even a study lounge area. Did I say that already?" He smiles and runs his hands across the counter, straightening bowls and placemats.

I study him. At a small college, an undergrad and grad student rooming together might be strange. But here, where so many students live off campus, it's not all that unusual. Still, it makes me wonder about this other roommate, what she's like, and how close she was to Ethan.

My gaze flickers from the curve of Spencer's cheek to the light slanting across the floorboards, the stars held by twine.

I could live here.

It's a fleeting and frivolous thought, but once it's there, I see it begin to form wings, take flight. I picture getting to know Spencer better, meeting Sadie, rummaging through Ethan's drawers and closets, and peeking into the boxes at the foot of his bed. It's the kind of access Oliver would kill for, and here it is, being offered to me on a faux marble platter.

Bad idea, I tell myself.

But my mind's already speeding ahead to the practical considerations. Homeowner's insurance covers additional living expenses while my house is being repaired. Taking into account the smoke and soot removal, fixing the roof and replacing the wall with water damage, then testing and retesting the air circulating through the house itself, the mitigation vendor estimated another two months before I can move back in. And it would solve some other problems as well—the loneliness, the boredom, the momentary flashes of anger at the parents who lied to me for the better part of almost thirty years. The hunger to be part of something, to solve a new case. *I need this*, I think.

"That's it." Spencer gives the fruit bowl a final push and looks up at me. "I can run downstairs and grab you an application if you'd like?" And when I hesitate: "It's just a formality. Even though you'd be subletting, the management still asks that we provide your information. You know, in case of an emergency."

"Okay," I say, surprised to hear the syllables leave my lips. Too late to bite them back.

"Great." A quick glance at his watch, smoothing of his shirtsleeve. "Give me two minutes."

Once he's gone, I move to the center of the room. Take in the floor that's worn from years of foot traffic, the tattered rug, the books stacked next to the television. Listen for whispers—a lovers' quarrel, the tail end of a lie.

The place feels different without Spencer. Larger, the street sounds more recognizable. A bit of the charm has disappeared as well. I notice stains on the cream slipcovers, dust that has escaped the broom under the dining table, cracks in the countertop, a broken windowpane.

I walk back to the archway and stand outside the closed door in the hall. Touch the handle. It doesn't budge.

For the first time since I arrived, I feel a prickle of unease. But I squash it down, remembering what it was like to have roommates stealing pens and laundry detergent, throwing impromptu parties. Guests who think every open room is an invitation.

The front door opens.

"Marley," Spencer calls.

"Here," I say, emerging from the hall. "Just scoping out the room one more time." *We're all liars*, I think. *It's the reason that's important*. "If the bed's staying, I'm going to have to buy full-sized sheets."

He checks his watch, and I remember that I caught him on his way to class.

"If you want," I offer, "I can fill out the form and bring it to the front office later."

"No need." He plucks a pen from his bag and holds it out to me.

What's the harm, I think as I list my Normaltown address. I can sleep on it and withdraw the application later when I'm thinking more rationally.

I write *Marley Caplan*, feeling a slight thrill at my duplicity—it's close enough to my own name to turn my head, but not close enough to pull up anything in a Google search. I include my phone number but linger over the age and birth date. This is primarily an apartment for students. Would it be strange for a twenty-nine-year-old to apply? Spencer shifts, glances at his watch again, and I scribble *24*. It's an age I hope I might pass for in a pinch—like Spencer, I'm just a graduate student with a limited income, another young person with crushing debt. Who's to suspect a disgraced former detective?

"Thanks," Spencer says when I hand him the sheet. He slips the application into a folder without looking at it. "I'll talk to Sadie, but you should hear something from us by tomorrow."

That soon? I think.

"Great." I smile.

Six

Wednesday, March 4, 10:00 A.M.

Outside, I take one last look at Artisan's Corner, sealing the building in my mind's eye.

"Kaplan?"

I turn at the sound of my name, wondering whether Spencer forgot something on his way to class.

But instead, a dark-haired man stands in front of Artisan's Corner, hands on his waist, glaring at me.

"Graves." I scowl.

This is the third time I've seen him in three days. It's a small town, but not that small. Before Monday, I hadn't seen him in four months.

Oliver glances at the building. "What are you doing here?"

I open my mouth to tell him it's a free country and he should stop following me but then remind myself that he knows everything about Ethan, the way he died, the reason Verena was pulled in, whereas she was left in the dark and I can only hypothesize. I need to play nice.

"Good to see you again, too." I smile sweetly.

He frowns at the change in my demeanor.

"Let me guess," he says. "Another 'friend'"— he puts the word in air quotes—"lives in this building."

I purse my lips, and Oliver shakes his head. "You're not a detective anymore, remember?"

A stab of something under my ribs, but I lift my hands innocently.

"I'm just looking to clear Dr. Sobek's name in the Title Nine investigation. Why are you here, anyway? The news reported the death as a suicide."

I think he'll threaten to arrest me again or at least tell me to mind my own business, but instead, he shrugs. "You remember how it is," he says. "Someone calls in a suicide, the reporting officers expect to find one. They assume things. Miss things." He hesitates, considering how much to tell me. Then something shifts in his face and his shoulders drop. "No pill bottles were found near the body. No needles or bags of powder. But the officers didn't mark this as suspicious. We had a death by apparent overdose, but there wasn't a single drug—not prescription, over-the-counter, or illegal—in the apartment. It wasn't until I showed up and had them do a full search that they noted their absence." He clears his throat. "So yeah, I'm treating the death as suspicious. And I haven't ruled out your professor friend yet."

I stare at him. He's given away this information too easily, which sets off alarm bells in my head. But what he's implying is preposterous.

"So what?" I say. "You think she poisoned him? Or they took drugs together, he overdosed, and she got rid of the evidence? That's ridiculous."

He looks at me seriously. "Is it? Someone thinks they got away with this. They didn't. They won't."

I open my mouth and shut it again. Then my eyes widen. "You leaked the suicide theory."

He might have even told Channel 6 he planned to take Verena in for questioning, which is how they got the footage of her leaving the building.

Oliver smiles. "Stay away from my investigation, Marlitt," he says, and turns back toward Artisan's Corner. "You don't know what you're dealing with."

I watch as the building manager ushers him through the front entrance. And the longer I stand there, the more convinced I am that it's true: Oliver leaked the information. He suspects foul play, but wants the perpetrator feeling safe, so he let the media run the story side by side with the news about Verena being taken in for questioning. Even if that means everyone blames her.

I call my mother. She doesn't answer. I check my watch. Call the house.

"Marlitt." My father's voice on the other end. "Of course," he says like we've been having a conversation for a while now, "I'd love to have lunch with you. That's so thoughtful—"

"Dad," I interrupt.

His laughter turns into a cough.

"I really wish you would—"

"Fine. Fine," he says like always. "If you're not calling with sandwich ideas—"

"I'm not—"

"—then I guess you're looking for your mother."

"Is she there?"

He sighs. "You just missed her."

"Oh," I say, disappointment arching into my voice.

"But maybe I could help? I have been known to change a tire, fix a faulty wire, and sing like Sinatra when no one's around."

I smile despite myself, and some of the tension falls from my shoulders. He can't help but wants to. That's something, isn't it?

"Any chance you also know how to get in touch with Verena?" I ask.

"Actually," he says cautiously, "I do."

The house is smaller than I expected. A short brick ranch with yellow trim and a distinct look of disrepair. It's possible it's always been this way—landlords don't take great care of rentals in college towns—but something in the bloated newspapers on the stoop and the flowers dying in the window box tells me this is a recent development. The grass is long and overrun with wild onion stalks. The metal box nailed to the front of the house overflows with envelopes and paper mailers.

My father told me Verena hasn't left since the investigation started. He knew her address because my mother's been having meals delivered to her door. One such box sits on the front step now. I wonder how long it's been there. If Verena's taking care of herself. And again, I think, *Sadness or guilt? Malaise or shame?*

"Can I come in?" I ask when the door opens.

Verena blinks and then steps back, pressing herself against the wall.

She looks less sturdy than the last time I saw her—leaner, too. Barefoot in baggy jeans and a long gray cardigan, hair piled on top of her head in a messy bun, drawing my eye to the new hollows under her cheeks.

She doesn't tell me to excuse the mess or offer anything to drink. She doesn't ask why I'm here. She doesn't say anything, in fact, just follows me, wordlessly, down the hall.

I find my way to a small living room occupied by a low coffee table and matching overstuffed burgundy sofas. They're too large for the space, and I have to angle my way between them so as not to disturb the collection of items scattered across the table—half-empty water glasses, a box of tissues, a pile of lined notebook paper, and crumpled aluminum foil. The heavy beige curtains are closed, and I can make out telltale signs of the dog that went missing—a foam bed in the corner, a collection of plush toys, chewed bottoms of furniture.

Verena doesn't seem to notice any of this. She's still standing in the hall, behind the burgundy love seat. It's her house, but she's waiting for me to take control.

"Why don't you sit," I suggest.

She looks at me a long moment, and then nods, folding herself into the corner of the opposite sofa.

"If it's okay with you," I begin carefully, "I want to talk about Ethan."

Verena squeezes her eyes shut. Dark lashes press against her skin.

"It doesn't make sense," she whispers. Her eyes fix on the floor and fill with tears.

"What doesn't make sense?"

"Any of it."

I nod. But looking around her house—all the lonely corners and sad decor—I think maybe it does, a little.

"You believe them," she says, her voice suddenly harsh. She's studying me now, meeting my gaze for the first time since I arrived. "What they're saying about me."

I open my mouth to deny it, but then hesitate.

She scowls and looks away.

"Yes, you and everyone else." She sucks in her cheeks. "Only your mother knows I didn't—would never—" She stares at the opposite wall.

"I don't know what to believe," I tell her. And it's true. Part of me can't imagine her having an affair with a student. Even more so, committing murder. But the other part knows that people are strange, unpredictable creatures. And even though I suspect Oliver's motives, I don't doubt his instincts. If he's interested in Verena, it's possible she's hiding something.

Her gaze flickers back to my face.

"But I want to help," I say finally. "And in order to do that, I need you to tell me everything—about Ethan, the class he was in, and anything else you think might be important."

She takes a long jerky breath.

I wait.

"Why don't we start with your general impressions," I suggest. "How long did you know Ethan? What was he like as a student?"

A tear slips down her cheek. She doesn't wipe it away.

"Ethan was in my intermediate class," she says slowly. "He started taking German with me his freshman year and continued taking my classes, so I had him three semesters—four, if you count this spring."

"Is that normal," I pause, "for a student to take so many classes with one professor?"

She nods. "Yes, if they like you. Sometimes," a tired smile, "even if they don't. They—what's the expression?—stick with the devil they know."

"And Ethan liked you?"

She shrugs. "He was a good student. Sweet. Thoughtful." She shakes her head. "I keep asking myself what I could have said." She stares at her palms. "The last time I saw him, I knew he wanted to talk. But I hurried him out of the classroom. I had a stack of tests to grade and edits for an article, all things that in hindsight don't seem important, and I keep wondering if I had stayed . . ."

"There's nothing you could have done," I say, realizing she—like everyone else—is talking about Ethan as if she believes the suicide narrative.

"I knew something was wrong," she blurts. "But, at the same time, I just—I didn't want to know." She blinks at me as if wondering whether I understand. "God, it sounds so selfish, but I was trying to make time and space for myself—to define clear boundaries, create work-life balance—and look at what happened." Blotchy red patches appear on her cheeks, and she wipes a tear away angrily. "I wasn't prepared for this," she says. "Half the students come to my office to complain about coursework, grading policies, the usual. The other half treat me like a psychologist. They tell me so many things . . ." She looks down at her hands, swallows, and collects herself. "They're going through so much—and I want to help, I do, but I wasn't trained how to respond to students in distress, when to intervene, what to say, how to buoy them up when I'm—"

Sinking, I finish for her. She doesn't know how to save students from drowning, because she's drowning herself.

She goes still suddenly, inclining her head and holding her breath.

"What?" I ask, my hand going instinctually for my waist, but finding no weapon there.

She sighs. "It's nothing." Then she gives a short, humorless laugh. "I think I might be going crazy."

I wait as her eyes linger on the closed curtains. "I just—I've had this feeling like someone's watching me. It's ridiculous," she says when my eyebrows lift. "I'm sure it's all in my head."

I glance toward the window. "Have you seen anyone suspicious? Someone lurking outside?"

She shakes her head. "Nothing like that. It's more of a sensation. I had the same feeling on campus a few times—outside the classroom, on the way to my office."

I lean forward. "Do you think one of your students may be following you?"

She pales. "I don't know," she says. "It's probably just stress." She exhales. "You know what the university counselor told me?"

Her question's rhetorical, but I shake my head anyway.

"He said their offices are seeing thirty percent more students every year. They're understaffed. Students have to wait days, weeks for appointments, and by that time . . ." She shakes her head, lips pressed together. "He told me they've stopped diagnosing students, because they latch on to words like 'depression' and 'anxiety' and shape them into identities. That so many students feel invisible. That all they want is to be seen. And I've tried—I've tried to see them, to let each and every one know they're important, valuable, that they matter, but it's not enough."

I take a breath. "So you were just showing Ethan you saw him."

She glares at me, trying to determine if there's a trap in my words.

I bite my lip and change tactics. "You said you knew Ethan wanted to talk. Had he told you something was bothering him before?"

She swallows. I wait.

"There are things I can't tell you," she says finally. "They might be important, but I promised Ethan."

"Verena." I lean forward, trying to get her to look at me. "This is serious. And it's about more than just the Title Nine investigation. The primary detective is treating Ethan's death as suspicious." I don't say "murder," but she doesn't look worried. In fact, she doesn't seem to register what I've said. "If there's anything at all that could clear your name, you need to tell me. And if not me, you should contact Detective Graves directly."

She shakes her head. "I can't," she says.

I stare at her.

"I made a promise."

"You can't keep promises to the dead." It comes out harsher than I intended, and she flinches. I soften my voice. "I want to help," I say. "We can clear your name. With the police. And with the university."

She sucks in her breath, eyes moving to some distant spot on the wall. "How do I go back after this? Face my students, my colleagues?" She sighs. "This isn't like other jobs. If I don't like it, I can't just transfer. Every year there are only fifteen or so tenure-track jobs in German in the entire country. Fifteen," she repeats darkly. "Guess how many applicants these jobs get. No, really," she says when I remain silent. "Guess."

"I don't know," I say, trying to remember whether my mother has ever complained of this. "Twenty?"

"Twenty?" Her voice arches incredulously. "Try four hundred. Four hundred people competing for fifteen jobs." She takes a breath. "Ten years in school. Ten years when my friends were starting their careers, climbing the corporate ladder, buying houses, getting married, having children—" Her voice catches. "And I was taking classes, writing a dissertation, living just above the poverty line, preparing for a job that doesn't exist." She shakes her head. "Do you know what you have to do to get a job now?"

"Publish or perish?"

She gives a harsh laugh. Shakes her head. "As if perishing is optional. Months of applying to jobs, writing cover letters, statements on teaching philosophies, research interests, begging for letters of recommendation. And then—if you're lucky—you get an online interview. And then an on-campus interview, three days of meetings, job talks, teaching demonstrations, all that time trying to bite down your nausea and ward off the fatigue and not get too attached to the city, the campus, the people, because you can't handle another rejection." I chew my lip. There's something there in the desperation, the stress, and the competition. "And you finally get the job, and then—" She lifts up her hand as if to say: *This is what's left.*

We're both silent.

"You know I have to ask," I say finally. "Where were you Friday night?"

She sighs. "Here. By myself."

"Can anyone—"

She shakes her head. "No," she says. "I was alone."

Back in the car, I try not to think of the haunted look in Verena's eyes. The crushing hopelessness stretched between the drawn curtains and open containers of half-eaten food. And I have the overwhelming sense that she can't wait any longer to clear her name, that the university is not on her side, or on the students', really, that they only want to cover their asses, and if that means laying the blame squarely on Verena, that's exactly what they'll do.

I still think the affair's a possibility—all this secret-keeping and the boyfriend leaving don't work in her favor—but I don't think she's capable of murder. I think she cared too much, and maybe got too close, and I feel a sudden urgency to protect her—to figure out what's going on, to help in the way I promised my mother I would but haven't really attempted until now.

Her

There's a chill in the air when I walk to class this morning. I've taken to exiting through the basement door and striding across the green grass to the other wing instead of ducking through the building. *Fresh air is good for the body*, I tell myself. And it's a welcome escape from the sticky layer of damp that clings to my office walls, the musty smell that seeps into my clothes, the bookshelves and manuscripts rising up, creeping inward as they tighten their hold on my chest.

Ahead, I see Anna and Kirsten. I slow my pace, not wanting to overtake them, and waiting until the very last moment to put on my teacher face, to engage, smile. They're giggling, Anna grasping on to Kirsten's arm as she doubles over, hearing nothing other than the sound of their own laughter, feeling the touch of each other's skin, so full of life they seem to spark and draw smiles from other students as they pass. I feel a stab of envy. When was the last time I was that in sync with anyone?

I stop just outside the classroom door, thinking I'll wait for them to get settled, wait for my breath to steady, wait just one more minute.

"—all busywork bullshit, anyway."

Travis. His voice so loud it's clear he hopes it carries.

"You can copy mine." Anna giggles. "She doesn't care."

"Fuck it. I'm getting a D in this class anyway."

"It's okay, really." Anna's voice is pleading, like he'd be doing her a favor.

"Nah, it's a bullshit requirement course."

Sound of Kirsten shushing him.

"Seriously, Sobek can go fuck herself."

My face flushes.

There's a clatter in the front of the room and the sound of a chair being scraped back.

"Chill, Haddock," Travis says. "Jesus. We know *you* want to fuck her."

"*Guten Morgen*," I force through my lungs.

I step out of my body. That's the only explanation. I must step out of my body and into Professor Sobek's skin, because Verena is still standing in the hall, mortified, taking deep panicky breaths into her laptop bag, shaking with impotence and fury.

Ethan's half out of his seat, his back to me, fists clenched. Travis's arms are crossed, but he's flinching away from him. Anna's face is pink, and Kirsten's eyes are wide as she glances at me. I pretend I don't see.

It's startling, the way the mouth can move, hands can log on to a computer, pull up a PowerPoint, gesture to slides, all while the mind is screaming and eyes are scanning the room, looking for pointing fingers and gnashing teeth, fingers curling into claws.

Anna slides a piece of paper to Travis. He hesitates, but then draws it closer, and begins scribbling in his notebook.

I ignore it. *See, Helena, I'm learning*. I ignore him sliding the paper back and then leaning over to murmur to Chase. I ignore Chase slipping an earbud into his ear. Showing Anna his screen. Kirsten shaking her head. And, finally, when I can't ignore it anymore, when his behavior becomes a distraction to the other students, I call on Chase to answer a question. He reddens and stammers, and I feel guilty.

Sometimes it seems like I'm teaching kindergarten. But that sounds cute—a garden full of daffodil children traipsing through the forest in overlarge boots and floppy hats, identifying tree bark and overturning rocks. Not catching students with mouthfuls of chewing tobacco, texting friends, copying answers from someone else's assignment, forcing me to scold them like six-year-olds or turn a blind eye and worry about the other lessons they're learning—like that they can cheat without consequence and there's no punishment for their lies.

Sometimes I think Ethan's the only one listening.

He stays after class today, lingering while the others pack up their bags and whip out cell phones, rushing to be the first to leave, when really, they were never present anyway.

"I'm reading the *Sonnets to Orpheus*," he tells me.

"Oh," I say, my eyes on Travis as he shoves Chase out the door.

"You mentioned Rilke in class the other day, and so I bought a parallel text to read the German, too."

I hear Chase tell Travis to fuck off.

Ethan follows my gaze. "I can talk to them, if you want."

I turn my eyes back to him.

He smiles.

"Oh," I say. "It's fine, really."

He runs his hand through his hair. "It's not, though. You're a good teacher. They're just assholes. I mean, excuse my language—"

I shake my head. "It's fine," I tell him, as if saying it enough times might make it eventually become true.

That was this morning, and all day I felt off.

I spent the afternoon working on my conference paper—it's less than two weeks away, and I still need to cut the length in half.

Christopher called around lunchtime. My office line—my cell doesn't work in the basement. *Just to check in*, he said. Sweet as always. I set the phone down on my desk so I could close the door. He wanted to know why. *Are you keeping me a secret?* He was teasing, of course. But also right, in a way. Not so much a secret but my personal life. It's separate. Plus, I know Maria can hear every word of my phone conversations, because I can hear every word of hers. The call was awkward after that. He said I was using my "work voice." But what other voice should I use?

By the time I got home, all I could think about were these two voices reflecting my two selves—work-me and home-me. I wanted to shed work-me like a second skin, but I couldn't shake Travis's scowl, or Chase with his arms crossed, mutely refusing to participate. And I could still hear the words "We know *you* want to fuck her" echoing down the hall.

Christopher greeted me at the door. He smiled and opened his arms wide. I stepped into his hug, but my shoulders were rigid, and I couldn't look at him. I knew that if I saw his happy face turn concerned, I'd break into tears. And if I give in to that feeling now, I'll never collect myself again.

He asked what happened, but I shook my head. I needed time to process, and I couldn't do that with him staring at me with that mixture of patience and sympathy, wanting to fix all my problems, waiting for me to open my mouth and all my fears to come pouring out:

I'm not the woman you think I am.

I've fractured—not just into work-self and home-self, but German-self and Turkish-self. My American-self is some transparent, ephemeral thing. A daughter of two countries, an immigrant in another. A tenure-seeking professor who can't finish a conference paper or stop her students from cheating. A girlfriend failing at the most basic communication. A human coming apart at the threads. A thousand versions of me so rough and splintered that I don't recognize my real-self anymore.

I'm scared.

But I'm angry, too. At him. For being kind. For being patient. For being too good to me. And at myself. For not being kind. Not being patient. Not being good enough.

When he slipped my bag from my shoulder and opened a bottle of wine, I had to stop myself from hurling the glass across the room.

There was no reason for it. I simply wanted some visual indication of the turmoil within.

Christopher ushered me to the kitchen table. He put on a Rolling Stones record and danced around using the spatula as a microphone while he cooked dinner. By the end of the night, I was laughing so hard, wine was coming out of my nose. It was almost enough to make me forget about what happened earlier today. Almost.

Seven

Monday, March 9, 8:00 A.M.

My few belongings are crammed into two suitcases and an overlarge duffel bag. Spencer called Friday night to tell me the sublet was mine. Now I spend Monday morning dipping and weaving through my parents' house, trying to convince my father I don't need help packing, and warding off the numerous questions that come with the sudden announcement I've found an apartment. I avoid his gaze and ignore the way his hand trembles when I give him the address.

My mother accepts the news with a nod, as if she's only surprised I hadn't moved out sooner. Neither suspect the move might have something to do with Verena and Ethan, but why would they? What I'm doing is too extreme, too ridiculous to consider.

I remind myself of this—the foolishness of my plan—as I turn onto Broad Street, but I can't help feeling a tiny bubble of excitement. *I'm free,* I think. Free of the lie, the slip of a boy I see running through their halls. If I hold my breath and plug my nose, I can almost convince myself I'm toeing the edge of a diving platform, poised to jump off the deep end, that this is an undercover case, and I'm working leads too dangerous for paperwork and red tape. But I'm not delusional. Not yet. My eyes are open, and I see this for what it is: me wanting to prove myself, an apartment full of grief, Verena about to lose her job, and my mother not far behind her, if she's not careful.

It's a gorgeous spring day. All blue skies, young trees spiraling up like lime cotton candy, pale blooms, and sun-kissed faces. The kind that invites students onto the quad, dog walkers to extend their routes, and townies to hunch outside brightly painted cafés smoking and drinking endless cups of coffee. The kind of day that makes it seem like nothing bad could ever happen in this city.

Artisan's Corner rises from the gray asphalt severing Broad in half—a dangerous intersection that will have drivers careening into oncoming traffic if they're not paying attention. Two roads diverging—one leads to exposed brick, secrets, and lies; the other slides past its façade to a breakfast place, biscuits and raspberry jam, a wide loop that returns me to my parents like I never left.

As the light changes from red to green, I think of Ethan and Verena, lives intersecting, the devil at the crossroads, and wonder if some stories aren't meant to be told. I think of wrong turns and right angles, paths bending in the undergrowth obscuring our view, and the different decisions that brought us here. But I'm the only one who still has a choice: left or right, forward or backward. To unearth the truth buried with Ethan, or to turn away unburdened and free.

Spencer's waiting outside the building, leaning against the wheelchair ramp with one foot pressed behind him. When I park and pop the trunk, he raises a hand and comes toward the car, smiling.

"Let me help." He grabs both suitcases before I can protest.

I fumble around the back seat for the duffel. See the slash of grease from Teddy's tire and ignore the low and urgent rush of a warning I hear in my ear.

We take the stairs instead of the elevator. My bag swings and bangs against the railing with every third step, a booming rhythmic echo that sends my heartbeat skittering as I breathe in the scent of old wood and dusty metal beams. And then we're outside number 23, and Spencer's opening the apartment door. I catch glimpses of gold in the clouds beyond the windowpanes, a rust spot on the metal duct, a bird spiraling out of view. And for a fraction of a second, just before Spencer hands me the key, he hesitates.

Here it comes, I think. He's going to tell me about Ethan, offer me one last chance to turn away, to leave the seal to Pandora's box unbroken.

But he only smiles.

"I think you'll like it here," he tells me, and drops the key into my hand.

I see a white stone that brings dark dreams, a row of doors, all open but one. I think of old stories where curiosity leads children into ovens and beautiful women disappear inside countryside castles. Monsieur de Montragoux, never-ending rooms full of riches, but the temptation of the forbidden is too great, and time and again, the final lock clicks open, the key swims in blood, and the fate of the inquisitive is sealed. The moral's always the same: curiosity draws the walls of its own prison. From knowledge learned, there's no escape.

Cold metal drops into my palm and my fingers wrap around it, the finality of its possession etched in my skin. But then Spencer holds out a potted plant and the vision dissipates.

"Oh," I say, breathless with surprise as he places the pot in my hands. "Thank you."

"You're welcome. But it's not from me. It's from Sadie." He gestures to the foliage surrounding the windows. "Plants are more her thing. She says only heathens are content to leave them outdoors." He shrugs. "She dropped it off this morning, said she can't wait to meet you, that she'll be back this evening, and that this is a fern," he smiles apologetically, "and it's supposed to bring you health, luck, and protection during your transition period."

"Transition period?" I furrow my eyebrows.

He nods as if this is completely normal. "She also said to water it regularly and that it does best in shade or partial light."

I smile and rub the fronds between my fingers, charmed despite myself.

"These," he says, withdrawing a pair of items from behind the counter, "are from me. Gifts to share when Sadie gets back so we can welcome you properly." He sets the bottles on the faux marble. "I didn't know whether you liked white or red, so I bought both."

"Wow," I say, overwhelmed. "This is wonderful. Thank you." There's something warm and fuzzy spreading through my chest. I try to tamp it down. Sooner or later, I'm going to have to lie to him and Sadie both, and don't want to feel too guilty when I twist facts into arrows to see what lands and what stings.

"We're just happy you're here. It's been a bit . . . quiet lately."

I nod, but my smile tightens. That hesitation again at the indirect mention of Ethan. A cloud shifts and the light from the window catches the edge of one of the bottles, turning it a violent shade of crimson.

Alone in Ethan's room, there's a prickling of the hairs on the back of my neck. I set the fern in the narrow slash of light on the windowsill. Spencer's left for class, and I'm supposed to be getting settled in, but my arms have snuck their way around my body, and I'm finding it difficult to unwrap them from my chest.

This was the bargain, I remind myself, eyeing the stripped mattress on Ethan's bed. Twenty-four-year-old you would have been delighted to discover free furniture in a rented room. Roommates who offer house-warming gifts. And since I'm not supposed to know about Ethan, I can't start freaking out now.

I sigh and begin to unpack the things I brought with me—a handful of hangers for the metal bar stretched in the corner, a pair of sneakers in the hopes I might get a few long walks in, jeans, and a collection of new shirts. I brought a laptop and a charger, too, in addition to a small stack of books for my father's research project. *Just like a student*, I think, with a smile.

I hold my breath as I pull the fitted sheet over the bed corners, tuck in the flat one, and throw the comforter on top. It's foolish, I know—the fear of his mattress. The sense that in touching it, I've disturbed the dead. But staring at the bed makes something catch in my throat. And the longer I stand here, blinking at Ethan's bare room—nothing but his nightstand, a lamp stolen from my parents' house, and the new comforter—the more claustrophobic I feel. It's the sensation of students waving goodbye to siblings, of moving into dorm rooms and dreaming of freedom, only to discover they've exchanged large and comfortable childhood bedrooms for temporary nondescript places, unknown roommates, and very little space to breathe. It's the knowledge that no one's waiting for them to get home, to check they've done their homework, fed themselves, dressed appropriately for the weather. There's no one to touch their foreheads when they're sick, ruffle their hair as they pass, listen to their heartbreak, their fears, and nudge them out the door. Those brief moments of love and human contact are no longer guaranteed; and suddenly freedom feels less like a relief and more like a burden. They must be responsible for themselves, drag their own bodies across the finish line, and they may have made a terrible mistake. But the papers have been signed, tuition paid. Classes are in session, and there's no turning back.

Focus, I think. Bite down on the panic, taste the blood on your tongue, and use it. Picture Ethan. Imagine him lying on his bed and reading with his feet up, leaving footprints on the wall, or pressed into the corner, furiously scribbling homework assignments. See him gazing out the window. Slip into his mind. Is he daydreaming about Verena? Or fantasizing a twisted revenge? Is he scared of some unknown person? Is there a dark figure at the edge of his vision?

I exhale and tug open his nightstand drawer.

There are no condoms or used tissues or Gideon Bibles. No fuzzy dust bunnies, pencils rolling from the back, or flecks of cedar shavings. Whatever things might have been saved and forgotten—ticket stubs, pennies pressed at the fair, foreign small change, rocks and seashells from a family vacation—they've been packed into boxes, tossed, or scrubbed away. And as much as I'd like to see these trinkets of the life he led, I know such insubstantial things can't tell me anything about the real Ethan. I'm just as likely to misinterpret their meanings as to get them right.

It hits me then—as I stand and let my eyes drift over the bed again and see the empty space Ethan left behind—how clean the room is. This isn't the once-over of management or courteous roommates, but a complete and thorough purification. I see a team in white protective gear, gloves, goggles, and surgical masks, removing biohazardous materials in little red boxes, shipping them off to certified waste disposal and incineration.

The realization is sudden, certain—Ethan died in this room.

I step backward, thinking of bacteria moving from the pancreas and intestines into other organs, breaking them down, and overflowing into the rest of the body. Skin disintegrating, causing tears, pathogens released into the air. But Ethan was found almost immediately, I remind myself. As soon as his body was removed, the premises would have been cleared by law enforcement and biohazard cleanup would have begun: sanitation with medical-grade compounds and special deodorizing chemicals. So the room is safe; cleaner, probably, than it's ever been.

I shift from one foot to the other. Mollified but not quite at ease. Why am I here if everything's been carted away? I think of Oliver's certainty that Ethan overdosed but the lack of drugs near his body. Would Oliver have fingerprinted the room? Questioned Ethan's roommates? Looked at traffic camera footage? Certainly. But there must be something he missed.

I examine the room from corner to corner, brush the top of the doorframe, the window, the night table. Crawl on my hands and knees and do a sweep of the floor. Still convinced that despite my eyes telling me there's nothing, Ethan must have left something behind. But after half an hour, I realize the room's as bare as a prison cell. No lover's note, lock of hair, or remnants of a broken heart.

I wander around the living room. Allow myself to breathe in the charm of the high ceilings, the mismatched pillows on the cloth-covered furniture, the scratched coffee table. All inherited throwaway pieces, the kind you find in basements or thrift shops—rough-edged with the continuity of ownership, wine stains on the edge of the couch, a large bite mark out of the corner of the coffee table, late nights and bruised knees and stories housed in objects that only the former owners could know. It's possible some of these pieces might have belonged to Ethan. But there are no initials carved into wood or names stitched into pillows. And again, I'm struck by the impossibility of my task.

Even if I could get a forensics team over here to inspect everything from the floor to the ceiling for fingerprints, strands of hair, or fibers from Verena's clothes and show without a doubt she never took a breath in Ethan's apartment, her absence doesn't mean anything—they could have met in a myriad of other places; and doing the same sweep of every apartment, hotel lobby, gym, or classroom within a twenty-mile radius still wouldn't prove anything, because there would always be a thirty-mile radius, forty-mile, the possibility they met in some green field, forest glade, or river bend. *There's Spencer and Sadie*, I remind myself. Who better to know if he and Verena were having an affair? If Ethan did drugs, held a grudge, or if their relationship was something else?

I draw my fingers over the window ledge and find it covered with flecks of dirt and dust. The potted plants have paper identifiers sticking from the soil with light and watering instructions. The large ones in the center are bay and basil. The smaller ones are chives and oregano. I touch an empty wine bottle with string lights packed inside, an unlit candle, a ceramic vase, and a small giraffe figurine.

With an alert ear for any noises in the hall, I move to the entertainment center—a small flat-screen TV standing on top of a misty glass-fronted cabinet. Someone's repurposed the cabinets beneath as bookshelves. Classics mostly, organized alphabetically—Camus, Conrad, Dickens, Dostoyevsky—mixed in with a few German titles that must have belonged to Ethan. I dig my fingers around the back of the shelves, searching for small fallen things or items hidden away with tape. Give each book another shake, but nothing comes tumbling out.

I stand, toeing a dark rust-colored splotch on the rug that could be anything. Then I drag the coffee table away from the center. There are four deep imprints where the feet used to be, but otherwise nothing unusual—no lost bits of paper or dark hairs curled around the legs. I move to the couch. The cloth beneath the slipcover is a thick-stitched dirty-brown-and-orange monstrosity that most likely was discovered beside a dumpster. But all I find between the cushions are a handful of lint, two nickels, and a blue pen.

I stand. I don't even know what I'm looking for anymore. Somewhere outside, a car alarm wails. There's a rushing sound from another tenant taking a shower.

I tuck the slipcover down again and think of Riley's hypothesis that someone framed Verena. Could Ethan have been murdered because of his relationship with her? My mother said she had a boyfriend. Could this man have followed Verena and Ethan here, waited until she left, and then—what? Faked Ethan's suicide, written a letter pointing the finger at Verena in revenge? I shake my head. It's too contrived, too complicated, too much like a long-running soap opera where three seasons later we discover that, in fact, Ethan's not dead but faked the whole thing and ran off with Verena's twin. I need to focus on what I know. Ethan was found here, in this apartment. The media suggested he died by his own hand. Oliver possibly leaked that information, but he himself doesn't believe it. No pills were found near the body. And in the course of his investigation, Oliver found something that implicated Verena, and whatever it was, Title IX is now looking into a possible violation. My mother thinks Ethan overdosed. Riley thinks he wrote a note. And if there was a note, then I'm left with the impossible task of disproving the dead.

I make my way through the kitchen. Discover more items that look like hand-me-downs or thrift-store finds: a heavy brown-and-tan Crock-Pot with plastic yellow colanders stacked inside, a collection of old cookbooks, mismatched glassware with beer logos.

A door slams down the hall and I jump halfway up the stove, feeling guilty. It dawns on me that when you live somewhere, poking around drawers and cabinets feels a lot more like snooping than investigating.

I chew my bottom lip, thinking. Take a deep breath and stride back across the open space. I try the handle to Spencer's room, but—same as the day when he gave me the tour—it doesn't budge. So I move on to the unknown roommate—Sadie. Her door's ajar, and I push it lightly with my fingertips.

I can see the trajectory of a whirlwind exit written in the jacket thrown over the bed, the pair of dirty socks landing on—but not entirely in—the plastic laundry basket, the metal jewelry strewn across the built-in desk, and the hairbrush on the floor.

I glance behind me again, feeling like either one of them could explode into the apartment at any moment. *Don't mind me, Sadie,* I think. Just your new roommate looking to borrow a pen, a hair tie, something innocuous that might be annoying but less invasive than poking through your dirty laundry and bedside table looking for evidence.

The photos on her wall are interspersed with magazine pages. Mostly workout routines and diet advice. *Eat your way slim. Snack smart. Reduce yourself entirely until we see nothing but your soul.* Models who are three shades too thin in vibrant colors—wisps of women photoshopped so they all but disappear when viewed from the side. And then there's a girl with straw-blond hair and smooth skin rolling beneath flowy blouses, an arm stretched over the shoulders of another girl with flowers in her hands. This is Sadie. Dozens of photos of her laughing. Summer days. Rugged Georgia farmland, stretches of blue sky, and rough-hewn wooden fences. There's a close-up shot, but here she's frowning, looking pensively off to the side. A family photo that's been ripped apart and taped back together. A dizzying number of snapshots, candid moments, and posed head tilts spanning the floor to the ceiling.

I step back to take in the entire wall, bump into the bed frame, and swear as my heart does another leap. Trace the photos left to right and top to bottom so I don't miss anything. And then, near the baseboard, I see him: Ethan.

Even though I've been looking for his face, there's a sudden lurch in my stomach like the hardwood's given way. There they are in the living room. Him—lounging next to Sadie on the lumpy couch, sharing the pale blue quilt that's now thrown haphazardly across her bed. And again—tossing something up at Sadie's face, a white blur that might be popcorn. There are others, too: spoon-feeding each other ice cream, a dollop of chocolate running down Sadie's chin. Asleep on the couch, Ethan's head tilted back, Sadie tucked under his arm. I feel a strange slash of envy as I look from photo to photo. *This is what it would have been like to have a brother*, I think—the ease of touching, teasing, dull-edged by time. Falling in and out of conversation like breathing, one thought streaming into the other, gaps in conversation rendered unintelligible to others but always understood because your sibling has already filled in the words in his head.

The unfairness of it slams me hard. It wasn't just the past that I lost, but the present and future, too. I shouldn't be here—reliving my twenties in some drafty apartment in Athens. I should have lived them with my brother and my best friend Craig. I see us all sitting around the table with my parents, who look less old, less tired because their house has new life, or rather never lost it to begin with. Picture the way we clink glasses, walk barefoot across the warm hardwoods, Craig laughing at my mother's perpetual insistence he take off his shoes. All of us—adults. Not stunted by an unfinished childhood. College years cut short. My brother—what? An accountant? No, I think, he would have gone on to be a doctor, specializing in the same congenital heart disorder that he survived. Craig would have been a business executive just like he planned—proud but also a little embarrassed every time he pulled up in his new BMW—instead of never finishing his degree. And me? I never would have become a detective, never met Teddy, never disappointed him, or resigned in disgrace. What would I have been?

The question nags at me as I scan Sadie's wall. Even in my imagination, I can't picture a different path. But I know at least one thing: I wouldn't be sitting here in a dead man's apartment, going through his roommate's things, if I hadn't lost something pivotal myself.

I snap photos with my phone, reminding myself that this isn't about me. Instead, I pick through Sadie's bedside table, surprised but not surprised to find an open box of condoms, a half-eaten bag of candy bars. Diet pills. ChapStick. Hand lotion. And a messy bunch of used tissues.

I drop to my knees and lift the edge of her comforter. A large cardboard box is wedged underneath at an angle, and I have to squash down the sides to drag it out. Five big letters are drawn across the top. I lie on my belly and, sure enough, pushed even farther back is another box. Here's the matching set I saw in Ethan's room when Spencer gave me the tour.

I glance at the girl on the wall. Notice the way her eyes are drawn to Ethan. Always her gazing at him, not the other way around. *She loved him*, I think, feeling something tighten in my stomach. She loved him and kept his things. And what's more, she hid them.

The tape on the first box has been ripped open, and I take out each item one by one. Folded clothes, still fresh with the scent of laundry detergent, sit atop textbooks for biochemistry, cell biology, German, and genetics. I thumb through the German one, scanning the notes Ethan's left in the margins, words he's translated—*Schwache*, *Begriff*, *Grund*—and conjugation charts.

It's not until I reach the back that I see them—the papers smoothed and pressed into the book crease so that at first glance they appear to be part of the binding. Homework assignments, essays, all chronologically arranged, and with short notes at the bottom, signed *VS*.

The notes start small. *Gut gemacht! Richtig!* With exclamation points and encouraging remarks. A teacher congratulating a student on a job well done, the rare joy of discovering a diligent pupil among a mix of cheaters and slackers and mouth breathers.

Page after page of As, 20/20s, 100/100s. Ethan scratching out mistakes and correcting them, penciling questions in the margins that Verena dutifully answers. *When was the "th" replaced with an aspirated "t"? If the Berlin Wall came down in 1989, why is reunification not celebrated until 1990?* But soon the questions grow longer. More personal. *German authors I absolutely must read? Your favorite poet?* The answers lengthen in turn. One sheet doesn't appear to be homework at all, but rather a poem in German that Ethan has transcribed and translated.

Verena's written at the bottom: *Yes! One of my favorites by Rilke.* And then on the side: *Your notations remind me of a short prose work by a Polish writer. I can't remember his name, but it's called "Episode in a Library."*

The following page is Ethan, who's drawn a girl seated at a desk bent over a poem and a smaller sketch of a lizard-like creature. In the margins, Ethan adds: *The author's name is Zbigniew Herbert. This text kind of reminds me of that passage from Hofmannsthal's "Lord Chandos Letter" where words swirl around and congeal into eyes. "They are vortices that make one dizzy" or something like that.*

Verena's finished the quote for him: *"and, rotating inexorably, lead into the void." You're right! Hofmannsthal's writing before Herbert, of course, but they're both interested in the failure of language—the inability of words to truly capture feelings of the ~~hea~~ soul. VS.*

What is this? I think. *Nerdy flirting?*

I stare at the crossed-out letters. "The feelings of the heart" is what she started to write, but then she corrected herself, went with the less weighty "soul." Freudian slip, or was she worried about Ethan getting the wrong idea? Still, if it was nothing, why correct herself at all?

I look back to the first poem—the one Ethan translated. I skim it twice, but my eyes keep catching on the first two lines.

You, from the beginning
lost Beloved, who never arrived.

I feel something cavernous yawn and open beneath me and have the sudden urge to put everything back in the box.

The poem continues:

I don't even know what songs are dear to you

The longing is so raw, so delicate, so obvious. Ethan speaking to Verena through Rilke. How could she not have seen?

All the immeasurable
images in me—the landscapes beheld in the distance,
cities and towers and bridges and
unforeseen turns in the roads
and the mighty lands where the gods
once intermingled:
rise within me to mean
You, who escaped.

"You, who escaped," I repeat into the silence. So not an affair?

I smooth the page, thinking of my mother's "Verena would never—" So what if she didn't do anything at all? What if she saw the signs, the furtive glances, the obsession, and ignored them? But in never reprimanding, never correcting, allowed Ethan to continue longing after her? I sigh in frustration. Again, it's proving what didn't happen that's the problem.

Oh, you, Beloved, are all the gardens
I have ever seen with such

hope. An open window
in a country house—and you nearly stepped out
thoughtfully, to me. I found alleyways,
you had just left
and sometimes the mirrors of the merchants' shops
were still dizzy with your reflection and, startled, gave back
my too-sudden image.—Who knows, if the same
bird did not echo through us both
yesterday, individually, in the evening?

Verena's made notes throughout, suggesting different words and highlighting the ones she likes—*dizzy, echo*—nothing too close to the meaning of the poem itself.

Beloved.

I shake my head. Perhaps it's one of those instances that are only obvious in hindsight. That, if things had turned out differently, would have ended with Verena's name in the acknowledgments section of his first book—*for instilling in me a love of German poetry,* he might have written.

I check the other textbooks for similar homework assignments tucked in the back. But Ethan didn't save notes from his other professors. I tug the Rilke and Herbert pages out of the binding, thinking they're unlikely to be missed, and leave the rest.

The second box is more of the same—clothes, notebooks, a pocketknife—but nothing from Verena, no more translated poems, words transcribed and accented like heartbeats bleeding from the page.

Back in the living room, I pull out my laptop and check the Athens police blotter and the university website for updates on Ethan's death and Verena's investigation. There's nothing new online, so I set up alerts for both "Ethan Haddock" and "Verena Sobek" and try to push down the feeling that she deserves it—the suspension, the ire—because, really, it's just a poem. Just symbols on a page related to the subject she teaches. If

Ethan read more into them and Verena failed to notice, that's his fault, not hers. Right?

I rub my palms into my eye sockets, swearing. I feel like I'm swimming in a sea of moral ambiguity. One with no bottom or distant shore, no sun on the horizon or way to orient myself in the muck.

Eight

Monday, March 9, 5:00 P.M.

In spite of everything, it's so comfortable—sinking into the old sofa amid the yellow spring light, a bird chirping somewhere above the slow hum of afternoon traffic, earthy whiffs of oregano and basil on the windowsill—that when the door opens and Spencer glides into the living room, I think I might be half asleep.

I shut my computer so quickly I almost miss the alert in the corner. Something new has been posted about Verena. I glance at Spencer again. He's carrying paper grocery bags from the bottom with both hands and gives the door a small shove with his foot. He offers me a tired grin.

Later, I tell myself.

"Don't get up, don't get up," he says with a laugh when I move to help. "Sadie texted to say she'll be here in ten." He slides the bags onto the counter and begins to unload containers of mixed nuts, olives, and cheese. "You're not vegan, are you?" he asks.

I shake my head. "I can pay—" I begin.

"No." Spencer smiles quickly and waves his hand. "My treat. And don't worry," he says as he pulls out two more bottles of wine, "we don't share groceries or anything like that. Too confusing and someone always feels they've been slighted." He gives a small shrug as if to indicate this person is never him. "But we have dinner together once a week." A pause as he pulls out another wedge of cheese. "Usually on Wednesdays. We switch off who does the main and then the other two make the sides." He hesitates and inclines his head. "Only if you want to, of course."

"That sounds great," I tell him. And it does. Charming, low commitment, the perfect opportunity to do a little background prodding on Ethan. "Are you sure I can't help?"

"I've got this," he says with a brief smile, meeting my gaze for a moment before returning to the board. "Why don't you change, and by the time you're ready, Sadie will be back, and we can open one of these bottles of wine."

Change? I stand there dumbly. It seems a bit antiquated—changing for dinner—but when I compare my jeans and T-shirt to Spencer's crisp button-down, I do feel suddenly underdressed.

He's still arranging various items on the board and doesn't look up when I move toward the hall.

I return when I hear another voice in the living room. I've chosen a navy blouse. It's polyester, but looks like silk and is the nicest piece of clothing I packed. The rest reflects what I plan on doing the next two months: walking to and from campus, sitting in the library, and rummaging around for whatever I can find on Ethan's life. Nothing professional or remotely fancy in the mix.

"There she is." Spencer smiles. I think he gives a short nod of approval at my attire.

"Marley, meet Sadie. Sadie, Marley."

Sadie, who's bent close to Spencer, her mouth a thin line and arms crossed, turns suddenly and smiles.

I blink. I expected the photographs from the wall to have come to life—a blond sprite, flowers flowing from long golden strands. But the woman in front of me has short inky-black hair, dark eyeliner, and leafy tattoos winding their way around her wrists. The similarities are there in the inquisitive eyes beneath the heavy-lidded mascara, but that's it. She stumbles across the floorboards and throws her hands around my neck. Almost a foot shorter than me, her head fits neatly under my chin. The metal zipper from her jacket presses against my ribs.

"I'm so glad you're here," she says into my shirt.

"Let her breathe, Sadie."

"I'm a hugger," Sadie says, releasing me. "You don't mind, do you?"

I do, actually. The press of her arm against my compression sleeve sends a jolt through my skin.

"Not at all," I say.

"Great." She smiles again. "I'm going to throw some things in my room. Then you can tell me all about yourself."

She trips down the hall, a quick backward glance at me as Spencer pulls wineglasses from a shelf.

"Counter or table?" he asks.

"Counter," I say, unsettled by Sadie's expression, the sense I missed something in the worried line between her eyebrows.

"All right." Spencer gestures to the stools. "Take a seat."

Sadie's back, checking her phone, plucking at placemats, and tapping her screen again. I study the botanical tattoos coiling up her arms.

"Rosemary, pansy, rue, and violet," she says, catching my gaze.

"Is that from—"

"*Hamlet*, yeah." She looks down so her hair covers her face. "I went through an angsty Ophelia period last year," she says. "Not that I would—" She stops, clenches her jaw.

I hold my breath, waiting. I feel something shift around the counter, small and weightless like lace, something important in Sadie's expression disappearing in the shadows. There's a slow drip of water in the sink. Slap of heels running down the hall. Orange globe slipping behind the opposite building. I see Teddy holding up his fingers to time the sunset, blink, and find Spencer staring curiously at me. Still, he's there in the stretch of silence, the way Sadie's eyes skitter across the floor, and Spencer's tight shoulders—Ethan.

"I was going to order pizza," Sadie says after a pause.

"It's apéro," Spencer tells her, scooping olives into a bowl. "You can order pizza later if you want."

Sadie rolls her eyes. They're wet at the edges. "Stop being pretentious."

"That's what it's called. It's French."

"Speaking French," she says, wiping the side of her face and plucking a slice of cheese from the board, "is pretentious."

Spencer shakes his head and returns to his setup, opening cabinets and drawers. Although he's not loud or careless, each slam of the cupboard sends a tiny shiver through my skin.

"What are you looking for?" Sadie demands.

"The knives," he says. "From the block on the counter."

Sadie pinches her mouth. "I threw them out."

Spencer turns. "You threw them out?" he repeats.

Sadie nods and then folds her arms defiantly across her chest.

"Why—" Spencer begins but then changes his mind. "What are we supposed to cut with?"

"There are knives in the drawer with the silverware."

"Those are butter knives."

Sadie shrugs.

I get the feeling if I weren't here, this would be a different conversation. Tonight, though, they're on their best behavior.

Spencer takes a deep breath. Smiles. "Fine," he says, grabbing a rounded knife from the drawer and bringing it to the counter. He's already poured himself a glass of wine. And he turns to pour one for me and Sadie.

"To our new roommate," he says with an outstretched arm. "Welcome to Artisan's Corner."

We clink glasses.

They're both striking in their own way, so radiant and pure that as I bring the wine to my lips I feel as if I'm sipping from a chalice, that between them and this apartment, they're offering me something akin to a new life.

Spencer and Sadie tilt their heads in sync, clink glasses again. Something flickers between them, and I wonder if they've slept together. Or if perhaps they've developed a more recent bond—the kind that forms around shared trauma, two open wounds stitched back together. Because I sense tension, too. There, in Spencer's eyebrow crease; in Sadie's wordless gesture to her empty glass.

They alternate playing twenty questions—all directed at me—lobbing them one after another—*Where are you from? What do you do? Where do your parents live? How often do you see them?*—and I'm beginning to feel dizzy, like being on the wrong side of the table in the interview room. I dodge and weave and answer truthfully when I can, but I'm growing tired with the effort, and if I don't flip the conversation now, I'm bound to begin tripping over my lies and everyone might go to bed without me having asked what I really want to know.

"What about you?" I turn to Sadie, inflecting my voice with wine-infused laziness although I've only had a few sips.

Sadie gives a long, dramatic sigh. "Calhoun," she says with disgust.

"That's not too far from here, is it? What, two hours? Do you—"

"Two and a half. And no. Not ever."

I should leave it. Spencer's giving me tiny headshakes over his glass, but I can't. Spencer's quite measured, but I get the impression Sadie's just dying for someone to ask her about herself. What's wrong? What's her story? Who is she really? She's figuring it out as she goes—latching on to the parts of her history that elicit sympathy, laughter, or outrage, deciding what's important in the retelling of those pieces, creating narratives, and testing theories in her head before she says them out loud. I did the same thing when I was her age, before I realized no one could tell me who I was supposed to be. And that identity wasn't a permanent or definable thing, but a shifting, movable shape about as finite and indestructible as a balloon.

"Why not?" I ask.

"Because my parents are assholes."

I wait.

She pushes an olive around with her fork.

Spencer clears his throat. But I see it, the spark in Sadie's eye—*Don't interrupt.*

"It's okay, if you don't want to—"

"Do you know what conversion therapy is?"

I shake my head, but I do know. And it's awful. Beyond the pseudoscience and humiliation of the treatment, the aftermath is brutal—depression, drug use, homelessness, or worse. Some states have bans or regulations outlawing it for minors. Georgia doesn't.

"Basically, my dad caught me kissing my friend Grace. He told her parents and then sent me to this conversion camp for the summer, because he thought kissing girls was a sign of a mental illness and could be cured." A sad smile. "Needless to say, it didn't work."

"That's awful," I say.

She shrugs, picks at her napkin. "My mother's the daughter of a minister. My father's a deacon at our church. They had created this perfect little family. We had a house with—I shit you not—a literal white picket fence. And they weren't rich, but over the years my mother scrounged up things from Big Lots to make our living room look like something out of a catalog. My bedroom," she grimaces, "was hot pink and she used to buy all these princess dresses and make me go on errands with her and when people would stop and bend down to say 'Oh, well don't you look nice,' she would laugh and come up with something like 'She dressed herself, so sweet, how could I say no.' I would protest, dying on the inside, and she'd just smile her beatific smile as if this contrived adherence to my wishes wouldn't be perceived as anything other than charming, and inevitably the older women would sigh and say, 'I remember when my girls were that age,' and my mother would just keep smiling and laughing, 'I really shouldn't give in.' I swear my nightmares are made up of her fake-sugary little grins." She takes a breath, looks at us, then bites down on a cracker and says through clenched teeth, "So yeah. That's me—failed princess, conversion therapy dropout."

"Wow," I say. "And with everything we know."

"Yeah, I mean, this was years ago and my mother apologized," she lays the stress heavily on the last syllable, "but, you know," another bite of cracker, "the damage had been done."

She sighs. "I thought telling her I was bi would make it easier. But she refuses to understand. 'It's one or the other, darling' is what she says now, acting like she's all enlightened since she and my father got divorced. But it doesn't matter. It's not like I have anyone to bring home."

She's waiting for me to ask about her dating misadventures, and I think about the condoms, the look on her face in the photos with Ethan, but I turn to Spencer instead.

"And what about you?" I ask. "Are your parents"—Sadie gives a wide-eyed shake of her head—"assholes, too?"

"My parents are dead," he says slowly. "It's okay." He waves his hand to wipe away the panicked look on my face. "It happened a long time ago. My junior year of college."

Not that long ago, I think, if he's a master's student. But the organization. The order. All of it suddenly makes sense. No time for arrested development or reliance on someone else to pick up the slack. He's had to take care of himself.

"How?" I ask before I can stop myself.

"It was a car accident." He sighs. "My mom was driving under the influence."

"I'm sorry," I whisper, feeling the thread of something like cool liquid slip through my fingers. I glance between them—Sadie's fists are woven into her hair and she's eyeing Spencer sideways through the strands. Spencer's broad shoulders etch against the failing light. *We are the broken ones*, I think. Battered, bruised, and burned. But here we are—together. Safe and warm in this lighthouse above the city streets.

"How'd you get the scars?" Sadie asks, breaking the silence. She mimes scratching her face with her nail-bitten fingers.

"Don't be rude," Spencer murmurs.

But he's watching my reaction. *Give a little, get a little*, I think. I'm not sure I'll draw much from Spencer either way, but I sense that if I pour out my troubles to Sadie, she's likely to spill hers right back. And that's what I need—a flood of heartbreak and tears and memories of Ethan.

"There was a fire," I say slowly. "In my house."

Sadie's eyes jump to the candles on the table.

"Oh my god," she says, puffing frantically to extinguish them. The flames dance on their bases.

"It's fine," I say, waving my hand dismissively. "I passed out. Don't remember anything except waking up in the hospital."

"But, I mean . . ." Sadie's eyes skim the kitchen, registering every flammable object, old outlet, and fire hazard. "How did it happen?"

I think of the boy with the lighter, the pillar candles by my bed.

"Extension cord," I say. I always liked that theory. A freak accident. Less my fault. Nothing to do with me at all, actually.

Sadie squeals. "No way." Panicked look at Spencer. "I have, like, a million in my room."

"You never told me what you're studying," I say to Sadie in an effort to change the subject.

Her face falls. "Undecided," she says grimly.

Spencer clears his throat. "Sadie's an art history major but thinking about changing to film studies."

Sadie frowns. "I never told you— Oh, fine." A flash of something. "I guess you heard me saying—" She fiddles with her hair and glances at me. "I can never make up my mind about what I want to do."

"Or whom," Spencer teases.

She tosses a grape at him. He catches it smoothly and pops it into his mouth.

"Speaking of," he turns to her, "guess who I saw today?"

"Who?" Sadie pushes olives around until they form a sad face on her plate.

"Madeline. She had her lap full of art supplies, and there was even a slash of cerulean blue across her cheek."

Sadie flushes and glances at the door.

"She can't hear me," Spencer laughs.

"Madeline's our neighbor," Sadie tells me. "Apartment Twenty-Five?"

I shake my head. "I haven't met anyone yet."

"She's an artist," Sadie says. "She has this crazy red hair—"

"She's also a bit *au naturel*," Spencer chimes in.

Sadie rolls her eyes. "What Spencer means is she doesn't shave her armpits."

"Or shower," Spencer adds.

"She does shower. Just not every day."

"And she burns incense. Constantly."

"Anyway," Sadie throws Spencer an annoyed look, "we bumped into each other one afternoon early last fall and she let me into her studio—that's what she uses her apartment for—it's a one-bedroom, so she sleeps there, of course, but she works there, too. She has all these canvases and easels set around the window so she can get the best light and there are tarps thrown across the floor, covered in paint. It's magical, really."

"Sadie was her muse."

"Her muse?" I repeat dumbly. My mind's wandering, trying to fit Ethan into this conversation. Am I his substitute and they're talking to me the same way they would talk to him, or did he fill another role? Was he the storyteller, the goofball, or would he have been sad and aloof? The kind of roommate Sadie might try to make laugh or Spencer might try to open up with a glass of wine?

"'Muse' makes it sound—different—than it was." Her voice falters.

"Madeline painted Sadie," Spencer tells me. "For weeks, she was the only subject she painted. There's one that's just Sadie's eyes, dozens of them, with eyeliner and irises."

Sadie waves her hand in mock embarrassment.

"It was for a project," she says. "On the female gaze. A reversal of the male eyes in some film montage."

"It was weird," Spencer says. "I think she was obsessed with her."

"I wasn't," Sadie protests.

"Not you. Madeline. I think Madeline was obsessed with you. Well, until—"

"Until she wasn't."

They fall back into silence.

"Anyway," Sadie says. "Now Spencer thinks I'm interested in her comings and goings. But only because of the one night I spent in her studio."

"Only one?" Spencer teases.

Sadie scowls. "He thinks I spent the night there all the time, but he only caught me once. But it's true. Only one."

Her eyes flicker to me.

"So don't be charmed by her paintbrush?" I manage weakly.

There's a painful beat where neither say anything, but then Sadie laughs and Spencer joins her.

"Exactly," she says. "The whole boho artist thing is just a ruse to get you naked."

"E— Our old roommate once offered to rescue the paintings of me in there. He was sweet like that—going to volunteer to pose and then steal them back, but . . ." The smile flickers and then dies.

"Madeline's only interested in the female form," Spencer tells me.

Sadie nods gratefully but doesn't say anything else. Her face has turned blotchy all of a sudden.

I could ask now—about this old roommate, why he left in the middle of term—but Sadie looks too fragile. Spencer too alert. I need them to come to me, I decide. To volunteer information about Ethan before I start asking my own questions.

I turn away from them to find the light has completely gone from the windows, but there are no curtains to draw. I imagine how we must look to people outside. Far enough away where they can't see my scars and Sadie's tears, we might appear to be the loveliest and happiest people in the world.

Later, in Ethan's room—I still can't think of it as mine—I ease myself onto the pillow, contemplating conversion therapy and car accidents. They're so different—Sadie and Spencer—and yet I can't help but imagine they're united by a sense of loss. They both learned early that parents can hurt you, abandon you. Just like I've learned how easily they can lie to you. Did Ethan feel that way, too? Did somehow, between these walls, the three of them form an odd alliance?

It's strange—me, here, sleeping in Ethan's bed, touching his things, talking with his roommates. And I know there's the potential this could all go sideways—that my presence could further implicate Verena and tie my mother to this case in a way that makes my involvement difficult to untangle. But she asked me to help, and here's my opportunity to learn more than I ever would as a detective. And I can't pass that up. That hunger for the truth still drives me. And Verena needs her name cleared more than anything.

I roll over, conscious of Sadie's steady snoring on the other side of the wall, the creak of Ethan's mattress under my body, the dull rustle of the comforter as I pull it around my skin. *I don't even know what songs are dear to you.*

My fingers brush something rough along the wall, just at the mattress line. It's in the middle of the bed, near my ribs, so I didn't notice when I tugged the sheets around the corners this afternoon. I rub my thumb over the jagged ridges, thinking it must be uneven drywall, but when I sweep my hand over the rest of the wall, it's smooth under my fingertips.

Sighing, I roll over, provoking another heavy groan from the mattress.

Sadie's breath catches, but then returns to normal. I count to ten and then flip on the lamp. I face the wall again, shifting so my shadow doesn't obscure the light.

Along the side of the mattress are dozens of small scratches—tally marks, roughly eight groups of five. I touch the lines, one by one, unsettled. Did Ethan do this? I count forty-four. The number doesn't mean anything to me, but why should it? Despite clawing through his room, Sadie's, the shared spaces, I haven't learned anything about Ethan at all.

I switch off the light and stare at the ceiling. It's low, much lower than the living room with its exposed beams and metalwork. And I feel its weight slowly pressing down on me.

If I weren't still awake, I might not have heard it, the faint whisper of movement outside my door. I hold my breath, completely still. I'm motionless so long, I think I might have imagined it, but just when I begin to breathe again, I hear the creak of a floorboard. And then there's the friction of the hall door being opened, the sound of running water, and the flush of the toilet. Spencer or Sadie using the bathroom in the middle of the night. The door opens again, casting a swath of yellow light into the hall, and then is gone. I lie back onto my pillow and breathe slowly as my heartbeat returns to normal. I listen for more movement, but hear only the hum of the standing fan, cars rumbling on the street below, and the muffled beating of birds' wings outside my window.

"Ethan," I whisper, "are you there?"

PART II

Him

He became so skilled at pretending. Good grades, debate team, crew captain. He made speeches, called hello to everyone in the high school halls, was a good student, son, friend. He pretended because that's what was modeled for him. He pretended because that's all he'd known. When did he first see the cracks? Realize that a sincere word had never been uttered at the dining room table, that the husband who clasped his mother's arm as they walked into church was only pretending to be that husband, that his mother couldn't give him what he needed. Ultimately it didn't matter when the first crack appeared, because once it was there, it split in two, and then three, and all of a sudden he was shattering from the inside out—so many sharp edges bursting from the seams of his sweaters, the threads of his jeans, he wondered how no one could see. He started watching others more closely. Watching them watching him. They all took for granted he was who he said he would be. They wanted this thing they could put into a box. Good students don't have shards of glass tearing them up inside. Dark fantasies where they rip the world's façade away to reveal the hidden caverns and the stitched-up abyss beneath. He took a microscope to his classmates, looking for their bruised souls, to see if they were real or only pretending. He wondered if he was just slow to come to the realization that it was all fake. If the rest knew and simply went on living, found ways to disguise themselves, or if they didn't see. But he saw them everywhere—the pretenders, the liars, fooling each other and themselves.

He found himself talking to strangers, going to coffee shops just to smile at the baristas, anything to force others to acknowledge him—to recognize his existence. But she saw him. Called on him by name. Smiled, even if her smile pulled tight at the edges. Even if she was coming apart at the threads. They were the same in that way. Him and her. Destined to come together and be whole.

Her

Sometimes I lie in bed wondering how I got here. To this square room with low ceilings and custard paint. To this city so far from home. I trace the decisions, all the various bedrooms I've slept in, cities, and moving boxes backward, feeling strangely weightless, wanting something solid to hold me down. I thought the job would do that—a tenure line, a profession forever, a symbol I belonged, was wanted—but tenure track makes for a flimsy tether, just a thin piece of twine snapping in the breeze. A storm, a pair of scissors, and I'm floating again. For a while, I found security in Christopher, but even his hand has lost its gravitational pull; and it's unfair to ask him to drag me to the ground whenever my feet begin to leave our street.

Lately I've been wondering if I got it all wrong—if I should have stayed in my hometown, close to my mother, if by now I should have had my own child, another being tied to me, rooting me in place, structuring my day with bath times, grocery runs, and birthday parties. Yesterday I saw a woman holding the hand of a toddler dressed in rain boots, taking small steps, one fist clutched firmly around her fingers, and was consumed with the sharp and sudden desire to be her. To come home to pealing giggles and tantrums and dirty diapers instead of student papers and never-ending emails and yet another round of revisions on my article and readers who shamelessly suggest I cite their books or furiously chastise me for neglecting their scholarship. I know there are women who do both—this balancing act between professor and parent—but that never seemed an option for me. It always felt as if it was one or the other. And it's the other that now haunts me. An ache widens in my chest and I realize I'm crying without quite knowing the cause. For this child? The life that could have been? Or for myself? An emptiness yawns on all sides. And I feel it again—the need to grasp something solid. To find an anchor before I become unmoored.

It's October. I pick my way through campus, watching the leaves scatter. Two girls recline on the weather-worn lip of a stone fountain, one with her head in the other's lap. The seated girl plucks a late-blooming dandelion and offers it to the other one, all freckles and golden-red curls, telling her to blow and make a wish, and then they're laughing—such joy, such innocence. A glimpse of what I always imagined but never see in my classroom. The students are either too serious, one bad grade from sending a flurry of emails and demands for extra credit, or completely careless, shuffling from class to class not sure of the day or the subject matter. But they're rarely present—fully cognizant of this fleeting time of their lives. The beauty of it. The impermanence. But there's something about these girls. I want to grasp the dandelion stem in my hands, tell them not to waste it in one breath, but to exhale gradually, and let the wind carry the seeds along with their thoughts and dreams so they float away and never touch the ground.

Perhaps I'm the one who struggles with being present.

Where am I? Oh, yes. Staring at a sea of disinterested faces. Chase hasn't done his homework and doesn't bother to hide it. Madison has her arms folded across her chest and is staring resolutely at a spot behind my head. Travis blinks at his phone under his desk, mouth twitching in response to whatever's on his screen. Kirsten nods at everything I say, but has no idea what I'm talking about when I ask her a question. Only Ethan takes notes. Raises his hand. Knows the answer.

When I started teaching, I was a lowly master's student, incidentally teaching the same introductory-level language classes as I do now. But at least I knew what was expected of me: Prepare lesson plans. Teach. Grade. Repeat. The students varied, but they were engaged. They stayed after class. Asked questions. I felt as if I had a small role in preparing them for their futures, broadening their minds, exposing them to another culture. And for a while, that was enough.

But now the students don't seem to know what they want. The hope that defined a generation is gone. Born post 9/11, they're the product of fearful helicopter parents and expect the same hand-holding from me. Or they refuse to respect my credentials and believe I'm the product of some kind of affirmative action policy. The university does nothing to counter either assumption.

At least Ethan thinks I'm a good teacher, I remind myself, as I call on him for the fifth time today. And isn't that all that matters? If I can get through to just one?

By the time I arrive home, I'm delirious from frustration and lack of sleep. Christopher meets me at the door with a sports bag swung over his shoulder and asks if I want to join him for a pickup game. He says he needs the distraction, something about his brother, but I tell him I can't. It's my last weekend to work on my paper before the conference, and I'm pretty sure whatever game he's playing is just an excuse to drink and lounge around outside anyway. "Another time," I say. He gives a short wave but doesn't bother pretending he believes me.

Inside, I fumble my way through the kitchen and make a pot of coffee while I read over my most recent revisions. Jagger hovers around my ankles, giving urgent little yips. I stretch out my hand to him, but he darts toward the back door. *The first paragraph needs work*, I think, lifting the pot before it's ready, missing my cup, and spilling half its contents onto the counter. *There's something not quite right about my argument. It's rudimentary, verging on essentialist. Oh god. I'm going to have to scrap the whole thing*. The words blur on the page, one morphing into another, until they don't make any sense.

I let Jagger outside, feel the rush of cool air on my skin, and he takes off after a squirrel. The little beast is too fast for him—up a tree with Jagger speeding past, looking around like the squirrel has vanished into thin air. I call him, but he runs farther into the trees. *Maybe it's not the argument that's the problem, but the wording.* I yell to Jagger again. "*Scheiße*," I swear, as he runs the length of the back fence, barking gleefully at the neighbor's cat, a falling leaf, nothing at all, until finally I slam my fist against the door. His head shoots up, but he still doesn't come. So I hit the glass again. And again. I have the sudden desire to put my hand straight through it, to watch the pane shatter, feel the sharp blades in my palms. I put my shoes on and walk halfway into the yard before Jagger finally responds to my calls. He races back to the house ahead of me, his front paws covered in dirt and looking truly delighted with himself.

I walk straight to the living room and bury my head in a decorative pillow to muffle my scream.

Nine

Tuesday, March 10, 9:00 A.M.

A siren wakes me, high and shrill, and I sit up, alert, confused by the light that streams in at the wrong end of the room, the smallness of my bed, the wall at my elbow. A suitcase lies discarded on the floor and T-shirts hang limply from a metal bar in the corner. I run my fingers through my hair and yawn. There's a heavy, metallic taste in my mouth and an empty hollow in my stomach, which reminds me of drinking wine and laughing but also the warning label on my pain meds. Memories of last night flip through my mind, disjointed images distilled like photographs in a toy picture viewer—Sadie bent at the waist, frowning. Click. Sadie smiling, arms outstretched. Click. Spencer offering a glass of wine. Click. An apartment aglow in the darkness. Each snapshot with a hazy orb at its edge. A smudge, blurred shape, flecks of dust particles, or mist. I try to sort them, these disparate moments, arrange them into a plotline that tells me something about Ethan, his life and death—to find a narrative in which I'm not a liar. A fake. A fraud, infiltrating the lives of two people who've suffered an irretrievable loss, whose betrayal will inevitably only cause more harm.

The smell of toast filters down the hall, and I hear someone humming, running the tap, opening and shutting cabinets in the kitchen. "Jesus," I murmur as another cabinet slams shut. It's like they want everyone to wake up. I grab my jeans and a wrinkled T-shirt from the floor, hoping breakfast doesn't warrant the same decorum as dinner.

In the bathroom, I glance at my face in the mirror. It's been months, but I don't think I'll ever get used to it—the distorted reflection, the arch of surprise in my eyes when I take in the scars, the shaved head, the spots where hair doesn't grow. I apply my salves, brush my teeth, open the medicine cabinet, and find nothing but toothpaste. Close the door, trying not to look but still seeing a boy with a shy grin and brown hair peering over my shoulder.

I convince myself to shower. Fiddle with the handle and knob on the faucet, not quite sure what turns on what, and the water blasts out of the showerhead, a sudden explosion of scalding liquid that has me tumbling backward and swearing.

The noises stop in the kitchen.

"Everything all right?" Spencer calls.

"Fine," I yell, shamefaced and kneading the back of my ankle.

Ten minutes later, clean and smelling faintly of lemons, I make my way to the kitchen.

Spencer is dressed in what I'm beginning to think of as his uniform—neatly pressed slacks, a button-down shirt, suede ankle boots—and looks like he's been awake for hours. A newspaper lies folded on the counter, the crossword puzzle completed, and his messenger bag hangs from a barstool all organized and ready to go.

"Morning," he says with a faint smile. "I picked up bagels."

I tug at my wet hair. The living room's so bright it makes my eyes hurt, and I blink in the rectangular pool of sunlight on the floor.

"I don't usually sleep this late," I tell him.

And it's true. I might laze in bed until eight, but usually I've been awake for hours, staring at the ceiling, wondering where things went wrong.

"What time is class?" he asks, unloading single-serve packets of cream cheese and jam.

It takes me a moment to realize what he's talking about—the lie, the first one, that I'm a student researcher. Told to explain my interest in the apartment. But now must be followed through with a second lie—that I go to class. That inevitably will be followed by a third, a fourth, a fifth, until every moment, every minute, I will have to be on my toes, lying as often as breathing. This simple falsehood morphing, taking root, and growing into something that colors every interaction I have with the others.

Spencer glances at me uncertainly. "It's just," he hesitates, "I thought we could walk to campus together. If you'd like?"

There's something in his expression that makes me want to please him. But I can't afford to form habits—walking to class, making up a fake course schedule, fabricated commitments that might get me into trouble later if he sees me striding across the quad at a time when I should be somewhere else.

"I would love to," I tell him. "Really, but I need to finish a paper . . ." I let the sentence linger, hoping he'll fill in the blanks, and am relieved by the sudden beeping in the hall, a groan as Sadie fumbles for her alarm. Her door opens and she shuffles across the floor in crumpled basketball shorts and smeared eyeliner. She stops when she sees me.

"Oh," she says in a small voice. "For a moment . . . I almost forgot."

Her lips pucker, and she looks away, drawing her hands into her sweatshirt.

"Bagel?" Spencer offers. He must feel it, too—the sudden chill—but he acts like nothing's happened. "Look, I even got blackberry jam." He slides a packet across the counter.

Sadie narrows her eyes. Shakes her head. "You know I'm low-carb," she mutters, swiping the packet before it falls on the floor.

"Not a morning person," Spencer tells me.

Sadie takes a breath like she wants to argue but instead marches to the table. "I'm not paying you back," she says over her shoulder.

I watch her drag out a chair and sit down heavily.

"Fine, fine." Spencer shrugs as if to say, *What can you do?*

He's watching me over the lip of his coffee mug. "How did you sleep?" he asks.

I think of the uneven gashes in the wall, the movement in the hall. "Not bad."

He nods knowingly. "First night in a new place is always a little rough. And the street sounds take some getting used to."

I frown. He's right, of course, but after hearing the noise in the bathroom I don't even remember falling asleep. No cars, nightlife, or other noises kept me awake.

"Marley," Sadie says from the table, "wanna split a bagel with me?"

"Sure." I grab a packet of jam and mouth *Thank you* to Spencer, before sliding into the chair across from her.

I'm beginning to see how they work: Spencer and Sadie. Spencer's a few years older, balanced and controlled—I bet he's the one who makes sure the utilities get paid on time and takes out the trash before pickup. He shows an almost-paternal care for Sadie, who expresses her gratitude peevishly—all eye rolls and little huffs to mask her discomfort at his doting—more like a teenager than a college student. *Where do I fit in?* I wonder as I scoot back in the heavy wooden chair. *Where did Ethan?*

Sadie cuts the bagel in half and puts one side on a napkin for me.

"I really am supposed to be limiting my carbs," she says, pushing the napkin across the table.

"I don't see why."

She holds up her arm and pinches the flesh underneath. "Because of that."

I frown. "It's skin," I say. Not discolored, thickened, and scarred. Just pale epidermis with moles and freckles and wispy tendrils of ink.

She shakes her head. "You wouldn't understand."

I blink at her, wondering what she sees when she looks at me, and how this could be any better than what she sees when she looks at herself. The size of her arm is normal and healthy, like the circle of skin bunching above her high-waisted jeans. But she's pushing her half of the bagel around on her plate, making minuscule incisions with her knife, before pinching them down with her fingers and sticking dime-sized pieces despondently into her mouth.

"There's more bagels if you want any," Spencer says as he slips an orange into his messenger bag. He smooths the front of his shirt. "I'm off to campus."

He catches my gaze in the dark mirror of the microwave, and I look away, surprised to feel my cheeks burn.

The door slams, and Sadie breathes a sigh of relief.

"Good," she says, standing with her plate. She walks to the trash can in the corner. "I didn't want to hurt his feelings." She dumps the remaining bagel inside. "I'm off, too. There are blueberries in the fridge if you want any."

She lingers a moment by the counter.

"Did you really," she looks down at her toes, "sleep well?"

I massage the back of my neck, seeing marks scratched into drywall. "For the most part," I say.

She bites her lower lip. "It's just—I thought I heard sounds in your room. Like you were—I don't know—maybe talking in your sleep."

I think of the nightmares of dark machines and falling out windows. The ones where I wake screaming—in English or German—never quite knowing what I've said.

"I had strange dreams," I tell her, which for the first time in a long while isn't true—last night, I don't think I dreamed at all. But she's given me an opportunity, and I watch her face as I form the next words. "And I kept waking up, feeling like someone was there."

Her eyes widen. She opens her mouth and then closes it again. I get the feeling she wants to tell me, but something stops her.

"Weird," she mutters, covering her mouth. Then she turns on her heel and stumbles back to her room.

Twenty minutes later, she leaves without looking at me.

From the window, I watch her cross the street, blond roots beginning to show beneath black hair. Her stride is half skip, half slouch, like she can't decide if the world is all blue skies and sunshine or about to crack open and swallow her whole.

The memorial announcement for Ethan wasn't public, but I know a couple of funeral directors from my murder days. And after some calls, I find out Ethan's service is this afternoon at a historic cemetery less than two miles from his apartment building. I can't drive my car—too recognizable. And so, I wear running gear—muted colors, nothing to attract notice, but new stuff that Teddy won't recognize if he's there.

When I worked Homicide, we often attended funerals in suspicious deaths. There were never any graveside confessions or murderers lurking behind the trees, making sure their victim was really truly dead, but it was a good opportunity to observe the family. See who showed up and who didn't. Who spoke. Who cried. Who brooded silently. Often, the quiet ones were the most likely to give you something. They were all dark looks and hooded glances—not because they had nothing to say, but because they felt like no one understood. So Teddy and I would stand discreetly at the back, nodding solemnly at family members we'd already spoken with, our presence offering reassurance. We understand. We're here. We're in control. We'll figure out who did this to your son, daughter, wife, sister. We'll listen to your heartache, your grievances, your suspicions about your aunt. You can talk to us.

By the time I arrive, the priest is closing his book, and people are standing with their heads bowed, hands clasped in front of them. The sky is a brilliant mocking blue, the late morning still and soundless, so that my footsteps echo loudly beneath me, and I worry about drawing unnecessary attention to myself. But they're focused on the casket, the words of the priest. There are no young people. Rows of empty plastic chairs where Ethan's friends and classmates should be. Toward the front, I see a man—

tall, with gray-blond hair—clasping a dark-haired woman by the elbow. These must be Ethan's parents. I'm not close enough to see the woman's face, but I can feel her anger in the way her body twists away from the tall man. Rather than accept his support, she's leaning heavily on a metal cane with one hand and holding a tissue to her eye with the other.

The casket's a heavy mahogany. It lurches once before it's lowered into the ground, a grating sound I can hear from my spot tucked beneath an aging oak on the opposite hill. The small group shudders. Then, one by one, they stand and scatter soil on the grave. A red-haired woman drops a single rose and then steps quickly away. There are lilies to symbolize the innocence restored to the departed soul. White tulips for forgiveness and hope. But nothing personal. No baseball mitts or diplomas. No tokens of the boy he'd been, the man he'd become. And I can't help but feel that whoever he was remains a mystery—not just to me, but to the ones he loved.

In the back, I see Oliver. There's no sign of Teddy. And no one who looks like my replacement either. Oliver's come alone. That doesn't necessarily mean anything—Athens PD doesn't always assign two people to every case, and even if Oliver and the new guy were called out in the beginning, they may have scaled back over the past week. His partner might be investigating other leads, or here, watching somewhere from afar. I hunch my shoulders and pull my hat around my ears, thinking of Oliver's warning.

Some guests linger, touch the shoulders of Ethan's parents, incline their heads and exchange comforting words. A squeeze of the arm. Quick hug. Oliver is the last to pay his respects. He waits for the other guests to leave and then moves toward them. Ethan's father shakes Oliver's hand, listens solemnly to what he says, and steps aside as his wife leans briefly into Oliver's shoulder. I frown, wishing I could read their lips, trying to understand what comfort a homicide detective might offer. If he's shared his misgivings about the missing drugs. Or if he suspects the family is involved. *Why are you here?* I wonder.

I wait until the last car in the procession has disappeared around a bend of spindly pines and then resume my stride, crossing the metal bridge over the river and moving past rolling green-gray hills covered by white tombstones, metal crosses, and dark spirals lifting from the earth. There was something, I think, in the way Ethan's mother raised her head to Oliver, the way she avoided her husband's touch. The fact that neither parent came to collect Ethan's things. I want to talk to them. Peek into their lives, try to understand. The urge is unsettling. It has nothing to do with Verena, the affair accusations, the whole reason I've involved myself in their lives to begin with. And I could say that it's to better understand Ethan, that his parents could provide insights to his character, tell me whether he's an addict, or has always had a thing for teachers. But I know it's deeper than that. And if I'm lying to everyone else, I need to at least be honest with myself—that at some point over the past week my interest in Ethan, his life and death, has become personal. And I need to solve this case to prove something to myself.

Around noon, I stop by my parents' to pick up a few items—clothes mostly, even a dress for our next roommate dinner—and my father jokingly asks if I've brought my laundry.

"It's fine, you know." His laughter turns into a cough. "When you were in Atlanta, you couldn't take advantage of living close to home. Had to go to that dingy laundromat around the corner."

"It wasn't that bad." I shrug.

In the beginning, my best friend, Craig, and I would pick up Vietnamese food and sit on narrow benches slurping noodles and watching the clothes somersault, timing the starts, and betting our fortune cookies on whose dryer finished first. I never minded until he died and I had to go alone.

"I thought I heard your voice." My mother strides into the kitchen, a quick glance at me as she digs through her briefcase. She's dressed for an afternoon meeting and nods in approval at the two of us standing together at the counter.

"Did your father tell you?"

"Tell me what?" I frown.

He shakes his head slightly, and she gives him a hard look.

"It's nothing," he says.

"Not nothing," my mother interrupts.

"Yes," he says firmly. "It is."

My mother pinches her lips, weighs the unusual force in his words, and decides to let it go.

"Well, if he didn't call you," a heavy pause meant for my father, "to what do we owe the pleasure?"

I glance between them, wondering what other secrets they're hiding. Then I decide I don't care.

"Just needed to grab a few things," I tell her.

Her eyes land on the dress in the tangle of clothes. "I see," she says.

"I told her to bring her laundry next time," my father jokes again, but some of the levity's gone out of it.

"Hmm," my mother murmurs, returning her attention to her briefcase.

"Have you talked to Verena?" I ask.

She sighs, keeps digging. "She hasn't been back to the office. I don't know if they told her to stay away, or if she just can't bear it. But"—a hopeful glance at me—"have you learned anything? I'll get you a list of Ethan's other professors, too. They'll be more likely to pick up on"—she pauses, finally locating her keys, and snaps her bag shut—"that kind of thing."

I think of showing her the Rilke translation with Verena's notes and asking her if that was the "kind of thing" she was talking about, but I don't. I need to decide for myself what to make of it before I show it to anyone else.

"Great," I say mildly, imagining myself sitting cross-legged across the desk from some blank-faced professor. *Did Ethan ever write you love poems? Beloved? No?* I remember Verena, the way she looked standing alone in the doorway of her house. "Do you think she's okay?"

My mother gazes out the window. "Okay," she repeats. "Such a vague and overused word." She takes a breath. "She's managing, I guess." She turns to me, puts her palm over my hand. "Thank you," she swallows, "for helping her."

I nod. "Of course," I say, and try to tamp down the feeling that swells within my chest.

That afternoon, I revisit my mother's first email and stare at all the unstarred students. Three names, I've highlighted myself: Chase Warren, Travis Hubbard, and Madison King. Chase and Travis are the boys Kirsten said tried to push Verena over the edge. And according to Riley, Madison hated her, too.

The problem is: they're not good students. Not the type to talk to a professor's daughter or volunteer answers to a police detective, whether they believe she's still employed or not.

I start with the girl. Her course schedule would be nice. But only her adviser would have that, and without my badge, I'm unlikely to get the information I need. Plus, anyone who knows about Verena's suspension and connects Ms. Marlitt Kaplan to Dr. Helena Schmidt-Kaplan might get us into trouble. So I turn to social media. Madison has a Facebook page, but it's private. I could create a fake account and friend her, but there's no guarantee she'd accept, so I don't bother. The more search result pages I sift through, the older I feel. How do people keep track of all these apps? Half the accounts aren't hers anyway. A middle-aged mom of three in Alabama. A self-proclaimed influencer with five-figure rates for attending parties in the research triangle area. A second grade teacher in Arizona. But I find her—UGA sophomore, Go Dawgs, Fuck Bama—on Instagram. This account isn't private, so I scroll through her feed—photos of margaritas at El Sol, the rooftop tiki bar at Allgood, a bedroom floor and a collection of Solo cups, under which she's written "waterfall queen #kingscup." There are other photos, too. Flowers on North Campus. A coffee mug next to a binder. Photos of her fake pouting as she points to the building behind her, "time for class" typed at the bottom. She posts almost once an hour. Perfect for me and every creepy stalker out there to learn where she is at any given moment. As I'm refreshing the feed, I see a new post appear: a half-eaten sandwich with a pregnant woman emoji, the hashtag "foodbaby," and the words "couldn't possibly eat any more" written beneath. I roll my eyes but then smile. I've just recognized the high ceilings and exposed wood beams in the photo background as the Bolton dining hall.

The lunch rate for those without a meal plan is ridiculous. Before, this would have pissed me off, but it's almost painful now that I don't have a steady income. I wonder how many things I can stuff into my pockets, and then remind myself that food is not the point. I need to find Madison before she throws that sandwich away and I have to start looking for her all over again.

I do a quick pass of the floor and catch what looks like the back of her head. She's finished that sandwich after all, and now there's an empty plate on her table pushed aside to make room for her notebook, which is open, but she's staring at her phone, refreshing her feed to see the messages reassuring her "she is so not fat" and her friends are "so jelly" she can eat whatever she wants.

I take a tray and pile on things at random—premade veggie burger, fries, a cookie—keeping Madison in the corner of my vision and praying no one grabs the empty table across from her. But it's late in the afternoon and there's plenty of seating, so that by the time I have what looks like enough food to feed a football team and justify the hefty entry fee, I position my tray so I'm facing her. And as soon as I sit, I pick up my phone.

"Hey," I say ridiculously to no one. "No, just grabbing lunch before class." I'm speaking at an annoyingly high volume and Madison's eyes flicker to me.

"Oh my god." I lower my voice a notch but not enough that she can't hear, and fake looking around. "I know. I heard. Crazy. I feel bad for him, but it serves that bitch right." I see Madison shift. She's still bent over her phone, but her eyes are fixed on the screen, not moving. She's listening to me.

"She tried to fail me, you know," I add for extra effect. "Yeah, whatever. I mean, everyone does. But who cares?" I laugh. "Yeah, okay. Talk to you later."

I'm still grinning at my phone when I put it down. Pick up a fry, meet Madison's stare over my tray. Raise an eyebrow.

She glances away, torn, I think, between the desire to look back at her screen and the need to find out whatever gossip I have.

"You were talking about Ethan Haddock," she says, not even pretending she wasn't listening. "You know Sobek?"

"Yeah," I say. Of course, at this point all the students are talking about what happened. Less worried than gleeful to see how the mighty have fallen, without realizing that an untenured professor is barely mighty at all.

I shake my head. "Fuck her."

She leans forward. "Right? Did you have class—?"

"Last year," I say.

She grins. She has me beat and knows it.

"I'm in her class now," she says. "Well, was in her class. She hasn't been back since last week. They've got some grad student teaching it. But I was in the one with Ethan."

"No way."

"Yeah, and I mean, it was so obvious."

"Really?" I ask. "You think they had an affair?"

Maybe I'm too eager or maybe she hears the hint of skepticism in my voice. Whatever it is, I've made a wrong move. Madison's leaning back now, hand sliding toward her phone.

"I mean," I scramble, "who would want to fuck her?" I try to muster the same disgust as Riley. "She's old."

The grin reappears. "Right? I don't know, though. Some guys are into teachers. Power thing." She gives a little shrug.

"Huh," I say noncommittally. "It's just," I swirl a fry in a package of ketchup, "my friend said she heard Sobek was framed. That the guy was murdered. And someone made it look like they were having an affair."

Madison narrows her eyes.

"I don't know." I stick the fry in my mouth, chewing with my mouth open like I don't care either way. "Whoever did it, I owe them a thank-you."

She closes her notebook. "You and me both," she says as she stands and grabs her tray.

She strides away without another word, but I see her pause just before she reaches the exit and shoot a puzzled glance back my way.

I pull out my phone and take a bite out of the veggie burger, determined to get my money's worth out of the meal since I didn't get much out of the conversation.

It didn't occur to me that someone else would have taken over Verena's courses. With class in session, it should be easier to find Chase and Travis. But as soon as I google them, I know it's a dead end. Online, I see that they're both members of Sigma Sigma. Just the thought of those Greek letters makes my skin itch. But the weekend of Ethan's death, there was a huge getaway. Both their Facebook pages have photos of the same lake house monstrosity. Pool floats. And bloody steaks on a propane grill. Someone doing a flip off a large water blob even though it was late February and the water must have been freezing. The student revenge hypothesis seemed like a stretch to begin with, and I curse myself for following this angle with Madison instead of trying to learn more about her thoughts on Ethan and Verena. As for the guys, they can hate Dr. Sobek all they want, but my guess is it was mostly talk. Pool floats and boat drinks seem more their speed anyway.

Later that night, I plug in my computer and check my email.

Fifty-six unread messages.

Shit.

One is from my mother: a list of Ethan's other professors and their email addresses. But the rest are alerts generated by Verena's name; the first is from over twenty-four hours ago. I remember the notice yesterday—right before Spencer got home. My stomach clenches. Something's happened. Verena's confessed. Been fired. Maybe the Title IX investigator found a slew of other documents. Love notes between her and Ethan. Maybe she outlined it all in her journal. Every stolen kiss. Every late-night visit. Case opened and closed before I even dipped my toes in.

But when I open the latest email, the update's not from the *Banner-Herald* or the university. It's from a social news aggregate, the kind that's only loosely moderated, where anyone can post anything but people often quote their sources as fact. I frown and click the link. It's a thread under the UGA topic, with a link to the same grainy video of Verena being escorted from Joe Brown that I saw on the news, posted by a user named u/milkywr0ngway, with the header: Has anyone else been targeted by sobek? Beneath, the person has written: Most rapists are repeat offenders. The university should fire her immediately.

I feel something cold clamp down on my chest. How did an affair allegation turn into an accusation of rape? I click the post. There are already over a hundred up-votes and twenty-one comments.

The first is from a user named u/serendipity2dragon: Reactionary much? She had a consensual relationship with a student. The news article said he was 20, so it's not like it's statutory.

u/milkywr0ngway: But I mean, was he the first? How many times do you think she's done this?

u/tobyboy11: I heard she was a ruski sleeper cell.

u/milkywr0ngway: This is serious.

u/nikfreak_atl_98: I heard she gives As for blowjobs.

u/lifegivesyoulimes: I was in Sobek's class 3 years ago. Saw her downtown and she offered to buy me a drink. Next thing I know shes trying to get me back to her apartment.

u/milkywr0ngway: You should report this to the title ix office.

u/lifegivesyoulimes: I didn't go.

u/milkywr0ngway: But still. That's fucked up. what happened when you went back to class?

u/lifegivesyoulimes: Nothing. She pretended it never happened.

u/69dckpuss69: Same thing w me. But I fucked her. Got an A.

u/milkywr0ngway: Yeah, I'm gonna say u/69dckpuss69 is full of shit.

u/thetruthisnowh3re: Says here, Sobek's only been at the university since last year. So looks like u/lifegivesyoulimes is full of shit, too.

Well, at least someone is fact-checking, I think as I keep scanning.

UGA should fire the slut.

Send her back where she came from.

Then u/milkywr0ngway pipes up again: This is serious, guys. We need to build a case against her. Get her out of the classroom.

u/faeryangelqu33n: I'm in the same class as the guy who killed himself. Sobek flirted with him all last fall but lately would barely look at him. I think she broke up with him and he lost it.

I shake my head. They're so casual in the way they talk about Ethan's death. He might as well be a character on television. Even the way they blame Verena—as if getting someone fired or deported is some game and not someone's life and livelihood.

u/milkywr0ngway: you have to tell the university.
She should be hung.
Found her email on the faculty page.
Found her number.

Fuck, I think, running my hand over my mouth. This is bad. It's not long before they find her address, throw a brick through her window, and pull out the tar and feathers. All while my mother's certain nothing happened. And I don't know what to believe.

My eyes begin to glaze. I feel dirty and angry all at once, but at whom? The students who say whatever they want regardless of the consequences? The professors who make passes at their students or do nothing to discourage them? The administrators, who let these professors stay, who don't provide training or acknowledge that the students need help beyond office hours? I have to stop reading. It feels too much like watching a train wreck without any power to stop it, and I have the feeling that it's Verena who's been offered up to divert the track while all the young people stand in its way.

There are two possibilities: Verena is guilty of the affair, all the claims are true, and I can stop poking around looking for evidence otherwise. Or someone has a grudge, Verena's innocent, and the news of Ethan's death inspired the online accusations. I try not to think of the third possibility: that I'm so desperate to prove myself that I'm inventing farfetched scenarios. And while the most obvious explanation is that Verena was having an affair with Ethan or at least encouraged his affection in some way, I can't help but think there's something else—some piece of the puzzle I'm missing.

I'm just about to switch off the light when I hear footsteps in the hall. A faint knock.

"Can I talk to you?" Sadie stands in the doorway. She's wearing a ripped T-shirt and plaid pajama bottoms that sweep the floor, a look of grim determination on her face.

I scoot back on my pillow and throw the comforter against the wall.

"Sure," I say.

There's nowhere to sit, and she pulses on her toes until I pat the bottom of the bed.

"Okay, yeah," she says, glancing around the room and finding no better option. "I guess."

"What did you want to—?"

"Wait a sec." She leans over to get a finger on the open door and nudges it shut. "It's just . . ." She takes a thin breath. "Spencer didn't think we should tell you—I mean, he thought we should at first, but I didn't want to talk about it, and then, well, now that you're here and have paid rent, he thought it might be better if you didn't know—ignorance is bliss and all, but I—" She draws her knees to her chin. "I can't keep pretending nothing happened. It's all too weird and feels like we erased him, and—"

I maintain a confused but encouraging smile—the kind of expression I might wear if I didn't know exactly what she was talking about, but my heart is hammering. *Finally*, I think.

"Oh god, this probably doesn't make any sense." She throws up her hands. "You must think I'm crazy." She looks at me and then down at the floor before continuing in a rush. "I'm just going to say it. And I'm sorry if it's blunt—I don't know what else to do." She takes a deep breath. "You see, the reason we needed a midsemester sublet isn't because our roommate left. He killed himself." She draws both palms to her face.

"Oh," I say. "Oh no, that's awful. I mean," I reach a tentative hand toward her arm, "really, really horrible. I'm so sorry."

She nods and mascara-filled tears trace charcoal lines down her cheeks. I wonder how certain she is about the manner of Ethan's death. If she's repeating what she heard on the news or if Spencer told her something specific.

"But don't you see?" She gestures around us. "He died here. This was his room. His bed." She shakes her head.

I look from her to the mattress and back again. I've had time to get used to the idea but try to remember how unnerved I was by the thought of sleeping in Ethan's bed and wear that feeling on my face. I crawl back to the headboard, as if attempting to get away from the sheets.

"I don't understand," I say, happy to hear a shimmer of wounded shock in my voice. "Why didn't you tell me earlier? I mean, I deserved to know that someone died"—Sadie flinches—"in my room."

I can tell by her pinched mouth that I've hit the right note—indignation but also playing into her guilt.

She squirms. "You're right, we should have told you, but I—I don't know, I thought if I didn't say it out loud . . . then it couldn't be true." An inky tear hovers at the edge of her chin and then drops onto her knee.

She looks truly repentant and it seems cruel to let her suffer any longer.

"What was his name?" I ask.

She sucks in her breath. "Ethan," she says. "We were—god, that's so weird, to say 'were'—but we were friends. Good friends. And I can't believe it. I can't believe he's gone."

I touch her arm again. This was always Teddy's role—comforting the survivors. I get too caught up in trying to think of the right words, the correct way to set my face, the appropriate tone. But Teddy, he instinctively knew those things. "I don't like to see people hurting," he said once. "I show them I care." Maybe that was the problem. I focused on the showing piece and not the caring. Because I didn't care, not really. To care would make me vulnerable, and I just wanted them comfortable enough to talk to me.

"Do you have any idea why," I ask tentatively, "he might have done it?"

Her lips tremble.

"Yes," she says, her voice a small whisper. "And I think it might have been my fault."

The tears fall freely now, and just when I think I should give her a hug or rub her back or say something—anything—I hear the front door open and close.

Sadie scrambles off the bed.

"Okay, well then," she says awkwardly. "Good night."

She's already standing in the hall when she turns. "I understand if you don't want to live here. We could find a way to give you back your money if it's too weird—or sad—but I would really like it," a shy smile, "if you stayed."

Then she's gone.

Him

Alone. Surrounded by other humans but all alone. Everywhere he looked were people together. They walked in pairs, in groups of three, slung their arms around each other's shoulders, called to one another across the dying grass. His roommates, his classmates. People snuggled together in coffee shops, dined together at restaurants. He was like the boy with his face pressed against the window of the candy store, always on the outside looking in.

That evening, he stood in the bathroom and studied himself in the mirror. He'd been told he had his father's forehead and his mother's eyes but he saw neither of them in his face.

The noises in the hall were growing louder. He recognized the laughter. He always thought he wanted to be a part of it, but now he unscrewed the cap and peered into the bottle. Blue pills. He held a second bottle up to the light and shook it. Half full or half empty? It was a question that revealed something about his psychology, but he knew there were exactly fifteen white pills. "Facts over feelings," isn't that what his father always said? In the back of the cabinet was another bottle with a label that had been ripped away. He touched the paper idly as footsteps pounded outside the door.

The door handle rattled.

"Come to dinner," a singsong voice called. "You can't stay in there all night."

He closed the mirrored cabinet and cupped his hands to drink water from the tap.

Wait, he told himself, watching as the cool liquid slipped through his fingers.

Her

The conference room is small. A table with four chairs and a podium, located in front of three rows of desks a striking distance away. A man already sits at the table. He wears a camel-colored suit, no tie, and arches an eyebrow when I enter.

"Take a seat anywhere you'd like," he tells me, and looks back at his notes.

When I approach the front, he frowns, but then stands.

"I see." He rubs his palms down his pant legs. "I didn't realize you were on the panel." He extends a hand. "Jack Klemper."

I nod, recognizing his name from the program. University of Louisiana, his paper has something to do with eighteenth-century spiritualists and charlatans. "Verena Sobek," I say.

"Right. '*Umgang mit Geistern*: Elisa von der Recke's Reckoning,'" he says, and I'm surprised to hear the title of my own paper recited back to me. "Catchy. Recke is fascinating, is she not?"

"Yes," I say, delighted to find someone who shares my interest, and, as the room fills, we chat quietly about her influence on everyone from Goethe to Catherine the Great.

My name is first on the list of the presenters. I stand. Read. And as always, as soon as I shut my mouth and sit, I can't remember a word I said. Did I stumble over "Cagliostro"? Did I say "um" too many times? But from the way the organizer smiles and a few people in the front row nod, I think I did an okay job. Only Jack seems a bit perturbed. He's presenting last and huffs to himself as he shuffles papers. His mouth morphs into a thin line and his body shifts away from me. *Must be nerves*, I think. He leaves immediately after so I don't have time to tell him how much I enjoyed his discussion of early freemasonry in Germany. But I catch a glimpse of him at the reception—a painful and uncomfortable affair during which academics much better suited to standing behind podiums or burying themselves in their offices are forced to mingle.

I'm just making excuses—the awkward-conversation-induced headache is real, after all—when Jack appears at my elbow.

"I can't believe Katrina," he hisses.

I turn to see our panel chair leaning her head back in laughter. "Oh?" I murmur. I have my coat twisted around my back and struggle to pull on the sleeves.

"Yeah, I mean . . ." He runs his hand through his hair. It occurs to me that aside from the smattering of graduate students gathered around the open bar, Jack and I may be the youngest people here. "What was she thinking?"

I raise my eyebrow.

"Putting us on the same panel," he clarifies impatiently. "Our papers were way too similar. You didn't notice?"

I shake my head. "Yours was about—"

"Cagliostro, same as yours."

"No," I begin, wanting to argue that his paper prioritized male influence, where mine centered on Recke's ultimate rejection of superstition, just as the headache lodges itself at the base of my skull.

"Yes, and she should have been able to tell based on our abstracts. Unless—" He gives me a hard look. "Unless you changed your paper topic."

"No," I begin.

"Not that it would be your fault," he continues. "Of course not. People do that all the time."

But he's still staring at me, so I say that no, I stayed relatively close to the same ideas I proposed in my abstract, that it's part of a larger paper I already submitted to the *German Studies Quarterly* for publication.

"You did?" A red flush creeps up his neck. "And did they—have you heard anything back?"

"Still waiting," I tell him, although the editors have sent it off to readers for review. "Look, I really need to—" He's still blinking at me as I edge around him. "Early flight," I say, and then race out of the room.

It's over, I tell myself on the way back to the airport the next morning. Now, maybe, I can relax. Spend time with Christopher, eat dinner at a regular hour. I'm exhausted from all the small talk and pretending. And of course, it takes longer to get to the airport than I expected, so I'm racing through the terminal and am almost the last to board. The only window seat is at the back of the plane, and I bump and make apologies all the way down the aisle. The man I sit next to is around my age, maybe a few years younger. He's good-looking, but that kind of thing rarely registers anymore. I've just dug my headphones out of my bag when he asks to borrow a pen.

"First time in Boston?" He leans toward me conversationally.

I tell him no, that I was there for a conference.

He gives me a funny look, like he's waiting for me to say more, but then he nods to himself and says, "Same," that he'd been in the city for a work thing. He seems just as exhausted as I am. And I feel a certain camaraderie, two poor souls downtrodden by their jobs.

"What do you do?" he asks as he flips open a notebook.

I tell him I'm a professor and wait for him to express his surprise. For the trite *You don't look like a professor*. But he doesn't. Instead, he asks where I teach. I tell him UGA, and he says he went there as an undergrad. "Small world," he says. I tell him I've only been at the university a little over a year, but that I teach German. He tells me he took Spanish but never uses it. He doesn't know where Joe Brown is on campus, so I give him directions from the Romance Languages Department, feeling marginally proud that I've learned how to navigate a campus the size of a Bavarian town. We laugh about how German departments are always housed in the worst buildings. We talk about Boston and what we did over the weekend. Everything is going smoothly, but then I make a mistake. He asks how I'm getting back to Athens, and I become flustered, realizing how strange it is that I haven't mentioned Christopher yet. This is something you're supposed to do when you first meet someone. You say "my boyfriend," or even "we," and then the other person knows you're a part of a pair and that lays down the boundaries for the rest of the conversation.

I panic, thinking maybe he was flirting, and I didn't realize it. So I tell him that my boyfriend's picking me up. He frowns, and I worry he thinks I've made up the boyfriend to reject him nicely. And then all I can think about is how loud the engine is, and the throbbing returns to the base of my skull. There are so many traps when you talk to people. I remember Jack's face after my presentation. His insistence that our topics were the same. I just can't do any more social math in my head. I gesture behind us to where I think the engine is, say that it's too loud, and motion that I'm going to put my headphones on. He nods distractedly, and again I feel like maybe I've offended him. But it really was loud! My throat is sore from yelling—like trying to talk in a club instead of on an airplane.

The pilot announces our descent. Soon the "Fasten Seat Belt" lights go off and everyone's standing and unloading their luggage from the overhead bins. My flight companion steps into the aisle and a man from another row moves between us as I gather my things. I think my companion will turn and say goodbye, but he doesn't. I watch him as I pull my bag across the seat. There's something in the straight line of his shoulders when he walks away—not a backward glance, not a wave, or "nice chatting with you"—that makes me feel guilty.

I take the long escalator up to baggage claim. I had hoped Christopher would be there, standing with the other families—some holding signs, others flowers—waiting to welcome me home. But instead, I'm met with all those unfamiliar faces, the barely masked disappointment that I'm not their sister, girlfriend, daughter, whoever they were hoping would emerge at that moment from the belly of Hartsfield-Jackson. I check my phone. Christopher's left a message that traffic's abysmal and he's running late. I sit on a bench near the bathroom watching mothers hug sons; husbands, wives; and groups of friends encircle one another. I look for the man from the plane, but he's gone.

Ten

Wednesday, March 11, 8:00 A.M.

It's a bright, sunless morning, the kind that wakes you up early but without any warmth. I brush the side of the wall, feeling line after line slip under my fingers, thinking of Sadie in my room last night. Her need to tell me about Ethan, nervous and anxious all at once, sitting on my bed like she was at confession. The chill is still there, and I shiver. I pull on a pair of socks before my feet hit the floor.

The living room windows capture the thick white clouds that have settled over the city, revealing only snippets of crooked red rooflines.

Sadie's sitting at the kitchen table. She looks strangely alert given the untouched mug in front of her. And her head whips around at the sound of my wool-muffled footsteps in a way that makes me think she's been waiting for me.

"Coffee?" she offers.

"Please."

She jumps up and runs to the pot. There's no trace of the tears I heard through the wall late into the evening. A splash of coffee lands on the counter and she laughs, wiping it with her thumb.

I scrape a chair away from the table as she skips back with a mug that matches her own.

"I'm sorry about last night," she says, sliding the coffee toward my hands.

"It's okay," I say, watching her face. "You were upset."

"I know, but to unload it on you like that, right when you were trying to sleep—it wasn't cool." She shakes her head. "I should have at least waited until morning."

"It's okay," I tell her again. "Really. I'm not upset. But," I'm prying now, counting on her guilt, "it would help, if I knew more about why . . ."

Sadie sucks in her bottom lip, and I hesitate.

"I know," she says finally. "You're right. You deserve to know." She puts her hands on either side of the table. "It's just, well, you might have seen it on the news, actually." A hopeful glance like if I'd heard about it, she wouldn't have to explain. I give a small, confused headshake. "Right." She takes a breath. "There was a professor . . ." I keep my face neutral, but my foot is pulsing beneath the table. ". . . and she and Ethan were having an affair."

"Oh," I say, gauging her tone. The accusation delivered as if it's a fact. "That's not good."

"It's fucked-up," she hisses as she brushes her hair out of her face. "I mean, I knew—as soon as Spencer called—I knew it had something to do with the professor. Ethan talked about her all the time."

"Had you met her?" I ask. "Did she ever come here?"

Sadie's eyebrows shoot toward the ceiling. "Here? Absolutely not." She crosses her arms over her chest.

"How do you know?"

"Because if they were in his room, I would have heard them." An angry flush rises up her neck. "And if I had known she was his professor, I would have told her exactly how fucked up it was for her to be taking advantage of Ethan like that."

"Taking advantage?" I repeat.

"Yeah, I mean, she was his *teacher*. What kind of sick power dynamics—?"

"I mean," I interject, hating myself before I even say it, "some guys might be into that kind of thing—"

Sadie looks like she's completely reevaluating what kind of person I am.

"Oh my god. Why do people always say that?" Her nose flares. "If it was a male professor with a female student, people would be all up in arms, but because it's a female professor and a male student, and she's, yeah, kind of pretty, I guess, all the guys are like 'Wish that was my professor' and 'Why would you kill yourself over a PILF?' 'Celebrate, dude.'"

I frown. "PILF?"

"Ugh. Yes. Professor I'd like to fuck." She's breathless, and the red splotches have moved to her cheeks.

"Ew," I say, and mean it. I don't ever want to imagine my mother being referred to that way. "Did you have any idea? Last night, you said—"

"I know what I said," she spits back. "Sorry." She looks down, bites her lip. "I just—it makes me so mad—" She exhales. Looks up at me. "It's not your fault. You didn't know Ethan. And maybe you're right. Maybe sometimes it works—those kind of relationships—and maybe it's true love and not messed up and abusive, or maybe both people are in agreement, know what they want, but Ethan, he was . . . delicate. Really sensitive, you know?"

I don't. "In what way?"

"Just—" She scrunches her nose. "You could tell he felt things deeply, in his soul, or whatever. Like the whole mess with Madeline—when I told him about it, he got all teary-eyed. He was sad for me, sadder than I was, I think. And for the past few months, he just seemed so raw—all of his emotions close to the surface. He was always tired and wasn't really eating. Sometimes I would ask him a question and I could tell he was somewhere else. He seemed"—she takes a breath, looks around the room—"lost. I knew something was wrong, and now it's so clear—that he was heartbroken. Something must have happened with her—that professor."

"But," I fiddle with my mug handle, "if she never came here, how do you know they were having an affair?"

Sadie sucks in her cheeks. "On the news, they said she was taken in for questioning. And he talked about her all the time. Why else would he—?" She gives a furious shake of her head, and I'm not sure whether she wants to scream or burst into tears.

"Maybe," I say after a pause, "maybe he had feelings for her, but they weren't reciprocated. Maybe he confessed his love, and she said it was inappropriate."

"No."

"And that's why—"

"No," she says, louder this time.

"But if you never saw them together, how can you be certain?"

"Because he told me," she shouts, slamming her palms against the table. "Okay? That's why I said it was my fault. Because he told me he had this secret, and it was eating him up inside, but he wouldn't say what it was because it would hurt someone he loved. And I didn't do anything about it. I thought if I just gave him time, he'd come to me on his own, but instead—" Tears spill over her lashes.

"How did he—?"

"I don't know." She cuts me off. "It doesn't matter, does it? Doesn't change anything." Her lips pinch, and I think she might cry again. "Spencer said I shouldn't ask. The way he looked after he found—" She shakes her head. "And he's right. I don't want to imagine—" She begins to tremble, and now that she's started, she can't stop. "It's just so horrible," she says. "To think all that time he was right there, suffering, and I didn't do anything." Spit clings to the sides of her mouth. "I hate her." She glares at the opposite wall. "I hope she gets fired and sent back to Germany. I hope she rots in hell."

She wipes her face determinedly with her palms, and her nose leaves a wet streak on her sleeve.

I soften a little. I understand her need to blame Verena. But the curiosity curls in the corner, stretches its claws, and begins to pace around me. I think of Oliver at the funeral. Ethan's parents. One more lie, I think, a harmless one, and then I'll stop.

"I almost forgot," I say suddenly when she moves to stand. "A man stopped by the apartment yesterday. Tall, midfifties. I think he said his last name was Haddock."

Sadie freezes.

"He said someone put things in a box for him."

She draws a breath.

I hesitate. "I told him I had just moved in and would ask, but now, I guess, it makes sense . . ."

She exhales, starts chewing her thumbnail, eyes darting from me to her room.

"I haven't seen any boxes, though." I shrug. "Have you?"

This performance isn't going to earn me any acting awards, but Sadie's too inward focused to notice.

She speaks into her hands. "I took them."

I experience a sudden swell of relief that she didn't lie. The feeling bothers me in ways I try not to investigate.

"You did?" I frown. "Why?"

She bites down on her lip, but a sob breaks through. "Because—he doesn't deserve Ethan's things." Her eyes flash. "He was an asshole. Ethan was torn up about his mom. She has MS, you know? The bad kind, primary something."

"Primary progressive," I say. I didn't know, but I remember the woman at the funeral leaning on her cane. The way she flinched away from her husband's hand.

"They were really close—Ethan and his mom. And his dad—he just didn't care. Or maybe he did, but he didn't show it, and so Ethan felt all alone. And—I just didn't want—" But I can't understand what she's saying through her sobs.

"Do you think he knows what's in the boxes?"

She blinks at me, swipes at her nose with the back of her wrist. "What?"

"Do you think Mr. Haddock knows what things Ethan left behind?"

She shakes her head slowly.

"I've met men like him," I say. "Even if he and Ethan weren't close, he'll keep coming here until he gets what he wants."

Sadie frowns.

"But," I continue quickly, "if he doesn't know what's in there, you could take something"—her eyes widen—"something special—that meant a lot to Ethan—and then, if you want, I can drop off the boxes at his parents' house later today." She opens her mouth. "That way his dad won't come back here again."

Her face falls again. "I don't know where they live," she says miserably.

"I'll handle it," I say. And when she lifts her eyebrow, I shrug. "He left his address." He didn't, obviously, since he was never here to begin with, but my skills of detection haven't deteriorated so much that I won't be able to find it.

In Sadie's room, she kneels in front of her bed like I knew she would. Beneath her knees are the deep scratches I noticed when Spencer gave me the tour of the apartment. She touches them absently.

"After I found out," she says, "I took a knife from the kitchen into my room." She touches her wrist. "And I thought about it. I really did. But the longer I held the knife in my hands, the angrier I got—at myself, but also at Ethan for leaving me and the professor for hurting him—and that anger needed to go somewhere." She sighs. Somewhere in the distance, a car alarm shrieks. "So I slashed up the floor instead. Then I took all the sharp knives and threw them in the trash."

The alarm is silenced midhowl, a door slams, and we're left with only the shallow sound of our breaths.

"Here they are," Sadie says, dragging the boxes from beneath her bed.

She looks up at me, and under her fingertips I see the tape that's been ripped open.

"I already took something," she says.

I nod. Wait. She steps to the giraffe on the windowsill, the one with a match in the living room. "There were three," she says. "I don't know what happened to the other one."

She runs her finger over the ripped tape. "They're not worth anything. I doubt his dad will even notice they're missing."

I nod solemnly, thanking Sadie for being too distracted to notice the contents aren't in the order she left them. "Let's get some tape, and I'll drop them off while I'm running errands."

She takes a deep breath.

"Marley," she calls as I move toward the bedroom door.

I turn.

"Thank you."

I smile. "Of course," I say, the truth of my betrayal bitter on my tongue.

Ethan's parents live a few miles past the university holdings in a sprawling neighborhood that surrounds a lake. Here, there are palatial-style mansions with marble-tiled pools looking onto the water and twice as many fireplaces as occupants. Home gyms and movie theaters in basements. Such obvious displays of wealth, it makes you wonder how it's possible so many rich people exist; and that if you can find them here, in this green pocket that feels like the middle of nowhere, they must be everywhere.

Compared to the others, the Haddocks' place is modest, but it's still larger than my parents' by four bedrooms and could fit my Normaltown bungalow in its garage. A curving sidewalk leads me up shallow stone steps to the front door, where I stop to take a breath. Prepare my speech. The lie to Sadie still grates. And now I'm about to do the same thing to Ethan's grieving parents. I squash down the nagging question about what that makes me and the moral dilemma of lying in order to help Verena.

When I knock, a woman answers. She's midforties, in a cropped black pullover and matching lounge pants, and even though I recognize her from the funeral, she doesn't seem at ease in the threshold of the large house.

"Mrs. Haddock?" I ask tentatively.

Her eyes sharpen on the box in my hands and the name scrawled across it.

"Ethan," she whispers, and fumbles for the side of the door. She's silent so long, the box grows heavy. I shift on my feet. "Of course." Slight confused headshake. "You can leave it there. Just inside the door."

I step forward. "Do you mind if I come in?" I ask.

A tremor in her hand. She frowns.

"There's another box in the car," I tell her.

Her gaze flickers past me to the driveway. She rubs her eyes, squinting, and her frown wobbles at the edges, but then she nods and turns away, leaving the door open. I slide the first box inside and return with the other, carrying it through the tall foyer into a large great room.

The space is beautiful but cold, like the house has been staged for a magazine shoot or a property showing where future owners can cast themselves into the home because nothing personal is on display. The woman settles herself into the corner of a leather sofa facing an unlit fireplace. Tall windows on either side are framed by long white curtains, but no natural light reaches the floorboards. There's a broken mug of tea next to the coffee table, a pool of dark liquid seeping into the pale rug, and she shifts her feet to cover it.

"You can put it there," she says, flicking her wrist to the foot of the stairs. "Maybe he'll trip over it."

"I'm sorry?" I turn.

"What's your name?" she asks sharply.

"Sadie." It's the first fabrication of many I've prepared for today, and my voice shakes.

She tilts her head as if trying to remember something, her mouth crumpling as she nods. "His roommate."

"Yes." I allow my eyes to mist.

"He didn't tell me about . . ." She waves her hand in the direction of my scars. "But he wouldn't, would he?" A small quiver of a smile. "That's not the kind of thing he would care about." Her voice trails off. "I guess there was a lot he kept to himself," she murmurs.

I hear the low rumble of a voice somewhere within the house, and as I turn toward it, I see a family dressed in formal attire crouching outdoors in a pale field. The photo's been hidden away in a far corner. The tall blond man I recognize from the funeral, the dark-headed woman in the living room, and a small boy. And it's there, I think, in the eyes, the fullness of his lips—the resemblance to his mother.

"When we first moved here," the woman says from the sofa, "everyone thought I was the housekeeper." A harsh breath. "People are better now, but they still refer to my husband as 'the one with the Mexican wife.' It used to bother me, but—" A shrug of her shoulders as if to say what her neighbors thought was the least of her worries.

"Angie," a voice thunders. "The doctor called—" A man in a gray suit rounds the corner and stops midsentence when he sees me.

"Ah, hello," he says, not unkindly, a small sideways lift of his mouth. "I didn't know we had company. Can I get you anything? My wife has trouble with mobility these days—"

"I'm right here," the woman snaps.

"Still has a quick tongue, though." He smiles again, that same private grin, and I have the feeling he might be flirting with me. I imagine it's more habit than sincere. He's the kind of man who takes for granted that women are attracted to him. Midfifties, tall, in good shape. The little grin and firm handshake are all he needs to slide by in life.

"This is Ethan's roommate," Angie says as I reach out my hand.

"Sadie," I add. But his grin has disappeared.

"Oh," he says, giving me a firm but brief handshake.

His phone rings.

"Right, I need to get to the office. Angie, call the doctor."

And he strides back in the direction he came, the heat of his hand still warm in my palm.

"Please excuse my husband," Angie says. "He's been a bit—distracted lately."

She looks at me evenly and I feel my face flush.

"Was there anything else?"

I've never been so happy to see the sloping bricks and crowded streets of downtown.

It must be close to Family Weekend, because the sidewalks are already filled with visiting parents, students realizing for the first time they're not so bad now that they're treating them to lunch and filtering in and out of the Clayton Street boutiques in search of tokens to illustrate their love. Tourists take photos with painted fiberglass bulldogs, and I spend ten minutes looking for a parking space. But I wouldn't trade any of it for the soulless house in the suburbs, the white walls, the endless number of unused rooms, and oppressive tension stretched between the halls.

I didn't get what I went there for. As I stared into Angie's eyes—Ethan's eyes—all the words I'd prepared disintegrated in my mouth. How could I ask this mother, who'd lost her only child, if he stalked his teachers? If he did drugs? Even if he was afraid of anyone? How could I look at her as she frowned after her husband while trying to hide her tremors and accuse her son of being a liar?

I'm so distracted by the thoughts of families and lies, the feel of the warm sun against my skin, that I don't notice the woman at first. She's lingering at the periphery of Artisan's Corner, head down, but looks up, alert and wide-eyed, when she sees me.

As I pass, I give her a second glance and slow when she holds my gaze.

"Do we know each other?" I ask.

She flinches, a sudden jerk of the shoulders to find herself addressed directly. Her blond hair is swept behind her ears in an angled bob. Everything about her is neat and polished. And I see the shift as determination settles in her face.

"We don't," she declares coldly. "But we have a friend in common."

"Ethan," I breathe, arching an eyebrow at her with interest.

She gives an exasperated huff, like I should know who she's talking about.

"Spencer," she corrects.

I frown. "Yeah," I say, confused. "I live with him."

"I know." She takes a step toward me. "And *you* should know that we're dating, and he's not interested, so back off."

I open my mouth and then shut it again.

She pauses just long enough to make sure her message has sunk in, turns on her heels, and strides purposefully back to the intersection. And as I watch her retreating form, I realize she's been lingering here with the sole intention of saying that to me.

"Wait."

She turns, and I catch the hot edge of a glare that doesn't abate when I lift my palms.

"I have a boyfriend," I lie. "I'm not interested in Spencer."

I can tell she doesn't believe me, but there's a slight loosening of her shoulders. It makes sense, I think, as I look her over. This woman and Spencer. She's petite and slim, wearing a tailored navy skirt and striped silk blouse. Not a strand of hair or smudge of lipstick out of place, she's dressed for the job she wants, not like a student on her way to class, not in an outfit thrown together from the bottom of a suitcase like me. A couple united by tidiness and ambition.

I wring my hands, try for humility. "Why did you think I was?"

Her mouth twists. "Just," a hesitation, "something he said."

I frown, irritated that Spencer's picked up on the minor attraction I feel for him, that he didn't tell me he had a girlfriend, but somehow managed to convey to her that I have a crush on him.

She shifts, decides something. "He hasn't spent the night in almost two weeks." A tight breath, pink blotches on her cheeks like she's just conceded something embarrassing. "I know about the awful thing with his roommate. We were together the night it happened. To think," she shakes her head, "we were in bed, when his roommate—" She exhales, getting control of herself. And there it is—her making sure I know they're sleeping together while simultaneously providing Spencer an alibi, not that he needs one. "But he hasn't been back since. Not even to see the dog." And when my mouth opens, "Yes, we have a dog together," she says, as if this proves something about their relationship. "He got him for me when we started dating, and he's been sick," she looks distractedly down the street, "not eating, that kind of thing."

"Oh," I say, bewildered by the change of subject. "I'll tell him when I see him tonight," I offer.

"I'll tell him," she says coldly, "when I see him in an hour."

She crosses the street, scowls at a car that turns in front of her, heels hammering the asphalt like she'd prefer it was me.

Her

A week before Christmas. We drive north, Christopher shielding his eyes against the late-morning sun, me fiddling with my seat belt.

We got a later start than we planned. Christopher kept packing and repacking his bags, checking his pockets to make sure he had everything, and then checking them again. He fit the luggage carefully in the trunk. All Jagger's paraphernalia went in the back seat. "It's like having a child," Christopher joked as he loaded his bed and toys. And I felt that familiar stab somewhere just under my breastbone. Jagger was already in my lap, his small paws placed on the windowsill and barking merrily at the squirrels racing up trees, when Christopher swore.

"I forgot the presents," he yelped, and turned a wide arc in the middle of the street.

Two hours later, we're watching signs for Greenville slip by and I'm calculating the ten hours we have left, what I could have done with all this time, and how he managed to convince me to travel home with him to Lancaster, Pennsylvania.

At some point between gas stations and rest stops, I must fall asleep, because when Christopher finally slows the car and turns off the engine, there's a quartet of people standing on a front porch, waving at us through the windshield.

A flash of panic. I'd been so focused on the drive, the time away from work, that I'd forgotten this part—the family, strangers who love Christopher and want to love me in turn but I know from overheard phone conversations aren't sure about me yet.

"Verena," his mother, Martha, calls as I step out of the car.

She's the quickest down the gravel drive, making an effort to hold out her arms to me, though I can feel the pull of her body toward Christopher, the maternal longing for her firstborn as she releases my shoulders.

"We're so glad you're here." She smiles. And maybe I imagine it, but something tightens in her face.

Then I remember: the negotiation. Christopher wouldn't come to Christmas unless I was invited. His mother insisted that of course I was invited, she just didn't think I celebrated. Neither of us knew whether she said this because she thought I was Muslim, atheist, or assumed I was traveling back to Germany. He told her it was both of us or neither, which made it impossible to tell him that I'd been looking forward to having the house to myself, catching up on my research, and finally giving in to the panic that has been building in my chest since August.

I glance sideways at Christopher—he has one of his brothers in a bear hug, but the other stands passively, arms by his sides, wearing an expression that makes it clear he's not interested.

I should have stayed, I realize with growing alarm.

"Let's get you two settled," Martha says after Christopher finishes embracing everyone: Eric, his middle brother, who's as tall as Christopher but less round; Susan, his brother's wife with petite clothes and measured blond hair; and James, his youngest brother, the distant one, who casts curious glances in my direction, shakes my hand shyly, and then slips away.

The sleeping arrangements had been another negotiation, with his mother insisting a shared bed would send the wrong message to his youngest brother. Christopher refused the idea that one of us should take the couch. And so again, his mother gave in. "As long as we're together," she said over the phone.

I felt a twinge of guilt when he relayed these conversations to me. A sense of foreboding that our first meeting came with so many compromises. And now I see the small concessions in the line of Martha's shoulders as she indicates the towels on the bed, points to the bathroom down the hall, and gives Christopher a knowing look before she closes the door.

He frowns after her.

"Don't worry," he says, taking me in his arms. I breathe in the comforting scent of his skin. "She'll come around."

"I thought she was nice," I murmur.

He makes a noncommittal noise, and I wonder if normally, his mother's personality resembles his own—gregarious and overly friendly, playing the clown to put everyone else at ease.

"I think it's just hard. Two couples under her roof now, it must remind her of how it used to be with Dad—"

He stops. His father is the one subject that's off-limits. He left Christopher's mother three years ago for another woman and no one's talked to him since.

"And of course, there was all that trouble with James recently."

I nod absently, feeling as if I should know this, that Christopher told me at some point but my head was somewhere else.

He gives me a funny look.

"The opiates," he says, trying to jog my memory. "He was buying opium tea online and selling it to his high school friends." And when my face remains neutral, "He got suspended for the rest of his senior year." A heavy breath. "Almost overdosed."

"Oh," I say, suddenly understanding the dark circles under his brother's eyes, his lethargy. I think of my own students and their increased stress and social alienation. "That's horrible."

"Yeah," Christopher sighs. But he's still giving me that look, and I wonder when he told me this, what I was doing, and how I responded in the moment. Did we have a long conversation? Did Christopher talk for hours, tell me all the details? I remember a phone call, Christopher running his fingers through his hair, an impromptu flight over Thanksgiving weekend. Did he come here? To visit his brother? I can't remember.

The next morning, Christopher gets up before me and makes a large breakfast.

Everyone's already sitting at the table when I come downstairs, hair limp from the shower, rushing because I heard the clatter of glasses and dishware. Snow speckles the windows of his mother's house, and the living room is packed with enough gifts to fill the tree skirts of a small village.

"I was just coming to get you," he says.

I begin to apologize, but he waves my words away.

"Tell them how you say 'pancakes' in German," he prompts, attempting to fill the silence ushered in by my arrival. "I was trying but making a mess of it."

"*Pfannkuchen,*" I say, emphasizing each syllable.

James grimaces as if he recognizes the teacher in me. Eric nods distractedly. But Susan smiles widely.

"That's so cute," she says, and then repeats it to her plate. "Hello, little *Pfannkuchen.*"

"There's nothing little about my *Pfannkuchen,*" Christopher jokes, bringing a plastic bottle of maple syrup to the table, and everyone laughs. Including his mother, who beams at him like he's the best thing in the world. She catches me staring, and her lips falter, but then she smiles. *You're lucky*, her look says, *lucky my son loves you, lucky to be here at this table*, and suddenly I feel it—the squeezing, the pointing finger, the voice in my ear growing louder: *Imposter, imposter, imposter.*

After breakfast I excuse myself, telling everyone Jagger needs his walk. It's cold—thick layers of wet snow—and he looks rather affronted when I show him the leash, but I need to get away and he's my only excuse.

It doesn't help that the house is in the middle of nowhere. If Christopher's mother lived in a city, I could walk through the streets, lose myself in the lights and noise, but here there's nothing but trees pressed against each other, blocking out the sun. I've been told not to wander far—getting lost the most likely threat, but there are coyotes and bobcats, too.

I sigh, feeling like I've been holding my breath since we arrived. The sky is a heavy gray, the air so brittle it cracks in my lungs. It's too much—his family, the expectation to fit in. Every interaction feels fake, forced. It's like I'm forgetting how to be a normal human. Like when I pull on my socks in the morning, I'm slipping into another person's skin, and at night, I don't know how to get out of it.

We don't walk far. Jagger keeps pulling to go back—too much excitement and food in the kitchen to stay away.

When we return, one of the cars that was in the driveway is gone, but I hear the murmur of voices in the kitchen. I delay the inevitable by walking through the house, touching the frames of pictures of babies and grandparents, aunts, uncles, and all sorts of people I don't know or recognize.

I remember the treasures my mother kept—leaf pressings, hand drawings, and good marks—nothing was too small to elicit her praise. But Martha has turned her house into a time capsule to her children. There's Christopher, dropped to one knee, memorialized in his football uniform at every age between six and eighteen. Trophies, snapshots, and hand-drawn family pictures pressed into frames, as if nothing has changed since they were children. Even photos with their father remain. In the pantry, she keeps bags of Christopher's favorite food. She washes James's laundry and takes Susan shopping. I swallow a lump of guilt—I am the reason Christopher lives so far away, the reason he's missed birthdays and weddings and funerals, the reason she clutches to mementos instead of the man himself.

I hesitate outside the kitchen door.

Christopher sits with his back to me, holding something between his fingers.

His mother's brow is creased with worry, and she covers his hand with her own. "If you're sure," she says.

I see the arch of disappointment at the corner of his mouth. Whatever they're talking about, this isn't the response he was expecting.

"Have you met her family?" Martha asks.

Christopher sighs. "You know I haven't."

"Don't you think—I mean, I know they're far away. But don't you think you should meet them first—"

"We'll visit," Christopher tells her, "when the time's right."

"I just— Isn't it strange, that in all the years you've been together, she's never been back?"

I edge away, not wanting to hear more, fearing that Martha has seen a deep truth in me: That I will flee when things get hard. That when Christopher needs me, I'll already be gone. Or maybe she just knows what I've always felt—that I don't belong, will never belong. I'm nothing but a rudderless ship passing through rough waters, leaving mothers, lovers, students, and colleagues forever in my wake.

"Your mother's right," I say.

It's almost eleven and I feigned tiredness after dinner to escape to the guest room while the rest played some complicated card game I didn't feel like pretending to understand.

Christopher followed me up the stairs, and I could feel the apologetic smile he left behind us as he told Eric to deal him a hand.

"Hmm," he murmurs noncommittally, peering at the collection of toiletries his mother has scattered across the dresser. "She'll certainly be pleased someone thinks so. She's been telling James, Eric, and me she's right about everything for years." He sniffs a bottle of night cream and wrinkles his nose. "Is she correct about anything in particular?"

"That I shouldn't be here."

"Oh." He blinks with the realization that I overheard. "She didn't mean— She just, you know, being a mother and all, can't imagine not getting to see her kids around the holidays. She thinks maybe that's why you've been distant—you'd rather be in Germany than here."

I open my mouth to say I haven't been distant, when I'm hit with a flash of Christmas markets and twinkling string lights, the taste of spiced mulled wine, and the feel of a warm mug through thick gloves. I think of my father surrounded by younger children, my mother in the house alone. A blanket of snow so pristine and pure it makes your heart hurt.

I always thought my mother should have fought harder—for my father, for us, for our family. In my mind, my father was golden, the treasure at the end of the rainbow, the man with the keys to the castle. It never occurred to me that he should have fought harder, too, because I understood him. His desire to leave that village—to see it only in the distance, a passing glance over his shoulder, dotted rust-colored rooflines from a plane window—filled my entire being. But it's the last look that gets you. Eurydice dragged back to Hades. Lot's wife turned to salt. For women, the pull of a place means you can never leave. So I haven't been back.

We pretend, my mother and I, that I'll return—over the winter holiday, summer break, when I finish my book, or have a tenured position with better pay and more stability. The same way she pretends she will visit—in the slow season, when she lets the garden lie fallow. She never says big events—when you get married, have a child—because that would be to admit that I'm building a future here. That just like my father, I loved her but refused to live her life.

"I wish I had my computer," I say miserably.

Martha has instituted a strict no-work policy. Our laptops are sitting in a box in a corner of the dining room. "It's Christmas. No one's sending you emails," she said when Eric refused. Yet another tradition Christopher neglected to warn me about. I know he thinks he's doing me a favor—a forced vacation, a mental break. But now I'm confronted with free time, myself, and the suspicion that without work I don't exist.

"What if they need me?" I ask.

"Who?" Christopher seems genuinely perplexed, which makes me feel foolish.

"My students."

"They're home." He moves to rub my shoulders. "With their families. They have other people to worry about them now," he says. "So you can take a break."

I open my mouth and then close it.

It is this: the assumption that everyone has a home like his to come home to—with a mother who rushes to the grocery store to prepare his favorite meals, organizes games for family bonding time, and pulls out the movies they've watched every Christmas since childhood—that drives complaints of the spoiled snowflake Z generation. Middle-aged people who return to houses with trees in the corners and stockings with hand-stitched names hanging from the fireplace, refusing to understand that not everyone has that. Some students won't go home to their parents at all. They'll stay with aunts who've taken pity on them, grandparents who shoulder the burden, friends and lovers who form new traditions for those who don't have anywhere else to go. And others will simply be alone—sitting in empty apartments, working the late-night shift, eating takeout dinners on their living room floor. I've been that student, and I know holidays don't necessarily mean reprieve—from stress, heartache, or yourself.

I wait for him to close the door, count to ten, and then reach into my suitcase for my phone. I imagine Eric secretly doing the same thing and am surprised Martha didn't confiscate our mobile devices.

She's right. Not many people are sending emails this week.

But I do have one. From our administrative assistant. It contains the student evaluations from fall semester.

My stomach immediately ties in knots. I shouldn't have looked. They're never that bad, but there's always one that makes me question everything. *Don't focus on the negative,* Helena says. *The students aren't qualified to assess our teaching anyway. The evaluations have high error rates. They're riddled by gender and racial biases and irrelevant factors like class size. It's just a popularity contest.* But that's the problem—I've never won at those. I feel the acid rise in my throat even before I open the PDF, scan the metrics—4.2 out of 5. Not bad, but not 5 out of 5, so not good either. There's still room for interpretation, for the chair to deny promotion. But it's not the numbers that worry me, that make Martha's sweet potato casserole curdle in my stomach. It's the comments.

The evaluations are anonymous, so the comments are fair game for the students to unleash their fury, avenge themselves for every moment they've felt slighted—by me and any other teacher in their life. I hold my breath as I scan them. The first likes the class, the second likes me. "Learned a lot, thanks." "Class was super organized." "Give her tenure." That's nice. But then: "Can't understand a word she says. Horrible accent." "Talks about politics in a language class—wtf. do your job." "Send her back to Iran." *Iran?* I swallow the bile in the back of my throat. My hands begin to shake. And then I read the last one: "Thoughtful teacher. Always there to answer questions when we need her. Patient with instructions. My favorite class this semester! Thanks, Dr. Sobek." I find my breath again. This must be Ethan, and I know I should read only his evaluation, focus on the positive, but my eyes keep skipping back to the negative comments.

Go back to Iran.

You don't belong here.

Imposter.

Fake.

Fraud.

Eleven

Wednesday, April 1

Sadie, Spencer, and I fall into an uneasy rhythm. Spencer gets up first, makes coffee, stays just long enough to say good morning, and then is out the door. I wake up, shower, and am already drinking my second cup by the time Sadie stumbles out of her room, swearing about not being on time, and complaining of a headache. She's often bleary-eyed and tangle-haired but still manages to drag herself out the door. Once they're gone, I check the social news aggregate feed. Although u/milkywr0ngway is still advocating punishment for Verena, the others seem to have lost interest. I head to the library to work on my father's research and spend the rest of the afternoon wandering around campus, studying faces, and haunting the spaces where I expect Verena's students to turn up. Some afternoons, Spencer comes home early and tells me about class or a book he's reading. We go on walks, and I tell him what I've learned about the university's architectural history. A petal blows across the wind and catches in my hair. Spencer plucks it out gently and tucks it behind my ear. I laugh. And for the briefest moment, I forget my scars, the smooth patches where hair doesn't grow. I could be anyone. We could be anyone. Just two semi-young people laughing in the sun.

Sadie comes home and we eat dinner together, even on days that aren't Wednesdays, Spencer creating more and more elaborate dishes, and Sadie tells us about growing up on a farm, the cow her mother rescued from a sinkhole, the cat that caught copperheads and left them at their front door. Spencer tells fewer stories, but on occasion he talks about his parents, their real estate business, and their parties—decadent affairs, which always ended with his mother asleep in less than respectable positions: on the stairs, a pool lounge chair, the dining room floor. He tells these stories with humor, but Sadie's eyes slide across the table to me, and I feel increasing sympathy for the son sent upstairs full with worry of where he'd find his mother in the morning.

On a Wednesday, almost a month after I move in, Sadie leaves for class—a tornado of stomps, slamming doors, and forgetting her homework that leaves me smiling but glad of the stillness that descends in her wake. So when there's a series of rhythmic knocks, I assume it's her, kicking with her foot, arms too full of books, snacks, and tote bags to twist the handle herself.

But it's not Sadie. It's a man with windswept dark hair and blue eyes who appears even more surprised than I am to find ourselves face-to-face again.

"Oliver."

His hand is still outstretched, prepared to knock again, and he lowers it slowly.

"Kaplan?" He looks down the hall as if he might have the wrong address, checks the door, and then turns back to me, his voice low. "What are you doing here?"

I have a strange feeling of déjà vu—he said the same thing to me a few weeks ago.

"What are *you* doing here?" I echo. There's a teenage petulance in my voice that I regret instantly. And I can't help but peek behind him, my heart faltering when I realize he's come without Teddy.

He folds his arms and rocks back on his heels, scrutinizing me.

I jut out my chin and move to block the doorway. It's this, my infinite stubbornness, that got me here, a civilian living in a dead boy's room. My best quality or my worst—it's the reason I had one of the highest homicide solve rates and also the cause of my current unemployment. But as I stare at him, I remind myself that he's the reason everyone blames Verena. And that in this way we're the same—or at least, we were the same: right now, he's willing to do whatever he wants to solve this case, not caring who gets hurt in the process.

Someone coughs in the hall, and Oliver whips his head around. It's not Spencer or Sadie, but a young woman with a head of red curls. She rolls by Oliver, lap full of canvases, and looks deliberately away from the apartment. There's a swift movement of keys in the lock and the door slams shut.

Oliver clears his throat. "Can I come in?"

I purse my lips, relishing the thought that I might have something he wants. That if I play my cards right, this may be my chance to learn more about Ethan's death than I ever will poking around the apartment or interviewing Verena's students. And if he's willing to forgo the rules to solve this case, I am, too. But I enjoy having the upper hand for once, so I linger, thinking it over, while Oliver shifts impatiently on his feet.

I widen the door wordlessly, and he steps inside.

Seeing him there between the kitchen counter and the sloping living room floors, backlit by the early-spring light, taking in the room slowly, methodically, looking for inconsistencies and incongruencies, knowing that I'm going to have to explain myself if I want to learn anything, the full force of what I'm doing hits me—a staggering sensation, like getting off a Ferris wheel and only then realizing you're afraid of heights. I feel light-headed, almost giddy. I'm not breaking any laws. Not in violation of some dumb protocol. *You can't make me leave*, I think defiantly, which is silly because until a few moments ago he didn't know I was here.

Oliver chews his lip, deciding how best to handle me.

"I came to talk to Ethan Haddock's roommates—the residents of this apartment."

Direct, I appreciate that, but it throws me off-balance. He's not looking at me, but at the matching mugs on the counter, Sadie's stained with lip-stick, mine with a brown splash of coffee. Do I admit or play dumb—*Oh, what a strange coincidence, I had no idea Ethan died in this apartment. No idea you were at the funeral.* I sigh, pretty sure that approach will get me nowhere. I know Oliver. If I want answers, I have to offer them, too.

"Well, you're looking at one," I tell him.

He blinks, taking that in. His eyes sweep to the hall with the bedrooms. "Where are Spencer Duplass and Sadie Parris?"

And then I realize—the stiffness, the formality—he thinks someone might hear us. And this is why he hasn't threatened to arrest me.

"In class."

Some of the rigidity falls from his shoulders, but he's still staring at me evenly.

"They'll both be gone at least an hour," I say, "but we should stay by the door in case one comes home early. Sadie has a habit of forgetting her things."

I see the curious flick of his eyebrow as he wonders how well I know them and if this knowledge will come in useful.

"Fine," he agrees.

I pull a barstool up to the counter and gesture for him to do the same. *See*, my movement says, *I'm at home here.*

"I'd offer you something but don't want anyone to think we've been having a nice long chat."

"Right." He folds his arms across his chest. "What the hell are you thinking?"

I decide to play nice. *Give a little, get a little*, I think.

"I moved in almost a month ago. My house is still uninhabitable." I pluck an apple from the counter and take a bite.

Oliver watches me. Calculates the time between my move-in date and Ethan's death, connects it to the day he saw me stalking outside the building.

"And so you're here," he muses, "trying to see what you can discover from Ethan's roommates, hoping for a clue we missed and that the Title Nine investigator can't be bothered to find."

His look says what I've been thinking, that the plan verges on idiotic, but I see a flicker of interest—he thinks he might get something out of my arrangement.

"Exactly."

"Did it occur to you that nothing you find will hold up in court?"

"I'm not planning on going to court," I say. This is my trump card. I'm no longer an investigating officer, tied to a rule book and warrants and affidavits. I'm a regular civilian, which means I can live wherever and with whomever I want. "Just looking to clear Verena's name. Why are you here?" I fiddle with a hangnail and watch him out of the corner of my eye. "Still considering the death suspicious?"

He leans against the refrigerator, eyes going over the room again, noting the pair of Sadie's boots flung by the door, the paper bag that missed the trash, the empty knife block.

I see him waver—I'm kicked off the team, thrown out of the rink, no longer welcome at the cool kids' table; inviting me back into the fold, even a little bit, is like feeding a stray cat, and probably won't do either one of us any good. But ultimately, he must land at the same conclusion as me: information shared means information gained.

"The thing is," he says slowly, "I knew him."

My eyebrows shoot up. Not what I was expecting.

If you know a victim, you're emotionally involved and shouldn't be on the case. Oliver should have told Truman immediately, and Truman would have had him reassigned. The fact that he's here, poking around, means he didn't say anything to Truman. Means this might be an unofficial visit—means he's verging into the same territory that lost me my job four months ago. And that this, more than anything, is why he's tolerated my involvement—he's desperate.

"Not well," he clarifies, seeing the look on my face. "He was a friend of my younger brother—Charles?"

I realize suddenly that I don't know anything about Oliver's family. It was Teddy whose mother invited me to dinners in their backyard, the long table stretched under string lights, his sisters teasing him endlessly but with the same adoration they might a pop star. When I try to draw up Oliver's world outside the station—anything he's told me about parents, siblings, romantic partners—my mind's blank.

"Ethan," he continues, unsurprised by my lack of response, "used to come by my parents' house all the time. Bright, playful little kid."

"When was the last time you saw him?"

His mouth twists. "Six, maybe seven years ago. I was in college. Charlie would have been—" He looks at the ceiling, counting backward. "I don't know, thirteen or fourteen. Ethan, the same age."

"I got the impression from his roommates that he was shy," I say, "a bit skittish."

Oliver chews the side of his cheek. "I mean, maybe he was, when he lived with them—like I said, it's been a while." He rubs a hand over his jaw. "He was outgoing, kind, possibly a little naïve. Thought the world glittered, you know? Everything was 'lit,' 'amazing,' 'awesome.' And of course he thought that. He had a perfect life. Perfect family. He and his dad would be outside every Saturday throwing the football. Sunday at the grill."

There's something wistful in the way Oliver says this. "I take it your weekends looked different?"

He blinks at me and then crosses his arms, leaning back to examine my face under his lashes. "You really don't know, do you?"

I open my mouth and then close it.

He shakes his head. "We worked together two years, and you don't know anything about me." He doesn't sound hurt, more surprised, and maybe even a little impressed by my complete lack of knowledge, as if people don't work side by side for years without knowing any more about their colleagues than the items on their desks, a photo of a wife, perhaps, children, a pet dog, never remembering if the daughter's the one who plays soccer or the son. But we're not colleagues in cubicles, we're detectives. Curiosity and observation are our livelihood. So why didn't I pay attention?

I search my memory.

"You have a brother," I say.

"I have three."

"You're the oldest."

"Second youngest."

"Your dad's a . . ." I've got nothing. I can tell you the names of Teddy's sisters, their birth order, career choices, and favorite ice-cream flavors, but I can't remember a single thing about Oliver's family.

"My dad," Oliver takes a breath, "was an electrician."

Was. Shit.

"He killed himself when I was nine."

I fumble for the words to apologize, but he holds up a hand.

"I didn't tell you or anyone. But Teddy knew. I assumed you did, too." Meaning that, at some point, he thought I would have been curious enough about the new guy to look him up, curious after seeing him at the funeral about his interest in this particular case, curious about him at all.

"Ethan's parents never came by to collect his things," I say. It's a weak offering, but it's something.

"What?" Oliver's eyebrows arch in surprise.

"There were two boxes. I dropped them off yesterday." I clear my throat. "As far as I know, Mr. and Mrs. Haddock haven't been by the apartment at all. Spencer ended up taking Ethan's books back to the library. Sadie packed his things." I hesitate. "And I've been sleeping in his bed."

Oliver stares at me a full minute before responding.

"That's strange."

"His parents' absence or the bed?"

"Both. The bed definitely." He frowns. "It's none of my business, but I know you and Teddy still aren't speaking—"

"You're right," I say. "It's none of your business." I don't like what he's implying. That the move into Ethan's apartment may have something to do with missing Teddy and my desperation.

He lifts up his hands. "Fine. How's Angie holding up?"

I think of the spilled tea. The tension between her and her husband.

"She seemed okay. Maybe a little tired. Withdrawn."

He nods. "She has trouble focusing. The MS—it's been hard on her. She took a couple bad falls. Ethan's the one who begged her to use the cane." He shakes his head. "I worry that with him gone—"

We're both quiet. And I know what he's thinking. That Ethan's concern for his mother proves something. But if Ethan's life was so perfect before, maybe having a sick parent changed something in him. Maybe he realized that life, love, health—all those things young people take for granted—were no longer a guarantee, and that knowledge unsettled his entire foundation.

I swallow the urge to ask about Teddy, how he's doing, if he's eating, if he misses me.

"There's something else," I say instead.

Oliver cocks his head. I know I'm showing my remaining hand, but I have the feeling we're playing that game where someone puts an item in one palm, holds both behind their back, and you've got to guess the right arm to win the prize. So far, we've both displayed our empty hands. I have to show what's in the right one, if I want to see what he's holding, too.

I lead him back to Ethan's room and pull the comforter away from the wall.

"It could have been another tenant, but seeing how the ridges line up perfectly with his mattress—"

He brushes down my comforter gently, and I'm aware of the intimacy of the space, the strangeness of Oliver leaning over my bed as he runs his finger across the wall. He looks from the jagged scratches to me and then back again.

"Forty-four," I tell him.

He straightens and turns to the window, hands on his hips and back to me. "Mean anything to you?" His eyes are on the adjacent roof, a red balloon caught in the power lines.

"No." I've racked my brain. It's not the number of days he lived here. Number of classes he had with Verena. Any significant number I can think of.

"We're missing something."

"I think you're right," I say, warmed a little by the "we."

I wait to see if he's willing to continue our game of show-and-tell.

"It's quite possible he was depressed. But—" That headshake again. "I still haven't ruled out the death as suspicious."

Here, there's an "I," not a "we." And I'm struck by the absence of a partner. The feeling that Oliver has made this decision alone. I have a flash of last fall when he tried to direct everyone's attention away from the fraternity. Remind myself that he can't be trusted. That he's part of a broken system, but maybe I can use its faults to help Verena.

"You still think the professor has something to do with this?" I fold my arms over my chest. "Because everything you have so far is rumor and hearsay." I don't bother telling him about the love poem.

He frowns. "It's up to the university to decide what to do about the affair allegations, but—" He hesitates, gauging how much to tell me.

"What?"

He takes a breath. "Remember how I told you there were no pill bottles?"

I nod.

Oliver runs his hands through his hair. "I requested an autopsy. It took a while to get the results."

Oliver would have pushed, but it's unlikely the case would have taken priority. In the past two decades alone, suicide rates have increased across all age groups, but the biggest uptick has been among people aged fifteen to twenty-five. It's the second-most-common cause of death among college students after accidents, which is horrible and sad, and more should be done in the way of mental health services. But it sounds like Oliver's investigating this on his own. And without Truman's approval, he wouldn't have been able to rush the findings.

"What did the tox reports come back with?"

In most toxicology screens, you're using antibodies to look for drugs in the blood. Generally, you're searching for alcohol, amphetamines, opiates, and barbiturates. Anything that might impair judgment, explain erratic behavior, or indicate the possibility of accidental overdose or poisoning. If the tox report comes back negative, then you can rule out substance abuse. If it comes back positive, a more sophisticated test is required. The whole process can take weeks.

"There were traces of eszopiclone, benzodiazepine, and antihistamines in his system."

Fuck. "Aren't benzos for panic disorders?"

Oliver nods. "They're used for a lot of things—anxiety, epilepsy, even insomnia, which would explain the eszopiclone—it's a sedative, pretty common in the major sleep aids. They're both generally considered safe, although there's always the risk of dependence and addiction. But together—" He shakes his head. "They could cause anything from further depression to decreased heart rate, loss of consciousness, and death."

I know about eszopiclone. I started taking it after the fire. At first, it gave me dry mouth and made me think I was coming down with something. I had all the symptoms of the common cold—fatigue, sneezing, a runny nose. It's possible this is why Ethan was taking the antihistamines—he thought he had allergies when really it was a side effect of the z-pills.

"Officially, we have an undetermined cause of death."

I stare at the mattress. Undetermined cause of death. It's not sexy—you'll never see a forensics examiner on television lead with that—but it happens. Not often, maybe only 5 percent of the time, but enough that coroners have a fifth category for the manner of death—after natural, accidental, homicide, and suicide, there's undetermined.

"What if he wasn't sure one drug would be enough, so he took the others to be certain he got the job done?"

"It's possible," Oliver concedes. "Dara found 'death by overdose' in his Google search history. Maybe he thought the combination would dull what he was about to do. Or he didn't know how the drugs would interact. But his mother said he wasn't taking anything. That he'd never had a hard time sleeping. Quite the opposite. She said he slept through a small hurricane on a trip to visit his grandmother in Florida recently."

I sigh. There's a lot his mother might not know. Students go through a variety of changes in college. They're still learning impulse control, have acclimation anxiety, poor diets, and bad sleep habits. They don't take care of their bodies, suffer from imposter syndrome, digital alienation, academic and financial stress, on top of other mental health issues. And if a student has a doctor at home, a doctor at the health center, a doctor in town, they could end up with quite the cocktail of prescriptions.

"Did you check with his doctor?"

"The family physician, yeah." Oliver shakes his head. "She hadn't seen him in over a year. No prescriptions for anything. 'All in all, a healthy kid,' she said."

"He could have bought them off a dealer," I muse, "stole single pills, or slowly borrowed them from friends."

Oliver nods. "But that requires careful planning and other people, and I would have found them by now."

"What about the note?" This is the assumption everyone's been making. I hope if I ask like I already know, Oliver won't hesitate to confirm. I hold my breath, thinking maybe I've pushed him too far. That he'll realize my presence here is a risk and accuse me of interfering with the investigation again.

But instead, he sighs. "Inconclusive," he says.

"What do you mean?"

About a third of suicides leave an authenticated note. They're more common in cases of drug intoxication and other poisonings than violent methods, like a hanging or a firearm, but if he wrote a note, then Oliver's suspicions wouldn't make sense.

He seems to be debating how much to tell me.

"Ethan used an unconventional surface."

"You mean like a mirror? A wall?" I think of the notches next to his mattress.

Oliver shakes his head sadly, frowns, and then says: "His skin."

I stare at him, picturing blue lines swirling over pale epidermis, children drawing butterflies on their knees, lovers writing sweet nothings on each other's ribs, dark tattoos blooming in the dark. I feel sick.

When I don't say anything, he continues, "The handwriting analysist said it was likely a match but there were variables in the authentication."

I swear. Anytime you have a note left on an unusual surface, you have to account for the differences—spatial constraints, awkward position of the writer, writing device not working effectively, and erasure over time. And, of course, there's the interpretation of the words themselves.

"What did it say?"

Oliver presses his lips together. The flesh in the middle turns white.

"He wrote 'I'm sorry' here." Oliver points to the palm of his left hand. "'Verena' here." He indicates the skin of his inner left arm. "And 'Verena,' again, here." He makes a slash across his right wrist.

"Shit," I say, running a hand over my mouth.

"Yeah," he agrees. And I know he's seeing it, the blood where the pen bit deep, the lighter indentation when the pills began to take effect, and Ethan's last words—so painful and personal that he felt compelled to carve them into his skin.

Him

In one fell swoop, his world cracked open.

How was it possible for everything he knew about life to change in a day? For years he'd been walking on glass, avoiding the cracks, only to find the entire floor had shattered beneath him.

He needed a kind word, an understanding glance. For someone to recognize his suffering.

He sat on a cold bench outside the building. Students dodged him as they quickened their pace to class. A tear slipped down his cheek, and he touched it with his fingertips. A girl looked in his direction and hesitated as if she might say something but only smiled, tugged on her backpack, and hurried on her way.

He heard her bike—its familiar stutter and squeak—before she pedaled up the lane. Another tear streaked down his face and he let it fall.

"Guten Morgen," he called to her, drawing her attention.

"Morgen." She nodded as she locked her bike to the metal rack.

He cleared his throat and looked at her with bright eyes.

But she didn't stop to ask if he was okay. Instead, she touched her wrist to indicate the time and raced up the steps, a heavy textbook clutched to her chest.

He reached out to her as the tears froze on his face.

Her

Ethan. My best student. Suddenly gone. Not gone-gone. He's there, sitting in the front, at the same desk with the pencil scratches on the corner. But it feels like over the holidays, some tiny part of his soul—the hardworking, happy, warm bit—has been replaced with an indifferent, cold, and lethargic spirit.

At first, I thought it was the general January gloom. Winter here is sunless and chilly but without the pristine beauty or excitement of the first snow. There's no ski week on the horizon, and spring break is too far away. The students seem like little Georgia sparrows fighting a natural inclination to fly south for the winter. Instead, they're weighed down by gray coats and fleece-lined jackets, succumbing to the short days and long nights.

I couldn't sit in my office anymore, so I took home a stack of personal essays to grade. Most were sweet. I can tell some of the students are homesick. They write about their pets. How they hate dining hall food and miss their mothers' cooking. One wrote that his dad died last year. I didn't know. He wrote about how they would go fishing every summer and how he can't look at a lake without thinking about him. I had only two more essays to grade and my mind was beginning to wander when I picked up Ethan's. At first, I was annoyed at how sloppy it was. No conjugations, riddled with spelling errors. It's like he's stopped trying. But a few words stood out—*allein*, *Depression*, *schlafen*. I didn't know what to do. I called Helena. She said it probably wasn't cause for alarm, but that I should recommend him to counseling services. Send him an email with the reminder that it's free and confidential. So, I did. But it didn't seem like enough. And so, I sent him my cell number—just in case. Now I'm wondering if I did the right thing. But I keep imagining him alone in his room, staring at the ceiling. The vision haunted me even as I took Jagger on a walk. But when I came home, I didn't have any new emails or phone messages. So I called Student Affairs. The woman on the other end was nice, but it was clear she thought I was overreacting. She kept saying things like "Ma'am, I'm sure he's fine," and "Yes, ma'am, we get calls like this all the time," and "It's nice to know you care. I'll see if I can't get his adviser to check on him," and the pointless, unhelpful "Don't you worry, dear."

I hung up and then screamed, scaring poor Jagger—he tucked his tail between his legs and wouldn't come out from under the couch until I bribed him with a jar of peanut butter.

Now I'm exhausted but can't sleep. It's 2:00 A.M. and my phone buzzes. When I lean over to check, Christopher gives a loud sigh, and I think I've woken him, but then he grunts and rolls over. His breath returns to an easy rhythm, and I touch the screen edge. It illuminates with a text from Jack Klemper. He wants to know whether there's been any news on the article. At two in the morning. I roll onto my back without replying.

Definitely not going to sleep now.

I stare at the ceiling and think about Ethan. The words of his essay melting down the wall. Alone. Depression. Sleep.

Normally students come to me with their dying grandparents, their ailing fathers, the dog that needs to go to the vet, the suicidal friend who requires watching. I suspect there's truth in these stories somewhere, but so often they're paired with requests for extensions, excuses for missed class, and demands for late work acceptance that I can't help but wonder whether they've commodified their grief into bargaining chips, and if at some point, this cheapening of life experiences will do real damage to their souls.

But Ethan has never laid his worries on my desk, asked for understanding or allowances. Whatever burden he's struggling under, he's decided to shoulder it alone. And I see it in the once-alert but now-vacant expression, the late assignments, and dark smudges of missed sleep under his eyes—he's collapsing under its weight. And so, I decide that tomorrow, as the others pack up their new laptops, pull on scarves and jackets fresh from Christmas boxes, I'm going to ask him to stay after class.

Twelve

Thursday, April 2

There's dew trapped at the corners of the window, faint water webs of morning. Spring is here in full force, bringing longer days and fitful afternoon storms, sticky heat that predicts a long summer. I sit up too quickly and fall immediately back on my pillow. My vision's gone oddly funny, and I blink out the filmy residue of sleep. Open and close my jaw with the sensation I might have been grinding my teeth.

Homicide changes everything. All night, I avoided this thought, but in the early light I see clearly. The words on Ethan's skin aren't a suicide note, but rather an accusation. That's what Oliver is thinking, isn't it? That's why Title IX is so interested in Verena, why Oliver brought her in. I think of how hard she worked to get her position. Maybe Ethan threatened to report her. Threatened to go to the university, to her chair. That's motive.

Is she capable of murder? I remember the hollows under her eyes, that vacant stare at my parents' table. I thought she cared too much, got too close, maybe, but would never cross that line. Now I don't know. Because no matter how I turn it, the fact that Ethan had Verena's name written on his flesh doesn't look good. Each and every angle suggests some kind of misconduct on Verena's part, and I know I need to speak with her again.

Can I trust Oliver? The look on his face when he told me about knowing Ethan felt real, as did the pain in his voice when he described his final words and the way they were drawn on his skin. But his suicide leak caused all the online vitriol against Verena. And then it turns out he doesn't even believe it. He thinks Ethan was poisoned. That's the other thing about everything that's happened the last few months—it's made me doubt my instincts.

I touch my cell phone. I want to call Teddy and ask him what he thinks. I want to bounce ideas off him like in the old days, to go back to the beginning, draw arrows, and highlight the minefields on the map. But I left the force for a reason, I remind myself. And although I'd give anything for Oliver's resources, I know not to trust him just because he's holding a badge. And Teddy? I can't ask for favors before I've made amends.

I sit up again—slower this time—and stretch the fatigue from my shoulders. Verena, I think. Victim? Perpetrator? Or something in between?

Outside Verena's house, the shades are drawn, but there's no evidence of bricks thrown through windows or scrubbed-away spray paint. No crowd with posters or men sitting in cars with their caps down low. Her online accusers haven't found her. At least not yet.

The door opens hesitantly. Verena stands in a sliver of darkness and says nothing, but gazes past me to the street. Has she read the most recent comments? *Destroy the bitch. Rape her dead. Kill. Them. All.*

She's managing, my mother said, but this—the exaggerated thinness, unwashed hair, glassy eyes—barely looks like coping, making do, or any other verb that would require an active state of existence; it feels more like enduring and, I glance at her face, a lot like suffering.

"I keep thinking about what you said the last time I was here," I say.

She opens the door wider and I follow her inside.

I turn to face her. "About how there are four hundred or so people who want the same job, who've trained for over a decade, who've already been pushed past their breaking point—"

Her mouth tightens, but she nods.

"And they're desperate." I pace the foyer, remembering Riley's hypothesis that someone made up the accusations about Verena. "Would do anything to get hired," I say. Her face darkens, and I decide to go with the vengeful-colleague angle. "What if someone really wanted your job? And you got it. Do you think they'd be capable of—I don't know—sabotaging you, setting you up somehow? All that pressure—that's enough to make someone crazy."

I don't add that this same pressure might be enough to drive her to cover up an affair. To do anything to keep the job she worked so hard to get. But that's the other reason I'm here, to decide once and for all whether I can trust what she says.

"Would you like something to drink?" she asks, gesturing for me to sit in the living room and walking away before I can answer.

She rummages around the kitchen, using the time to collect herself. I move to take a closer look at the shelves on the opposite wall. There are no loose pills or bottles, but I discover a photo face down and right it. A man with caramel-colored eyes and light hair laughs back at me. He and Verena are sitting on a picnic blanket, a small dog asleep on Verena's lap.

I hear her return just as I'm replacing the photo. She stiffens and sets both glasses on the coffee table.

"That's Christopher." She sighs. "He left without a word. I just got home and . . . he was gone."

I frown. "Was that like him? To leave without saying goodbye?"

"No." She shakes her head. "I called and called. Worried something bad had happened. But he'd packed all his things." She looks toward the chair by the window, and I wonder how long she sat there waiting before she realized he wasn't coming back. "We had been fighting but were trying to make things work. I guess . . . he just couldn't anymore."

"When was this?" I ask. If Verena was having an affair, who would have a greater motive for murder than the scorned boyfriend?

"A few weeks before . . . Ethan."

I glance around the room again. So the boyfriend discovers the affair.

Moves out. Bides his time and then—what? Sees Ethan at a bar? Slips crushed pills into his drink? Breaks into his apartment and force-feeds them to him? I look back at the smiling man, telling myself not to be deceived by his friendly face and that he's the first line of inquiry I'll be following when I leave this place.

She reaches out her fingers for the photograph.

"And then Jagger." Her voice wobbles. "I don't even remember leaving the gate open." She shakes her head. "Poor puppy. I put up posters, called animal shelters, even the police . . . I just don't know how he could have gone so far so quickly. Why he didn't come when I called. He must have seen a squirrel. I—" She closes her eyes. "I've been imagining the worst—him being hit by a car, scared and alone by the side of the road, or lost, cowering by a tree." A tear slips down her cheek. "I've started hoping that someone stole him. Maybe someone found him and didn't want to give him back. I keep looking—anytime I see someone with a small dog. But I would prefer that, honestly, if someone took him, because then I would know he was safe . . ."

She hands the photo back to me and sits, drawing up her knees so she's cross-legged on the couch.

"You know," she says softly, "the year I was studying for my qualifying exams—when I think back, it's just blank." She closes her eyes. "I mean, I know what I had to do—locked in a room for hours on end, five days of tests, writing essay after essay to prove my knowledge of a thousand years of literary history, an oral defense in front of the faculty. I know I did it, but those months are just gone—like my brain decided they were too much and that time was too miserable to keep."

I rock back and study her face. Is she trying to tell me something? That the combination of stress and fatigue could make her capable of doing something—something bad, possibly—and blocking it out?

I have a sudden unbidden memory of my mother—I'm six, maybe seven, sitting in the back seat of the car. I spent the afternoon in her office, scribbling on coloring books, while she stayed late for a meeting.

We're at a red light, and suddenly she grips both sides of the steering wheel and lets out a bloodcurdling, animallike scream. After she's finished, she catches my eye in the rearview mirror, surprised. "I forgot you were there," she says. Then the light turns green, and she drives under it like nothing happened.

Why? I think. What is it about loving a job that means we allow it to destroy ourselves? Destroy our relationships, well-being, and all the other good things in our lives? Wouldn't it be better just to find a job that pays the bills? Tedious, meaningless work, but at least at the end of the day, you could leave it at the office, the bank, the counter of a restaurant, or in the back rooms of a clothing store. A job you don't have to carry with you, allow to define you, control you, until you don't know the difference between your suit and your skin, professor and person. Detective and human.

I try to remember my question. "Can you think of anyone who might have wanted your job that badly?" I ask. "Who might have set you up?"

"Wanting it, yes. Sabotaging me, no." She smiles sadly. "Who would have the time?"

"So you can't think of anyone at all," I press, "anyone who would want to damage your reputation?" I remember Madison. "Students who were angry with you? Colleagues who might be jealous, or, I don't know, could maybe advance in their own careers if you weren't in the way?"

She rubs the bridge of her nose. "I've had issues with students cheating. Who think I assign too much work, that kind of thing." She shrugs as if to say none of this is out of the ordinary. "And there are some who don't like me." She shifts in her seat. "But what you're suggesting—" She shakes her head. "It just seems too far."

"What about the online posts?"

Her mouth forms a grim line. "What about them?"

"You've seen them?"

She nods, rubs her hands up and down her arms. "The Title Nine officer showed them to me. She wanted to know if I've ever met students at a bar or offered them alcohol. If I've asked for sexual favors. Had sex with my students. Here or anywhere else I've taught. If I close my office door when I meet with students. She kept asking. 'Open or shut.' 'Shut or open.' I told her I leave it open—always—as a matter of policy, but she said there was a message on the university's anonymous report line. Several messages. About closed-door meetings. And inappropriate touching. Comments that made students uncomfortable. She said they have to investigate any and all accusations."

"Even the Russian sleeper cell?"

She rolls her eyes. "I pointed that out. She said no. I asked if that one wasn't considered a credible accusation, why were the others." Her lips twist. "She said they wouldn't be investigating that complaint because being a Russian sleeper cell didn't violate Title Nine policy."

"What about the threats?"

"She said threatening someone with physical harm is a criminal offense, and I can report it to the police or apply for an injunction through civil court, but again, that it has no bearing on the Title Nine investigation."

I exhale. That's what I was afraid of.

"Do you think any of the accusations might have been written by your current students?"

The question's layered. She notices, and that flash of anger is back.

"There's not a word of truth in them."

"That's not what I'm asking," I tell her, although it was, a little. "Do you think any of your students might have made them up, to get you into more trouble?"

She looks sad. Tired. "Yes," she says finally. "It's possible."

I have her write their names on a sheet of paper. Two of the boys match the students Kirsten said wanted to push her over the edge.

"What about colleagues?"

She shakes her head. "All our disciplines are different. There's no overlap, no need to compete, anything like that."

"Funding opportunities? Scholarship? Research?"

"I haven't had time to apply for anything. There's not much money in the humanities for grants anyway, so I mean, even if there was one, it would be three, maybe four thousand dollars. Although," she takes a breath, "I mean, it's probably nothing, but—" She shifts in her seat. "I have received a few strange emails from a colleague. A couple late-night texts, too."

She hesitates again, unsure, and I nod in encouragement.

She clears her throat. "We were on a conference panel together in October. Our topics were embarrassingly similar—I don't know how the organizers missed it. But I got the feeling my research was further along than his. I told him I had already submitted an article to a journal in our field and he seemed angry at first. Like I had stolen his idea when it was clear we'd been working on it simultaneously. I mean," she flexes her fingers, "I didn't know anything about his work until he presented." She shakes her head. "Anyway, he sent me a few emails asking whether I've heard back from the editors."

"And what did you tell him?"

"The truth—nothing final yet. But," she sucks in her cheeks, "that's too much of a stretch, isn't it? He lives in Baton Rouge. Doesn't know Ethan. Why would he target me because of a journal article?"

"You said yourself that academia does crazy things to people."

"Yeah." She exhales slowly, drags her nails through her hair. "I guess it does."

She adds the name of the conference guy to the list of students, and then we go through the online posts one by one. She received her computer back from the station yesterday and already has the page pulled up on her screen. But she can't identify any student in particular who might have authored them. Her gaze lingers on the violent ones. The threats of rape. Death. And I wonder how many times she's read them. Thought about the horrible things these people describe doing to her. And if there's anyone who might follow through.

On the way out, I peer through the glass back door. The yard is cornered off by a low fence and half overgrown with kudzu. There's evidence of happier days—a cast-iron firepit, two chairs, a rope toy, and a yellow tennis ball—but the firepit and chairs are grime-covered, the rope frayed and waterlogged, the ball sunken into dead leaves. And there's a small crack in the center of the door like someone tried to put their fist through it.

I call Oliver and leave him a message about Verena's boyfriend. I still don't trust him, but I don't have the resources to track down Christopher. So I cross my fingers and hope we'll continue our information sharing. Then I turn my attention to the colleague bothering Verena about that conference paper.

I spend the next hour at the library on a university computer poring over Jack Klemper's faculty page. He's an assistant professor of German, specializing in nineteenth-century literature, with a focus on representations of the supernatural. And that is the only interesting thing about him. In his school-issued photo, he's thin-skinned with the kind of light hair that makes it impossible to tell whether it's blond or gray. I check Rate My Professor, a website that once allowed students to comment on everything from the professor's "toughness" to their "hotness," leaving chili peppers for the ones they found attractive. Ridiculous and demeaning, according to my mother, for students to evaluate a professor's teaching like they're leaving a restaurant review. But for me, it can only be helpful. These aren't the gold-star students voicing opinions that could be traced back to them. Heaven forbid they say something awful and then need a letter of recommendation. These are the ones looking for easy As and free passes, who'll angrily say whatever they feel like, given a platform and the pretense of anonymity.

Their complaints are childish and banal. "He never smiles," one student writes.

"Unfair grader," another adds. "Makes you feel stupid if you don't know the answer."

"German snob."

Compared to the online thread about Verena, this is nothing, but it's clear Jack Klemper is not well liked. If these reflect his official evaluations, then he'd need to be even more prolific in his research to compensate, which brings me back to the messages he sent to Verena. The anger when he realized they had unknowingly been pursuing similar topics and that she submitted a paper before him that was now under review. But is there anything else?

His office number and email are listed, and I decide the best way to find out is to get him on the phone.

"Klemper." His voice is high and nasal, a bit aggravated.

"Hi," I say. "I'm looking for a German professor I met at a conference last weekend."

"Yes," he says impatiently.

"I'm studying—"

"What's the name of the professor?"

"Well, you see, I don't remember. He had blond hair—"

"Young lady," he says sternly. I almost laugh. *Young lady?* "This number is not an information service. If you couldn't be bothered to learn the person's name, then I'm afraid I can't help you."

"Wait," I say quickly. "I was calling, because, well, I thought maybe it was you."

He snorts. "I wasn't at a conference last weekend."

"Oh, did I say last week? It was a few weekends ago. The last week of February."

"I wasn't at any conference then either. I was here in my office, working, because I'm incredibly busy and that's what I do," he adds unnecessarily. "So, if you don't mind—"

And he hangs up.

Well, at least now I see why his students don't like him. The conversation lasted less than thirty seconds, but I got what I needed: he's an arrogant ass but claims to be in Louisiana the weekend Ethan died. It shouldn't be too hard to verify if he's telling the truth.

I begrudgingly message Oliver his name, too, and call my mother on the walk back to Artisan's Corner.

"Do you know Jack Klemper?" I ask when she picks up.

She clears her throat, torn between irritation and impatience. Like Klemper, she hates when people call her at work. "Should I?"

"He's a German professor."

She sighs. "That's like me asking if you know someone just because they're a police officer. Where does he teach?"

I want to argue that there must be a hundred times more police officers than German professors but I leave it. "University of Louisiana, Baton Rouge."

She thinks a moment. "Haven't heard of him. What's his area?"

"Nineteenth-century literature."

"Really?" She pauses, and I can hear the frown in her voice. "He must not have published anything significant."

I want to laugh. And Jack Klemper's students think he's a snob.

"Why do you ask?"

"He's been emailing Verena about an article submission."

"Well, I suppose that's better than the other emails she's been getting." She sighs. "You know, the police finally gave her computer back."

"I know," I tell her. "That's good."

"Is it?" I hear her fiddle with something on her desk. "I don't think so. All she does is hit Refresh on that website with those hateful comments." She sighs. "There's so many ways people can terrorize you these days."

I wonder whether she knows the extent of it. Just how violent and specific some of the threats are.

"So how's the new apartment?" she asks. I pause at this abrupt transition. Ponder whether this means that somehow she's connected my move with Verena's suspension.

"Fine," I say. "I like being closer to coffee and campus."

She hesitates. She's never understood my affinity for coffee shops when I can make coffee at home.

"And your roommates?"

My cheeks burn. I know she's asking because of the dress.

"They're fine, too."

"That's good," she says, clearing her throat. "We haven't seen you much the past few weeks. And you know your father . . . well, he's gotten used to you being here."

"I thought you would have had enough of me these past four months." I laugh.

She tsks dismissively. "Of course we like seeing you. And you really should visit—spend time with your father."

"I will," I tell her, though I'm not sure why the sudden insistence. Before I lived with them, we would go months without seeing each other. "This weekend," I promise.

Sadie's home early, eating miniature candy bars and staring at her laptop.

"Tough day?" I ask, dropping my bag in a chair.

She looks up and I see her eyes are wet. "Tomorrow will be five weeks," she says.

"Oh." She's right. "I'm sorry."

"And they still haven't done anything about that professor." She throws up her hands. "Suspension? What does that even mean? Gah." She clicks Enter and slams down the screen.

"Do you ever wonder," I say hesitantly, "if maybe there was another reason?"

She glares at me. "What do you mean?"

"Did Ethan have a lot of friends?" I ask.

"He had me." She folds her arms over her chest.

"I know," I reassure her. "I was just wondering if maybe he was lonely. Or maybe," I say quickly, before she can lay the blame squarely on Verena again, "if he was being bullied." It's a roundabout way of asking what I really want to know: *Would anyone hurt him?*

She sighs. "Everyone liked Ethan," she says. "He was sweet and funny, and—" She stops abruptly and her eyes bulge at me.

"What?"

"Well, there were these two assholes in his class—he said they were making everyone's life miserable. It's the only time I ever heard him talk bad about anyone, and—" Something frightening streaks across her face.

"What?"

"One day . . ." She grits her teeth angrily. "He came home with a split lip. He said he tripped and fell, but I wondered."

"Do you remember their names?"

The flash of anger turns on me.

"Why?" she hisses. "What are you going to do about it? Why do you even care? You didn't know Ethan."

I lift my hands and step back, not liking how her tone verges on suspicion. "Sorry," I say, thinking of two boys who didn't get along with Ethan, who wanted to push Verena over the edge. "I just," I soften my voice, "hate seeing you blame yourself."

"I don't blame myself," she mutters. "I blame her. And maybe them. Chase and Travis," she says suddenly. "I remember, because even their names sounded like douchebags."

She turns away from me, conversation over, and clicks on the television.

I take my laptop to my room. My fingers shake as I open the lid and scan through their Facebook profiles again.

Chase Warren and Travis Hubbard. Both are finance majors, members of the UGA Hermes Society, and have impressive internships: Chase at a local bank and Travis at J.P. Morgan. And both were enrolled in Verena's class, the one Ethan was in.

I tap my finger next to the keypad. In high school, it's more the goth-type kids who take German, but most universities have foreign language requirements as part of their gen ed curriculum, so you'll find a variety of students in the lower-level language classes whether they want to be there or not. And it's clear Chase and Travis didn't, even if knowing German might have helped them with their careers.

I turn to the photos from that weekend—the one of their lake house getaway, when Ethan was discovered dead. But as I click through images of brown-green water, a three-story house, and men in swim trunks, I realize something: though there are dozens of photographs on their two pages, Chase and Travis aren't in a single one. Not among the smiling auburn-haired boys drinking beer on the dock. Not passed out on beach towels, flipping burgers behind the grill, or playing volleyball in the pale grass. Not in the group picture, arms slung around their brothers, cheering with red Solo cups.

"Where are you?" I murmur as my eyes scan the photos again.

The weekend party would make for the perfect alibi. The location tag indicates Lake Oconee, which is less than an hour away. It's a quick drive back to Athens and the other brothers would be too drunk to notice whether Travis and Chase were imbibing, if they left for a few hours, or changed their clothes. I inhale. Imagine them inviting Ethan to a bar, slipping drugs into his drink, following him to his apartment. I blow out my breath. Why, though? Just because they didn't like him? It's too farfetched. But so is an overdose with no drugs found in the apartment.

I sigh, mind still spinning, and decide to pull up the social news aggregate thread, knowing Verena's doing the same.

At the top is a new post from u/milkywr0ngway: it's been over a month, the slut should pay for what she did.

A shiver sneaks up my neck.

"I'm afraid," Verena had said earlier as we scrolled through page after page of threats and accusations. "Afraid of what they'll say next—not because it will be true. But because it could be worse, so much worse than unwanted touching and buying drinks. And even if I prove they're wrong, people will believe it—now and always."

A tear had slipped down her cheek then. "And you know what's the most horrible part of all?" She blinked at me. "It's not fair to Ethan, to his memory, for this"—she gestured to the screen—"to be his legacy. Because he was a bright and sweet student. A kind and sensitive soul."

I stare at my laptop as the number of up-votes on u/milkywr0ngway's post grows. As it elicits more calls for action. For violence. It occurs to me then, even if I can prove something else happened—that Chase and Travis were involved, or there never was an affair to begin with—it might not matter. Not for Verena. And not for Ethan.

Her

I made a mistake.

"They lack impulse control," the university counselor warned me. "You need to regulate the situation for them. Otherwise, they'll tell you everything and leave your office feeling overexposed, and you won't know what to say, what campus resources to call. Why do you think we limit our sessions to fifty minutes?"

But it's not until after I dive in headfirst that I realize I'm in no position to help anyone. That I don't know how to swim.

Ethan starts to cry before I even ask. We're standing in the classroom. I tell him I read his essay and am concerned—not just about what he wrote, but also about his recent absences, the decline in his participation, the change in his behavior. Large tears begin to roll down his cheeks. Another student rushes back into the room, and he dries them quickly. Others are lingering outside the door waiting for their next class, so I invite him downstairs to my office.

He asks if he can shut the door. Normally, I would say no, department policy, for his protection, and so forth. But there's something in his voice—I can tell it's important. And so, I tell him it's fine and to take a seat. *This is my first mistake.*

"I need advice," he says, sitting on the edge of the chair. "And you've always been kind to me, and I don't know who else to ask."

I should direct him to counseling services, walk him to their offices myself. But he seems so desperate, so vulnerable, I just want to calm him. To reassure him. To show him that he's seen. So I tell him I'm happy to help if I can. Willing to listen. *This is my second.*

"I don't know how to begin," he tells me.

"Okay," I say, only now worrying that maybe I should have left the door open, should mention counseling.

But then he takes a breath and says, "My dad's having an affair."

At first, I think I've misheard him, but he keeps talking, like if he doesn't get the words out, they might swallow him instead.

"I was at home this weekend watching the Super Bowl. It's a tradition—my father and I always watch it together. We've done it since I was a kid. Anyway, he got up to do something, and so I sat in his chair—this big, comfy leather armchair—and I realized something had fallen down next to the cushion—so I reached down and found a phone."

"A phone," I repeat dumbly.

"Yeah, I mean, it's not that strange, I guess. But I knew it wasn't his phone. It was this cheap boxy-looking thing. I heard my dad coming back, so I slipped the phone in my pocket. Just to think about it, you know, before I asked." I nod because that's what he seems to be expecting. "But he was acting really weird. And looking around. Asked me to get up, rifled through the cushions. And I knew something was off. When I asked what he was doing, he said he was looking for his keys, but was super vague and guilty-sounding. Then he said he must have left them in the car and went outside again. While he was gone, I flipped through the phone—his password was my birthday—and wrote down as many numbers as I could. There were only a few, which I guess should have been another clue. And when I called the first number, a woman picked up and said, 'Hey, sexy.'" He blinks at me, as if surprised to hear the words said out loud, and then he puts his face in his hands. "I can't believe he'd lie to me or do that to my mom. She's sick—really sick—and this would destroy her." He takes a breath, looks at me anxiously. "What should I do?"

I blink, startled that this is why he's come to me for help.

"I don't know," I tell him. Subject-verb agreement, dative verbs, an analysis of the Gretchen episode in Goethe's *Faust*—these are problems I can solve. But give advice to a student who's just discovered his father's cheating on his ill mother?

He stares at me expectantly. And then slowly, I see him realize that I can't help. He registers me for who I am—a tired woman in a basement office with moldy walls, empty shelves, and a desk strewn with papers and dirty plastic containers from yesterday's lunch—and understands that I am not in the position to be giving advice to anyone. He sits quietly a moment and then says, "Sorry for telling you all this. I know it's not your job, but thanks for listening." He stands slowly and opens the door. "Just, um, please don't tell anyone. I know, you wouldn't, but still—"

Behind him, my colleague Maria walks by and pauses to see if I need her to intervene. I shake my head slightly.

"It's okay, Ethan," I say. "I won't tell anyone. I promise."

Maria lifts an eyebrow but continues to her office.

After, walking to my car, I think of Ethan's face. The dawning realization that I didn't have any answers. That despite my years of experience, I was no better prepared to meet this world with all its injustices and disappointments than he was.

I feel the wind of traffic fly by on the street, and I step off the sidewalk, just as a car turns. An arm reaches out and pulls me away. I spin around to face a tall, dark-haired man who looks vaguely familiar.

"You saved me," I say, because, well, what else do you say when someone stops you from doing something stupid? He looks just as surprised as I am. He smiles and murmurs something about Athens drivers being crazy. Although, by the way he studies my face, I think maybe he knows it isn't the drivers.

So that was my day filled with mistakes. Now it's late and I've been tossing and turning for what feels like hours. I give up hope of sleep and settle on staring at the ceiling. Christopher snores lightly next to me, his thoughts undisturbed by students' tears and the crushing sense he's failing some undefined responsibility, failing everyone, including himself.

Next to the bed, my phone vibrates. Another text from Jack requesting news. *What's taking so long?* he writes, with a head-exploding emoji. Maybe I should just tell him the article was rejected. It's bound to happen anyway.

Thirteen

Friday, April 3, 10:00 A.M.

I position myself on a bench outside the Joe Brown side entrance. It's not the first time I've watched Chase and Travis, so I know they always choose the quickest exit. The day is bright and clear, and some of the fog I've felt these past few days has lifted. The perpetrator must be connected to Verena and Ethan—it's the only thing that makes sense. And here are two boys who hated one and bullied the other. As I wait, this certainty grants me a kind of stillness. The heightened focus of the cat in the grass, the hawk lifting from the branch, the wolf at the edge of the forest: I see you.

Travis appears first. He's narrow-shouldered and weasel-faced, trying to mask his adolescent features with a patchy brown beard and an adult-looking messenger bag. He grasps a phone in one hand and taps it grimly with the other. Chase emerges a few seconds behind him. Heavier set and clean-shaven, he has an arm around an auburn-haired girl, who kisses him and then races off in the opposite direction.

Travis waits until her ponytail disappears and then shoves his phone in Chase's face.

Chase glances at it and laughs, and I catch something that sounds a lot like "idiot."

"You'll make it back next time," he says.

"Fuck you," Travis growls. "There won't be a next time. I'm out."

But Chase only grins. "You always say that." He offers a fist bump, but Travis shakes his head.

I lean forward. This is an interesting development. A break in their usual camaraderie.

Chase shrugs and shoulders his backpack. "Call me when you change your mind," he says, and takes off down Baldwin.

Travis stares after him, jaw working under his skin.

And I'm left with a decision: Chase or Travis?

There's a clatter on the stairs as Travis drops his phone. Or maybe he throws it. "Fuck," he shouts, running his hands through his hair. Two girls passing him jump.

He bends to retrieve the phone, mumbling under his breath, and when he stands, I see his hands are shaking.

It could be stress. It could be girl problems. It could be a lot of things other than guilt or the fear he might be caught for killing his classmate. But his strange behavior makes the decision for me.

Travis slices through campus on foot. It's a path I know well. Strewn with bamboo and brick pavers, it's the quickest way from my mother's office to downtown. To Walker's. Artisan's Corner. To Ethan.

I watch the scruffy back of his head, study the uneven cuts of his hair. See the vein pulse at the side of his throat.

Every minute or so, he drags the phone from his pocket, swears, and shoves it back again. Otherwise, he keeps his shoulders up around his ears and his fists clenched.

I expect him to turn down Broad or Clayton. It's almost lunchtime, and the three blocks that make up downtown have a number of popular restaurants. Students stand in line for burgers and fried chicken, balance books on their knees, sip smoothies and coffee.

But Travis keeps walking. He doesn't look behind him. Doesn't notice me pausing and hesitating and matching his pace.

I wonder if he followed Ethan this way. Him and Chase both. If they haunted his step. Looked for signs of weakness. If they shadowed Verena.

Lingered outside her house. But the clarity from earlier has left me. And I start to wonder if what I'm doing—tracking a student in broad daylight on the unlikely chance he poisoned his classmate—is utterly ridiculous.

Bass pulses from a passing car, a bird shrieks when I near its nest, water rushes from an abandoned hose, and all the while I keep Travis in my peripheral vision. He crosses over Washington and then Hancock. Takes a left on Dougherty and a right down a narrow side street.

He doesn't stop until he reaches a blue house with a white front porch and an Atlanta United flag hanging from the entrance. He lingers on the sidewalk, scuffing his shoes on the concrete, and almost turns back. But then he takes a breath as if mustering his determination. He walks past the house to a chain-link fence. A shack-sized building rises behind it, squat and square with a heavy door and a solitary dark window. The shades are drawn, but fingers pinch the blinds as Travis lets himself through the gate.

I step behind an oak tree.

Maybe Travis bought the benzos on the underground market. Maybe he's worried the drugs can be traced back to him. Or his dealer put two and two together and now wants more money or for Travis to start selling.

Travis knocks twice and the door opens. The stillness is shattered by a blast of electronic music and laughter. Even from twenty feet away, I can see Travis's shoulders tighten. The panic underwriting the resolve. Somewhere deep within the house comes a sound like flesh hitting flesh, and I have a sudden image of those fight clubs that were popular in the 2000s.

A hand reaches out and the room swallows him.

Adrenaline pumps through my chest. I almost follow, unlatch the metal gate, and succumb to the impulse that got me into so much trouble last year. And maybe it's the thought of that case that makes me look up, to proceed with more caution than I used to, but as soon as I do, I see the rectangular boxes. The blinking red eye of the camera watching the front door and side fence.

I glance behind me. Even though the house is tucked off the road on a residential street, I have that sudden alertness you feel in the woods just before a snake darts across your path. That half beat where instinct works before your brain, alerting you to danger, the predator lurking in the dark.

I turn in a full circle, looking for it. But there's nothing. Just the pulse of my own heartbeat in my throat. The feeling that whatever Travis has gotten himself into, it's out of his control.

When Travis reappears, he's pale-faced and shaking hands with someone I can't see.

I watch as he slinks off in the direction of campus. I count to fifty, and then I knock, the same rhythmic pattern I heard earlier.

I hold my breath. But nothing happens.

I try again, conscious of movement behind the door, the sense of someone peering at me through the peephole.

The door opens a fraction and with it I'm hit with the smell of burning, microwaved things, ammonia, and cigarettes.

"Who the fuck are you?" the voice says. He's backlit and has a thick accent—British or maybe Australian. A gold chain glints around his neck, and in the sliver of light behind his head I see a table littered with soda cans and neat stacks of cash. At the far corner of the room is a heavy rectangular cabinet that glows like an arcade game. The man pulls the door tighter and obscures my vision.

"Travis sent me," I say.

There's a bark of laughter from behind him and someone swears. The sound of jingling metal and hands slapping backs.

"Travis," he repeats, and I feel his gaze creep from my legs to my neck. "The balls on that kid." He shakes his head and then leans forward, so close I get a heavy whiff of aftershave, an oppressive scent of stale whiskey and hot leather. "You tell that fucker not to send friends until he makes right the two stacks he owes me."

The door shuts, followed by another rumble of laughter. And I retreat with the feeling of eyes on the back of my head.

The sun's drifted behind a cloud, wind sends pale leaves skittering, and I wonder if I can catch up with Travis again.

"Learn anything interesting?"

"Shit," I say, turning fast.

Oliver lifts his hands. "I saw you cross Broad."

"You were following me."

His smile says I'm in no position to judge.

"Don't you have better things to do?"

"That depends," he says slowly, "on what you found."

I tilt my chin and keep walking.

He matches my stride. "You shouldn't be doing this," he says.

I scowl but don't look at him.

"If you have any reason to believe that kid is involved with Ethan's death, you shouldn't approach him. I'm serious," he says when I snort. "He could be dangerous."

I think of the piles of cash. The tremors of his hand. I'm not sure Travis is dangerous, but whatever he's involved in is.

I turn my head from side to side, trying to decide what direction Travis went.

Oliver reaches a hand out to my arm, but then decides better and drops it. "What are we doing here, Marlitt?"

I laugh. "You want to define our relationship?"

His mouth twists. "You've been sending names for me to look into. Names that may have something to do with Dr. Sobek and the Title Nine investigation, but also might be leads in my case. And now you're acting cagey about this kid."

"You were fine when I was showing you the notches by Ethan's bed and telling you about Ethan's parents. If you're worried about my involvement, just say I'm an anonymous tip."

"Except you're not anonymous."

"I'm sure you'll find a way around it," I mutter. I feel the bitterness and resentment from our last case rise in my chest, and stride away from him.

"I looked into Dr. Sobek's boyfriend," Oliver says, picking up his pace.

I glance at him. He never responded to my message, so I assumed he ignored it. This admission softens me, a little.

"And?"

"Dead end. He's been in Lancaster, Pennsylvania, since mid-February staying at his mother's. Credit cards, gas purchases confirm. No flight records with his name on them. Lancaster to Athens is an eleven-hour drive—one way. It wouldn't have been possible for him to leave in the middle of the night, drive to Athens, and be back without her noticing."

"She could be lying."

He nods. "He went out with friends Friday night. They confirmed his whereabouts until one A.M. Even if he hit the road right after, he wouldn't have gotten into Athens until noon."

And by that point Ethan would already be dead.

I sigh. In some way, I should be relieved. If the boyfriend did kill Ethan, it would reaffirm the probability of an affair. But it was our most promising lead. Chase. Travis. Hating another student enough to kill him. The whole thing seems so unlikely.

"And Klemper?"

Oliver gives me a sideways glance. "Didn't use his credit cards all weekend. His department admin says he spends most weekends in his office, but she'd be damned if she came in on Saturdays, so couldn't vouch for him. It's an eight-hour drive, so technically he could have driven to Athens after his Friday classes, but—"

But Oliver thinks this line of inquiry is even more farfetched than the boyfriend theory and has dropped it.

I chew on my bottom lip and keep walking.

"So," he says. "Who's the kid?"

I quicken my pace. "Travis Hubbard," I tell him. "One of Verena's students. Had class with Ethan. I heard he was mean."

Oliver lifts an eyebrow.

I shrug. He doesn't get to question my instincts.

"And what was going on back there?" He jerks his head in the direction we just left.

I take a breath. "I'm not sure. There was cash. Other men in the room, but not many. I'd say three or four besides the guy who answered the door. But it felt"—I think of the cameras, the man's gaze on my neck, the sense that I'd walked into some foreign territory with its own rules—"tense."

"Drugs?"

"Maybe," I say.

"Well, why don't we ask him?"

I realize we've stopped next to a patrol car. A woman walking her dog glances between us and the vehicle with undisguised curiosity.

"A buddy of mine picked him up," Oliver says, flicking his wrist toward the back seat. "Jaywalking." He shakes his head. "A dangerous thing in this city. Don't you think?"

I turn to Travis, who's staring out the window, the fear stripped bare on his face, and then to Oliver, unsettled by a familiar feeling—*Just because he's a cop, he thinks he can do anything.*

The uniform gets out of the car.

I don't recognize him—tall with clipped blond hair—but he nods at me.

"I'll grab a coffee," he says to Oliver, and walks away.

"It's just a friendly conversation," Oliver murmurs when I glare at him mutely. "I thought you might want to join."

Of course, I want to join. I've been dying to interview someone, to wave a badge and get answers to my questions, instead of sneaking around, having courteous conversations with my mother's students, and scrounging for scraps of information around Ethan's apartment. Oliver knows this. And is relying on my desperation because he needs me. He has no idea why I'm interested in Travis. He picked up the poor kid on a whim, because he saw me following.

I grit my teeth. "I ask the questions."

"Fine." Oliver lifts his palms.

I open the driver's door. Oliver walks around to the passenger's.

"I didn't do anything," the boy says frantically, as soon as we're inside.

"Travis," I say, turning my body to face him in the back seat.

He blinks and starts trembling. His eyes dance over my scars and his whole body presses away from me. "Who—how do you know my name?"

"I know a lot about you," I say. "Finance major. Senior at UGA. Intern at J.P. Morgan." I tick each fact off with my fingers.

He pales.

"Quite the impressive résumé," I say with a barely concealed lack of sincerity. "But I know other things, too." I lean forward. "Like how often you visit that house back there," I jerk my head in its direction, "and that you missed your fraternity's weekend getaway at the end of February."

He claws at his shirt collar, breathing hard through his nose.

I pull up his Facebook profile on my phone. "This is you, isn't it? Travis Hubbard. Age twenty-one. Lives in Athens, Georgia. From Dunwoody."

His pallor changes from white to green.

I swipe through the photos. All the beautiful boys swimming in the lake.

"These aren't yours," I say.

His eyes widen.

"I—"

"You're not in a single one." I brush each with my fingertip. "Not doing keg stands. Not fishing on the dock. Not on the boat." I give him a hard stare. "Where were you that weekend?"

"I was there," he stammers. "I took the photos—"

"Really?" I speak over him, fake baffled. "Then how do you explain the duplicates on your brothers' pages?"

I pull up the others I've bookmarked. "Randy Smith has that nice one of the dock. Tucker Williamson, the one of the boat. Should I keep going?"

Travis opens his mouth and closes it again.

"And you know who else isn't in these photos?" I pause, watch his expression grow wide. "Chase Warren."

His eyes bulge. Oliver's head swivels between us, and I get a secret thrill knowing I've found something he's missed, even with his resources.

"You know what I think?" I say to Travis. "I think you wanted everyone to believe you were at Lake Oconee. But really you were somewhere else. Someplace you weren't supposed to be."

He closes his eyes.

"Maybe it was just a prank," I say. "You didn't mean to hurt anyone. Not really. What did you do?" I lean closer. Conscious of Oliver's eyes on the side of my neck. "Tell him the drugs were Tylenol? Slip crushed pills into his bottled water? Maybe you didn't think it would kill him. Just make him a little sick."

His eyes shoot open.

"What—"

"But that wasn't enough." I speak over him. "You wanted to see what happened. To witness the drug's effects. So you drove back to Athens and paid a visit to Ethan Haddock."

"Ethan?" Color returns to Travis's cheeks, and he looks genuinely confused. "The kid who killed himself? What does he have to do with anything?" Then he pales. "Unless . . . Did he— Did he owe him, too? Oh my god, and he . . . He . . ."

Now it's my turn to look confused.

"Owe whom?"

He blinks. "You know, and that's why . . . that's why—"

His mouth crumples, and I hold my breath. *This is it*, I think. *This is when he confesses.*

"Please don't kill me."

"What?" I glance at Oliver.

"I lost it, okay?" Travis buries his face in his hands. "I made some back today. But I don't have the rest."

I furrow my brow. "Lost what?"

He gulps for air. "The cash, the chips, all of it."

I frown.

"Start at the beginning," Oliver says.

The story unfolds long and slow, with Travis stammering and correcting and twisting his seat belt in knots. The shack is a slap house—essentially an illegal gambling ring. Some are operated out of vacant storefronts, others from the backs of people's homes. This one is small-time, but run by an Irish guy with a penchant for American gangster movies who sends scary dudes to threaten to cut off your fingers if you're late on a payment. He makes exceptions for boys with rich parents like Chase and Travis. They get extra opportunities to win their money back—or double their losses. He has a good hustle going with the college students in town. Targets business majors mostly, the kind looking to fund their investment portfolios, get a jump start on that imaginary penthouse. Chase and Travis got in over their heads. Between the two of them, they owe almost twenty grand. And both have been caught on separate occasions gambling at work. Illustrating his generation's strange proclivity for passive self-awareness, Travis insists gambling addiction's a real thing; it was threatening their coveted internships. But there was a high-stakes poker tournament in Biloxi the last weekend of February. An opportunity to win it all back. Their fraternity getaway was the perfect excuse for missing work on Friday. They put up the photos to cover their tracks, but lost more than they came with.

"Tell him I'll get the money back. I'll go to Mississippi this weekend—"

I raise an eyebrow.

"I'll ask my parents," he gasps. "Just don't hurt me."

He blinks at Oliver and flinches when I lift my hand. And suddenly, I see myself from his perspective. With the scars and the partially shaved head—I look like a villain.

Oliver lets him go with a warning about illegal street crossing.

I open the door and stand with my arms folded over my chest, watching Travis slink away.

Oliver steps out, too. "He thought we worked for the Irish guy," he says over the hood, shaking his head. "And what? The police are in his pocket?" He gestures to the car. "He's seen too many movies."

I lift an eyebrow. "Has he?"

Oliver frowns.

"You're going to have to report this," I say, eyes still on Travis.

Illegal gambling dens are hotbeds for criminal activity. Follow the money and you often find human trafficking, unlawful firearm possession, illegal drug distribution. At big casinos, you might have women coming around with drinks to entice men to keep playing. At these places, they hand out meth.

Oliver swears. Travis hasn't even made it to the corner, but he's already checking his phone.

"It's not going to end well for him, is it?" I say.

Oliver sighs. "I still don't understand why he bothered with the fake photos."

"He was covering his tracks."

"How is getting wasted better than posting nothing at all?"

I shrug. "Who knows what college students think."

"You know," he says, "Teddy asked if I'd seen you."

I feel my throat constrict. "What did you tell him?"

"I said I was just following an anonymous tip."

"Right." I cross my arms and look away.

Oliver sighs. "I'll double-check everything Travis said. Follow up on the Chase kid. See if the Irishman had anything to do with Ethan. But,

Marlitt . . ." I eye him warily. "If we're going to do this, next time you have a lead, call me."

He doesn't specify what "this" is, but I suppose it's better for both of us that way.

"Okay, boss," I say sarcastically. Then I turn and follow Travis down the street.

Walker's is crowded. I catch the eye of the barista, and she slides me a paper cup. I drop money in the tip jar while she lists suggestions to an indecisive customer.

Caffeine, I think, as I press the lever to the airpot, *is the elixir of the gods*.

But the way Oliver picked up Travis nags at me. So does the other officer's acquiescence—he didn't ask any questions. Just left me and Oliver with a scared kid in the back of his car. No camera or audio recordings. No caution.

I sip my coffee, burn my tongue, and put it down again.

Oliver's proximity to the case makes him dangerous. He knew Ethan. His willingness to look the other way in my own involvement, although advantageous, is telling. It's a one-track-mindedness I recognize in myself and my behavior last fall. From the outside, it's so obvious—the risks, the stakes, how easily I hurt the people closest to me—that I suddenly see everything clearly: my mistake and what I have to do to make things right with Teddy.

"I saw your friend a few days ago," the bartender says.

I blink, pulled from my thoughts to find she's detached herself from the cash register and has made her way down to me. A grimace as she lifts a fresh pot onto the counter. I notice the brace on her wrist and focus on the black Velcro, but the heat still rushes up my neck. It's as if she knew what I was thinking.

"White guy, prim, likes hair gel?"

So not Teddy. Oliver. Of course. Some of the color drains from my face, and I gesture at her hand, wanting to change the subject.

"What happened there?"

"The curse of the barista." She shrugs. "Carpal tunnel."

The customer at the other end seems to have made up his mind and shifts impatiently from foot to foot making exasperated gestures.

"He said you were investigating that student death. The one down the street."

It takes me a moment to realize "you" means us in the collective—Homicide, the team to which I no longer belong. And it hits me—that this earth-shattering thing, losing my job, my partner, my purpose in life, has caused very few reverberations in the outside world. She doesn't know anything's changed, thinks I'm still working alongside my old colleagues. She might have even seen Oliver and me talking outside the coffee shop a few weeks ago and assumed we were working the same case.

I make a noncommittal sound in the back of my throat—one that doesn't confirm I'm employed as a detective but doesn't deny it, either.

"He showed me a picture, asked whether the guy ever came in here."

I nod. It makes sense. Walker's is one of the few places downtown open all day—catching the early birds for coffee, the late-night crowd for mixed drinks. There's a good chance that if Ethan went out at all, he'd wind up in one of their booths.

"I told him I'd never seen him before. But then, last night, I was wiping down the bar, looked up, and—"

Saw him, I think.

"Remembered."

Right.

"He was in the corner booth. There." She points behind me. It's the same booth I usually choose—against the far wall, it's the most secluded, private. "And with a woman."

My heart gives a sudden lurch. I put down my coffee.

She shakes her finger knowingly. "It wasn't the professor. It was a young woman. Short. Cute. Kind of mousy features." She looks past me. "Dressed in all black. They were all over each other, but both seemed pretty hammered—glassy-eyed, stumbling."

I wait.

"That's it," she says. "It was just a flash. I probably went back to whatever I was doing at the time, but I'm sure it was him. And he was with another woman."

I know what she's getting at, that if Ethan was with someone else, it throws the affair or at least the devastation over Verena into question. But it's not that simple.

"When was this?"

"Middle of January. I remember because it was cold, and I felt bad kicking them out, but I was closing up the bar." Another shrug.

The man at the end of the counter is waving his arm furiously now.

"Fine," she growls in his direction. "Tell your partner I'm sorry I didn't think of it sooner."

I nod without any intention of sharing this fact with Oliver and make my way back to the entrance. Hear her snap "Yes?" at the customer and him fumble over his order.

Outside, I see Roger. He's sitting in the sun and casting dirty looks at a pair of well-dressed alums who've occupied his regular patio table. Across the street, a child wails about a dropped ice-cream cone and a group of hungover students lingers outside the Grill. There's a shriek as a girl runs up from behind and throws her arms around her friend. A table of indie kids roll their eyes so emphatically you can almost hear them.

It's the little things—a boy and girl pressed into a corner booth, photos taped to a bedroom wall—that give me pause. And this mystery woman, short with cute mousy features and a fondness for black clothing—I can't help but think I know someone who matches that description, and she's spent the last few weeks lying about her relationship with Ethan.

There's broken glass on the sidewalk. A father clutches a young boy's arm, and as I edge around them, I almost run into a student carrying a stack of books with both hands. If Sadie and Ethan were sleeping together, she would have every right to be furious that he was having an affair with his professor, but it changes the narrative of the sad boy, helplessly in love, distraught by rejection. It turns him into a player, a ladies' man, someone who views romance as a series of conquests and is deceptive and manipulative—the kind of person my mother hopes I identify in Ethan, but I'm finding increasingly difficult to believe. And it doesn't align with what Sadie told me—that Ethan was delicate, crushed by a secret. Her certainty this secret involved Verena. But she's been quick to cast stones. First she accused Verena and then Chase and Travis, having me look in every other direction except the most obvious: the person closest to home.

Before I go back to the apartment, I make a phone call. One I should have made four months ago.

"Hey," I say, surprised the woman on the other end picked up. "Do you have time to talk?"

Her

It's Valentine's Day, and I'm making an effort. A knee-length cocktail dress, a faint brush of mascara. Lipstick instead of balm. Christopher reserved a table at an Italian restaurant in Five Points. Three months ago. He looked sheepish when he told me.

"Otherwise everywhere gets booked and you have to eat at four o'clock when they open or at some depressing chain where they serve fried onions as appetizers."

My Christopher. He does know a thing or two about food. There are also chocolate-covered strawberries hidden behind a bag of peas in the freezer. Clearly meant to be a surprise, so I pretend not to see.

I'm just putting in my earrings—my mother's gold studs with tiny diamond flecks—when my phone rings.

Christopher appears on the threshold. He looks handsome—everything pressed and slicked back into place—and eager to leave.

I reach for the phone.

"Whoever it is," he says with a nervous smile, "tell them you'll call back tomorrow. We've got plans this evening."

His eyes are bright, and I realize with a sudden twinge of panic he must be referring to sex—something we haven't been doing a lot of lately . . . and something he must be expecting tonight.

I take a breath and answer the call without registering the number, prepared only to deliver the message as Christopher instructed.

"It's my dad," the voice on the other end breathes.

"Dad?" I repeat.

"Your dad?" Christopher echoes. Torn between impatience and concern. "Calling from Turkey?"

I blink at him. I must have repeated what I heard. The voice on the other end is still talking.

"Is everything okay?" Christopher asks.

"Slow down," I hear myself say, feel myself sit on the edge of the bed.

Christopher's eyes widen, and he waves his hands trying to catch my gaze, pointing at his watch.

You can talk to him in the car, he mouths, still under the impression it's my father on the other line. He moves his arms like an aircraft marshal trying to direct me toward the door. "We'll miss our reservation," he whispers.

"Just breathe," I tell the voice on the other end. "Everything's going to be okay."

You have to set boundaries," Christopher says later that night.

His tie lies crumpled on the dresser. His shirt is back on its hanger. We never made it to dinner. The velvet box he's been carrying in his pocket since Christmas is back in its hiding place in his sock drawer. And I can't help but feel a tiny shiver of relief.

He thought it was my father calling from Turkey. That's why he wasn't upset. When I tell him it was a student, he stops short, but looks more worried than angry.

"The university shouldn't give out your phone number," he says. "They expect enough from you as it is."

"I gave it to him," I say without thinking. Then I see his face and add, "In case of emergency."

He takes my hand. "That's not your job," he says firmly.

I rip my fingers away. "Of course it's not." I think I might be crying. "But what else am I supposed to do?" I blink at him, like he might have the answer. "How could I live with myself knowing that he hurt himself, and I did nothing?"

Fourteen

Saturday, April 4, 9:00 A.M.

I begin to see him. Of course I do. I've been staring at his photo for days and sleeping in his bed. I catch his reflection in the bathroom mirror, find him lounging on the sofa. Hear him catch his breath. "What," I ask, "did you say?" Ethan gesturing. Opening cupboards. Pointing. Look, open your eyes. Ethan spilling my drink. Trying to get my attention.

I wake drenched in sweat and with a horrible headache, picturing Sadie gazing at Ethan in a dozen photographs, her eyes always on him, and not the other way around. I think of the deep scratches on her bedroom floor and her holding a knife in her hand. Her saying that Ethan had a secret and Verena insisting on keeping secrets to the dead. Threats of violence and retribution, Sadie and Verena, two women who claimed to care about Ethan. I need to talk to both again.

I listen for movement. First Spencer—the clip of his fast, determined footsteps. There's no vacillation, no forgetful returns to his room. His habits are so routine, I can picture him moving through the kitchen, grabbing a coffee filter—then, yes, I hear the faint whir of the grinder—flip of the switch, grab of an apple, fingers perusing the newspaper, coffee into his travel mug, and just the faintest hesitation. Then the door's falling shut behind him. Sadie takes longer. The frantic beeping of her alarm, a hand shuffling under a comforter, phone flying across the nightstand. For a long minute, the alarm continues to beep, and I know she's fallen back asleep, face smothered by her pillow, hand hanging from the mattress in an abandoned attempt to silence it. When it goes off again, she swears and ends the beeping midchord. She'll be late to her 9:00 A.M. class, but the front door finally slams. I count to twenty in case she's forgotten anything, and then wait another minute more. Because what I need is on her wall.

Last night, I talked to Teddy's girlfriend, Cindy. We hadn't spoken since that evening late in November when I used her as a distraction so I could investigate the dark corners of a fraternity basement. Of course, I didn't think of it that way then—that I was using her for my own agenda—but it's true. And it was the final straw in my relationship with Teddy.

It was bad enough that I'd ignored the racist whispers and history of microaggressions he'd face investigating Greek life in order to have him with me on the case, I also flaunted the rules with the full knowledge that every time he backed me up, as a Black man, he took a greater disciplinary risk. I was no better than Oliver, doing whatever I thought would bring me closer to the truth, not caring whom I hurt in the process. And I hurt Cindy. She trusted me, was a good friend, and I let her down.

"I wanted to help," she told me. "I just wish you'd been honest with me about what the case meant to you and let me decide my own role."

It occurs to me that I'm doing the same thing with Sadie; not using her per se, at least not in the same way, but not being truthful about my intentions. And I want to be absolutely certain about her involvement with Ethan before I approach her and cause any more pain. Because right now, the only reason I can imagine that Ethan would tell his professor his secret and not his roommate is that the roommate was the person he was afraid of hurting. That what was tearing him up inside was that Sadie loved him and he loved someone else.

I peel myself from the bed, touch Ethan's ridges for luck, and slip into Sadie's room.

I'm struck by how easy it is. No lock picking, no credit card slipped between the door and the frame. The implicit trust that her roommates would never do her harm.

What I want is a photo of Sadie—easy, she's in at least half of the glossy images on the wall. But I need to pull one she won't miss, so I look for a picture near the floor. I examine the images like I did the first day, noticing how my impression of them has changed. The person I once saw in these photos, only a girl with round cheeks and large eyes trying to cloak her childlike face in dark swoops and hard edges, has transformed into Sadie, who sings when she's happy; Sadie, with a fondness for popcorn and ice cream and bad TV shows; Sadie, who, in spite of everything, clearly misses home. And I feel it again, that nagging thought: *Please don't be Sadie.* But there's a problem with my wish—it's too raw, too personal, too biased. I stare at the wall. Sadie in pigtails. Sadie with blond hair. Strips of pink. Red. Blue. Black.

And then I have another, entirely new, euphoric realization—I'm allowed to not want Sadie to be involved. To feel this sudden urge to protect her. I don't have to bury my feelings—that never worked anyway. Not for me. Not for Oliver. Not even Teddy. I look closer and see that almost every third picture is of rolling farmland, a blue-gray creek, girls with wild hair on bikes spiraling across grassy trails, a strange but beautiful rock garden. A photo of Ethan, smiling. Another Ethan with haunted eyes. There's a photo I don't remember from the first week here. One that's been ripped and taped back together. Three people sitting on the couch in the living room—smiling in the half-surprised, half-purposeful way that indicates the presence of a timer—Sadie with a red-haired girl and a brown-haired boy: Madeline and Ethan.

I shake my head. I never pictured Madeline in this apartment. I always saw Sadie in her studio, sitting on a stool, leaning on a chaise lounge. I didn't imagine them hanging out here, watching a movie, cooking dinner. This whole time I've been thinking of Sadie, Ethan, and Spencer as a threesome—imagining myself as taking Ethan's place. *But that's not true*, I realize, staring at the photo. I've taken Madeline's spot on the couch, her place at the kitchen table. It's Spencer who's taken Ethan's role. And there he is: Spencer in the background of the photo. Not front and center like Madeline. Not with his arm flung around Sadie's shoulders like Ethan. But a blurred image moving behind them, head twisting to the side, some features still visible: the arch of his eyebrow, the high tilt of his cheekbones, the downturn of his lips. Ethan and Sadie in the foreground, a bundle of knees and elbows on the sofa, smushed together in a manner that suggests camaraderie but not romance, while Spencer's on the way to his room. And in the smudge of his face, I see a flicker of something in his eyes—jealousy, anger, pain—what exactly, I'm not sure.

I slip the photo into my bag and move a few others to cover the negative space. And then I'm out the door.

It's a beautiful morning. A pale sun casts misty blue shadows on the sidewalk. A dog trots obediently behind its owner, a leash in its mouth. The wind whispers through the trees. A bicyclist zooms by at breakneck speed. And I feel it—the world rushing past, the truth out there, waiting, just beyond my reach.

It's still early, but when I call, Verena's wide awake. Her voice sends a flicker of despair through my chest. I can't bear the thought of her house with its drawn curtains, a dark cavern of tears, half-eaten food, and abandoned dog toys—it's too claustrophobic. So I tell her to meet me at the cemetery. Not because I've developed a new desire to haunt tombstones, but because it's a place besides her living room where we don't have to worry about students, where I don't have to look over my shoulder for Sadie or Spencer; or Madeline, for that matter. And it's a place you go to contemplate death, your own mortality, and legacy of actions that transcend time—and yes, I hope all of these things might snap Verena out of her self-flagellatory slump, her refusal to defend herself, and her insistence on keeping Ethan's secret.

By the time I get off the phone, I'm already through the stone gate with a view of the sexton's house—white front porch with balusters and corbels as fine and delicate as paper snowflakes. Scattered across the rolling hills, small statues are all but eclipsed by long grass. There are Greek Revival mausoleums and Victorian Gothic headstones. It's the burial place of so many famous men. University professors and trustees, football coaches, Georgia governors, my father's much-loved Ben Epps, a founding member of the B-52s. Men who have streets named after them, like Baxter and Thomas. Men, like Lumpkin, who enforced the treaty that led to the Trail of Tears.

The enslaved men who built the university were not buried here on the hills with their scenic views, but instead in the floodplains, where there were no monuments, no families allowed to visit, their graves marked by uninscribed fieldstones, paved over as the university expanded, unearthed during construction, and left in shallow fields to rush into neighboring gardens after heavy rains. Whoever said death is the great equalizer has yet to walk these overgrown, tree-lined streets and see only white faces listed in registers of notable lives led.

I've walked deeper into the cemetery than I realized, and turn just as Verena's bike comes into view. Her head swivels from left to right, not looking for me but taking in the slips of stone and pine, the chiseled crosses, and the metal gates forming their own caskets.

When I step into the narrow strip of road and call to her, she pulls off to the side and drops her bike.

"I've never been here before," she says quietly, her voice a reverent hush as she unstraps her helmet.

She's wearing the same baggy jeans as the last time I saw her and a shapeless blue sweater that seems too warm for the sunny day. Her hair's pulled away from her face, leaving hard angles scrubbed raw. She falls in line with me as I meander up a dirt path.

"Have you thought any more about what I said?" I ask. "About keeping promises to the dead?"

Pebbles skitter under our feet, and I turn to look at her.

She gazes at the stadium looming in the distance. "It's wrong that this is how Ethan will be remembered."

I nod. "But if we find out what happened, we can change people's opinions."

She sighs. "Do you really believe that?"

I bite my lip, and she looks away. Then she shakes her head. "The police—they know this already. But I gave Ethan my phone number."

My mouth drops open.

"I was worried about him." Her voice takes a defensive edge. "It's not like I teach those big lectures with towering rows of a hundred students. In small classes—you get to know them." She frowns at my face. "I didn't say anything because I knew how it would sound." She takes a breath. "But sometimes he would call—late at night. Sometimes his speech was slurred, and I was afraid he'd been drinking. He said he was tired but couldn't fall asleep. He was anxious, felt like he'd been asked to carry the world, and it was slipping from his shoulders. But it was never . . . he never once said anything to make me think that he had feelings for me—god, honestly, I thought the students considered me ancient. I mean, as a graduate student teacher, I had issues. But now? It never crossed my mind—and if it had, I would have stopped it immediately." She lets out a breath. "I was worried about him."

I study her face and realize that I believe her—that she wanted to help, that she wouldn't have encouraged his calls if she thought he was looking for love or sex or anything resembling a romantic relationship. But I also think that he filled in the lonely hours, gave her the purpose she no longer found in teaching, a reason to get out of bed in the morning.

"But nothing happened," she insists.

We both turn our heads at the sound of metallic clanking and watch one of the plot fences sway in the wind.

"And the secret . . . ?"

She looks at me. "I don't know how telling you will change anything."

"It may not." I shrug. "But it might. And like you said, Ethan deserves to be remembered for who he was. His memory shouldn't be overshadowed by a scandal and affair allegations."

She pinches her mouth. Nods slowly. "I'm not even sure where to begin."

"Start at the beginning," I tell her.

"I noticed a change in his behavior in January," she says. "He had been falling asleep in class, missing entire weeks. Some students do that, but not Ethan." She shakes her head. "Then in February, he wrote this essay—that he was depressed and felt alone." She sighs. "I asked him to stay after class. If everything was okay. And he just," she looks out across the cemetery, "broke apart."

"His mother has MS," I say. "It was pretty bad and getting worse."

She nods. "Yes, I think that was part of it. But Ethan . . . he discovered a phone, a secret one, and realized his dad was cheating on her. While she was sick." A tear slips down her cheek. "And he didn't know what to do."

I think of the funeral, the way Angie refused her husband's support. The tension stretched between those large white rooms.

"So he asked you."

She nods. And I see it in her slumped shoulders, this burden she's been carrying.

"I couldn't think of a single word that that wouldn't be trite or cliché." She takes a breath, gaze lifting from the tombstones to the bridge in the distance. "And so, I said nothing at all."

We sit in silence. This whole time I had focused on the love poem. But I had forgotten the Polish story, the drawing Ethan made of the girl in the library. The sense that words fail us when we need them most.

A quarrel of sparrows lifts from the trees and spirals up and out of view.

"I need to ask you something," I say, and withdraw the photograph from my bag. "Do you recognize either of these people?"

I point to Sadie first. The camera has caught her unawares, the last tip of laughter before it morphs into the predictable frown.

Verena gazes at her vacantly, and then shakes her head.

"Should I?"

I stare at her a long moment, but she seems certain, and I exhale a breath of relief.

"What about him?" I move my finger to Spencer's retreating form. Caught at a three-quarter angle, his features are sharpened, his cheekbones as fine as a knife's edge, his nose hooked like a bird.

"He looks familiar," she says slowly, brows crumpling into a frown. "I think I've seen him around campus."

"Makes sense. He's a student."

"Maybe even in Joe Brown."

I frown. That's a little weirder. As far as I know he doesn't take classes in German or comparative literature.

"Are you sure?"

She nods, but I see a flicker of doubt. "Why?" she asks. "Who are they?"

"Ethan's roommates."

Him

It was a cool gray dawn. The class was sluggish, uninterested. She tried to keep them engaged while simultaneously fighting a cough. He'd seen her ride into campus on her old bicycle, and she looked exhausted as she locked it outside the building. But he was there for her—every question, he had a ready response, nodding along, showing her that they were in this together. The others rolled their eyes but didn't say anything because his diligence allowed them to stare out the window and doze with their eyes open. But even that wasn't enough. It was clear in the way the pauses between her questions and his name lengthened. The desperate lift of her voice when she called on a different student, only to be met with shrugs, papers shuffling. *I don't know. I didn't really understand.* The reprimand was on the tip of her tongue, he could tell—but she was too nice to embarrass anyone and moved on.

She let them go early. Blamed their poor performance on the weather. He took his time organizing his pens and papers, filing them neatly into his bag.

"No one did their homework," he said.

She flinched, surprised to find him still there, leaning against his desk, bag slung over his shoulder.

"Oh," she sighed. "I know."

She pulled on her coat and moved to the hall. He followed. She paused in the doorway. It was the same dance they'd done before. Him asking questions, talking to her as she collected her things and began the slow, book-laden walk back to her office. But this time she was distracted. There was no excuse, tired smile, or half-hearted wave. Instead, she let him keep talking. He observed things about her he'd never noticed before—gold flecks in her irises, the way she tugged at her hair when she was thinking. Even the stairwell, the rough banister, looked different with her by his side. The doors opened into the brown lawn speckled with yellow leaves, and that too had transformed into something secret, a magical place shared between them. He attributed her awkwardness to the hierarchical nature of the student-professor relationship. Which was strange, since she wasn't much older than he was. She just had a few more degrees. So he imagined they were colleagues instead, chatting after class.

"Have you heard of the Socratic method?" he asked.

She blinked, and he realized that even though he'd met her stride by stride, talking about class, and his irresponsible classmates, she was somewhere far away. It irked him that he didn't have her full attention. *Don't you see how hard I work?* He wanted to grab her by both arms and shake the awareness into her. *I do it for you.*

But no, he'd learned control. If this year had taught him anything, it was to master his emotions before speaking.

Instead, he told her that the Socratic method might be helpful in the classroom, a different way to engage the students. They had just discussed it in his philosophy course, and he imitated the professor, who gave long, self-congratulating descriptions of its merits and then waited for a student to observe that it was the same pedagogy he practiced in his own classroom.

They were almost to her office now. He imagined her inviting him in for coffee, wanting to hear more about Socrates, about philosophy, himself. But she stopped abruptly, avoided looking at him by rubbing the bridge of her nose. He realized that she was angry, offended, even, when he was just trying to help. Suddenly he saw himself from her perspective—not as a colleague but as a student who had presumed to tell her how to do her job. She was working out how to communicate this to him. He saw it in the way her eyes leaped from his face to the door of her building. Should she put him in his place or excuse his hubris as the unrecognized ego of a twenty-year-old? He wouldn't be satisfied with either, so he saved her the trouble. "Just a thought," he said, then turned on his heel and walked away.

He punished her by missing class. Let her deal with a room full of students who didn't bother to do their homework. Let her stand there in front of the room like an idiot when no one answered her questions. Even when he returned, he sat in the back, resolutely keeping his hands folded, his eyes down. Let her know that she'd wounded him, and that there were consequences.

Fifteen

Saturday, April 4, noon

I pull myself up on a flat gray stone wall and dial Oliver.

"Listen," I say, before he has time to answer, "you thought Ethan had a perfect family, all cookouts and throwing footballs and ice-cream parties, right?"

A pause. "I don't remember saying anything about ice cream." I hear the tug of a smile on his lips.

I snort. "Well, what if Ethan discovered that it all was a lie? The happy family? The perfect parents? Nice-guy dad?"

Oliver sighs—and I can hear the slump of his shoulders, the way he runs his hand over his mouth. "You're talking about the phone and his father's affair?"

"How did you—?"

"Dr. Sobek's journal. She wrote about all her meetings and various interactions with students. I assume this is why she didn't want us to have it. Ethan asked her not to tell anyone."

"She was keeping his secret."

"If she wanted to keep it a secret, she shouldn't have written it down," he snaps. He clears his throat. "Sorry, it's just—I always liked him, Mr. Haddock, he was like a—"

Oh shit, I think, too late. *A father figure.*

"Anyway, I looked into it. He was in Atlanta all weekend. With the woman—the one from the secret phone. She confirmed and so did the concierge at the front desk, the bartender at the hotel, the server at a very nice sushi restaurant."

"They seem to have made quite an impression."

"Yeah," Oliver says stiffly. "They did. She was redheaded and young. Really young. Not," he adds before I can ask, "below the age of majority, but yeah, young enough compared to him that people took notice."

I'm thinking of the woman at the funeral, the one with the rose, and I register it a half beat late.

"You thought Haddock Senior killed Ethan?"

A pause. So long I think the connection's dropped. But then Oliver clears his throat. "Honestly, Marlitt. I don't know anymore."

Hearing him say my name warms something in my chest. For a moment, it almost feels like we're friends. This Oliver, unsure and vulnerable, is so unlike the man I worked with last year. The man who insisted on being two steps ahead, proving himself, being better, the best, pretending to play by the rules, but bending them when it suited him. But there's still that voice that whispers he can't be trusted.

"Then why did you check his alibi?" My tone is hard, accusatory.

Oliver clears his throat.

"To rule him out. If he learned Ethan had discovered the affair . . ."

"That would be—"

"Awful, yeah." Another tug of breath. "But like I said, his alibi was solid."

He's silent a moment.

"You know what the worst part is?" he says after a while.

"There's a worse part?"

He gives a tight laugh. "Yeah, there is."

I wait.

He exhales. "Angie knew about the affair—the other woman—all of it. MS . . . it can mess with your sex drive. And I guess, she thought, I don't know, an open marriage would make things easier."

"Shit."

"Yeah." I hear him rub his hand over his mouth. "They didn't tell Ethan. Obviously. But that whole time, he thought he was protecting her . . ."

"And she knew."

We're both quiet. I kick a pebble with my toe and watch it scatter across rocks.

"Then why did Haddock Senior have another phone?" I ask. "If Angie knew, why the secret?"

"Does it matter?" I hear the impatience in Oliver's voice, the annoyance that this is the detail I've latched on to. "Maybe it was to spare her the pain of seeing the other woman's number on their bill."

"How considerate."

I bite my lip and let the anger and disappointment settle in my stomach. *Back to zero*, I think.

My gaze lifts to the blue-gray sky. Two small birds dive after a larger bird with something clutched in its talons.

"Both of Ethan's roommates had alibis, right?"

"Of course. Why? Are you second-guessing your living arrangement?" I hear a mild chuckle in Oliver's voice. "A little late for that."

"It's just that Sadie and Ethan seemed particularly close. And Verena thinks she's seen Spencer around Joe Brown, but I can't think of any reason he'd be there as an MBA student."

"Want me to pull his transcripts? See if he's been slumming it with some humanities courses?"

I blow out a breath. "Maybe. I don't know."

A feeling nags at me. Some unspooled thread snapping in the corner of my vision.

"How do you prove something didn't happen?" It's the thought I've gone over again and again, finally framed and spoken aloud.

Oliver sighs. "I think you're asking the wrong question." I wait as the phone shifts beneath his ear. "How do you prove something did?"

"That's the opposite—"

"Exactly. You need to prove something opposite happened than what everyone thinks. Otherwise, you're right, you can't prove it didn't happen. So prove what happened instead."

I rub my temples, feeling like we're talking in circles.

"Ethan's dead," I say. "He died in his apartment. With the words 'Verena' and 'I'm sorry' on his skin. He died of an overdose. But no drugs were found near his body. So if he didn't kill himself . . ."

I hesitate. Even though he can't see me, I shake my head, unable to finish my sentence. We both have different reasons for wanting this to be a homicide, but wanting something doesn't make it so, and with Verena's boyfriend, Chase and Travis, and even Mr. Haddock ruled out, the list of people who might want to kill Ethan is shrinking fast.

The walk back to Artisan's Corner is long. The heat has settled like a sticky wet blanket, and I find myself dragging my feet and mindlessly scratching the burns on the side of my face.

When I reach the end of South Thomas, a white paper catches my eye. Taped to a lamppost, it flutters under colorful concert posters, rental advertisements, and offerings of tutor lessons: a photo of a small terrier. I drop my hand, step forward to get a closer look, and see a cropped image of the picture from Verena's living room. Below the photo are the words: *Missing dog. Answers to Jagger. Call Verena Sobek* and a phone number. Someone's circled "Verena" with a red pen and written "whore" with an arrow pointing to her name. I frown. Now that I've noticed this one, I see others papered down the street. I feel a twinge of sympathy for Verena, envisioning her haunting store windows and telephone poles from her house to Mama's Boy and Trapeze. One's been half ripped down. Another has a large X drawn across Jagger, *she got what she deserved* scrawled beneath. A shiver sneaks down my neck. I imagine townspeople with burning torches, men brandishing irons with the letter *A*, villagers binding women and pushing them off seaside cliffs, only believing their innocence after they drowned.

By the time I make it back to the apartment, the sun is a brilliant white. Sadie's sitting on the sofa with her feet on the coffee table, humming as she paints her toenails a dark shade of blue—not quite black—which I take as a good sign.

A fleck of polish lands on the corner of the table, and she swears, a quick glance in the direction of Spencer's room.

"Good thing he's not here," she murmurs. "Otherwise, he'd be right behind me cleaning it up." She shakes her head in mock annoyance, examining her toes in the sunlight. "Really, I preferred our messy life. Who cares if there's clutter on the counter and dishes in the sink? But no—now everything's double- and triple-washed, stacked, and put away before you're even finished with it."

"I thought Spencer had been here the longest," I say, sitting on the arm of the sofa.

She laughs. "You would think so," she says, "with the way he cleans and organizes and gets mad if you forget to take out the trash. But no, he's only lived here since January. Ethan and I had another roommate—Sarah. She was nice but spent all her time at her boyfriend's and eventually decided to move in with him." She gestures, as if to say, *What can you do?* "Ethan put up flyers all over campus, but Spencer was the only one who called. I guess not too many people look for midyear rentals." She shrugs and then grins at me. "We lucked out with you."

"Ah, thanks," I say, knowing full well that luck had nothing to do with it. But my mind catches on Sarah, this old roommate and new information.

"Sarah," I say casually. "Does she still visit?"

"Nah." Sadie shakes her head.

"Did she get along with everyone?"

"Of course, she just got along with her boyfriend more." She winks at me. "So . . ." Her voice goes up an octave, and I look down to see she's beaming at me. "Guess who I ran into today?"

"Who?" I ask, thinking of boyfriends and girlfriends and affairs.

"Madeline," Sadie squeals, breaking my train of thought. I can tell by the way her voice lifts that she's been waiting to talk about her this whole time. "We passed each other outside. She was leaving with her paint box and a bunch of canvases, and I was coming in and so I said hi and held the door. And she looked really awkward, but then she said, 'So you're talking to me now?' And I was like, 'Yeah, you're the one who's been ignoring me,' but then she said, 'What about me taking advantage of you?' and I was like, 'What—taking advantage?'"

I'm having a hard time following her monologue, still thinking of Ethan's father's affair, that this was the big secret, the one he was trying to protect from the person he loved, that this person wasn't Sadie, and that his mother knew already.

"And so, she said that I sent her a note saying I thought she was taking advantage of me and that I didn't want to speak to her ever again. And she was hurt and confused but wanted to respect my wishes." Sadie takes a long breath. "Anyway, it was just a huge misunderstanding and we're going to grab drinks tomorrow."

So this explains the humming—it's the happiest I've seen her since I moved in.

"Wait, then who wrote the note?" I ask.

"I don't know. Maybe another one of her muses." She lifts an eyebrow. "She has a lot of models, you know."

"But why did she think it was from you?"

Sadie scowls at me. "I don't know. And I don't care. We're talking now, so," she dips her hand, "water under the bridge."

"But," I push, "think of all that time wasted. You could have been together these past few months. Madeline would have a million more Sadie-paintings."

Sadie frowns. I've gotten through. "Yeah," she says finally. "You're right. I'll ask her tomorrow."

I nod. "Good," I say, looking away from the tiny line that's formed between her eyebrows.

"Just be careful, okay?" I say.

Something nags at me. Oliver's assertion that Ethan was well liked, a happy kid. His belief, it wasn't suicide but poison. What if the killer mixed up the target? Slipped into the apartment, injected the drugs into Sadie's milk, and Ethan drank it? A glass on the counter meant for Spencer?

"Why?" Sadie cocks her head, and I shrug self-consciously.

"When you told me about Madeline before, I don't know, you seemed so sad. I just"—I look at her—"would hate for you to get hurt again."

I think she'll laugh off my concern or give me a sulky "Whatever." But instead, she caps the nail polish and flies at me, wrapping my arms in a tight embrace.

"Thank you," she whispers. Then she withdraws shyly and returns to the sofa. "I'll be fine," she murmurs.

I think of the taped-together photo—Madeline in the same spot where Sadie is now.

"Can I ask you something?"

She scrunches her face. "No." And when I frown, she laughs. "Just kidding," she says airily. "What's up?"

"Was Madeline friends with Ethan?"

Sadie nods. "Madeline hung out here all the time—movie nights, Sunday brunch, cocktails—Spencer called us the three musketeers. But I think he was just jealous. He was always invited but we never really hung out."

"What about roommate dinners? I thought you switched off making dinner once a week."

Sadie shakes her head. "Nope. He likes to cook, so sometimes he'd make a big thing of pasta and let us eat the leftovers or finish a bottle of wine he'd opened, but we didn't really talk much until you moved in."

I frown.

She lifts an eyebrow. "He told me you suggested it," she says. "The dinners—so we could get to know each other."

"Really?" I shake my head, trying to remember the conversation the first night. "I got the impression you'd been doing it for a while."

"Well, I guess Maddie, Ethan, and I would do stuff like that, but not with Spencer."

I'm still digesting this new bit of information when my phone rings.

It's Verena.

Sadie goes back to painting her nails and I move to the kitchen counter.

"I keep thinking of the photo you showed me," Verena says.

I cup my hand over the speaker, an eye on Sadie. "What about it?" I murmur.

"It's just—the man in the background. I think I've met him before." She clears her throat. "Before I saw him at Joe Brown."

"Spencer?" I say, and Sadie shoots me a curious glance from the couch.

"He didn't tell me his name." She takes a breath. "I met him on a plane."

PART III

Him

She found him, really. It had been a long week. Boring meeting after boring meeting. The lawyers were attired almost identically: dark slacks, light dress shirts, sleeves rolled up to show they were getting down to business. Their predictability made him sick. He even created a game of it: anticipating their unimaginative responses to the handling of his parents' estate before they opened their foul, coffee-exhaling mouths. And worse, because of a scheduling mishap, he had to fly on a commodity airline. The kind where you don't get to pick your own seat and exhausted mothers let their toddlers drill you in the back with their heels. He sat in the rear of the plane, hoping it wouldn't fill. It did. She was one of the last to arrive, looking haggard, smiling vague apologetic smiles at every seat she bumped. Something oddly familiar about her movements, but he forgot about her almost as soon as he looked down, returning to emails, sneering at the lawyers' grammatical errors. "Idiots," he murmured. And then there she was, standing beside his shoulder. She gestured to the empty seat next to him. He unclasped his seat belt and stood to let her pass. She smelled like sweat and honey. She wouldn't sit still. Kept bending to withdraw things from the overlarge purse she shoved in front of her. He watched her reach for her headphones. Waited for a flicker of recognition. Nothing.

"Do you mind if I borrow a pen?"

"Oh." She glanced at him and smiled the kind of impersonal smile you give someone in the odd closeness of a passenger plane. "Sure. There's usually some rolling around the bottom of my purse."

Still nothing.

"What were you doing in Boston?" he asked conversationally as she reached down again.

She fiddled with her headphones. "Conference," she said.

"No way. Me too," he lied.

"Really?" She seemed delighted by the coincidence. "I haven't been back in a few years," she told him. "I was in Cambridge."

He thought of the brick walkways frequented by students and dog walkers. Iron lampposts under heavy-limbed trees. It would have been nice to stay there, instead of the gray shithole by the airport.

"Same," he lied again.

She nodded as if this made perfect sense.

"Do you live in Atlanta?" he asked.

"Athens, actually."

"Really," he said, surprised for the first time. "Me too."

She smiled. "What do you do?"

"Real estate," he said, although it was not entirely true. "You?"

"I'm a German professor." She flushed like she was expecting him to contradict her.

"At UGA?"

She nodded.

They chatted for almost an hour. And still, she didn't recognize him. He smiled through gritted teeth. He'd sacrificed so much. And yet, for her, it was as if he'd never existed. But he saw the way she tucked her hair behind her ear when she talked about herself, the way her breath quickened when she mentioned teaching, the way she didn't notice when he redirected her questions so she'd talk more about herself.

"Is someone picking you up from the airport?" he asked.

For the first time, a line appeared between her eyebrows. "Yes," she said, "my boyfriend."

He frowned. The boyfriend.

She saw the downturn of his mouth and could tell the boyfriend comment displeased him. Acted embarrassed, like he'd asked for her number.

"You know," she said, "I think I'm going to put my headphones on. The engine's really loud."

And then she proceeded to ignore him. Did she think she was too good for him? A humanities professor? With her dazzling life of department meetings and grading papers, an existence slowly subsumed by debt and boredom?

The pilot announced the plane was descending. He watched her shift and settle. Glance at him from the corner of her eye. When they landed, she took her headphones off, but he didn't start the conversation again. Let her wonder if she had offended him. Let it bother her the whole drive home, with or without the boyfriend.

When it was time for their row to depart, he grabbed his satchel from the overhead bin and walked down the aisle without a word. Another man stepped between them as she gathered her things, but he knew she was watching his back fade from view. He kept her pen.

Sixteen

Sunday, April 5

Sleep eludes me. I pace the floor like a night animal, listening for sounds in the dark. Predator or prey, I'm not sure. There was no roommate dinner last night, no lounging together on the sofa reading, or Spencer bemoaning Sadie's poor choices in television. Just a shared bottle of wine, and then I feigned a headache and went straight to my room—Ethan's room—our room. They followed suit, disappearing—Spencer out into the night, Sadie to bed.

I'm beginning to think of the living room as a stage, where we're all performing from different playbooks. My role is obvious. But the others? I grind my palms into the hollows of my eyes. I just need to figure out how they connect. The pills. The fatigue. Sadie and Madeline. Spencer and Sadie. Ethan and Verena. I need to breathe, organize my thoughts.

I stare at the ceiling and watch the shadows cast by late-night drivers dance across the wall. I listen to students yell goodbyes after barhopping, listen to Sadie snoring, listen for sounds of Spencer, until eventually I hear nothing at all.

I oversleep my alarm. Sunlight streams through at full force, indicating an hour well past morning. There's a stale taste in my mouth and the feeling I've forgotten something important. Something I'd rather not remember, but need to.

My phone rings. I have the odd sensation it's been ringing for a while now. That if it hadn't rung, I may not have woken up at all.

It's Oliver.

"Are you alone?" he demands.

I crane my neck, listening for sounds in the hall.

"I think so, yeah."

"I need you to be sure."

His urgency sparks something in my chest. "What is it?" I ask, slipping soundlessly from the mattress.

"Just check first."

"Okay, okay." I'm trying to be quiet, which is hard on the old floorboards. My legs are unsteady. Limbs heavy.

"Well?" Oliver whispers.

"No one's here," I say finally, standing in the center of the living room with my eyes on the front door. The edge in his voice makes me think I'm either going to need a quick exit or to apprehend the first person who walks in.

"I've been going through Sobek's journal again. The Title Nine officer called—"

"You haven't given it to them yet?" I think of Verena twisting her hands, waiting for something—anything—to exonerate her as the accusations keep rolling in.

"And here's the thing," Oliver says, ignoring me. "Sobek attributes the changes in Ethan's behavior to his mother's MS diagnosis and his father's affair—it's a lot to handle for anyone, right?"

"Okay," I say, not following.

"But when I compared her journal to their emails, she had already been in contact with him in January, worried about him missing class."

"So?"

"So," he gives a short, aggravated huff, "so his mom was diagnosed last summer, but he didn't discover his father's affair until early February. We assumed he'd been handling his mother's illness fine—or at least as well as could be expected given the circumstances—until he found out about his father."

"Then why the change a month earlier?" I finish for him.

"Exactly. And I looked back at what he was complaining about—fatigue, dizziness, memory problems. They're all symptoms of unbalanced medications."

I frown. "So he'd been taking drugs the whole time?"

"At least since January. And in excess. But again, that begs the question why. And that plus the increased alcohol usage suggests there was something else, some other reason he was self-medicating—"

"But that means it's likely he did overdose. Accidental, maybe. He kept increasing the dosage— Wait," I say, mind speeding ahead of what I'm saying. "Alcohol. You didn't say there was alcohol in his system."

Oliver hesitates. "Yeah, and his liver showed signs of inflammation." A pause. "You still there?"

My heart slams in my chest. I barely hear Oliver. What changed in January? I think of Sadie complaining of Spencer's tidiness. All the new rules. Madeline suddenly ousted from the group. And Spencer pulling out bottles of wine.

We've been trying to figure out if Ethan was depressed, and why he was experimenting with a cocktail of pills like a human petri dish, but what if the depression wasn't the reason for the pills, but the result? I think of Ethan's confusion, his erratic behavior, sudden mood swings—he must have thought he was going crazy. And yet, so many students struggle with their mental health that when Verena sounded the alarm, no one took her seriously.

"When is the first email about Ethan's performance in class?" I ask Oliver.

"Mid-January."

Only a few weeks into spring semester. A few weeks after Spencer moved in.

I think of Verena. Trying to be a good teacher. Seeing her best student falling behind—noticing the signs before everyone else but misinterpreting them. And eventually . . . dismissing them. Who could blame her?

How many times a day do students lie to her? *My grandmother's in the hospital, my pet needs to go to the vet, my car broke down, computer crashed*—eventually all Ethan's excuses must have seemed like more of the same. Discovering his dad was cheating after his mom's MS diagnosis would explain a lot, but could also be one final desperate lie.

"Do you know the exact date?"

"I have it here." There's a shuffle as he presses the phone to his shoulder, flips a page. I hear Teddy's voice in the background, the faint rumble of Truman's, and my stomach clenches. But I can't lose focus. Not now. Not anymore.

"The sixteenth."

I do the math in my head. Forty-some days between then and the end of February, give or take. Forty-some days between Spencer moving in and Ethan's death. Forty-four scratches on the wall. Could Ethan have been marking the days like Edmond Dantès—not a prisoner in his room but in his head, trying to keep track? Like how I've begun to rub my fingers over those same marks in the morning, reminding myself I'm awake?

I think of the lethargic haze that stays with me throughout the day, one blending into another. I'm taking shallow breaths, blinking at the empty knife block on the counter but seeing Spencer turn his back and then hold out a glass of wine.

"What did you say his symptoms were—the early ones that he complained of to Verena?"

"Dizziness and fatigue." Oliver thumbs through his notes. "Lethargy. Clumsiness."

"Right," I say, gazing at the bruises on my knees. The splash on the counter from Sadie's spilled coffee. A napkin on the floor that missed the trash can. "I'll call you back."

I've been so stupid. Breathtakingly ignorant and idiotic.

I picture a bird's-eye view of myself floating down a river, unaware of the thundering waterfall, the crashing rocks below, and now suddenly I'm swimming as fast as my arms can take me in the opposite direction.

But to do what needs to be done I'm forced to break my silent promise to Sadie with yet another betrayal of trust.

I'm back in her room, at her desk, picking through jewelry and pens and abandoned staples—a torn hand fan, a broken watch, a seashell, a woven bracelet—until I find what I'm looking for: bobby pins. The first is buried under a lipstick-blotted tissue. The second is stuck in the bottom corner of the drawer. I dig it out with my fingernail, swearing when a rough edge catches my skin. But I've got it. The pin. It's sticky with some kind of hair product, but it will work. I bend the flat piece back and strip it of its rubber knob, twisting the other side up so I have a lever. *This is silly high school shit*, I think. If I find something, I'm going to have to call Oliver, who will have to get a warrant, prompted by a mysterious tip, and pretend like he doesn't know what he's looking for or exactly where it is. I grumble, sitting cross-legged in the hall in front of Spencer's room, bent over the bobby pin, feeling like I'm doing Oliver's dirty work, but if I'm right, then this is what we both wanted.

With a cautious ear to the front door, I think of the barrel and pins inside the lock—tiny chambers and metal cylinders forming the barrier between privacy, secrets, and truths. A grating in the hall stops me. I scramble up, but the sound's already moving away. Something on rollers—a suitcase, backpack? I sit down, this time on my knees, and work the lock again, hearing Verena's voice. *I recognized him. Sat next to him on a plane.*

It was the middle of October. She'd been at a conference. A two-hour flight. The sensation that she'd offended him. But that was all she could remember. She was distracted. Blamed the conference. The fatigue. It's odd, picturing the pair of them side by side between metal wings, the heavy rumble of an engine, recycled air blowing from overhead vents. But this whole time I've been looking for a connection, some line from Ethan to Verena besides the obvious one. And Spencer might be it.

I feel the last pin move and hear the click. The handle turns. I don't want to look, but it's too late. The door's falling open of its own accord—a breathing, living thing beckoning me. I think of the young bride discovering the murdered wives, Alice tumbling down the rabbit hole, and have the strange feeling that whatever I do now, when I return to this place I've called home the past weeks, it will have transformed. The true meaning of "there's no going back" is not that the deed cannot be undone, but that although the floorboards will still slope and warm in the afternoon sun and the scent of wine and Italian dinners will remain, I will see this place, my safe lighthouse and shelter, differently.

I take a breath and slip the pins into my pocket for safekeeping.

Unlike Sadie's, Spencer's room is meticulously organized—no dust gathering in corners or taking on its own fuzzy mass under furniture, no clothes thrown over the backs of chairs, no giraffe figurines on the windowsill or photographs taped to the wall. Nothing other than papers stacked on his desk so neatly they might have been measured by a ruler, a solitary pen, and clothes hung precisely at their creases. A handheld steamer sits on the floor, and even it is tucked neatly below a pair of slacks. I realize suddenly that he might have anticipated this—me rummaging through his things, running my hands over his pockets. He might have cleaned his room last night while I tossed and turned. Might have stuffed incriminating evidence into his messenger bag this morning to dump in some city trash can on his way to campus.

I slide my finger over his desk like I'm expecting a false bottom, a hidden compartment, anything other than the same nondescript, built-in pine boards nailed together in my room and Sadie's. I return to the papers. There's no typed confession, no *all work and no play* repeating script. The top sheet reads: "A Conceptional Basis for Uncertainty: Marketing to Generation Z." I don't dare move it aside to look at the others—the edges are too perfectly aligned for me to replicate. I spin, taking in the size of the room. It's still small, but larger than Sadie's and mine put together. He has space for a queen-sized bed in the middle, rather than the full I have pressed against the wall. Real curtains hang over his window and a woven rug stretches beneath the bed. Although the room's quite bare, these two additions add a sense of comfort—no worrying about piercing streetlights or the bite of morning cold against your sockless feet—but they also provide privacy—no prying eyes from outside or ears to hear you moving around in the dark. I drop to my knees and peer beneath the bed, but of course there's nothing. I tug open the top drawer of the heavy wooden nightstand. Again, nothing. It's empty just like Ethan's when I moved in. I rock back on my heels. That's strange, isn't it? No tissues, no bedtime reading, not even a phone charger. I suck in my breath and turn back to his makeshift closet, thinking maybe I'm too late. Maybe he's gone. But his clothes are still here. I move to the solid dresser on the opposite side of the room. Here, too, is evidence of a return—socks folded Marie Kondo style, ties rolled and organized by color, even underwear in neat little rows. I would laugh, but there's something unsettling about the tidiness. I think of Sadie miming robot arms, arching her eyebrows like Mr. Spock. There's a sudden change in the air, and I freeze, holding my breath as I listen, but I don't hear anything above the sounds of traffic and the rumbling AC.

I close the drawer silently. Maybe the plane ride was just a coincidence. Two people traveling to Atlanta from Boston who both happen to know Ethan. Nothing more, nothing less. The kind of small-world fluke that's bound to happen at least once in your life and perhaps more frequently now that people cross oceans for work and book flights online at any hour. But it nags at me, just like the picture-perfect room, the tidiness, and the complete absence of personality in all the neat tucks and folds.

An hour later, I've settled myself into the crook of the living room sofa opposite the front door, going for cool and casual, but my heart is hammering. I've been googling Spencer Duplass and Sadie Parris. There are a few photos of Sadie—backlit by a sunset on a lake, doing a handstand on the beach, sandwiched between two other girls on a woodsy trail—a private Facebook page, a quote: "Life's too short to be anything but happy," her name in a list of high school tennis champions (no photo, but the high school's in Calhoun, Georgia, three years ago, so it must be her—I try to picture her in a white tennis outfit and fail). But the only Spencer Duplass I find on Facebook is a forty-two-year-old white male who lives with his wife and three children in Pocatello, Idaho. Twenty-something-year-old Spencer has no photos, no social media pages or suggested friends. I find an article on the deaths of his parents, Samuel and Julie Duplass, car accident four years ago, so at least he's not lying about that. A reference to the sale of their real estate empire by their surviving son, which explains why he doesn't have to work while he completes his MBA. But that's it.

I touch my phone. To tell Oliver or not? But tell him what, exactly?

I've found nothing incriminating on Spencer. It's simply that in this day of everyone posting snapshots of their lunch and TikTok videos, I haven't found anything at all, and that bothers me. Then there's the plane ride with Verena, but what does that prove? The change in Ethan's behavior. The wine. The symptoms he experienced in January that seem oddly familiar. Nothing but feelings and conjecture. And even though it doesn't matter, even if Oliver will be the person to put Spencer behind bars and no one's keeping a record of my solves, I realize I need to do this. To find out what game Spencer's playing. For Verena. For Ethan. And maybe even for myself.

Footsteps in the hall. I hit Exit, delete my search history, and pull up the Word document with notes for my father's book. I try to make it look like I've been nodding off and barely mask my sigh of relief when Sadie stumbles through the door.

"Have you been outside today?" She marches to the sink.

"No," I mumble, "working from home."

"It's brutal. Jesus." She breaks off a paper towel and starts dabbing her face. "I mean, it's only March. And everyone wanted help with their groceries out to their cars." She stops. "Wait. Why aren't you at the library?"

"Like you said, it's hot." I gesture to the coffee table. "I have some books here, figured I could type up my notes."

She's frowning at me, her head tilted to one side.

"It's just . . ." She stops. Shakes her head. "Forget it."

"What?"

Twist of her mouth. "You haven't been at Maddie's, have you?"

"What?"

"I mean, I'm sure she'd love to paint you—scars make for the best portraits, and all."

She's wringing the paper towel in her hands, and I laugh. I can't help it.

"Paint me? Are you serious? I can't even look at myself in the mirror. Why would I let someone stare for hours at my scarred skin?" The truth, always better than a lie. It slips off my tongue easily, and I'm hit by the accuracy of it. This confession of my vanity. The weight of the change in my physical appearance—not so different from Sadie grabbing at belly rolls and pushing food around her plate.

"So you haven't—"

"No."

"Right." A furrowed sliver between her eyebrows and then a smile. "Sorry." She moves from the sink to the sofa, sits on the arm—our roles reversed from the other afternoon. "It just feels too good to be true, you know? Being with Maddie—I keep waiting for someone to sweep in and take her away."

I close my laptop. "I get it," I tell her. And I do. I know better than anyone how many forces can rip someone you love from your grasp. "But how could you ever think that I—"

"I know, I know." She waves her hand. "I'm sorry. It's just something Spencer said about wrinkles and scars being more interesting to an artist's eye. And it made me think of you and Madeline."

Of course it did, which was no doubt his intention.

I give a thin laugh. "How did that even come up?"

Sadie laughs, too. "I don't know. I think I was watching a makeup tutorial. Random, right?" She shakes her head, grabs a bottle of water from the fridge.

No, I think, not random. Not if Spencer's trying to generate a divide. A small stab here, quick jab there, tiny paper cuts that over time would bloom into one giant wound. I think of the look on his face when he saw the two of us on the couch, Sadie leaning over the counter to taste my sauce before dinner. He doesn't want us close.

"Do you ever feel hazy," I ask her, "for no good reason? Or maybe you only have one glass of wine, but you feel super hungover—unusually so—in the morning?"

"All the time," Sadie says, laughing. "I'm a lightweight."

"But we drink almost every night," I say. "You'd think you would have built up a tolerance."

She shrugs, screws the cap back on the water, and offers it to me.

"No thanks," I tell her. Swallow. "Did that ever happen to Ethan?"

"What? Hangovers? He was worse than me," Sadie says, smiling sadly. "What's wrong?" she asks suddenly.

I realize I've frozen with an ear to the hall.

I hear footsteps. They seem to hesitate outside our door, but then continue. I breathe a sigh of relief.

"Whoa. Paranoid much?" Sadie raises an eyebrow.

I laugh. "Just exhausted." I shake my head. "You know what?" I say. "I think I'm done for the day. Want to make popcorn and watch *Sabrina*?"

"Really?"

"Why not? I read you should take a work break every fifty-two minutes. And I've been staring at my computer for at least three hours."

I stay in my spot with half an eye on the door, half on the television, throwing pieces of popcorn every so often in Sadie's direction, so she's laughing, the mood so light it could take wing and fly away.

The television's loud enough that I don't hear his footsteps, but just as the door swings open, I toss a popcorn kernel in Sadie's direction and she dips, catching it in her mouth and throwing her arms in the air like she's just scored a shot from the free throw line. She's giggling, and I'm laughing, but also watching from under my lashes as Spencer enters the room. And it's there, in the split-second hesitation, the way his lips flatten razor-sharp before he sees me looking and grins—he's not happy at all.

"I have a surprise for you two," he says cheerfully.

Sadie shushes him. "*Sabrina*." She gestures to the television.

His gaze flickers to mine, but I can't quite muster the same conspiratorial smile we've shared the past four weeks.

"What surprise?" I ask to cover its absence.

"Ice cream—for dessert. I thought I'd make dinner tonight."

Sadie's face is upturned, grinning at Spencer like this is the best news she's heard all week. I feel a sharp pang like I've lost in some divorced-parent bribery game and my child's allegiance has shifted away from me.

"But it's Sunday."

He shrugs and begins to unload packages from paper bags. "Variety's the spice of life."

"What kind?" Sadie asks.

"Rocky road."

"My favorite."

Spencer smiles. "I remember."

A shadow of something on Sadie's face, but it vanishes as she leans over to dig a last handful out of the popcorn bowl. I think of Ethan, Madeline, and Sadie sharing a carton, nestled together on the couch, Spencer observing this on his way to his room and pocketing the information for later.

My eyes meet Spencer's again, and whatever he sees there seems to satisfy him. He begins humming, scouring the fridge. Sadie shushes him half-heartedly and returns her attention to the television. Glimpse of tree limbs and pale fingers. A bright light flashes across the screen.

I sit straight-backed and alert, knowing that dessert and humming only mean Spencer's upped his game.

The ending credits roll, and Spencer clears his throat.

"I have an idea," he says. "Let's make this a proper dinner. Get dressed up. Light candles."

Drink wine, I think.

"Put on some music," he says.

"Okay," Sadie agrees before I can answer, "but I get to pick."

"Great." He smiles at her, a warm, genuine smile like he couldn't be more pleased that she's happy.

A strange pang. *I don't want it to be you.*

We shouldn't, of course, but we always have a favorite suspect. If we bothered to look, we'd probably recognize our biases are linked more to childhood trauma than statistics or evidence—I've got it for the guy with acne scars because he reminds me of that asshole who made fun of my braces in sixth grade, or the fraternity guy for a million personal reasons I'd rather not investigate. We also have our least favorites—the soft-spoken girl who doesn't look like she could kill a cockroach never mind a guy twice her size, the grandfather who keeps telling you stories about his kids and mixing up who's who. But we all have our tipping points. I've sat with a perfectly normal-looking middle-aged man who showed me his wedding photos, bawling, swearing he'd get the guy who killed his wife, only to find her body buried next to the hammer he hit her with. The grandfather suddenly convinced his children are possessed by demons smothering them in the middle of the night. And although the perpetrator's usually the one with a record, a history of violence, or from that neighborhood where they built a prison instead of a school—it's best to keep an open mind.

And right now, that desire for it to be anyone other than Spencer is warring with something else, something I only notice now that I'm paying attention—that when he disappears to his room to change, he's carrying the bottle of wine.

I follow quickly but can't allow myself to pause at his door. I listen, holding my breath as I pass in a whir of near-silent footsteps, for the faint sound of a cork being removed, pills being crushed, the exhale of a syringe emptying contents. But I hear nothing as I pass his room, Sadie's, and then enter mine, sniffing the blouse I wore for the last roommate dinner to see if it's clean.

I rip off my T-shirt and then pause, the blouse halfway over my head. What is all this business with changing for dinner? *Control*, I think. Controlling our meals, our clothes. Our respective roles in the household. Testing to see how easily we'll comply.

Sadie's singing, and I know it's Madeline who made her happy. Perhaps aided by the break in the routine, our roomie television, and now dinner with ice cream, no less. The sky outside is bubble-gum pink with strips of cotton-candy clouds, and a part of me knows that this is the last dinner. I wonder if Spencer knows this, too, but don't allow myself to dwell on what that means.

On the way back to the living room, I stop in the bathroom. Glance at the mirror. For a hairsbreadth of a second, I catch Ethan behind me, a scattered reflection that I take as a look of warning. And I think the thought I've been avoiding all day, the thought I know will vanish as soon as Spencer's eyes crinkle at me, when his smile sends warmth through my skin. Because standing in the bathroom makes the thought real, solid, as heavy as metal—that if Ethan overdosed, then Spencer forced his hand.

When I finally step into the living room, Spencer's facing the stove, his back to me, and Sadie's pulled herself up on the countertop next to him, legs swinging loosely below, her head thrown back and laughing at something he's said.

For a moment, I hesitate. I see how easily he's won her affection. He's zeroed in and given her exactly what she needed—a little attention, nurturing in the form of a meal, teasing like an older brother.

Is it for show, I wonder, like me with the television and popcorn? Is he matching me move for move or are we each playing our own game with Sadie caught in between? I stare daggers at his shoulders, looking for vulnerable spots but seeing only the pressed lines of his button-down.

Half an hour later, Sadie and I are setting the table—dutifully obeying Spencer's request to dig out the cloth napkins. He follows us with two silver candlesticks—"Found them under the sink," he says, like there's a treasure chest down there and not just pipes and extra hand soap—and taper candles, which he lights ceremoniously. Sadie trots over with a vase from the windowsill. It's overflowing with violent red wildflowers that give off sweet and citrusy notes of cherry blossoms and vanilla.

The wineglasses appear. Of course, because this is the point of everything. Upping the ritual, more reasons to drink, more reasons to toast, waving around bottles like a magician's assistant with one hand, slowly poisoning us like the magician himself with the other. His glass, I see, is already full. Sadie thrusts her glass out to him and the warning dies in my throat. What can I say that won't tip him off? And that's it. Nothing's changed. I'm willing to risk Sadie's well-being, just like I risked Cindy's, took advantage of Teddy's friendship, jeopardized both of our jobs. And for what? I resigned. Ethan's dead. No amount of digging is going to change that. But what about Verena? *And the truth*, I think.

Spencer gazes at me strangely as he proffers the bottle. For a flash, I see it. The dare: *Will I, or won't I?* I try to muster the same foolish eagerness to drink I've displayed every night since I've arrived—to feel my body loosen with the sound of liquid hitting the glass, to allow its small waves to envelop me, and carry me out to sea. But his eyes linger on mine thoughtfully. I wonder if there was something I missed, a broken piece of tape stretched across the back of his bedroom door, a drawer left open the exact width of an ink pen, anything to indicate that someone had been in his room, going through his things.

He fills the glass a splash higher than usual—*Whoops, you don't mind? No? Didn't think so.* After all, what can I say? Sadie's already taken a large swig, cheeks bulging like a goldfish, before Spencer finishes his pour.

"Cheers," he says. "To the best meal I've ever prepared." He laughs and his eyes flicker between the pair of us as we drink.

Focus on the tip of my tongue. I don't notice anything unusual, no hazy cloud, no strange smell, no salty taste. But would there be? I think of all those date rape drugs—Rohypnol, GHB, and ketamine—chosen for that very reason: no color, no smell, no taste when added to a drink. *Or food*, I think, my stomach souring.

Spencer moves to the kitchen, lost in the clatter of silverware and plates. Sadie trips back and forth between him and the table, dancing on her toes, remembering the music, and biting her fingernails as she wavers over the best song to match the occasion.

The evening is perfect. Flickering candles bathe us in a soft glow. Spencer's prepared some kind of Sicilian pasta with chubby spaghetti-like noodles, sundried tomatoes, and almond pesto. It's the kind of meal that warms you from the inside without feeling heavy, striking that balance between comfort and lightness—greedy bites and second helpings stretched between Sadie's chattering, guitar strums in the background, and small but deliberate sips of wine. It would all seem normal, or at least resemble the sense of normalcy we've established during the past few weeks, except that I can feel Spencer watching me under his eyelashes, Sadie sweeping in to fill my silences, not a break in the conversation, so an observer might not notice they were there at all.

Spencer stands to grab more wine, and when he returns, his hand brushes mine as I pass him my glass. There's a whisper of something at the back of my neck, and I bristle, knowing that for weeks I've been leaving my armor at the door, slipping around the warm floors in nothing sturdier than gossamer, assuming the world outside was the problem. I think of the heavy lid of Pandora's box. It's not true what they say—the truth will set you free. The truth only means you see the walls of your cage.

A wry smile plays on Spencer's lips, and I wonder if he knows what I'm thinking. If he spotted my knowledge, my new wariness, as soon as he walked in the door. I bite the inside of my lip. *Pay attention. Be present.* But the room is falling away. Falling like a cloud from the moon, a glass from your fingertips, watch it from high above, laugh because what else is there but your foolishness? Let Spencer clean it up because you might slice open your palm, smear blood across his face. Put your hand on his shoulder for support, the vulnerable spot, mark *M* for murderer. *Where is the blind man with the balloon*, you think, and then laugh and begin to hum "In the Hall of the Mountain King." Sadie throws a tomato at you. It misses and hits Spencer instead. The sudden movement unbalances her and she stumbles first into the chair, then to the side of the table, and then fully onto the floor. The glass spills from her fingers. For a split second, there is nothing but wine, a tangle of legs and skirt. "I'm okay, I'm okay," she's laughing, but winces when Spencer gathers her up under the elbows. She dusts off her knees and examines her shin. It's all falling away, but you don't miss his flash of anger.

Him

She had told him so much about herself, tracking her down was easy. A simple Google search. And there she was on the university faculty page.

It was an unflattering headshot. Her head tilted in a way so that he could hear the photographer's voice through the frame: *Just angle it a bit more, a little more, there*, snap. Something about the liveliness of her was missing, eyes a little unfocused, smile strained. She looked younger, too, less tired than she had been on the plane. But it was her. And right under her photo was a building name and office number.

He was curious, that's all. In the beginning, he didn't have a plan. He just wanted to see where she worked. What she looked like from a distance and without the background of the gray-and-blue plane interior. He decided to make Joe Brown a part of his nightly run. He would take Thomas to Baldwin and then circle the building, wondering which of the lamplit windows was hers.

It was a while before he went inside. He changed his joggers to slacks. Walked up the stone steps, noting the few students who used the Lumpkin Street entrance. Her name was listed on a black felt letter board. Some names had probably been there for decades, but the crooked white letters reminded him that they were all replaceable.

After circling the first floor twice, he found himself striding down a dark stairwell to the musty bowels of the building. He learned her class schedule. The faces of the students who congregated around her. He ducked, afraid to be recognized, but she was distracted, explaining to a student that she didn't accept late work because it wasn't fair to the others who turned in their work on time. He shook his head. Some things never change. But he registered a familiar stab of disappointment. He wanted her to acknowledge him. He began to fantasize about meeting for coffee. Strolling through the small garden he discovered during his many trips around the building, he imagined long conversations with her like they had on the plane. He positioned himself just outside her classroom. Sat on the floor like the others, a book in his lap, priding himself on being inconspicuous, picturing how he would stand at just the right moment so her eye would be drawn to him. But she was always surrounded by those goddamn mouth breathers asking dumbass questions that he could have answered himself, until finally he decided to take matters into his own hands.

"Excuse me," he said after bumping into her. He felt a jolt run through her body and relished the moment their skin collided, that he'd hit her harder than he planned.

"I'm sorry," she apologized as if she was the one who deliberately ran into him. He waited for the moment of recognition—the *Do I know you? Have we met before?* He waited long enough that the pause became awkward. She gave him a small smile. "I should really watch where I'm going," she said. "Always so distracted." That faint hint of the German accent was there, but it was clear she didn't remember him.

"It's okay," he said, and forced a smile through clenched teeth. "No problem at all."

Then he began to watch her in earnest. It was on a Wednesday before the winter holiday that he saw one of her students, a pretty boy with perfect teeth and curly brown hair, post a flyer on the hall corkboard.

LOOKING FOR QUIET ROOMMATE / ONE ROOM / AVAILABLE JAN 1. The student had printed his number at the bottom of the page vertically in narrow strips, so people could pull off tabs and call later. He waited until the boy rounded the corner and then ripped the entire sheet from the wall. At the time, he wasn't sure why he did it. The plan didn't begin to form until later.

It wasn't hard to discover where she lived. An unexpected advantage of her not remembering his face was that she didn't recognize him waiting outside the building or walking two steps behind a pair of female students, his footsteps lost beneath their mindless chatter. This was how he learned where she parked her bike.

The following afternoon he arrived half an hour before he knew she would leave for the day and watched as she shoved her laptop bag and armful of papers into the front basket. This was how he learned where she lived.

She rarely closed the blinds. And even when she did, he could see shadows moving in the light. This was how he learned the boyfriend was not a fabrication. That he liked to sing while he cooked and swirled around the kitchen grabbing spoons and spatulas. That if she was alone, she left the television on until she went to bed, even if she was in a different room. That she sat in a chair by the window for hours, reading, writing, grading.

It was easy. Too easy. Had it been difficult, he might have given up, but at every stage, she made it simple, like she wanted him to find out these details about her life. She was a creature of habit. This was how he learned of the dog—a small yappy thing she called Jagger—which she walked promptly at 7:10 in the morning and 4:30 in the afternoon and let out the back door do its business in the backyard right before 9:00. This was how he learned the routines of the boyfriend, who left just shy of 8:00 and returned after 5:00 carrying grocery bags and bottles of wine, who was clumsy and overweight, harmless and nondescript—the kind of safe guy he would imagine her with but not the kind she deserved.

Seventeen

Monday, April 6, 9:00 A.M.

For the first time since moving in, I lock my bedroom door. It looks like I attempted to drag my suitcase in front of it, too, but gave up halfway. It sits abandoned in the middle of the room—a silent reminder of stumbling around in the dark after dinner.

Last night I dreamed I opened all the windows. A bird flew in and couldn't find its way out. Feathers slamming against the top windowpanes. Shattered glass on the living room floor. And the sound of weeping behind a door.

I wake to sunlight beating against the glass, a sour taste in my mouth. For a split second, I forget where I am. Then I roll over to face the wall, and my fingers find Ethan's scratches. I count them, for comfort, for penance, I'm not sure anymore—the grooves and their individual inconsistencies as familiar to me as the chalk they leave under my fingernails. The first is a deep gash, the second one, too. Three and four are slightly shorter, not marked with the same force. Five, a heavy perpendicular slash, not at an angle like a tally, but drawn through the center, splitting the other lines in two. The middle ones have their own slight variations in depth and height, but it's the last line that draws my attention—it's thin, a wisp of a pencil stroke, almost rubbed smooth by my fingers. Number forty-four. The one that required the faintest touch but the most determination. Because with all the strength leached from him, Ethan still tried to leave his mark.

I force myself to sit, my body empty and heavy both, like my insides have been scraped out and filled with sawdust. There's a fresh glass of water on the night table I don't remember filling.

Sounds of traffic rise from the street below, the rush of the world outside. It's so loud and unsettling that at first, I don't notice the stillness.

I scoot farther up my pillow and incline my head toward the door. But there's no clip of Spencer's footsteps, no whine of the coffee grinder or flip of the switch. I press my ear against the wall and listen for the irregular pattern of Sadie snoring and am met by the steady beeping of her alarm. I think of Ethan, the stutter of his heartbeat, the slowing of his inhalations, the decrease in oxygen to his brain, skin turning blue-purple, body going limp. I'm already halfway to the door when I hear a sputtered gasp, feet on the floor, and the beeping stops. Sadie drags herself from the closet back to the bed, springs creaking, from the bed to her desk, her desk to the bathroom, whir of the fan, water splashing the sink. Her trajectory is slow and painful. *My fault*, I think. My fault for not putting my hand over her glass. My fault for waiting. When the proof was in our blurred vision and slurred speech, Ethan's tox report, and all the signs I refused to see.

It's my fault. I looked at Verena's students, Ethan's parents, Ethan himself, when the obvious answer was right in front of me. Who bought the wine? Insisted we drink the first night? The second? Whose interest did I misinterpret as kindness? How long has he suspected?

I wait until the door slams. But I know. I know before I step into the hall. Before I touch the door to Spencer's room, before I test the handle and find it unlocked—he's gone.

He noticed I didn't finish my wine. What else had he seen? He may have witnessed Oliver leaving Artisan's Corner on Wednesday, me meeting with Verena at the cemetery, he may have even followed my car to Ethan's parents' house. He may have already withdrawn cash from the bank. Rented a car. But surely, he'd also have done his homework. He'd know a rental was risky. That he'd have to show his license, proof of insurance. That there'd be a record of his movements. Would he have sold his car? Bought one on Craigslist? He's been one step ahead the whole time. I have no doubt he'd find a way. The question is, can Oliver? A fine pricking of my ego. *Not without me*, I think.

Sadie's left a half-eaten apple on the counter. The smear of her dark lipstick on a coffee mug. There's a sour smell in the kitchen, like she might have been sick before she darted out the door.

I can't stay in the apartment any longer. Can't feel Ethan's accusatory glare, the sense that I failed him and Verena both. Can't think of the botanical vines winding their way up Sadie's arms, the tangle of Ethan's hair, the pair of them on the couch, laughing, while Spencer lurked in the background. I don't want to picture Ethan walking through campus carrying his terrible secret. Verena in her office leaning in to lift the burden off his back and carry it on her own.

I grab my jacket on the way out the door.

Outside, I move like someone's chasing me. I skirt the parking lot first. Spencer's car is gone. The space where he usually parks is empty except for a glistening pool of oil and a piece of broken glass. I turn it over with the toe of my shoe. It's sharp and pointed in a way that suggests a violent end—slash of a wrist, jagged edge held to a jugular—but I know what it is: the remaining half of a shattered giraffe figurine.

I glance down the street and am met by a strip of orange cloud, a sweep of hot breeze coming off the passing cars. I turn back to the brick buildings of downtown, look at the faces of the people huddled at crosswalks, watch for blue lights, and a sign—some kind of direction, a trail of bread crumbs, broken branches, or a coat slashed with paint.

I pass a woman with a toy poodle. Something tugs at the corner of my mind. And I turn, a question forming on my lips, but then my phone rings.

Oliver.

"I can't talk right now," I say.

"I've been going over Ethan's roommates' transcripts," he says, ignoring me.

"And?" I ask, watching the woman turn the corner.

"Spencer Duplass went to Tufts."

It takes me a moment to realize what he's telling me.

"He and Verena—" I begin.

"They were there at the same time. She was a graduate student, finishing her PhD. Spencer was a finance major. And get this—his foreign language was German."

"German," I repeat, mind drifting to the books on the living room shelf. I assumed they were Ethan's, that Sadie had forgotten to include them when she packed his things.

"I pulled the course catalog from the years he was enrolled, checked his classes, and guess whose name was listed as the instructor?"

I stop walking. Stop right in front of that pole. The one with the missing-dog poster, where someone scrawled that Verena was a whore. Except now the poster's been ripped away or pasted over. It's gone and hasn't been replaced, like Verena's given up hope, like even if someone found Jagger, she believes they'd keep him out of spite. But what if Jagger didn't run away? What if none this was ever about Ethan? What if someone wanted to hurt her? The girl with the dog is on North Campus now, the bright pink of her sweater still visible between the gaps of the trees.

"When did Verena's dog go missing?" I ask.

"Her dog?" Oliver repeats, confused. He pages through his notes. "On February twenty-fourth. It was a Monday."

"What about Christopher?" I ask. "When did he leave?"

"The week before the dog. The eighteenth. Why? What are you thinking?"

I start walking again—quickly, in the direction of my car. Spencer's a former student of Verena's. He knew her before. I struggle to grasp this, even as I run through the timeline in my head. Spencer sees Verena on a plane in October. Moves in with one of her students in January. That same student shows signs of lethargy, forgetfulness, and cries in her office in early February. Christopher leaves the eighteenth. Jagger disappears the twenty-fourth. Ethan dies the twenty-eighth. That's a lot of tragedy for one person in a few short weeks.

I bite my lip. "I'll call you back."

I stare at the phone in my hand, begin to dial, and put it away again.

I take a breath, mind flying down Lumpkin to Verena telling me about Christopher, the strange way that he left, the dog who ran away only a few days later. Then my thoughts race back to Artisan's Corner. Standing outside the building. A woman telling me about her new puppy. The one Spencer gave her.

I have no other option.

Finally, I lift the phone to my ear. "Mom," I say. "I need your help."

Him

He stood so close, he could feel the heat radiating off her skin. For the first time, he felt the power of her, the strength of a magnet, pulling him closer. Saw the way her fingers brushed the side of her cheek, the way she tugged her hair and revealed the smooth part of her neck.

He leaned in, placed his hand on her arm.

She jerked away.

"If that's all." A gesture to the door.

Flash of anger, a smile to hide it as he dropped his hand. "I just wanted to thank you for a great semester. I learned a lot."

She nodded. *"Das freut mich zu hören,"* she said, but there was no joy in her voice.

"Do you know what I've done for you?"

It must have been something in his tone, because she took a step backward and shifted her bag like a shield in front of her chest.

"Forget it," he said.

She looked at him for a long moment. And then she nodded.

"Auf Wiedersehen, Spencer."

Spencer.

Him.

Not Ethan.

He was first. He knew her longer, better. Yes, their fates aligned to a point. So much so that someone reading their stories might confuse one for the other. But he was the one who saw her for who she was. A liar and pretender.

And he chose to do something about it.

It was four years ago, but he still remembered the way her eyes flickered to the hall. Her desire to get away. He blocked her path. He was just a kid: twenty. The same age as Ethan. His parents had died. A dark stretch of the road, a patch of ice that ripped the world as he knew it apart. All he needed was a kind word. For her to see him. Acknowledge his presence. His pain. All the fucking hard work he put into her class. He sacrificed so much for her. And after a semester of calling on him and sharing private smiles, now she pretended she didn't care. Where were his concerned emails? Where was his shoulder to cry on? Just because he did what he was supposed to—kept going to class, doing his work, and never making excuses—he was left out in the cold. He was not a fool. He knew the affair allegations were bullshit. That she would never meet in a seedy hotel room. Invite Ethan to her house. That she sure as hell had never been to the apartment. But the point was that she cared about Ethan. The missed classes. The strange malaise. She wanted to know what was wrong. His mother had MS. Poor kid. At least he had a mother. His father was a philanderer. Big fucking deal. At least he was alive. But no, she was there, inviting him to her office. Letting him cry on her shoulder.

The phone number was the last straw. He heard them. Late at night. Ethan's choked voice: "Dr. Sobek?" And then pouring his heart out. Every sad thought. His delayed realization that life wasn't fair. His horrible secret. She knew he was depressed. He told her he couldn't bear it anymore—this burden of the truth. So even though she tried to comfort him, it wasn't enough. And now she knew that Ethan's death, her precious Ethan, was her fault.

He remembered the unsettled line between her eyebrows. The thought that he could do it. Force her to see him. Tell her everything he'd done for her. But that wasn't the point. The point was that he shouldn't have to. He stepped aside and she pushed past, walking away without a backward glance. It was the last time he saw her—her back a rigid line, books pressed against her chest—until that night on the plane. He graduated and took over his parents' business. But their employees resented him. He was young and inexperienced. So after two years of snide remarks and barely concealed loathing, he sold the business, refused to give referrals, and moved south for his MBA. A clean start.

He had no idea she had done the same. He hadn't followed her. Not for a long time, anyway. Hadn't thought of her, and when he did it was only to imagine her small life, schlepping books to and from classes, grading papers in the dwindling light. He figured she had dumped the fat, sloppy boyfriend, and lived in a basement apartment where the pipes froze, her only company a couple of cats. But he didn't think of her—eating TV dinners alone, slowly losing her eyesight, ugly glasses slipping down her nose—had almost entirely forgotten the clipped sound of her *Ts*, the tight breath when someone gave the wrong answer, her small private smile when he provided the right one. He didn't think about her at all until she sat next to him on that plane and acted like she had never seen him before in her goddamn life. It was just a coincidence that he ended up at the same university where she now taught. Serendipity that they were on the same flight. That he moved in with her favorite student. What were the chances, really?

Her

Christopher's gone. No goodbye. No note. Nothing.

When I walked into the house, I could feel his absence. We had been fighting. Ever since Ethan's call, tension stretched between us. Not screaming matches or silent treatment. But long, drawn-out arguments, where Christopher implored me to reflect on my work-life balance. To unplug. To stop trying to do it all and consider the emotional toll of investing so much in my students. To set boundaries. If not for him, then for myself. And so, I set boundaries. I told Ethan he couldn't call anymore. That I was sorry and sympathetic to what he was going through, but that he needed to talk to the university counselors. I did that for Christopher. Even though I saw what it did to Ethan. The look on his face like he'd lost his last hope, like he'd already succumbed to the darkness. Christopher insisted it was for the best. For my well-being and the students', too.

I throw my keys on the entry table and wait for his voice to boom from the kitchen, for him to wrap his arms around me. To ask how my day has been. I'm already preparing my responses. Fine. Normal. I will say nothing of the fact that Ethan was absent again. The odd hollow I felt in my chest when my eyes skimmed his empty seat. The sense of foreboding that followed me through the halls. But the house is silent aside from Jagger, who whimpers to be let outside and then claws at the door.

I put on his leash. We step onto the stoop. The wind whips through

Him

He didn't believe in coincidences. That one of her students posted a want ad for a roommate and this same student appeared to have a minor crush on her was not an accident. It was simply the universe telling him that he was right. This was his opportunity, and fate had delivered it to him on a platter—*Here,* fate said, *have at it, rearrange it as you will until it serves your purpose.* Because life does that. Most people are too weak to see all those opportunities to bend the world to your will—but not him; he sees and he acts. And after that abysmal meeting with the lawyers in October—the one where they told him his parents' business had been mired in debt and the profits from the sale had been less than anticipated—he could no longer afford the townhome off Barnett Shoals. He needed to share rent.

But Ethan was more difficult than he anticipated. Sometimes the universe makes you work for it. Ethan was friendly in a shy way, keener to ask questions than to answer them. He kept to his room, which he didn't bother to lock, but he was so quiet when he was home it was impossible to know if he was there or not. He knew Ethan liked her. This was perhaps part of the original appeal. There was something in the way Ethan lingered after class, the way he haunted her office hours, asking benign questions with obvious answers that amused him. He wanted to see what happened.

Sadie was another creature entirely—a wrench in his plans. She never shut up and was always whining about something. It was when he realized that she was exhausting his energy that he decided to zap her of hers. Again, too easy. No one questioned his generosity. His sudden desire to prepare meals, the bottles of wine that appeared without anyone having to replenish them. They were both young enough to remember their parents' kitchens where food appeared as if by magic. And so, they ate the pasta sauce and drank the wine. Downed the coffee. Never suspecting the crushed pills—the inheritance left to him by his mother in her medicine cabinet. He remembered counting them during one of her parties. "Blue is for peace," his mother would say. "Red for sweet. White for sleep and to forget me." Popping each into her mouth like candy. "People think love solves everything," she told him, "but it's not love, it's money." She sighed dreamily. "And Xannies."

He introduced it slowly, of course, so slowly he wasn't sure it was working, but then just another quarter of a crushed pill added to a bottle of cabernet one evening, and the next morning Ethan overslept his alarm. Sadie managed to get up, but she was confused and groggy and didn't say a word as she headed out the door. He spent a blissful morning sipping his coffee and reading the newspaper, gazing out the windows onto the sunlit street, proud of his work.

And now there was time to devote to her. The drugs had an added benefit. He knew that she—typical German—didn't tolerate tardiness or absence. Ethan's perfect student star fell in her eyes. But then something happened that he didn't expect: she became concerned. He discovered emails on Ethan's laptop asking if everything was okay, saying she was worried by the sudden change in his behavior, recommending university counseling services. He couldn't believe it—only Ethan with his softness would elicit such attention. It was unfair that when you presented yourself as capable and actually handled your shit that no one bothered with you. It was the weak ones who sucked up everyone's energy.

But he could tell that Ethan's late-night calls were wearing on her. He'd told her his secret. Forced her to share his burden. But at some point, she couldn't carry him further. Everyone has a tipping point. A moment when self-preservation kicks in. And between Ethan's excuses, his lethargy, and his clumsiness, she must have wondered how much was true. Maybe she was wrong about him, and he was like every other student—give them a little and they'll take it all. Every advantage, every extension, playing to your pity, your guilt, your feeling of responsibility—perhaps you've created this soul-sucking, responsibility-shirking monster because you were not firm enough in the beginning.

At some point, she must have forgotten Ethan was ever a good student. Her response times became longer, the tone more formal. And Ethan panicked, not taking the hint, and sending her almost-daily accounts of his maladies and excuses. She still emailed weekly follow-ups, but they were more direct: you missed three classes, now four, now five, this is the attendance policy, this is the student counseling service phone number. Ethan was distraught. He stopped going to his other courses as well and wandered the apartment like a ghost.

It was Ethan who gave him the idea for the message to the boyfriend.

While Ethan was out cold, he found a folder marked "German" and then a paper with a handwritten evaluation from her. It angered him, this old note, praising Ethan's accomplishments, his "natural talent," as she called it, in ways he refused to dwell on. He took the evaluation to the window and set another piece of paper on top of it. The story he penned to the boyfriend was brief—she was overburdened with responsibility, couldn't focus on both him and her career. She had made her choice and needed him gone, preferably yesterday. It must have hit a nerve, drawn on what the guy already suspected, because after he discovered the letter taped to the front door, he left almost immediately. Packed his bags while she was in class, so he was gone by the time she arrived home. What a loser. He was just disappointed he couldn't be there to see her face when she realized what happened.

Almost a week later, he allowed himself to observe the damage. Watched her pace back and forth in her living room. Realized that it was almost 9:00 P.M., and like clockwork, her little rabbit of a dog was going to be let out. So he unwrapped the package of beef jerky he happened to have in his glove box, and opened the gate. The idiot dog didn't even bark. He whistled softly, waved the jerky in one hand, and then scooped up the small creature in the other, the dog unperturbed, chewing merrily on its cow stick. He drove away just before she tore frantically out the door.

The girl from marketing class was delighted with her present—didn't even bat an eye that after only a handful of late nights, he was suddenly overwhelmingly in love and thought they should get a dog together. Apparently, she was under the impression they had been "dating" for a while. Idiot. He should set his sights higher next time. She thought the dog was "adorable" and wanted to know if it was a puppy. He had no idea, but when he told her it was, she really lost it. He had to make all kinds of excuses to leave the following morning. But in the end, he thought he'd played it nicely.

Her

Jagger's gone, too. I am alone. Entirely alone, and the walls are collapsing all around me. I was never supposed to be here. In this house. Without Christopher. Without Jagger. With only myself. And my thoughts are screaming louder than ever now that there's no one left to drown them out.

I keep imagining the worst. It was late. I must not have been thinking. I let Jagger outdoors to do his business. But instead of coming right back in, he took off around the side of the house. By the time I put on my shoes, he had disappeared into the night. Gone. Just like that. Just like Christopher. No note. No warning.

The back gate was unclasped. I don't remember opening it. Helena said sometimes people from the county come by to check the water meter, and they may have left it open. But I would have noticed when I got home, wouldn't I? I wanted to call their office and scream, but what good would that do? Because now he's gone, and no amount of screaming will bring him back. Helena came over and helped me scour the neighborhood. We yelled for hours, until my throat was raw, my whole body sore, limbs shaking. She told me to get some sleep. Tomorrow, we'll call animal shelters. I'll make signs with his photo and my number to call. But I can feel it—he's gone, and it's my fault.

I lie in bed picturing my father gazing at my mother, turning away from the gable roof of her familial home. Me watching the green countryside disappear from an airplane window. *I love you, but I can't live your life.* Is it any surprise, that I should suffer the same fate? But there's no "I love you." Simply empty rooms. A smothering sense of absence. The understanding that my boyfriend, even my dog, can't live my life.

And I'm not sure I can either.

Spring rain sounds poetic and sweet, all scents of lilac and catching raindrops on your tongue, but there's nothing soft and peaceful about Georgia thunderstorms in early March. Lightning slashes the sky followed by cracks of loud thunder.

Every late-night fear. Every worry. Every frantic email and call to counseling services. The signs were there, and now the prophecy's come true.

They suspect me for the wrong reasons. It wasn't any action on my part, but inaction. I don't have the energy to correct their mistake.

Every time I drink water from a glass, I have a sudden impulse to bite down, to feel the glass crunch between my teeth, slice through my tongue and the inside of my cheek.

I check the online feed, constantly refreshing the page. My punishment.

Slut.

Whore.

Go back where you came from.

And all I can think is that Ethan's gone. And I didn't do enough.

The loneliness is so real I can hold it in my hands. It is a physical weight crushing me. If only there were some way to be free.

Eighteen

Monday, April 6, 10:00 A.M.

The girl's full name is Gillian Redfearn. She's a first-year MBA student, enrolled full-time, and working at a local public relations firm. I don't ask how, but my mother manages to get me her address.

"If you don't hear from me in an hour," I tell her, "call Oliver Graves. Tell him Spencer's gone and give him Gillian's name. And you should check on Verena."

"What's going on?" Her voice is tight with worry.

"I don't have time to explain," I say, which is true, but I might also be wrong and don't want Oliver to bear witness if I've made a mistake.

It's turning into a golden spring day, the kind that masks the shadowy cracks at the edges, the warning this picture I've painted myself into with bright broad strokes might hide a darker one beneath.

The address is for a multiresidential Victorian on Hill Street. A family home once, with a pencil-drawn archway, rocking chairs on the porch, and bustling servants in the kitchen. Not as old as the plantation-style homes on Milledge but old enough. Pale green paint, the color of mint ice cream, three stories, with an attic converted into a loft on top. Stab of jealousy. Not because of Spencer, but because she calls this place—where fresh-cut grass blows across the sidewalk and sun catches corners of the stained-glass window—home.

I park on the opposite corner, pat my jacket, and step out of the car.

I don't wait long. A hollow opens behind the door and Spencer jogs down the steps, a bag thrown over his shoulder, clutching something in his fist.

The breath catches in my chest. A part of me thought—hoped?—feared?—he would already be gone.

"Spencer," I call.

He flinches when he sees me.

"How did you—"

"I ran into Gillian on campus," I say. "She told me you'd be here."

He frowns but is too focused on maneuvering through the cars, putting distance between us, to ask how I know Gillian.

"Well," he shoulders his bag, gives me a quick impersonal glance, "I have to get going."

He presses a button on the key fob and the headlights of a car farther down the street flash. His own car's nowhere in sight, and I wonder where he left it. At the Greyhound station? The Athens airport? Someplace to throw Oliver off.

A shiver sneaks up my spine. This is why he's still here. He knew the police would trace his car, so he abandoned it. He knew he couldn't rent one without there being a record so he waited until Gillian left for campus. I imagine him running his hand along the top of her doorframe, bending to lift a welcome mat for her house key. He would have known that she walked to campus, that she wouldn't notice her car missing until the end of the day. He didn't need to hotwire a vehicle. And despite what all those heist movies suggest, few people know how to do that anyway. It would be much easier to wait and simply let himself into Gillian's apartment.

"Take me with you," I say as he turns in the car's direction.

I could call Oliver now, but then what? There'd be no confession. No explanation. Only that twisting feeling in my gut, and that's no basis for a conviction. If Spencer leaves now, I would have shaken Pandora's box for no reason, and never get what my mother wants, what Ethan's parents and Verena need—the truth.

He hesitates. And I know he sees it, the desperation in my face, the neediness in my voice. It isn't hard for me to find it in myself, to put it on display.

He shakes his head—and I see it, too: the disgust behind the veil of pity. He strides to the rear passenger door and slides his bag across the seat.

I follow him, two paces behind, and try again. "You're the only one who gets it," I tell him.

His right hand is on the hood on the driver's side, his left fingering the keys. He looks at me. *What does Spencer want more than anything?* Attention. Admiration. To have not only been invited to hang out with Sadie and Ethan, but begged. Wanted. Appreciated. To be seen by Verena. Cherished and respected. For the world to conform to the megalomanic narrative in his head, where he is the hero of this story. I can't give him Verena. But I can give him me.

"You're not like the others—who see only my scars," I tell him, realizing that all along this is what I wanted, using my blind spots, hammering them into daggers. "You see people for who they are." His thumb on the handle. "You're smarter"—opening the door—"better, and"—half his body inside—"I don't know what I'll do without you." My voice reaches a frantic pitch, high and pleading, and I resist the urge to look around for witnesses to my humiliation, knowing if I break eye contact, acknowledge the presence of anyone other than Spencer, this whole monologue will be for nothing.

"I know about Dr. Sobek, Jagger, all of it," I say, "and I don't care."

He stares at me a long moment and then scans the tree-lined street. He sighs. "Okay," he says.

"Really?" I ask, unable to hide the surprise, using it to inflect my voice with relief.

He studies me, then smiles. "Under one condition."

"Name it," I say, my voice high.

"You throw your phone out the window once we hit Eighty-Five."

I swallow. I expected as much, but that he's decided this quickly sends alarm bells off in my head.

Inside the car, there's a faint whiff of what must be Gillian's perfume, vanilla and lilac. An overhead light blinks on, and Spencer fumbles to turn it off. A charging wire curls around the center console, a pair of earrings lie at the bottom of the cupholder. As he surveys the dashboard and runs his hand over the gearshift, it occurs to me that he's never driven Gillian's car before. He takes his time, moves his seat back, positions the mirror just right, and adjusts the safety belt.

I glance at his profile.

It was a good plan. Abandon his car. Steal hers. Oliver might never have made the connection. But I did. Because Spencer made a mistake. He didn't know I knew about Gillian. Didn't count on her jealousy. Or her approaching me.

"All right," he says finally. "Let's go."

"Let's," I echo.

The early-afternoon sun skims off his smooth complexion, the fullness of his mouth. We might be a young couple, playing hooky, off on an early weekend getaway, buoyant and free, the heart beating beneath my ribs with love instead of trepidation. Spencer drumming his fingers on the steering wheel with anticipation rather than annoyance. People see what they want to see. They'll glance at us and think Spencer must have a good heart, because why else would a handsome man choose someone who looked like me?

We drive in what might be a companionable silence, but I know our thoughts are skittering ahead. Spencer debating if he can trust me, second-guessing whether my performance was real. Me, wondering what I've started, if I know how to finish it, and where to go from here.

"I didn't want any of this, you know." He turns his body toward me, moves his right hand to the gearshift, so close to my arm we're almost touching. I see it now, the shimmering charm in the head tilt, the edge of the smile, the slivers of affection in his movements, all fake, but designed to make me work for his attention, to want more.

I force myself to relax my fists and slip one hand in my jacket pocket. This delicate dance requires tiptoes, not plodding feet. Any curiosity I display needs to put his pride at the center, not his motive or his weapon, but the strange turn of events that brought him into the middle of Ethan and Verena, and me on the sidelines of this sexless threesome.

"I don't understand," I say.

"It's not complicated, really."

I shift my knees in his direction but remain silent.

He chews his cheek, perhaps realizing that nothing about this is simple. Then he shrugs. "He didn't deserve her."

"Who?" I ask.

He flexes his fingers, says the name with a sneer. "Ethan."

I swallow the thick layer of disgust in his voice, the large hole worn in his charm.

"I don't understand," I say again. "Ethan didn't deserve whom? Sadie?"

A flash of impatience. He jabs his finger at me. "Don't pretend," he hisses. "Not Sadie. Never Sadie. God." He runs his hand over his face. "She was just as bad—just as annoying, always weeping, whining about how hard life was." He shakes his head. "Wastes of space, both of them, wastes of resources, energy, time."

Something clenches inside my chest.

"So you decided to kill them." I nod, forcing my voice to stay even, as if this is a completely reasonable course of action.

He looks at me with one eyebrow raised, the hollows of his cheekbones and the curl of his lip outlined by the headlights of a passing car. "Of course not."

He slows, veers into a turn lane.

Fuck, I think. *I blew this already.* But he doesn't tell me to get out, doesn't shove me through the door.

"That was Ethan's own damn fault," he growls, and then accelerates, moving his hand away from my leg. "Antihistamines, really?" He clenches his jaw. "How was I supposed to know?" He shakes his head. "She was always there for him, telling him how great he was, that he should major in German, chatting with him in her office about poetry." He spits out the last word. "Her favorite student."

I lean back against the cool leather, trying to stop the crushing sensation I feel rolling over my chest, the bottomless pit I've tumbled into. Somewhere an ambulance screams. Spencer's eyes shoot to the rearview mirror. There's nothing but darkness reflected in them. And I realize that, despite everything, I was still hoping to see light.

"Yeah," he says finally. "He wasn't special. Wasn't even that smart. One missed class here, another there, and he started failing." An edge of a smirk. He looks proud of himself.

"But," I say, leading despite my intentions.

His lips twist. "But then she got concerned. Started emailing, worrying about him. She even"—he grips the steering wheel hard—"gave him her phone number." He grits his teeth. "I heard them talking—" He glances at me, raw fury slashed across his face. My eyes meet his, and I don't know what he sees there—too much curiosity? Contempt? The dark cavern every word he utters carves into my soul?—but he scowls and turns away.

We sit in silence. I try to draw a map of the wide fields and narrow bends in my mind, but he keeps to country roads and avoids highways. There are mile markers but few street signs. And although when we started, I was certain he was heading north, now that the sun has set, I'm no longer sure. I don't think he has a clear idea where he's going either.

He fiddles with the radio, sneers at the stations Gillian preprogrammed, but blasts the music anyway.

I lean my head against the seat belt.

He rolls down the window, massages his jaw.

"I can drive," I offer.

He smirks. "I don't think so."

"Fine," I say. "I'll sleep." I feign a yawn. "Just don't nod off and drive us into a ditch."

I lean my head against the window and feel his eyes on the side of my neck.

Although it seems impossible given the hammering of my heartbeat, the frantic tumble of my thoughts, the importance now more than ever to stay awake, I must doze, because the next thing I know, the car has stopped beneath a broken security light.

The motel's one of those nondescript, sinister-looking brick buildings you've seen off a thousand highways and forgotten or driven by and wondered who would ever be so down on their luck as to check in. A sloping awning held up by scattered metal poles, rectangular air-conditioning units, and square windows, all with their curtains drawn shut.

Spencer parks at the opposite end of the glass-windowed lobby. He turns off the engine and pockets the keys.

"Wait here," he tells me.

I watch him stride across the parking lot—the straight back, hard set of his shoulders, a man comfortable moving through the dark—how did I miss it?

The car beeps and I realize he's locked the doors. A warning, I think. Or a test. I could open the door now and run, but if I do, it would set off the alarm, and he'd know I can't be trusted.

I sit on my hands and take deep breaths. Consider Spencer as he crosses the yellow threshold. Behind the fluorescent-lit cube of grime-covered glass, the motel attendant reclines at his desk and glances up warily when Spencer enters.

I open the glove compartment, stick my fingers into the sides of my seat and underneath, searching for a spare phone, a weapon. Look for signs along the deserted highway. Study the chipped paint of the vacancy sign.

Then I withdraw the rectangular object from my pocket. Press Play.

"It's not that complicated, really." Spencer's voice is muffled through the fabric, but I can make out every word. I breathe a sigh of relief as I slip the recorder back in my jacket. It's not a full confession. Not yet. His motive is becoming clearer, but I need specifics about the drugs. So I go over every detail I know about Spencer. The small facts about his life that slipped through the cracks—the pill-rattled mother, the car with his parents careening off the ledge. Looking for something, anything I can use against him.

But what do I really know about this man, who reappears in the slash of the security light and opens the door for me?

If the motel lacked curbside appeal, the inside is much worse—one queen bed opposite a low wooden dresser and cracked box television. Stained threadbare carpets squish under my shoes.

Spencer flicks the light switch and a green-tinged electric lamp flickers beside a lumpy red comforter.

He gestures around the room. "I paid for two nights, but we'll be gone by morning."

I nod.

He gives a thin smile, locks the dead bolt, and then draws the latch across the door.

"The place seems a bit sketch," he says. "Would hate for anyone to break in." He looks at me. "Or out." A hollow laugh. "But you're here of your own volition." He inclines his head. "Because you want to be."

I nod again, my mouth too dry to speak.

"Then make yourself comfortable," he says, dropping his bag on a wooden chair and striding toward the bathroom.

I hear the fan crank on, the running of water, and am overcome by my own need to use the facilities. I check the clock next to the bed. It's just after 1:00 A.M. We've driven fifteen hours, only stopping once for gas. Gillian's car must get great mileage. The pressure on my bladder increases. I debate stepping outside, relieving myself in the bushes, but

I can't risk Spencer hearing the door open and doubting me now. Any wrong move might cost me.

I dig my fingers into my palms, force my attention there.

After what feels like an hour, the water stops, the door opens, and Spencer steps out in a towel.

"I need to get in there," I say, pushing past him, and closing—not locking—the door behind me, trying not to think about all that skin, about what he thinks might happen, if he even wants something like that from me.

I step back out as soon as I'm finished—not wanting him to think I've shut myself in the bathroom for good.

"Better?" he asks with an amused smile.

"Better," I say, feeling an odd shift in the room—as if my need to pee has put us on equal footing, he's remembered I'm only human, with human needs.

I see he's changed his clothes. The slacks traded in for jeans, the button-down for a T-shirt. They look unnatural on him. Then I notice the plastic cups on the night table.

"Not the type of establishment to provide proper glasses," he says. "Or wine, but I always keep a few of these in my overnight bag." He holds up a pair of miniature liquor bottles. "Hope bourbon is okay."

He's already emptied the contents into separate cups. I blink at him, remembering the first night, when he held the wineglass out to me, the spark I felt as our hands touched—not desire, I realize too late, but a warning.

Still, I let my fingers linger against his as I reach for my drink.

"Why don't you take your jacket off? Make yourself comfortable."

He pats the side of the mattress next to him. I slip the jacket from my shoulders and lay it casually on the foot of the bed, recorder pocket up but fabric in a pile so Spencer can't see the shape of it. Then I sit on top of the comforter next to him, my back against the wall, legs outstretched.

"Cheers," he says, and we touch the edges of our plastic cups.

"To a new life," I murmur.

"To the next one," he says, and tilts back his drink.

The room feels suddenly small, pressing in on me and him, locking us together in this farce, this strange game of truth or dare, words and drinks.

I estimate I have fifteen to thirty minutes before the drugs kick in. Enough time to find out where the pills came from and how Verena's name ended up on Ethan's body. I hesitate, but I've already come this far, so I take a breath and swallow mine, too.

Him

The hard-earned peace began to dissipate with Ethan moaning to Sadie on the couch—the pair of them growing closer, commiserating about their lost loves and rejections. Sadie, ever the drama queen, chopped off her hair and then dyed it. Started wearing only black clothes and writing Madeline's name on her arms. Anything to get the girl to notice her. But she didn't, and wouldn't. He'd made sure of that.

He just wanted a quiet weekend. Was that too much to ask? He had an exam coming up. And couldn't be bothered not to act annoyed when the common area was constantly occupied by two sniveling twenty-year-olds. He suggested a weekend away—*A little rest and relaxation, you deserve it*. Only Sadie agreed with his logic and decided to visit a friend in Atlanta. Ethan decided he didn't deserve anything, nice or otherwise. So he upped his sleeping pills, it was barely anything, especially with the number Ethan had adapted to. How was he to know he was taking antihistamines? He enjoyed another peaceful morning. Coffee. The newspapers at the table. He stretched out across the sofa with his books and relished having the place to himself. But then he remembered he wasn't alone. Ethan was still in his room, poised to come out at any moment. So around four, he made another pot of coffee without the usual additions and knocked on Ethan's door. He found him spread across the floor. Vomit smeared across his chin. He acted quickly. It was clear he had overdosed. Not to panic. The problem was the drugs. If they did a toxicology report, they would realize Ethan didn't have a prescription and wonder where he got them. At least he didn't have a prescription either. *Thanks, Mom*, he thought wryly as he rummaged through Ethan's folders. But still, a note would make things easier. He found a handwritten essay. Practiced the odd swirl to Ethan's *S*s. The tilt in his *R*s. An early life spent forging his parents' signatures meant he knew about masking the deliberate strokes of the pen, trailing off instead of leaving a sharp stopping point. That strange skill set had come in handy lately. The note to Madeline. To the boyfriend. He shook his head. Who would have known parental neglect would leave him with so many useful talents? It was Sadie who made him think of writing on Ethan's skin. The faint outline of Madeline's name still shimmered on her wrist. So dramatic, but better—more room for error than on a piece of paper. He slipped on gloves and took a steadying breath. He knew he only had one chance as he picked up Ethan's pen and wrote "I'm sorry" on the flesh of his hand. "Verena" on his inner arm. He entered a search for overdose methods on Ethan's computer just to make sure everything pointed in the right direction.

Then he left. Bought groceries. Prepared a meal for Gillian. They laughed. She got drunk. He spent the night. Congratulated himself on this alibi should he need it. And lying in her bed, he had a stroke of genius. A way to tie up loose threads. He thought of the words of their marketing professor from earlier that week. They floated back to him as he stared at the ceiling. "All you need is a narrative," he had said. "Give people a story they can fit themselves into—the new car and the hands-out-the-window road trip. The lonely man who brought beautiful friends together around a galvanized tub of low-calorie beer—and they'll buy whatever you want." So he built a narrative that people would believe because they could see themselves in it. Even as they murmured their disgust, he knew it was because they could recognize themselves in the story. The unhappy professor. The sensitive student. It was already there—all the phone calls and emails between them. The fire was burning, he just lit another match.

He returned to the apartment Saturday morning and called the police. No one questioned his story. After all, it was becoming increasingly normal for young men to die early. Suicide was the plague of their generation. The dark-haired officer was the only one who didn't seem convinced by the markings on Ethan's skin.

The missing drugs. That was his mistake. He thought the detectives might look into his family history. If they had dug deeper into his parents' deaths, they would have noted the similarity between his mother's tox report and Ethan's. The news described a car crash. And it was true. His mother drove off the road. He just helped her along with an extra dose of her trusty pills. They'd always refused to see his potential. Ignored him. Insisted he hide himself away during their parties. But—a controlling stake in their company, a salary, a respected profession, that's what he deserved.

He could have waited, but he'd done it for her. So she would see him, not as a student but as a peer. More than that—he'd rescue her from a life of drudgery. No more schlepping books from classroom to classroom wearing bargain-bin clothes, no more grading papers and riding that rickety bike to work. Instead, with money from his parents' business, they could sleep in and have analytical conversations over afternoon coffees. He'd bring her to industry parties. "Yes," he would say, "she was my professor. But now look at her, my brilliant wife." And his employees would laugh and everyone would be jealous. They'd go to the theater and have box seats. Dine at the best restaurants and drink the best wine.

But now he understood—she led him on. Then she met that fat boyfriend. He saw the way she giggled at the idiot's jokes like she was someone else—a silly teenager, a fraud, not the respected professor she pretended. He tried to remind her. To be the bigger person. But when he thanked her for a good semester, she looked at him like he had overstepped, like she hadn't spent the whole year smiling at him, chatting after class on the way to her office. The way she said *"Auf Wiedersehen"*—like he was a stranger, a threat. But the words don't just mean "goodbye," they mean "until we meet again." So really, she should have known one day they'd cross paths.

But still the pills—it would have been better to scatter some across the floor or put them in a plastic bag. Instead, he had carted them off to Gillian's, thinking he might need them again. He did, but their absence made the detective suspicious. And yet, he sensed there was something not entirely aboveboard with him anyway—takes one to know one, right?

He hadn't counted on the female detective, though. Former detective. Retired detective. Whatever. He saw her outside a few days after the story aired—watched the way she lingered and scanned the windows. It was clear she was looking for a way in. After the news report, a few neighbors knocked on the door. Offered their condolences, took curious looks around, but this felt different. A hastily scribbled note in the window and then he was walking past her in a hurry, in case he was wrong. In case she was just waiting on a friend, looking to bum a cigarette. But then she stopped him. Took the bait.

She wrote a fake name on the rental application. But it was close enough to her real one that he found her. He googled the fire. Of course he did. How many house fires a year did she think happened in Athens? The police department hadn't updated their website, and at first, he thought he had been made. But when he called asking to speak with Detective Marlitt Kaplan, a testy woman who sounded to be about a hundred told him she no longer worked there. When he asked if she had been transferred, she gave a wry snort and told him she doubted it. So, not a detective. But still, it wasn't a coincidence.

He could have told her they found someone else. Sorry. But he wanted to see what she knew. Keep your enemies close and all that. He removed everything incriminating. Started keeping the pills on his person and locking his bedroom door. In the end, though, maybe that was the mistake. Locked doors invite more suspicion than open ones. But at first, she made him doubt himself. She seemed to genuinely enjoy living there.

Laughing at dinner, drinking wine, getting drunk, albeit more so thanks to his trusty little pills. It was the last dinner when he noticed the change. She accepted the wine, but only sipped it. He caught the furtive glance when he came back to the table. She had been watching him closely. Of course, there was the bobby pin, too, found in the middle of his rug despite the door being locked. That's when he knew he had to leave.

But then she showed up at Gillian's. She thought she could play to his ego. Get him to confess. But he wanted to tell someone. Ethan, the boyfriend, the career, even the dog—it was all so perfect. And here was his chance. A pity she wouldn't remember. And even worse that he wouldn't be there to catch his old professor when she fell, to see her face when she realized she needed him, to sweep her up after she broke into pieces. A missed opportunity. But it didn't matter. He could always come back.

Nineteen

Tuesday, April 7, 2:00 A.M.

Swimming in blackness, not liquid, but sticky tar, dragging me back, filling my lungs, a heavy pressure on my chest, foreign breath on my tongue, a crushing sensation in my ribs, a mouth pressed over my own. A sputtered cough, and I'm rolled over on my side, where I vomit on myself, vomit on a faded red comforter, see the other side of the bed is empty, reach out and feel that the mattress is cold.

"Oh my god, oh my god, oh my god."

The voice is familiar but strained.

"Jesus, fuck, Marlitt. I thought for certain—" Oliver is white-faced and shaking, running his hand over the back of his head. And I realize it was his mouth pressed against mine, his breath filling my lungs, him saving me from the darkness, which means my mother did what I asked. She gave him Gillian Redfearn's name, and he tracked her down, got her license plate number, and followed us here. A warmth spreads through my chest.

"The ambulance is on its way."

"Spencer," I say, the realization dawning with a sickening crunch, "he's gone."

Oliver shakes his head. "He's not."

I blink at him, and he points to the left side of the bed and then the floor.

"Looks like he rolled off and hit the night table."

I shake my head, not understanding. "He's still here?"

Oliver sighs, and it's then I notice the blue lights jumping off the bathroom wall, hear the screams of the ambulance. Or maybe I'm screaming, I'm not sure, because the next thing I know is Oliver's holding me, telling me not to look, as medics lift Spencer's body from the carpet and his arm drops limply from his side. His eyes are open and for a brief moment, they rest on mine. But they're unblinking, and there's a dark fluid crusted around his mouth. I lean over and vomit again.

It seems the vomiting is far from over—that's all they want from me in the hospital—stomach pumped, sick into metal bowls, too sick to hold up my head, sick all over myself, sick that I didn't see this coming. That I thought it was my life he was after, and it never occurred to me he would take his own.

"You don't know that," Oliver tells me. He's standing at the foot of my hospital bed.

"He killed himself," I repeat numbly.

"You took the same amount."

I shake my head. "That's not possible."

"It sounds like he'd been dosing you for weeks. You developed a tolerance. He hadn't."

"So he wanted to kill us both?"

"Or just grant you a good night's sleep. He might have slipped in a little extra, not thinking it would be fatal, since he'd been giving you and Sadie close to the same."

My stomach is hollow, but I feel oddly like I might be sick again.

"What are you saying?"

"I'm saying we can't know what he was thinking."

A metal cart rattles in the hall. He takes a breath. "You know you shouldn't have—"

I shoot him a look.

"But thank you. Now at least Ethan's parents—" He purses his lips. "Well, at least they know. And the professor, she can clear her name."

I gave Oliver the recording. In the minutes before I passed out, Spencer told me about the drugs in the wine. He even admitted to writing Verena's name on Ethan's skin. And it's this—his late-night confession—that makes me think it wasn't his plan to grant me a long sleep so I couldn't follow him. That he must have known either or both of us would die.

"I still can't believe it," I say. "He did all that—moving in with Ethan, poisoning him, stealing a dog—just to hurt Verena."

"Classic narcissistic behavior," Oliver says. "The desire for control. It's the only way they can support the narrative they create for themselves—to manipulate others into seeing them the same way."

"I should have known."

He sighs. "Yeah, well, me too."

"But I spent so much time with him."

He shakes his head. "They learn to spot vulnerabilities, to prey on them, use them to their advantage. I—" He rubs his hand over his mouth. "I saw him as myself, grieving, the way I did after my father—and Spencer, well, he let me feel sorry for him, let me say all the things I wished people had said after it happened. It didn't even occur to me that he wasn't devastated, that he wasn't sorry." His lips pinch together so hard they turn white. "That he was using my own pain to blind me."

He's right. It was all there. The sense of self-importance, the air of success, and small actions to assert control, but in ways that we would thank him for it, feed his ego. I was an idiot not to see.

"Do you think you'll ever come back?"

I blink at him. "To the force?"

"Well, not here, obviously," he says, and I flinch at his tone, the certainty I'll never work at Athens PD again. "But somewhere else. A friend of mine in Atlanta told me they were hiring. I could put in a good word for you."

"Thanks," I say with a wave of my hand. "But I'm not interested."

He clenches his jaw. I know he's trying to help. But to serve and protect you have to believe in the system. And I don't. Not anymore. Not after last fall. Not after watching how casually Oliver sacrificed Verena. How easy it was for me to do the same to Sadie.

Oliver shifts on his feet. "There's something else," he says.

I groan.

"Everything's okay, but . . . it's why I'm here. And not your mother."

I try to sit up. "What's wrong? Is she okay?"

"She's fine." He pushes me down gently. "Everyone's fine. Your father—"

"My dad—"

"He's resting now. But he's here."

"In the hospital?"

"Yeah," Oliver says. "They came as soon as I called."

"My father hates hospitals." I shake my head, thinking Oliver must be wrong. My father hasn't been in a hospital or doctor's office since my brother died almost thirty years ago. Didn't even visit me after the fire.

Oliver frowns, not understanding why I'm arguing.

"He collapsed in the waiting room. The doctor said he was dehydrated, but they took him in for testing."

I take a deep breath, thinking of my father's recent weight loss, the coughing and fatigue, trying to wrap my brain around the fact that he actually came to the hospital to see me.

"Oh," he says over his shoulder as he moves toward the door. "You were right about Haddock Senior. And the phone. It wasn't just for the girlfriend. There were some sketchy business contacts—"

I blink at him. I don't care about Ethan's dad. His stupid phone and affair. I want to know more about my father. What tests? Did he hurt himself when he fell?

Oliver smiles sadly. "I think I should let you rest."

He leaves without another word. And I'm determined to stay awake until a nurse or doctor appears so I can ask what happened, but my eyelids grow heavy again.

When I wake, a nurse stands over my bed.

"You look better." He nods as he checks my vitals.

I grimace. My throat's dry. Mouth tastes sour and my breath does, too. I wrinkle my nose.

"Alcohol and benzodiazepine." He shakes his head. "Not a good mixture."

I think of Spencer's body being lifted from the floor. "No," I agree. "Not good at all."

"We gave you an emetic medication to induce vomiting. Flumazenil in your IV. We'll hold you another hour or two for observation and then you'll need someone to take you home. Is there anyone you can call?"

"There's no need." My father strides into the room. I expected him to be dressed in a hospital gown, but he's wearing his usual slacks and sweater. Like he's here only to visit me and not like he himself was admitted just hours before. "I'm here." He says this as if the nurse should know who he is. As if he's Superman and should have his hands on his hips, chest puffed out.

The nurse lifts an eyebrow, no idea what an impressive figure my father makes. Almost thirty years without stepping foot in a hospital and here he is.

"And you are?" the nurse asks.

"Her father."

"I see." The nurse clears his throat. "We can discharge her now, then."

"That's it?" my father asks. "What about medication treatment, motivational therapy, and an offer to meet with someone from mental health services?"

I can tell my father's been doing his research.

The nurse blinks at him. "I can give you some pamphlets on recovery and treatment centers."

My father waves him away. "She doesn't need that. But the hospital should provide coordinated care, referrals for people to get further help."

The nurse looks from him to me.

"It's about the principle," I tell him.

"That's right." My father nods.

The nurse backs away. "Okay," he says slowly. "I'll bring it up to the board."

"You do that." My father nods again, like he really believes the nurse will do any such thing.

"What happened?" I ask, when he finally returns his attention to me.

"I could ask you the same thing."

I shift in the bed. "You first," I say.

"It's no—"

"Don't say it's nothing."

He grimaces. "I fell. The doctor said I was dehydrated but wanted to do tests. I think your mother's behind it. Now that I'm here, she wants me to get a lifetime of checkups."

"But why? Do they think something's wrong?"

He hesitates.

"No more secrets," I say, looking at him evenly.

"No more secrets," he repeats, holding up his palms.

He sits in a plastic chair, facing me. "I don't know, honey," he says. "The truth is I haven't felt my best recently."

I think of his sallow skin, the laughter that turns to wheezy coughs. All of a sudden I realize that the moments I assumed I'd have with him, finishing the book, seeing him holding it in his hands, Thanksgivings, birthdays—they're no longer certain. I imagine the years slipping by like water, each anniversary passing like ripples cast by a sinking stone.

He squeezes my hand.

"I should be comforting you," I tell him as a tear slips down my cheek.

"That's never been your job," he says.

Then he clears his throat. "Your mother told me you had a visitor earlier," he says.

"Oliver? Yeah, I saw him." I shift on my hip. "There were some . . . things to wrap up."

My father shakes his head at this but doesn't ask.

"No, this was a different visitor." A slight smile as he sees me realize.

I blink, needing to hear him say it.

When he doesn't, I ask, "How is he?"

"Honestly," he says, "I think he misses you."

Twenty

Monday, June 8

Summer arrives with little fanfare. Children still run through lawn sprinklers but teenagers disappear inside. College students have abandoned the city in droves, returning to suburban houses and cramped apartments to wait out the long days and hot nights until September ushers them back to campus again. The flowers bloom in Verena's window boxes, and she makes me promise to water them when she travels to Germany next month. Christopher plans to visit, but beyond that they haven't figured anything out yet. There were tears on Gillian's end, but Jagger's back with Verena, safe and sound.

The Title IX investigation is over. The investigator wrote a letter determining there was insufficient evidence supporting the accusation that Verena violated Title IX policy. Her suspension was lifted just before the end of the semester, contract renewed for the following year. But she doesn't plan on going back. After all, the university hasn't offered a solution in terms of workload and burnout or the increasing need for mental health services for students and faculty. Her name's been cleared, but she would return to a campus that hasn't changed. And it needs to, not just for students like Sadie and Ethan, but for professors like my mother and Verena.

I linger outside my house, oddly nervous as the breeze brushes my skin. But everything is different today. There are no pumpkins decaying on doorsteps, bare tree limbs, and dispensed candy wrappers littering the street. No smell of smoke, sound of splintering wood. The sun is shining, the grass is green, squirrels bark at each other, disappearing behind thick tree leaves.

I open my front door cautiously, remembering warnings of toxic particles and mold. But my house is finally safe to live in. And I run my hand fondly over the bookshelf and the back of the sofa. I open all the windows and chase out the bugs that have occupied the place in my absence. *If it's safe for you*, I think as a ladybug crawls across my palm.

The house feels changed, stripped bare, vulnerable and exposed, and a little the worse for wear. But I'm changed, too. That's the thing about removing all those protective layers—it's only once they're gone that you see your raw strength.

A piece of caution tape is caught in a holly bush, and I tug it free, thinking of the day Spencer plucked a flower from my hair and I felt beautiful. A knot forms just under my breastbone as I head back to the car for another box, remembering the comfortable lapses of silence, the familiar teasing, the way it felt like I had known him my whole life. I shake my head. Of course he felt familiar. He was reading me, mirroring me, showing me what I wanted to see. Just like he had with Sadie, Ethan, even Verena—he saw our vulnerabilities and exploited them.

I think of Teddy, the ache of his absence, the gap he left in my life. Spencer must have pegged me from day one—how to get close. I was so obvious.

Oliver told me that narcissists often convince their victims they share a special bond. Was it just about control? Exerting his will over the others? Spencer didn't like Sadie all gooey and happy, ignoring him in favor of Maddie and Ethan, so he sent Madeline a note. Didn't like Ethan being smarter than him, so he started crushing up pills, making him miss class. Didn't like the sympathy his absences elicited from Verena, so he upped the dosage. But the one thing I don't understand is why he took his own life.

If Oliver's right, then he completely lacked empathy. He wouldn't have felt sorry for what he did to Ethan, to Verena, to me. He wouldn't have feared being caught. In the story Spencer told himself, all his actions would have been justified. And taking his own life—isn't that antithetical to narcissistic behavior? Oliver says this isn't true. That narcissists do commit suicide. But he doesn't believe that was his intention. He insists that Spencer, with the false assumptions of indestructability common to narcissists, thought the drugs wouldn't harm him. It was us—Ethan, Sadie, me, his mother, even, the weak ones—who were susceptible to their influence and damage.

After the hospital, I went back to Artisan's Corner one last time. My earlier suspicion was right; it did feel different. Not tinged by poisoned wine and a poisoned soul, but empty. There were no more whispers, just-missed reflections, or movements out of the corner of my eye. Ethan was gone. He was finally free.

"Hello," I called. Because that was the other thing I was there for—not just to collect my belongings, but to talk to Sadie. I'd been imagining her frantically trying to get in touch with Spencer and me, worried when neither of us came home the night before, worried to find Spencer's door open, his room bare, wondering what it all meant. And I knew I owed her an explanation—of who I am, why I took the sublet, and what Spencer did to Ethan. Where Spencer was now: awaiting formal identification. But Sadie wasn't there.

I packed my bags slowly, pausing every so often when I thought I heard the clip of her laughter, the stumbling skip of her feet . . . until I realized where she was.

My few things assembled and zipped away, I knocked on number 25.

I heard music and voices lift in unison. And then Sadie opened the door.

"Marley," she said, eyes bright. "It's like we summoned you! I was just telling Maddie she should paint your portrait— Wait." Her mouth dropped open. "What are those?" She pointed at my bags.

"Can I come in?" I directed the question at Madeline, who appeared just behind Sadie while we were speaking.

Her apartment was full of canvases. I saw Sadie's face a myriad of different ways, and other images, too. The four-faced clock on Broad, distorted and mixed with a white lily and curls of poetry. She told me the painting was for Ethan. That it was the beginning of a series in his honor.

And I told them everything, from sneaking around Sadie's room to drinking with Spencer that final time. There were tears, so many tears that I worried I'd stripped away their laughter, that whatever renewed feelings they'd found for each other had been soured by my words, by the truth that I was so determined to unleash.

But Sadie only squeezed my hand and left the room. She returned with a giraffe figurine.

"For his parents," she said, pressing it into my palm. "There were two big ones and a small one. A family." She shook her head. "They were silly and sentimental, but they meant something to Ethan. Maybe they'll mean something to them, too."

I thought of the broken giraffe on the asphalt, the smallest one, the reminder of what had been lost.

"You keep it," I told her.

Madeline said she had never liked Spencer. "The way he looked at people." She shivered. "Always creeped me out."

I nodded and wished I had felt that way.

It's strange to think that I only lived in that apartment five weeks. It seemed longer and shorter at the same time. Long, because I feel connected to Sadie. Short, because after I moved out, sometimes I would wake and feel as if it were all a dream. *And Spencer*, a small voice asks. *The neglected child? The orphan?* I feel a tug as I imagine him sent to his room, finding his mother unconscious, feeling invisible, scrambling for power and attention. But he wasn't a boy lashing out; he was a man, methodical in his revenge. And, in the end, he was like a spider that got stuck in its own web—the lies and manipulation so twisted, he forgot which threads were safe and which were spun to control his prey.

The movers arrive with furniture from my parents' house. They gifted me the bed and dresser from their guest bedroom. Now that I finally adjusted to the mattress, they didn't see any use in me buying a new one. Instead, the small desk from the laundry room has moved in front of the guest window, so my father can stare at the trees outside while he works on his book. It's more convenient, too. After his fall and the tests at the hospital, he was diagnosed with thyroid cancer. The doctors caught it early, before it spread, and they're optimistic. But since he started treatment, he's had difficulty sleeping. Now he can move between the office and the bedroom, filling the night with his words. Sometimes when I can't sleep, I wonder whether we'd ever gotten my father to the hospital if it hadn't been for Spencer's heavy hand. That I feel an odd sense of gratitude for being poisoned is proof of how much he wrecked my head.

I've been officially let go as my father's research assistant. My skills at deduction would be better applied elsewhere, he told me, as I sat with him during his second treatment. I can't say I blame him. I have very little work to show for the past month. But clearing Verena's name and discovering the truth about Spencer has earned me a reputation in unofficial channels, including a local private investigation agency. I start on Wednesday.

After I unpack, I spend the afternoon in the backyard stretching string lights from limb to limb, setting up a long table, chasing away mosquitoes, and organizing plates of food. I light citronella candles and wonder if there will ever come a time when the smell of smoke doesn't make me sick. But it's almost five and I allow myself to be hopeful. Hopeful this attempt to make amends, to let people in, marks a new beginning.

Verena's the first to arrive. "Happy birthday," she says, handing me a bouquet of amaryllis and following me into the house as I hunt for a vase. "Welcome to thirty."

I grimace, and she laughs. "It's not all that bad."

"Whatever happened with that article?" I ask over my shoulder.

Her mouth forms a grim line. "Rejected. I got the news a few weeks ago."

"I'm sorry," I say, and as I search my thoughts, I find this to be true. She deserves something good to happen for a change. "Did they say why?"

She shakes her head. "Both the readers' notes were minimal. If anything, they suggested that I should revise and resubmit. But the editors had some convoluted reason for turning it down." She sighs. "So I reached out to an acquaintance from grad school who's on the editorial board. She told me—off the record—that the editors had received an email forwarding them the link to the online accusations and said that they worried what it would look like to include my article before the Title Nine investigation was over. They didn't want to wait, so they went with a similar submission."

"Jack Klemper's."

"She didn't say, but yeah, probably."

"Do you think he sent the email?"

She shrugs. "Honestly," she says, "I don't care."

"What if he wrote some of those posts? Oliver can get someone to match the IP addresses."

She shakes her head. "It doesn't matter anymore. When I think of all the stress—that I was focused on that stupid conference, instead of on Christopher. That the article is one reason, maybe, that I was too distracted to help Ethan . . ."

I open my mouth and shut it again, knowing that no matter what I say, she will blame herself.

"I can't stop thinking that I failed him somehow," she says.

I run the tap. "Do you ever wonder if we give ourselves too much credit?"

"You think I'm egotistical?" She lifts an eyebrow.

"I think we both are. We're so certain we can control events by searching, knowing," I take a breath, "being there, saying the right thing. But really"—I gesture to the repaired ceiling, the new wood—"what is this place except a reminder that we don't control anything?"

She purses her lips.

"I could have—"

"You couldn't," I say.

I don't tell her about the concoction of pills Spencer had been feeding Ethan. The investigation is still ongoing. Oliver has quite the caseload and paperwork in front of him. After my motel misadventure, he went back to the apartment and collected all those wine bottles on top of the cabinets. Thanks to my mother's voice recorder, at least he could prove to Ethan's parents that their son didn't poison himself. And although I know she doesn't believe me, I tell Verena again that there was nothing she could have said to prevent what happened.

Soon, the backyard is humming with voices. Cindy is here, and so is Dara. Aisha's going through my rooms methodically, making notes on what a house looks like after a fire renovation. Seeing if she can spot the signs of its destruction.

Even Oliver's come, looking a bit unsure, and glancing at Verena every few minutes out of the corner of his eye. It must be strange after everything that's happened to see her in a social setting.

I watch them, these people I worked with, laughed with, almost died with, and feel suddenly overwhelmed.

Cindy slides up beside me and gives my arm a squeeze.

"I can't believe you all came." It's the thought on the tip of my tongue, the vulnerable and anxious truth, the birthday girl who fears no one will attend her party.

But Cindy only laughs. Then she looks at me seriously. "We've just been waiting for an invitation."

I don't feel worthy of any of them. It's mind-boggling that they see past the scars, the selfishness, the insecurities to find anything worth saving in me.

My eyes trip back to Oliver. He's staring at Verena again, but nods when he catches my gaze.

Oliver saved my life. The doctor made that clear. Had he not arrived as soon as he did, given me mouth-to-mouth, and called the ambulance, I would have died. And I'm grateful for that, but there's still a nagging thought, a persistent doubt, the same feeling I had on the last case we worked together, that even after all we've been through, he's hiding something.

I think of Pandora lifting the heavy lid, Ethan discovering his father's phone, Verena closing her office door. All the warnings about curiosity and yet our persistent desire to unmask the truth. But here's the thing. The difference between me now and me six months ago: I don't need to know. Not *it's not my job to know*, although that's true, too. But I don't need to know why Spencer did what he did. What Oliver's hiding. What I do need is to make things right. With Cindy. With Teddy. But most of all with myself. And I don't mean bandaging up my wounds and slapping on armor so nothing like this happens again. I mean taking a good hard look at my scars, cleaning them out, and letting them breathe. Healing is painful. It's awkward and uncomfortable. It starts by admitting my faults—all of them—and asking for forgiveness. Being willing to accept that I might not get it. But doing it all the same. I have to let go of my ego to grow and be free.

I hear the crunch of his bike on the gravel drive before I see him. Smile at the sound of him locking it, just like he used to, through the back gate.

And so here it goes. One foot in front of the other. The screaming selfish child left behind. The long-overdue in-person apology sincere on my lips. And since he's walking toward me, I hope this means enough time has passed that he's ready to hear it.

"Marlitt?" A crinkling around the eyes.

"Teddy."

Epilogue

Her

We aren't born insecure, are we? We open our eyes to the world, blink at all the shapes and colors, wrap our fingers around shirt hems and earrings, and believe they exist simply for us. Then we toddle through rooms demanding things, pulling books from the shelves, and kicking Bavarian garden gnomes. We destroy laundry piles and upend boxes, and leave their contents scattered for others to step on and clean up. Never second-guessing, worrying about consequences, anxious about the books tumbling down until they're landing on our heads.

It's the pointed fingers that make us second-guess ourselves, words shot like arrows when our backs are turned. At first, we don't understand. But slowly, their meanings seep in. They transform us from the inside out. *Fake. Fraud. Impostor.* Until every step is laden with thoughts of consequence, seen from the outside, our identity viewed from everyone else's lens. But there was a time when we knew how to think for ourselves. How to take what we wanted and act without fear.

And that's how I find myself at the police station watching Detective Oliver Graves from behind the wheel of Helena's car. She agreed to wait to call him until I got here. In return, I promised to make sure Marlitt was okay. After all, she saved me—Marlitt. If she hadn't told her mother to check on me, I'm not sure what would have happened. But now I know what I have to do. Helena thought Marlitt found Ethan's killer. That the information she gave her would lead Oliver Graves directly to him. And the detective exits the station with the determined look of a man who knows where he's going.

I follow him through the night. I thought my hands would shake, but now that I've decided, I feel oddly calm. And I can almost see the pieces of my life shift and slide around me. Now that I understand who broke them apart, I know what needs to be done to put them together again. The sun dips behind power lines and settles beneath the trees. And still we drive. Detective Graves, a steady fifteen miles over the speed limit. Me, slowly, but always catching up around a bend. It's just after two in the morning when he turns on his blinker. This adherence to the rules when he's spent the last few hours flying down dark country roads amuses me for reasons that must be tied to fatigue more than anything. I keep driving and then circle back. Park in the vacant lot next to the motel.

Detective Graves walks around a silver car, peers in its dark windows before striding into the lobby. He exits a minute later, gun drawn. The manager follows, but Detective Graves motions for him to return inside. He stops in front of a red door. Listens and then withdraws a key. He pushes the edge with his fingers and slips inside. But there are no raised voices. No gunshots. All is silent. And for a moment, I hesitate. But the time for indecision has passed. I am here and no longer passive. Now is the time for action.

The door is cracked, and a slash of yellow light illuminates the stained carpet. Detective Graves stands over Marlitt. I know it's her, although I can't see much more than the bottom of her shoe. He checks her pulse. Then he turns to the man, who's watched him from the bed without altering his position.

Detective Graves motions to the plastic cup on the table. "Drink," he says.

The man doesn't move.

Detective Graves lifts the cup, but still the man doesn't stir. Not in acquiescence. Not in protest. Whatever contents are in the half-drunk liquid have rendered him incapable of even turning his head.

I lean forward and the door creaks under my weight. Detective Graves whips around, pointing his gun. A jacket falls onto the floor.

The man's eyes move to me and widen in surprise. I recognize him then. My student. The one who followed me from class all those years ago, who lurked in the halls and haunted my steps. His hair is different. He looks older, more confident, even though the eyes that follow me are uncertain. I see the man he became, the one from the plane who asked so many questions, the hardened, dark soul who ripped my life apart and then killed Ethan.

"I'll do it," I say, closing the door and taking the cup from Detective Graves's hand.

I place my fingers on the man's jaw and tilt the liquid between his teeth.

"For Ethan," I say.

Because what kind of professor would I be, if I didn't teach my former student a lesson?

Acknowledgments

Anne Lamott writes that "we are a species that needs and wants to understand who we are." In many ways, this book is an attempt to understand the world I occupied while writing it. I was a professor, working on a college campus and navigating professorial expectations alongside a growing concern for my students and the rising mental health crisis sweeping dorms and classrooms. Therefore, this story is as much a mystery as it is a novel about campus life, professor burnout, and student-professor relationships. Although this is a work of fiction, I shared my own teaching experiences with professors who became colleagues and colleagues who became friends as we navigated faculty meetings, office hours, conferences, and publication expectations. And so, I want to begin these acknowledgments by thanking my inestimable peers: Valentine, Sandrine, Kristina, and Mine—being able to laugh in the most stressful situations is a gift and I treasure it. Of course, teaching is a futile task without students. Emily, Daniella, Damon, Luca, and so many others: thank you for reminding me why I love teaching. And Sarah: you were a bright star, and you are missed.

My heartfelt thanks to my incredible editor, Zack Wagman, for his enthusiasm, wisdom, and critical insights. And to the entire team at Flatiron Books: thank you for working so tirelessly to bring this manuscript to print—thank you, Bob Miller, Megan Lynch, Maxine Charles, Erin Kibby, Claire McLaughlin, Cat Kenney, Morgan Mitchell, and Kelly Too. Thank you, Christina MacDonald, for the thoughtful copyedits. And to Julianna Lee: thank you for designing yet another striking cover.

To Alex Lloyd and everyone at Pan Macmillan Australia: thank you for giving Marlitt a second home.

To my marvelous agent, Hillary Jacobson, thank you for believing in Marlitt from the very first read. I am grateful for your endless support, guidance, and acute editorial eye. And thank you, Josie Freedman, Sophie Baker, Lucy Morris, and Tara Wynne, for continuing to champion Marlitt.

To my mom, who will share this book with everyone she knows (including the mailman); my father, who'll place it on his desk as a talking point in his office; and my sister, who's been my rock this year and every year: your love and support mean more than I can say.

To my Georgia friends of twenty-plus years who have supported and encouraged me every step of the way, my new friends in Nashville who welcomed me with open arms, and those friends in California, Virginia, and every place in between: thank you.

And to Gray, you were my first reader, biggest supporter, and true love. I'm grateful for you. Forever and always.

About the Author

LAUREN NOSSETT is a professor turned novelist with a PhD in German literature. Her debut, *The Resemblance,* won the ITW Thriller Award for Best First Novel. She currently lives in Nashville, Tennessee.